ALONE

OUT

HERE

RILEY REDGATE

HYPERION

Los Angeles   New York

First Edition, April 2022
10 9 8 7 6 5 4 3 2 1
FAC-020093-22049

Printed in the United States of America

This book is set in Fairfield LT Std/Monotype
Designed by Samantha Krause

Library of Congress Cataloging-in-Publication Data
Names: Redgate, Riley, author.
Title: Alone out here / Riley Redgate.
Description: First edition. • Los Angeles : Hyperion, 2022. • Audience:
    Ages 14–18. • Summary: When the president's daughter—eighteen-year-old
    Leigh Chen—ends up on the only ship escaping a dying earth, she and a
    group of teenagers must grapple with the challenges of what it will take to
    survive as the last remnants of humanity.
Identifiers: LCCN 2021011160 • ISBN 9781368064729 (hardcover) •
    ISBN 9781368065344 (ebook)
Subjects: LCSH: Survival—Juvenile fiction. • Environmental disasters—
    Juvenile fiction. • Teenagers—Juvenile fiction. • Space flight—Juvenile
    fiction. • Interpersonal relations—Juvenile fiction. • Outer space—Juvenile
    fiction. • CYAC: Survival—Fiction. • Environmental disasters—Fiction. •
    Space flight—Fiction. • Interpersonal relations—Fiction. • Outer space—
    Fiction. • LCGFT: Psychological fiction.
Classification: LCC PZ7.1.R427 Al 2022 • DDC 813.6 [Fic]—dc23

Reinforced binding
Visit www.hyperionteens.com

For Li An,
first first reader

TELL ME WHAT YOU CAN'T FORGET,
AND I'LL TELL YOU WHO YOU ARE.

—Julie Buntin, *Marlena*

WE LONG ONLY FOR THE WORLD WE
WERE BORN INTO.

—Emily St. John Mandel, *Station Eleven*

I REMEMBER ONE NIGHT MORE CLEARLY THAN THE REST. It was the hottest July on record, and I was fifteen, lying awake and sweaty on the faded linen sofa in Lilly's basement. With the way the crickets were squalling, Lilly couldn't get to sleep, which meant no chance of sleep for Marcus or me, either. So the three of us were talking ourselves out into the universe, fantasizing in scratchy voices about God and death and the first day of sophomore year, and around two a.m., we wound up whispering about the end of the world.

We'd kicked the questions around before. Maybe you did, too. If the Apocalypse hit tomorrow, which five people would you pick for your zombie survival team? Which three things would you take down to the nuclear bunker? What would you save from the wasteland?

We never settled on answers. Lilly drifted off halfway through, and the next morning, Marcus kept swapping his choices back and forth, clarifying the rules over breakfast. "Is there internet in this wasteland?" he asked, thumbing his glasses up. "If I brought my headset, could I have unlimited games?"

Lilly rolled her eyes and said, "God, Marcus, what kind of amateur apocalypse do you think this *is*?" and I lay back in her window seat and laughed, loose-limbed, careless, because everything we were saying felt unreal.

That was three years ago. Now, most nights, I lie awake and watch those moments replaying across the backs of my eyelids. I retrace the pikes of sunlight angled through the kitchen window or feel the frayed threads of the sofa, the patches that Lilly's golden retriever pawed to death when he was too young to know better. I hear the way my best friends sighed after they laughed, deep and contented, like they'd just taken a cold drink on a hundred-degree day. It hurts to remember, knowing that two months later, the announcements froze that world like amber engulfing a living thing. But I can't make myself stop.

I wish I could show it to you, too—really show you. I wish I could scan my old life out into VR space so you could walk all the way inside. We'd step through Lilly's messy little kitchen like archaeologists through some perfectly preserved temple, and I'd pause the scene, point to the scar on Lilly's chin, and tell you that happened when we were thirteen, the day she hacked off a foot of her hair with a pair of garden shears on a dare from Marcus. He wasn't even being serious, and as for me, I stood there and watched with a stupid grin on my face, not believing it would happen until it did. And maybe you'd say Lilly sounds reckless or impulsive, and Marcus and I should have known better. And I'd say, probably, but that's Lilly, that's Marcus, that's us. That's what I'd save.

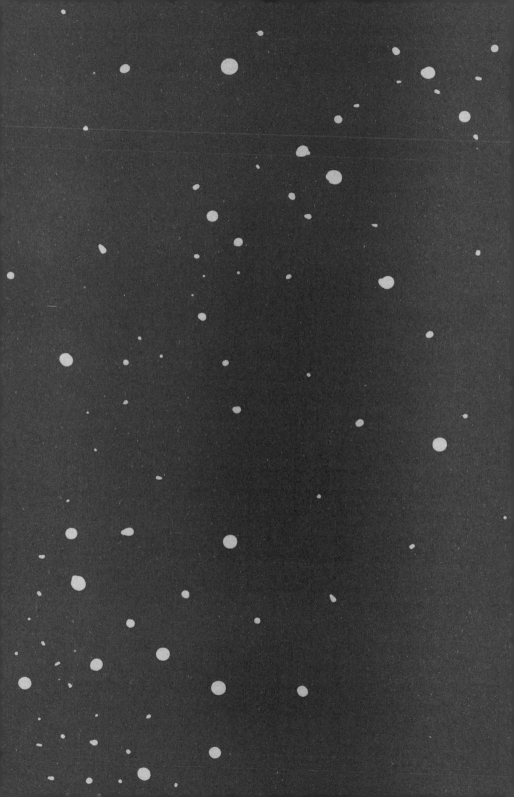

PART ONE

FLIGHT

CHAPTER 1

JULY 19, 2072

I startle awake to a world that's alive. Everything is a tumult of sound and motion, a siren howling overhead, a glow pulsing through the barracks' windows, a bare bulb over my bunk trembling like a furious fist. I sit bolt upright as the screaming starts.

For an instant I can only stare at the rows of bunk beds in chaos. I know exactly what's happening—I just don't understand how. The eruption isn't due until next spring. *Soon* is the shorthand that news anchors have been using, as in, soon, cubic miles of lava and ash will explode from Mount Shasta, a peak in Northern California, and cause a chain reaction that will render the planet uninhabitable. Since the announcements, we've watched the ground swell like an abscess and waited for the lance to drop, hoping and praying for more time.

Now I don't hope. I don't pray. I'm rolling out of my bunk and cramming my feet into my sneakers. If the last three years have taught me anything, it's that denial is useless. Only the facts matter, and there's just one fact to cling to now: The *Lazarus*, one of the generation spaceships that were meant to save millions of people, is standing half a mile outside our barracks door.

I seize my backpack from the floor, but the strap snaps taut, caught beneath my bed frame. "Move," I grunt, pulling harder. "Come on, *move!*"

It isn't coming free. I need to open my hand and run, I know that—but a protective panic is blazing up in me, the thought that this is all I have.

Someone lets loose a string of Arabic behind me, and a pair of hands heave the frame upward. The bag flies free. As I hug it tight to my chest, I cast a wild look around, but the speaker has already disappeared in the mayhem.

I wrangle the bag onto my shoulder and sprint for the exit, darting between the shadowy, muscular bodies of soldiers. Warren and Jones, my Secret Service detail, passed me to these officers yesterday—six high-ranking military officials assigned to safeguard our group. Last night, on the way to the cafeteria, I heard them muttering mutinously to each other about babysitting. Now they're barking commands over the siren, trying to corral stricken eleven-year-olds into line.

I join the cluster of people at the door just as a girl flings it open. She cries out, clapping her hands over her ears. In pours the sound, the undertow of rolling bass, the gut-shaking drop of the earth tearing apart.

Our cluster recoils, stunned by the roar and the sea of haze outside. Mount Shasta is a hundred miles away—but then, that's nothing to this kind of explosion. Two hundred years ago, the Krakatoa eruption shattered eardrums fifty miles out; people three thousand miles across the ocean heard sounds like gunfire. The last Yellowstone eruption dropped ash from Los Angeles to the Mississippi River.

A high voice yells, "Kimbieni!" The Kenyan president's daughter, Caro Omondi, darts through the crowd and over the threshold, small and nimble, her long braids cascading out of their black silk scarf. The spell is broken. The rest of us plunge after her into an oppressive heat as tangible as water.

We hurtle across a concrete plain that glows dully under stands of floodlights. Thick haze rolls through the light like cumulus clouds in rapid time-lapse, shrouding most of the complex. The Vehicle Assembly Building, where the ship was constructed, is a shadow in the distance, and the Launch Control Complex—which looked yesterday like flecks of static fuzz breaking the horizon line—is completely invisible.

Only the *Lazarus* is clear, looming dead ahead. The ship is X-shaped and aerodynamically sharpened, like the tip of a Phillips-head screwdriver. Even half a mile away, the size of the thing is staggering. Booster rockets are bundled to its four wings at intervals, tall and sleek and alabaster white, and the whole apparatus sits astride a positronic impulse launcher a hundred feet high. Most of that bulk will unbuckle during liftoff and tumble down into the Pacific.

As we run toward the launchpad, an unexpected calm closes around my head. Caro and the others diminish into splashes of color, just another field of contestants in another race. I imagine lines spray-painted on tufts of grass, guiding me toward a clock suspended at a finish line. As concrete scrapes beneath my sneakers, I feel the mile repeats I used to run in suffocating August heat, and the ache of an oncoming shin splint, and the cramps that dug like a fork's tines beneath my ribs. All these painful tools that forged me into an instrument of survival.

Then I'm leaving the group behind. I'm passing Caro; I'm speeding by a Thai girl who's pressing her glasses to her face; I'm overtaking a younger boy whose lips are quivering as if he's on the verge of terrified laughter. Lilly used to laugh when she ran alongside me at the end of a practice. She never had my endurance, but she could sprint like no one else. She'd cut halfway through the route and reappear near the end, challenging me, crowing as we flew toward the finish line, "Is that—the best—you can do?"

I push harder until only one figure remains at my shoulder: Sergei Volkov, a sandy-haired Russian boy I recognize from our tour of the *Lazarus*. A head taller than me, he holds pace as we match kick for kick. Soon we're skidding to a stop at the base of the access tower.

I pummel the elevator call button, my throat burning, while Sergei stares back into the haze. The door opens, and I dart inside, about to hit the button labeled SHIP ACCESS, but Sergei seizes me by the wrist and speaks urgently. The words are inaudible under the siren.

"What?" I yell.

He yells something back in Russian and points toward the dark figures growing out of the haze, then stretches out an arm to hold the doors open for them. I feel a shock of guilt and do the same.

We wait until two dozen kids have crammed themselves in, packing the elevator wall to wall. Then the mirrored doors glide shut, dulling the noise outside. Coughing follows, a flurry of hands brought to mouths. Everyone's eyes are rimmed pink and streaming from the haze, including Sergei's, but he nods to me. I nod back, wiping my face clean, tying my hair up into its usual high ponytail.

At last I have a second to think, but none of my thoughts are reassuring. Our barracks are a temporary building constructed miles nearer to the ship than any other. The Launch Control Center is nine miles away—any closer, and their delicate instruments would have shattered under the thunder of the *Lazarus*'s engine tests. The crew's living quarters are even farther out. How quickly can they cross that distance versus how quickly will tectonic aftershocks ripple down the fault line of the California coast? How soon will the ash fall thicken like a blizzard versus how soon can we seal the doors?

In the long term, the ash cloud by itself would have been survivable. The death knell is what scientists found when they probed beneath Mount Shasta: impossible quantities of methane that will blast out from deep geological reserves, transforming our atmosphere forever. Three days from now, the outgassing will be complete. Within two weeks, Earth's cloud cover will have begun to expand, trapping in ever more water vapor and heat in a vicious cycle, and after a month, the air at half of Earth's latitudes will be unbreathable. Then, as the ice caps melt, the sea will climb to flood most major cities. In the coming decades, our oceans will boil away altogether until Earth resembles Venus: a dry-surfaced, 800-degree wasteland.

Before 2069, hardly anyone knew the term for this process, *runaway greenhouse*. Now it's one of those phrases you hear so often that it feels almost meaningless. Images of fires and floods war in my mind as the elevator rises at an agonizing crawl. A girl jammed in at my side is speaking in Arabic, her voice small and terrified. Soon she's hyperventilating, repeating a phrase again and again until it's a cry. Finally she punches the wall of the elevator so hard that the car shivers. Half a dozen others yell back at her, their languages mixed into an unintelligible clot.

"Hey! Hey." I touch the girl's back, and she twists toward me. She looks maybe thirteen. Her dark eyes are enormous, and she's breathing so hard that her lips are fluttering like paper.

"It's okay," I say, hoping she knows some English. "We're nearly aboard. We just have to follow the launch process."

I expect the girl to snap at me, or maybe to burst into tears, but she hesitates instead, searching my face. I glance at my reflection in the elevator door and see what she sees. I'm as straight-backed and composed as my mother delivering a speech. My fear is invisible.

"What process?" the girl says, still shaky. Some of the other kids are watching, too—the ones who toured the Launch Control Center yesterday instead of the *Lazarus*. Their group must not have gone over the procedure.

I raise my voice. "Passengers go up to the cabins and follow the instruction cards in the bedside tables. Just stay calm. The crew will be here soon."

The words have hardly left my lips when the elevator door cranks open. We clatter out through the access arm, and at the end of the passageway, we have a stroke of luck. The hull door is already open. After crowding into the airlock, we find the secondary bay doors open, too.

We step into the *Lazarus*. The ship is another universe, quiet, still, and dim. We've emerged in the atrium: the intersection of the four wings, the center of the ship's X. Overhead, walkways curve like ribs through ten stories of space, joining one wing to another, limned with traces of light. I wonder about the lights, why those recessed spots are already glowing like eyes in the jungle.

"Syuda, syuda," Sergei calls, waving everyone toward a ramp that spirals up the wall, leading to the ship's interior elevator bay. I'm about to follow when my gaze snags on a Korean boy's profile. In the half-light, shaggy black hair disheveled and glasses askew, he looks like Marcus.

Right now, is the Cho family driving to the nearest bunker site, Marcus's sister watching the eruptions on her phone while the fiery pictures flicker across Marcus's enhancement lenses? Is Lilly flying around her bedroom, snatching up mementos while Mrs. Dionizio yells for her to hurry?

If my mother were here, she would take one look at me and say, *Leigh, are you with us?* It's a phrase she says brusquely, like a teacher checking on a distracted student during class, but to me it's always been reassuring. *I notice you're gone*, she's saying. *What can I do to bring you back?*

The thought of her wipes out every other thought, the way a dead bulb in a string of lights makes the rest go dark. My parents are in Geneva for a summit of the Global Fleet Planning Commission, and there's nothing like a launch site anywhere in Europe. Besides the *Lazarus*, our prototype, every ship in the fleet is still a half-finished husk. The other kids and I traveled out to California to learn how our ships would operate next year, like a field trip. We were supposed to be tourists here, not permanent residents.

I shove my hand into my backpack, groping around for my watch and earpiece. I have to call my parents. Lilly and Marcus, too, before they're underground and out of range. I rip at zippers, stretch elastic, but halfway through searching the front pocket, I lose my momentum, because suddenly I remember the watch's milky solar strip glinting, half-covered by the pillow where I stashed it last night for safekeeping.

A high-pitched noise builds in my throat. *Safekeeping.* I want to fling my bag across the atrium, but I can't move.

Even if I were back there, if I could call and they could answer, we'd say—what? What could we fit into this last shred of time? What could I possibly say that would be enough?

"Leigh!"

I startle back into myself. Sergei is at the top of the ramp, Caro at his side. He makes a frantic motion toward the elevators.

"I'll wait for the rest," I yell back, pointing toward the bay doors. Sergei balks, alarm crinkling his forehead, but Caro tugs him back into the elevator with the others.

I turn to the gap in the hull, staring down the pale artery of the access arm, and tighten my ponytail until pain radiates across my scalp. My momentary loss of control has passed. It won't happen again.

For eight years, I've had to be a counterpoint to whatever is collapsing around me. After the Washington Monument bombings late in my mother's first term, when the whole country was screaming war, my parents trained me on a list of talking points so I could fend off any questions at school in a sober, level-headed way. After the eruption announcements, the whole world was terrified, so my parents and I had to look calm whenever we walked onto a stage. The First Family means stability. Leigh Chen is an establishment, a First Daughter before anything else. She's an illusion that matters immeasurably more than I do.

A second group of kids rushes into the ship, dripping sweat and gasping. I direct them toward the elevator bay, but I don't follow. The crew must be close now, bundled into trucks and speeding toward us. Any moment they'll appear in the elevator, any second . . .

One moment I'm on my feet. The next I'm flung into the air like a flicked insect.

I crash onto my hands and knees as a colossal *boom* thunders through the walls. I know what the sound is instinctively: thousands of tons of molten rock punching out of the earth's crust.

I scramble upright, my palms scraped and stinging. Faint screams issue from the Residential Wing, where the second group disappears toward the cabins on an upper balcony. I move to follow them, but a cool voice stops me. It arrives from everywhere, radiating through the empty atrium and throughout the immense body of the ship: *T-minus five minutes to liftoff.*

I stare up past the walkways in disbelief. Someone went to the ship's bridge and started the launch sequence with none of our personnel aboard.

Before I've made a conscious decision, I'm bolting up the ramp toward the elevator bay. They have to stop this. When I know nothing else, I know we have to do what we're expected to do.

The elevator deposits me on the tenth floor. I sprint around the balconies and into the Command Wing. The floors are spongy black mesh, bouncing me forward. *T-minus four minutes,* the voice says.

"No," I gasp out. As I race forward, the lights and walls begin to tremble, and I don't know whether it's the earth moving beneath us or the *Lazarus's* forty Cerus engines purring in preparation. I wheel around a bend and flinch back, burying my face in my hands. The hallway ends in an open door to the bridge, where a brilliant glow pierces the windshield, banks of floodlights glaring into the ship.

I lurch over the threshold, peering through my fingers. A dark-haired girl is standing at a dashboard so long that it wraps around in a boomerang curve. Beside her, someone in the commander's seat is navigating the launch gear with quick, fluid motions. The grid of buttons and joysticks is cast in graduated relief, like the skyline of a model city. Overhead, a low female voice says, *Error. Clear launch pad. Error. Finalize inertial measurement unit alignment. Error. Final leak checks incomplete.*

The person in the seat flicks a switch and presses a palm down on a screen. *Retracting access arm,* says the voice.

"What are you doing?" My scream bursts out over the rumble of disturbed metal as the auxiliary power hums to life. "Nobody's boarded yet!"

I clatter down the dozen steps, hand outstretched to wrench the seated figure back, but then the chair revolves to face me. I stop dead. The woman in the seat is as tall and broad-shouldered as an Amazon, a frizz of honey-blond hair floating around her face. This is the *Lazarus's* head pilot, Commander Sara Jefferson. Now I recognize the dark-haired girl as her daughter, Eli, who stood at the commander's shoulder yesterday like a lieutenant, eyeing our tour group with wary interest.

They must have been here already when we came aboard. They're why the doors were open, why the lights were on like a welcoming home's.

Commander Jefferson scans me sneakers to ponytail. If she recognizes me from TV or the press, she makes no sign.

She rounds back to the dashboard and says, "We have people aboard. Fifty-four of them." She points to a screen that shows live video of the hull door, which is now sealed shut. "We've been counting."

"But the crew is still—"

"The crew knows we have to save who we can. The aftershocks are already starting. Every second on the ground is a risk we can't afford."

Speechless, I watch the pilot's hands play over the controls. I thought the countdown was the work of some terrified kid, throwing away hundreds of lives out of fear. This is different, a calculated risk assessment, a matter of protocol. But it feels just as brutal.

"Eli, get her a suit." The commander aims a finger toward the bunks set into the wall. "Then both of you strap in."

Eli throws open a cabinet and tosses me a packet of white fabric. *T-minus two minutes,* says the voice overhead as I tear the pressure suit out of the package.

A hiss makes me glance over. Eli has hit the vacuum seal on her suit, making its exoskeleton constrict her silhouette. As her visor slides into place, I meet my own eyes in the translucent mirror of its surface and see my face layered over hers.

"Suit up," Eli says. She swings into a bunk and draws the straps into place, moving as efficiently as a dancer or a boxer. It all looks practiced, as if she knew, but—of course—she lives on this complex. For this girl, every waking second would have been colored by the fact that, soon enough, it would be time to go.

The commander's voice blares over the PA and rings down the halls behind us: *Attention, passengers. Pressure suits are stored beneath your bunks. Put them on over your clothes, press the vacuum seal at your left shoulder, and strap in as shown by the instruction card at your bedside.* The orders translate themselves into Mandarin, then Spanish, as the commander springs from her seat toward the last bunk.

Halfway there, she goes still. She's paled to the color of the moon. Her lips move fractionally as the PA repeats her words in Hindi, French, Arabic, Swahili.

She breaks for the exit. By the time she reaches the stairs, she's in a full-out sprint.

"Mom?" Eli yells after her, but the commander has already reached the bridge's upper level. She's flying down the hall, a splash of golden hair disappearing.

The voice overhead says, *T-minus one minute.* I look down at my pressure suit, knowing it's time to strap in. I have my orders.

But faces are flashing through my mind. The younger kids paralyzed with fear, clinging to their bunks, and the soldiers trying to urge them forward. The engineers and technicians and astronauts on their way, not knowing that we're about to abandon them.

I could force the ship to wait. After years of wishing I could do anything to help anyone, I could do this one thing.

The pressure suit falls from my hands. I go for the dashboard.

"Hey," says Eli. "Stop!" I hear her struggling against her harness, bucking against the straps like a restrained animal. The belts are locked. "Get away from that!" she yells. "What are you doing?"

Truthfully, I have no idea. My fingers skim grids of buttons that clatter gently in their frames. There are hundreds upon hundreds, acronyms printed on every surface. A heading that reads PIL SEPARATION has dozens of keys grouped beneath it, divided into inscrutable combinations of letters and numbers. I scan them, hunting for a kill switch.

As the voice says *Thirty,* my eyes land on the screen where the commander was typing. The launch sequencer is playing through its final checks. *Vent valves locked,* it reads. *Positron shuttling fields active. Orbital frame aligned.* And there, in the corner, above a list of override codes, is a button pulsing red: ABORT LAUNCH?

I lunge for the screen, but with my finger an inch away, I freeze. Commander Jefferson is the professional. She's right about the risks. What if I press the button, a tremor rocks the ship, the launch pad slips askew, and we die along with everyone outside?

The red words blink, tantalizing me. What should I do? What do I think is right? I can't remember the last time it mattered what I thought. I feel utterly and terrifyingly free.

T-minus ten, says the voice. *Nine. Eight.*

The ship's engines roar to life. My mind becomes a circus of hysterical thought, a whirl of *No, no, please wait—not yet not now—give me more time.* Not even all the time I want, not even measured in years, not even enough time to say goodbye. Just enough to answer the questions knifing through me: Is it better to stay or go? To risk it all or run for your life? Is it better to live knowing what you've done or die knowing what you are?

Seven. Six. Five, says the voice, calm and sweet. Whoever recorded it was smiling, I think.

The deep-tissue roar in the air swells, and as the metal casings over the windshield ease toward each other, I look up, shivers skating across my body, finger still suspended over the kill switch. Through the haze, a fiery light is shattering the horizon, and I think of a sun bursting out from our core, I think of a spirit erupting from a body at the moment of death. *This can't be true,* I think uselessly. It can't be real, because only hours ago, before I fell asleep, the moon was gazing through the barracks window. The real world is that stillness, that held breath of anticipation. Not this—this panic, this mess of smoke. Maybe this is just another nightmare, in the same genre as my last three years of nightmares, and at the end of the countdown, my eyes will snap open, and I'll breathe heavily for a minute before rolling out of bed, wanting water.

I look down to see a blank screen beneath my fingertip.

Four, says the voice. *Three. Two. One.*

Pressure lands on the crown of my head like an anvil. This is not a dream. I topple into the commander's seat, and it locks backward into a horizontal takeoff position. Spots explode in my vision as millions of pounds of machinery blast off. We move slowly at first, and then accelerate mercilessly, gravity compounding on my skull, my throat, my wrists, pulling down at the soft tissues of my eyes. I begin to slip out of consciousness, choking, my body pinned and trembling like prey, and I feel ashamed, naive, for expecting myself to wake up. The old true world has evaporated, the way old truths do all the time. People used to think the moon was fixed in a crystalline sphere. People used to believe Earth would last forever. The truth is always an unshakable thing until it's a story people used to tell each other.

CHAPTER 2

ALONE

For a while I keep myself under. I nearly float to the surface of consciousness every so often, but there's too much up there that I don't want to confront. I hold myself in this halfway place instead, not asleep and not awake, seeing blurry flashes of red—the pulsating vessels in my eyelids—and of neon blue, the edges of some dream I can't pierce my way into. I hold myself under like someone trying to drown.

———

Eventually my eyelids glide open. Above is pumice-gray plating and light so white that it reminds me of dentistry. There's no moment of confusion or denial. I remember everything.

A high-pitched whine skewers my eardrums as I ease up in the commander's seat, touching my temple gingerly. The bridge is motionless. Eli's bunk is empty, and the alerts on the dashboard screen have been replaced by an abbreviated list of ship systems. The item at the top reads *COMM*.

Something tightens in my chest. I stagger out of the seat and hunch over the screen to press *COMM > BASE*. A speaker emits a static hiss, and a world map fills the display. It's the Robinson Projection, Alaska shrunken, poles flattened, pulsing red dots littering the continents like a pox.

I magnify the United States and tap our launch site, an icon of a spaceship labeled XPLORER INC. COMPLEX. The icon blinks yellow, issuing ripples into the Pacific as a dial tone keens.

But after five rings, I cancel the call, giving my head a hard shake. Trying our launch site is idiotic—of course none of the crew would stay. Hopefully they're halfway across Nevada by now. I zoom out, ignoring the dozen other icons that stretch down the West Coast toward San Francisco. These complexes used to house the space tourism giants, Spacescape and Hyer and YouMoon, until the world's astronautical facilities were ordered to focus on designing a ship like the *Lazarus*. If no one is left at the Xplorer site, the others will be deserted, too.

I touch CAPE CANAVERAL, FL, and the dialer starts up again. This time, someone will answer, someone who can tell me what's happening on Earth. Any moment now.

After eleven tones, the dialer goes dead.

"No, come on," I whisper. I press WALLOPS ISLAND, VA, then KODIAK, AK. I hit bases near Cairo and Buenos Aires, near Moscow and London.

"Hello?" I say over the dial tone, beginning to feel dizzy. "*Lazarus* to Earth. Come in. . . . Is anyone there?"

The tone is a relentless middle C. The map seems to expand before my eyes, Madagascar spreading away from Mozambique, Ireland from England, Sri Lanka from India, the oceans opening infinitely, every landmass huge and empty.

The stations are abandoned. We're alone.

I lift my bowed head and feel as if I'm falling slowly into the sight beyond the windshield. One thick layer of transparent ceramic is the only thing that separates me from the silvery webwork of the galaxy. At home, I used to watch the night sky through my bedroom window to calm myself down. The stars were perfect, remote, untouchable, everything I aspired to be. Now I'm among them.

I take a step back from the dashboard, then turn on my heel, jaw set. I don't need to make contact to know what's happening on Earth. I know the emergency protocol. After the eruption, autocalls and texts would have hit every watch, phone, headset, and earpiece in the world, and by now, millions of people will be filing into sprawling underground bunkers. Three hundred eighty-eight thousand of those complexes were constructed in the US alone over the last three years; the fact swims up from nowhere to bolster me, and details follow. Capacity five hundred per bunker. Highest number of bunkers per capita in West Virginia, lowest in Alaska. I can always trust myself to remember too much.

So, with any luck, Lilly and Marcus will already be belowground with their families. As for my parents, they'll have been among the first to reach safety. My mother is probably in some Swiss bunker near Geneva. She'll be making an address from a White House in VR space right now, her hands folded on a digital Resolute desk while my father stands behind the camera with the press team, his thumbs-up bent backward in that hitchhiker's angle. Once they get word that the *Lazarus* has launched, they'll find a way to contact us. That's right. That has to be right.

As I start up the steps, I turn my thoughts to the fleet. The *Lazarus*'s blueprint was only finalized for mass production a few weeks ago, but maybe some supply line will have time to manufacture the parts. Maybe a team far away from California will build more ships before the atmosphere becomes too hot and humid to breathe. Maybe . . .

I reach the top of the steps, and my thoughts of Earth vanish.

In the silence, I thought I was alone, but Eli is standing in the threshold. Sprawled out on the tiles at her feet, blond hair clotted with something dark that hasn't quite dried, is the commander.

For a moment they're both so still that the image is unnatural. Then Eli looks up at me. Something has gone from her face. Before takeoff, the flush in her cheeks was violent, her red mouth so thin and taut that it looked like a welt across her milk-white skin. I remember her features distorting behind her visor as she yelled, *What are you doing?*

That person has sunk into her now. Her narrow face is pale, her lips colorless. Long dark hair shadows one eye, while the other, an electric blue spot like laser light on a plaster wall, moves over me unseeingly.

"What happened?" I manage to ask.

"Not sure. . . . I found her in one of the Planters." Eli's voice is husky, and her mouth hardly moves when she speaks, like a ventriloquist's. "She slipped and fell, I think. Hit her head."

"You carried her here?"

Eli nods.

Our gazes move downward together. The previous day seems to shrink before me into a video that I am watching over and over again, unable to understand the sequence of events. Not even twelve hours ago, I was stepping out of an SUV onto the complex with a rare feeling of optimism. The sight of the *Lazarus* glowing against the blue sky made me think, *This could actually happen*—the fleet could be ready by spring, and when I went home to DC on Monday, I'd describe the ship to Marcus and Lilly, and in September their families would get drawn in the passenger lottery, and everything would be as close to okay as we could reasonably expect. Just hours ago these things felt plausible, and now, somehow, I'm hurtling away from Earth, standing over the body of the one person aboard who was trained for this.

A squeak of foot on tile cuts the air. Eli is making for a bank of lockers set into the wall. Only now do I register that while I was unconscious, she changed into a ship's uniform. These are dark suits ribbed at the knees and elbows, but cut strategically loose at the armpits and groin—"To prevent friction and sweat collection!" said our tour guide yesterday, bursting with enthusiasm. "With this material, these things are never going to wear out!"

Eli throws open locker after locker. She rummages through orange suits and silver tanks, through manuals and wires. I feel a dull, hot stab of pity. She must be searching for medical equipment. She must still, somehow, think there's hope.

"Eli," I say.

She doesn't turn. I'm not sure she heard, rifling through a locker full of power tools.

I raise my voice. "Eli."

"Yeah, what," she says mechanically.

"If you're looking for the first aid kit, I think it's on the lower level."

"First . . . no, I'm looking for . . ."

She trails off as she opens another locker. This time, she's in luck. She seizes a tablet from a charging pad inside and scrolls through, lips shaping words but emitting no sound.

I wait for her to explain. No explanation comes. Finally I ask, "What's on that tablet?"

Her face turns in my direction. I'm used to people looking through me, but Eli's stare is so unfocused she could be sleepwalking. "Diagnostic tests. Maintenance was supposed to make sure nothing got disrupted on launch. We don't have maintenance, so. I've got to start on the list."

"Wait. You don't—"

She's turning away, already receding from the conversation again. "Then the walk-through. Inventory . . . Check everything for the gravity strapdowns . . ."

"*Eli.*"

The sound of her name seems to bring her back to herself. She swallows and blinks hard, as if trying to restart her senses.

I don't let my gaze stray back to her mother. "You don't need to worry about any of that right now."

Her mouth tightens to a thin line. "Yeah, I do. Of course I do. This has to get done."

"It will get done. I'll do it."

"You'll—what?" Disorientation passes across her face. "No, I have to . . . I can do this," she mutters, her chest rising and falling quickly. She's looking around at the bridge, at the cabinets and windshield and dashboard, everywhere but at her mother. "Just give me ten minutes. I'm fine. I'll—"

"No." I say it gently, but she breaks off at once like I've shouted. "I'll handle everything out there. You stay here and take all the time you need."

Clutching on to the tablet, Eli shifts her weight from dirty sneaker to dirty sneaker. Her free hand tugs at her uniform's collar, then works through a snarl in her dark hair. Her body is all restlessness. It's obvious that she doesn't want pity, but the feeling intensifies in me like a stomachache.

I approach her the way I'd approach a skittish housecat. "Trust me," I say. "I'm not a careless person."

I feel her attention alighting on my features in little bursts of self-consciousness. She glances to my chin, and the cluster of acne there seems to burn. She looks to my eyes, and a muscle twitches up against my lower lid, shivering against my eyeball. Under her sharp expectancy, I feel slow and groggy.

"I know," she says finally, her voice so quick and quiet that I have to strain to hear. "I saw you in those PSAs they plastered all over the internet. Trying to tell everyone to stay in school as long as possible."

I grimace. "Those weren't my idea."

Eli's mouth twitches. Her hackles seem to settle.

I rest my fingertips on the tablet. After a long, final look of evaluation, she releases it into my grip.

I scroll through a checklist titled *Manual Diagnostic System Checks*. It must be a thousand items long. Under subheadings like *Radiation Sail, Hull,* and *Water Treatment* are lists of jargon that mean little to me: power dispersal gauge 90.211c, ionomer skins, pressurized seals.

"So," I say, "you know how to do these checks?"

"Yeah. They're basically automatic, um, just need a human monitor." She mumbles her way through an explanation of where to find the handheld monitors, where to place them to read the equipment's signals, and how to find positive reads or error messages.

"Great. I'll show the others so we can divide them up. Do we have to finish tonight?"

She shakes her head. "It's supposed to be a three-day process. Any major damage would self-report up here."

"Good." I turn off the tablet's display. "I'll come back soon, see how you're doing, all right?"

Eli jerks her narrow shoulders, a do-what-you-want motion, but I think I see surprise or even gratitude in the look she sneaks at me. There's something sullen, something childish about the way she won't just say, *Yeah, see you soon.*

Half a dozen steps down the hall, I glance back. Eli is standing at her mother's side again, looking down into the commander's lifeless face.

"Go," she says, not looking up. "I'll be fine."

———

The halls of the *Lazarus* hide what's ahead. They bend and meander, designed so that the ship's interior feels organic, like a system pushed into place by a thousand hardworking ants. As I wind through the Systems Wing with buckets of equipment, voices ring off every curve, echoing strangely. In one moment it sounds like someone is standing at my shoulder. The next, they're a mile away. The walls and ceiling alike are the delicate gray of a sky about to snow.

Only when I emerge onto the balconies do the voices clarify. Down in the atrium, the group has knotted up around an artificial fireplace playing across a fifteen-foot screen. Digital flames wave ceaselessly, randomized, never-ending. Before this hearth, sleek black sofas are bolted to the floor in formation, making the atrium resemble something between an oversize living room and a hotel lobby.

As I ride the elevator downward, I watch the other kids through the glass walls. A sandy-haired figure is waving one hand to try and quiet them. It's Sergei, towering over everyone else, a harried expression on his round, earnest face.

Of course he's getting nowhere. No one's wearing a translator, and the tour group is an international hodgepodge, all ages, with no unifying interests. We have exactly one thing in common: Each of us has at least one parent who's a member of the Global Fleet Planning Commission. Some are political leaders like my mother, others top scientists or engineers or consultants. The whole concept of this tour was to show international cooperation, an attempt to smooth over years' worth of enmity at GFPC summits. So, while we flew to California to tour the *Lazarus*, our every movement fawned over by cameras, our parents flew to Geneva, where I assume they were shouting and arguing until the last second.

The elevator slows. I fish a silicone translation earpiece out of a bucket, rotate its dial to the English setting, and slide the fleshy nub into my ear. Then I focus on my breathing. Back home, I developed a ritual to prepare myself before I walked between curtains onto a stage, or down an airplane's steps onto the runway, anywhere that brought me into open space. I squeeze my fists, then let go, imagining the tension streaming down to my heels and puddling around my shoes. I imagine stepping out of my body and leaving a husk of shed skin behind. By the time the elevator door glides open, my mask is in place.

"Everyone's okay?" Sergei is calling in Russian. "No one's

hurt?" As he finishes each phrase, my earpiece translates, automatically matched in pitch and timbre to his voice.

For decades, translation earpieces have been outfitted with more and more advanced AI, so at this point, for dozens of languages, they're as good as human translation. The fewer native speakers a language has, though, the less well-trained the AI, so with regional dialects and rarer languages, you run into the problems old translation technology had. Flat, emotionless voicing and hyper-literal colloquialisms. Awkward grammar and limited vocabulary.

"Everyone, please quiet down," Sergei calls. "We need—"

He breaks off, spotting me at the foot of the ramp as I wave and lift the bucket of translators. The noise quavers, and the crowd parts to let me through to the fireplace.

Sergei brightens as he plucks a translator from the bucket. "I thought you went back," he says, slotting the device into his ear. "I'm glad you didn't get left behind."

"Me too," I say, forcing a smile. "Help me pass these out?"

Sergei and I step up onto the hearth, a smooth black ledge the length of a sedan, and distribute the translators. The smallest of the group to scurry up, a tiny Irish girl, looks around thirteen. Did the soldiers even get the youngest kids past the barracks door? Did they faint from the punishing heat, break down hacking in the smoke? Did they take the elevator up the access tower only to find the arm retracting, while they screamed for us to wait a moment longer, please, just a second, open up?

If I'd pressed the kill switch, they might have made it aboard. An entire crew could be here, reassuring us, preparing to operate the ship as planned. I might not be standing here with this tablet in my hands.

As the last kids back away from the hearth, tucking in their earpieces, someone calls out, "How did we take off?"

"Yeah," says another kid, "who's flying the ship?"

I tamp down the guilt and regret. There's no time for either. These kids don't need to know about my indecision, or about the commander's death. They need some reassurance.

"The head pilot's daughter is in the bridge," I reply. "Elizabeth Jefferson. Eli. She sent me down here."

"Are we in touch with Earth?" Sergei asks to signs of hope in the crowd—craned necks, parted lips.

"Not yet," I say carefully, "but it's barely been an hour since the eruptions. We'll keep sending out signals, and hopefully we'll hear something soon."

I try to strike a balance with my tone. Pure optimism would sound like a lie, but I don't want to sound grim or wooden, either. I need to channel my mother, steady and reassuring, as relaxed in front of ten thousand people as she was at our dinner table.

It seems to be working. No one's going into emotional meltdown, anyway. They're all watching, waiting for more. I see myself in their eyes as if from far away, a girl like a plastic figurine, hands clasped behind her back.

"Okay." Sergei, clearly rallying, claps his hands together. "Okay, so, we're going to Juventas."

"That's the plan," I reply.

There's some uncertain whispering, so I add, "The ship's course is charted for an exoplanet called Juventas, which is in Alpha Centauri's habitable zone. That's 5.4 lightyears away or so, about as close as we could hope for, and it's point nine times the mass of Earth. Pretty promising from a statistical standpoint."

"How do you know all this?" someone calls.

"They told us on the ship tour."

"And you memorized it on the spot?" says a skeptical voice.

"I took notes," I say, which is true, and easier than explaining my memory. The instant recall isn't just a knack for numbers. One skim of a textbook propels me through any test. Phrases from favorite speeches fall out of my mouth verbatim. Lilly used to tease me mercilessly about that. "Of course you have favorite speeches," she'd say with that teasing grin. "God, Chen, you've really out-Chenned yourself."

Trying to shake the sound of her voice, I go on, "We—we also have coronagraph images showing that Juventas's surface is bluish. That's another good sign the planet's habitable."

"Hang on. We don't know if Juventas is *habitable?*" a tall girl says in Russian. "We're just flying at the nearest blue thing?"

I study the girl, trying to decide whether she's joking. The translator makes it hard to tell. Even in the big four languages—English, Mandarin, Hindi, and Spanish—the one thing that still often fails to come through is sarcasm.

The girl's fine blond hair is as short as a cap, forming a soft triangle at the nape of her neck, and as I study her full cheeks and long, feathery eyebrows, I spot the family resemblance.

Sergei looks down at his sister with annoyance. "Irina, none of us is going to know better than every astronomer and space agency on Earth."

Irina scowls. "I'm not saying I know anything. I'm just saying it's risky to fly toward some planet we don't know is safe." She looks back to me. "Why don't we go to Antaeus instead? We were trying to make a colony there anyway."

"True," I reply, "but the Antaeus settlement was supposed to be temporary. That's a minor planet without much of an atmosphere. We're looking for a place that's sustainable forever, not a spot for a terraforming experiment."

I cast around for a segue, not wanting to linger on the topic of high-profile space disasters. The Antaeus mission launched when I was thirteen, a crew of two hundred sent into interstellar space, and we lost contact eleven months later, days after they landed. The last sound that came through the transmission was a rumble that blossomed into a roar, the noise of a catastrophic explosion. That's the last thing we need in mind right now.

"The truth is," I say, keeping my tone conversational, "in terms of our lifetimes, our destination won't make much of a difference. The *Lazarus*'s average sustained speed is just under point four percent of light speed, so Juventas is eleven hundred years away, and that's one of the closest possibilities for a permanently habitable planet."

A hush falls. Eyes dart from left to right, everyone sneaking furtive looks at the people nearby. I know what they're thinking. This ragtag group of fifty kids—this is it, for the rest of our lives. These are the people we'll grow old with. The people we'll start families with.

My mouth goes dry. I've never wanted to have kids, but now there's no other option. We'll have to populate this place with as many children as possible, so that the future inhabitants of the *Lazarus* will be genetically diverse. How long will it take for our lives to become a cycle of pregnancy and birth and childrearing?

For a moment, the wrinkles of agitation are ironed flat by the huge, warm weight of the future. Then a tearful voice rises out of the group: "Maybe it's not too bad yet on Earth." It's the tiny girl who was panicking in the elevator. Her tan skin is practically gray now, her sky-blue hijab askew over her forehead. "Can we go back to find survivors?"

"Yes," Irina says immediately. "We should go back to Earth and stay in orbit! There must be a way to get more people on board. Weren't we supposed to have space elevators, to get the water for the ships up out of the atmosphere?"

"None of that has been built yet," I say. "We only selected the *Lazarus* as a prototype last month, so the matching infrastructure for the fleet was supposed to go up over the rest of the year. As it is, we've got dozens of elevator sites and no elevators yet."

An alarmed-looking Italian boy blurts out, "You mean we don't have any water?"

"No, we do," I say quickly. "NASA built other prototypes in orbit, like the rotary frame that handles our gravity and a filling station. Over the past couple years, they've been sending water to that station in small payloads. So, after we took off, the *Lazarus* flew there on autopilot to fill our tanks."

The Italian boy relaxes, but Irina doesn't look satisfied. "Okay, so we don't have the elevators," she says, "but can't we go back down to get more people?"

"The planet's gravity is too strong. If the ship reentered, we'd need a new launch apparatus to get up here again."

"We can't even try?" asks the tiny girl with the hijab.

"Are you an idiot, Fatima?" snaps another Arab girl nearby. "Go back down. For God's sake. Do you want to die, too?"

Voices surge up, but I speak over the swell: "We're not going back, and we're not going to die." As my words rebound toward me from the reaches of the atrium, I look between the fearful faces. "We're going to Juventas, like Sergei said, because

Earth's experts decided it was our best chance. It's possible that they could finish more ships on Earth before the collapse fully sets in, but we need to focus on the *Lazarus*."

"What is there to focus on?" asks a dark-skinned boy with glasses. He's so soft-spoken that I'm impressed my translator picked the words up. "Aren't the systems automated?"

A slender Latino boy near the front shoots him a scathing look. "We don't have any of the ship's personnel," he says, smoothing down his sleek black hair, which is such a perfect wave that it could be carved from ebony. "That means we have to make sure everything is in order ourselves."

"Exactly," I say, lifting up the tablet, "and this is the first step."

As I relay Eli's explanation of the diagnostic checks, everyone's eyes rivet on the tablet. There are no protests.

"So," I finish, "raise your hand if this is your first time aboard."

Half the group's hands go up.

"I'll show you around the *Lazarus*. Everyone else, I brought monitors and—"

I break off as Sergei nudges me and whispers, "Have a heart. They need to rest."

Looking more closely at the crowd, I realize he's right. They're bleary-eyed, swaying in their nightclothes, and one of the younger kids has nodded off on a sofa.

I clear my throat. "We'll get started in the morning. The locks on the cabin doors work on fingerprint recognition, so we'll look up how to set the privacy IDs, and then we can pick our rooms."

"I already set mine," says a high, musical voice. "I can show you how."

We look over to see Caro Omondi lounging against the end of the hearth, tying her headscarf into a complicated knot. The logo of *Silverwing*, a vintage VR game, is splashed across her T-shirt, and a black canvas purse is slung across her body.

"Perfect," I say with a grateful nod. "Follow Caro's lead, choose your cabins, and try to get some sleep, everybody."

Caro saunters toward the elevators. "This way, runts," she sings—either a translation error or heavy irony, since Caro can't be taller than five foot one. As she passes, hands in her pockets, she gives me a good try at a casual grin. I'm too jarred by the sight of a smile to respond.

As half the group tags along behind her, Sergei and I climb down from the hearth. "Sorry about my sister," he mumbles, tugging at the neck of his T-shirt.

I sigh. "I'm sure she just needs some sleep."

"You expect us to sleep?" says a crisp voice. Sergei and I turn to find the sleek-haired Latino boy listening to our conversation. His arms are crossed, one finger tapping a quick, agitated beat against his bicep, as if he's marking every second of his life that we're wasting.

"I couldn't rest if I tried," he goes on. "If these checks are really so important, we should start them now."

"We have three days, Francisco," Sergei says with a smile. "Leigh, this is Francisco Quispe, from Bolivia. He was telling me at dinner about the cable cars in La Paz."

Francisco's face contracts as if he's felt a stomach cramp. He seems to struggle. Then he says, "We'll need longer than three days. We were supposed to have a hundred trained crewmembers aboard, and in case you've both forgotten, we have half that number and no idea what we're doing."

I measure him up, his dissatisfied tone, his ramrod-straight posture, the sharp, easy arrogance that hangs around him like expensive cologne.

"You're right," I say in confidential tones. "It would be best to get started, but I have to give that tour of the ship, and half these kids are close to passing out, and we need a plan before we start." I offer him the tablet. "If you're staying up anyway, would you figure out how to tackle this list over the next few days?"

Francisco's eyebrows rise. Then he softens visibly, his shoulders loosening. "Of course," he says as he takes the tablet from me. "I'll have it ready for the morning."

Sergei claps him on the back, maybe a more forceful gesture than he intended, given that Sergei is roughly the size of a house. "I'll help. I won't be sleeping, either."

Francisco glances up at Sergei, dark eyes shrewd, before saying, "Okay. Thanks." He perches on the arm of a nearby sofa. "Let's make groups of two or three to prevent individual error. Younger kids paired with older ones, I'd say."

"Sure," Sergei says, "and we should make sure everyone has plenty of time for each check. We don't want to rush any . . ."

As they fall into discussion, I retreat toward the tour group. The kids clustered around the hearth go quiet as I approach. They all look younger than me. Some of them seem ridiculously tiny, the way the first-years did when I showed up to senior orientation last fall. By then, hardly 10 percent of the student body was still attending, but my parents kept me enrolled, in a well-publicized move. There were so few students, so few teachers, that Lilly and Marcus and I took classes with fourteen-year-olds who looked like these kids do—like puberty hit them about thirty seconds ago.

I have the sudden realization that for the rest of my life it'll be like this. I'll always be part of the oldest generation, watching the world grow younger and younger around me.

"This way," I say, going for the elevator. "We'll start at the top."

CHAPTER 3

THE NEW WORLD

"All the railings and walkways," I call as we cross from one balcony to another, "basically the whole internal structure, is made from a superstructure of carbon nanotubes called anathylene. It's a hundred times lighter than steel but twelve times as strong." A line of heads is peeking over the rails at the atrium below.

"If you're wondering about the gravity," I go on, "it works through constant acceleration. After launch, we buckled into a rotary frame that we built in orbit. Right now, the ship is accelerating that way"—I point upward—"at one g. Once we reach our top speed, the ship will rotate in its frame a hundred and eighty degrees, and two days' negative acceleration is next.

After that, we'll keep cycling through positive and negative acceleration." I draw a waveform cycle in the air with my finger. "So, we're moving forward the entire time, but at varying speeds. At the end of every accelerative period, we'll be doing about 1.75 million meters a second, and at the end of every negative period, our speed will be closer to three-quarters of a million. Any faster, and—"

I cut myself off. According to our tour guide, if we traveled at a high enough velocity, ambient hydrogen would pierce through the ship and jack up our risk of cancer to near certainty. But space radiation is up there with the Antaeus explosion on the list of subjects I'd like to avoid.

I clear my throat. "When we attached to the rotary frame, we also plugged into the *Hermes*, which is the filling station I mentioned earlier. It's equipped with automatic pumps that supplied our treatment plant with enough fresh water for the journey."

No one reacts. Actually no one has said a word since we started the tour. They look dazed, and as I run my palm over the smooth railing, I wonder if they're envisioning what the fleet should have been, a snowfall of silver ships, thousands upon thousands flurrying through space. If the fleet effort had gone to plan, we'd have saved 1 percent of Earth's population: 75 million randomly selected passengers, plus a quota of 15 million Necessary Personnel, mostly technicians, doctors, and astronauts. The number was ambitious but not impossible. With the upswing of space tourism in the past few decades, the infrastructure for mass-produced spaceship parts had been accumulating for a while. So, at first, the outlook was hopeful.

A year and a half after the announcements, though, the fractures started to show. Prototypes were getting axed left and right—not durable enough, not fast enough, not scalable enough. Factories were producing materials that didn't hold up under stress tests. Hurricane season swamped Central America and the US Southeast, typhoons slammed down on Bangladesh, and hundreds of half-constructed launch sites were reduced to rubble.

Three weeks ago, when the Global Fleet Planning Commission greenlit the *Lazarus* as our prototype, I felt hopeful for the first time in a year. We were behind schedule, but I thought there was still a chance we could catch up. Now, here we are, fifty-three survivors in place of ninety million. One ship where there should have been ninety thousand.

"Let's go take a look at the Menagerie," I suggest too brightly, hoping the sight of the animals will enliven the group. A few faces show shy hints of interest.

"What's the Menagerie like?" asks Fatima as we file into the elevators.

"I haven't seen that floor yet, either. It wasn't part of the tour."

"Will the animals be awake?"

"I doubt it. I'm guessing the launch sequence released some sort of gas tranquilizer." As we file into the antechamber to the Menagerie, though, I realize I have no idea how its inhabitants were protected from the launch pressure. And even with the scale of the *Lazarus*, how will they have enough space?

Then the inner door slides away, and freezing air engulfs us, gloving my bare arms.

When I heard *Menagerie*, I pictured ecosystems like dioramas, filled with shrubs, grass, and landscaped enclosures. I imagined a glass-walled aviary rattling with the sounds of birds. But there's no Noah's Ark here, no cantering pairs, two by two by two, awakening from a peaceful sleep. We're standing in a cavernous chamber awash with white-blue light. Frosted glass cubes are stacked up to the ceiling in grids, forming long aisles, fixed in place by silver frames.

As I approach one of the grids, I see the glittering cubes illuminated from behind. Each is a foot or so wide and contains dozens of vials, boxed up and iced over, DNA samples preserved indefinitely in cryogenic cases.

I draw a deep breath and regret it instantly. The acrid scent of disinfectant hangs on the air. Every surface is as sterile as an operating table. Everywhere the light lands, it glazes, never penetrating.

I turn around. "Let's go," I say. The others look stricken, Fatima's frail body shivering, Irina Volkova's face like marble in the glow.

"It's all right," I say faintly. "Let's just go."

The Menagerie seems to have sucked the warmth from the ship. The *Lazarus* was built to house a thousand people, and as we move through its warren-like corridors, its tremendous size and emptiness presses in. We pass hundreds of cabins that will stay unoccupied. We hover at the threshold to the canteen, which has nineteen empty seats for every one we can fill. We pass through rooms of worship that feel ghostly, with metal altars and plastic basins for ablutions, stainless crucifixes attached to bare walls. I keep thinking of those frosted blocks containing the last remnants of everything we left to die on Earth.

It isn't until we reach the full-immersion virtual reality chamber—the portal to a million worlds, the luxury we used to tell Marcus he'd never have—that the others show signs of life again. As I roll the door open, revealing the dark curvatures of the chamber's walls, someone pipes up, "I get the first go!" An Indian girl with red-tipped hair has darted up to the front of the group, teetering at the threshold as if she can already see something in the dark.

There are decent VR games made for headset alone, but the best ones are made for TPS, or Total Physical Surround. In a full-immersion chamber like this one, the player can choose between ambient sound, headset sound, or a mixture of the two, which professional gamers swear makes the difference. Wearing enhancement glasses adds layers of detail between you and the wallscreens, meaning 360-degree interactivity. Slip on your kinesis gloves, clip motion-capture beads to your joints, and find your body transplanted into another universe.

"I call second," somebody else chirps.

"That's not—"

"You can't—"

"We'll make a sign-up system soon," I break in with a tired smile. "We're almost done. The Catalog next."

We descend through the Preservation Wing to the Catalog's entrance, an imposing arch. I touch my fingertip to the entry pad, and with an echoing beep, the door glides open, revealing a semicircle of half darkness. Looming silhouettes are visible in the low light, each branching toward the ceiling, and when the door slides shut behind us, the quality of the silence changes. It's reverent now. Church silence.

Yesterday, when our tour guide led us down this six-floor spiral that houses thousands of Earthen artifacts, the place felt mysterious, intriguing, like the scent of another person's house. Tonight, it feels like a tomb. Qin Dynasty bronze and James Brown records, Senegalese medallions and Anasazi ceramics are heavily cushioned in towering displays. Dim, indirect lights spare the treasures too much exposure.

As we pass a section of exhibits on the fourth floor whose placards are dated between 2050 and the present day, a lump forms in my throat. A lot of these artists are still alive. So are the art communities who nominated them for inclusion in the Catalog, and probably some of the mentors who helped sculpt their imaginations. With those people trapped on Earth, what a ridiculous waste for me to survive.

I shouldn't even be here. I told my parents that I wanted to go to the GFPC summit with them, that I would visit the *Lazarus* when they did. "Besides," I said to my mom in the car as we whizzed along the highway to the maglev station, "why do I need to tour somewhere I'll be living for the rest of my life?"

"It's not about the ship," she told me. "You and the rest of these kids will have to be leaders once we're aboard the fleet. Besides, it's important to set an example by cooperation."

This seemed hilariously hypocritical, since the GFPC hadn't had a meeting in a year that hadn't ended in an icy standoff. By now, a whole coalition of leaders was boycotting summits, so there was no way they'd let their kids travel to the *Lazarus*'s site. Some example of cooperation, when anyone who might disagree was already removed from the equation.

Obviously I said none of that. I didn't scowl, didn't sigh, didn't roll my eyes. I looked out the window and stayed silent.

"Perk up, bao bao," my dad said brightly. "It's just one weekend."

The lump in my throat swells. If I'd known it wasn't just one weekend, I would have hugged them goodbye at the station. Maybe I wouldn't have boarded at all. Maybe I'd still be standing there in their arms, refusing to let go.

I'm shaken out of my thoughts by an "Oh!" from Fatima. We've reached the Catalog's ground floor, a section that houses a dozen carousels of priceless books, but the last carousel is empty. Books are scattered across the floor, covers overlapped like shingles, pages bent into loops. Storage boxes lie gaping nearby, packing foam and latex gloves drooled out around them.

Distrustful muttering builds up among the group. A boy in an Egyptian soccer jersey stalks toward the strewn books.

"What happened?" Fatima squeaks.

"It looks like they were still loading these," I reply.

"But if they didn't finish this," she says, her voice accelerating the way it did in the elevator before takeoff, "they weren't done with the ship. What if there's more? Do you think anything else is wrong?"

"Obviously," says Irina, nudging her way out of the group. "The ship wasn't meant to take off until next year. Why should everything be ready?"

The others are angling toward her. She addresses them, chin high. "If there's one flaw in the air filters or the water treatment plant, you can guess what's going to happen. We're not the fleet planners. We have no experts." She turns back to me, and I can see the fear under her defiance. "Well? You seem to know it all. What are the odds that we last longer than a month? What are we going to do after your diagnostic tests turn up some disaster?"

She's right, I think before I can stop myself. There were supposed to be engineers and mechanics to manage every valve and duct of this ship, technicians to diagnose an issue within moments of an error. Now that the only person aboard with any working knowledge is Eli, how long can we possibly survive?

Eleven hundred years seems like an insane, unimaginable goal, and if we don't reach Juventas, isn't it all meaningless? Why even bother trying?

Two dozen faces turn my way. At once, the spiraling thoughts halt. I hear myself replying as if on autopilot. "There's a perfectly good reason for the *Lazarus* to be ready. It's the prototype. Its systems were approved last month so that the Global Fleet Planning Commission could use it as a model for the other ships."

"So . . . you think the ship's okay?" a tentative voice asks.

I pause. After everything we've been through, I wish I could say, "Yes, I guarantee it, I know we're safe." But if I make up something too confident and Irina turns out to be right, the others won't believe another reassurance out of my mouth or anyone else's. I have to keep to the facts.

"The riskiest parts of the journey are liftoff and landing. Right now, we're hundreds of thousands of miles in, with no leaks or alerts. That's a good sign."

Irina smooths back a pale lock of hair, seeming to chew over my words, but a decisive scoff comes from another source: the Egyptian boy standing by the sea of books and foam and gloves. I fix my eyes on the back of his head, a mess of black curls. "Do you have something to add?" I ask.

He rounds on me, holding one of the books in a latex-gloved hand. "No," he says. "But you're good at not answering questions."

Someone in the group snickers. My toes curl, straining at the mesh ends of my running shoes. It's not that I don't want to state my opinion. It's that formulating an opinion at all is a risk. Once you figure out which direction your needle points, that belief becomes something other people can coax out of you, and they'll never let you go back on your first instinct, and just like that you've betrayed yourself.

The others watch me, obviously waiting for a retort, but I've been stifling comebacks my whole life. "Look at your mother," my dad always says. "Does she waste time in the LiveLy comment warrens, defending her reputation? No, she's busy trying to make people's lives better." The subtext, as always, is that if I roll around in the muck, slinging insults, I'll undo the image my parents built for us.

I consider the boy for a moment. He strips off the latex gloves as he looks back at me, steady and unrelenting, eyes as dark as earth after rain. His voice sounds familiar, although I don't know why it would, since he wasn't with our tour group yesterday.

Eventually I turn away from him as if I couldn't be less interested. "If that's all, let's check out one of the Planter floors, and then we're done for the night. This way."

As we leave the Catalog, I overhear Fatima remarking to the boy, "Good thinking, wearing the gloves."

"It's a habit," he says. "We have that kind of thing at home."

"Why?" she asks.

"My dad's an art conservator. He helped design the Catalog cases for the GFPC."

Filing the information away, I sneak a glance over my shoulder. The boy is stretching the gloves into sheer white lines. I realize how tired he looks, circles stamped under his eyes like thumbprints, nearly black against his golden-brown cheeks.

I lead the group into the Systems Wing. On the tenth story, we enter the topmost Planter floor, a brightly lit hall terraced with hanging soil beds. The rich, mineral scent unknits some of my tension, but as I describe the types of crops we'll grow and the manure recycling system, I'm still aware of the Egyptian boy in the corner of my eye. He isn't studying the soil beds or the piping, isn't squinting up at the grow lights like the others. His critical gaze is fixed on me again.

"Okay, everyone," I say at last. "Caro should still be in the Residential Wing. She'll show you how to program the cabin locks, and we'll regroup in the morning. Thanks."

I steel myself as they file out of the Planter hall. As expected, the Egyptian boy stays put. Once the door has slid shut at the others' backs, he approaches me with near-military posture, jaw set, shoulders squared. I affix indifference onto my expression as he stops before me.

"I know you agree with what Irina thinks," he says.

"Irina seems to think a lot of things," I reply, keeping my tone mild. "Which bit do you mean?"

"You know what I mean. The books in the Catalog. The ship. If you didn't think anything else was wrong, you wouldn't have let her finish that speech down there."

I fold my hands behind my back. "I heard her out because I wanted to be polite, not because I agree. Actually, I think speculating like that is pretty irresponsible right now."

The boy shakes his head, making his curly hair tremble. "It's not 'irresponsible' to be honest about what could happen next."

Annoyance twists up in my chest. He says "be honest" as if it's easy, as if honesty doesn't become a hundred times more complicated when you're talking life and death in front of a petrified crowd. I wish I could release a patronizing sigh.

Instead I ask, "What's your name?"

"Anis Ibrahim."

"Anis. Okay. I'm Leigh Chen."

With a note of incredulity, he says, "Yeah, I know that."

I can't help a small smile. Surprise eases his frown, but not for long. "Answer the question," he presses. "Do you think the ship's operational or not?"

My smile fades. "It doesn't matter what I think. It matters what's true."

"Oh, brilliant," he says, cheeks darkening. "Of all the people to make it aboard, we had to get a *politician*."

As his words gather heat, that nagging feeling of familiarity returns. I open my mouth to reply, but then the memory resurfaces: my hands chafing against my backpack in the barracks, trying to yank it free.

That's where I've heard his voice before. He was the one who heaved my bed frame up that crucial inch on Earth.

My annoyance untwists. The beginnings of my response die on my tongue. For an instant, the tension I always hold in myself goes slack, and the boy in front of me seems to turn translucent. I still see him as an obstacle, digging in his heels on this meaningless debate, but there, just beneath, is someone who helped me immediately and unquestioningly, at a time when every second's delay could have meant the difference between life and death.

I wonder if he's even connected me to that panicked girl in the barracks. He hasn't shown a single sign of recognition. I left my backpack in the bridge, and it would have been hard to get a good look at my face in the chaos.

All this has whirled through my mind in a few seconds. He's starting to look confused that I haven't retorted, or even reacted, to his jab.

"Aren't you going to say anything?" he asks.

"No, I think you covered all the major points." Meaning it as a peace offering, I give another smile. Anis's eyes stray down to my mouth. He shakes his head hard, looking even more confused, and stalks back through the door to the balconies.

As the door shuts, I stand looking after him for a long minute, and little by little, my annoyance rises to the surface again. Maybe he knows exactly what I owe him. Maybe he even thinks that because he helped me on Earth, he automatically gets some moral high ground.

His accusation begins to echo around me. *A politician.* What else does the guy expect me to be, knowing who I am? His father was an art conservator. He has no idea what it's like, being a public figure. He doesn't know how it feels to stumble across the so-called jokes online, posted by people who hate my mother and decided to take their politics out on the shape of my hips or breasts or eyes. No one's ever generated a deepfake of *him* saying or doing humiliating things.

I was only ten when my family moved to Washington, DC, and within days of our arrival, I was already seeing notelets about myself online. They were dressed in child-friendly language—"Look How Cute Leigh Chen Is at This First Family Trip to the Zoo!"—but I looked at the candid photos, my mouth in an oblivious O as I pointed at the elephants, and I got the message. There is nowhere to blend in, nowhere to be normal. I am being watched all the time.

The extent of that fact became clear several months later, at the end of fifth grade. I was a shy kid, but three of my classmates had befriended me, inviting me over for birthday parties and even sleepovers, whispering excitedly when they saw Secret Service stationed outside their houses. Eventually the three of them asked if they could come over to mine. I said yes. I gave them a stammering tour through the private upper floor of the White House, not realizing they were wearing video-capture contacts, recording everything they saw.

The videos showed up on the front page of LiveLy the next morning. Tabloids spent weeks gleefully ripping apart the walk-through, theorizing that my father was a closet alcoholic, zooming in on my mother's prescription bottles in the bathroom. "Olivia Chen Has a Duty to Disclose Her Mental Health Status!!" they wrote. "The Presidential Bedroom: What Are They Into??" Even now, thinking about the shots from those videos makes me feel a sickened, anxious flutter.

My parents told me that I couldn't have expected it, but secretly I began to read about other First Families, and I realized that what my classmates had done was the rule, not the exception. I found tell-all after tell-all from former friends or acquaintances of First Family members. They gave interviews, wrote books, sold movie scripts. *Charlie Arthur and Me: My Years Among the Arthurs.* Here was a long-form piece by someone who'd gone to high school with Briana Whitney, a First Daughter in the '40s, musing about how—even then!—there had been signs that she would someday be involved in that insider trading scandal. There was a video with 140 million views from someone who said Jason Ness, a First Son, had slept with her when he was on vacation and this was what he liked in bed. All immediately available.

At ten years old, I didn't understand everything I was seeing, but again, I absorbed everything that mattered. Strangers began to scare me; I didn't know what else to do besides close myself off from them. Starting in middle school, I gave one-word answers to questions, and when people kept badgering, I learned how to expand the answers into boring, canned replies. I made up presidential excuses not to see anyone outside school. During lunch, I strategically sat at a near-deserted table: at one corner, my homework and me; at the other, the two kids nobody liked, Lilly Dionizio and Marcus Cho. Everyone said Lilly was a megabitch and Marcus was the most obnoxious kid in the whole school, but they didn't seem so bad to me.

Don't think about it, I tell myself, my eyes burning. *Don't think about them.*

I focus on the Planters' comforting scent and allow my mind to empty out. Thoughts of Washington, of school, fade away as I roam up and down the rows of soil beds. I scrub my mind clean of Anis Ibrahim's insistences. I settle into my numbness, no longer fighting the twitch in my upper lip or the slouch of my shoulders.

Eventually, after what feels like half an hour, I come to a halt. Everyone else must be in their cabins by now. It's probably safe to leave.

I move toward the exit, but near the door, I hesitate. There's a dark smear on the edge of the last soil bed. I crouch, frowning, and touch it. My fingertip comes away crimson.

My throat contracts. I shoot to my feet, frantically rubbing my hand on my running shorts. Eli found her mother in one of the Planters. Commander Jefferson died right there, slumped against the edge of the soil bed.

I'm on the verge of fleeing for the door when a question forms, one that makes me feel pinned to this spot. Why did the commander come here? I remember the way she froze, then ran as if her life depended on it. Something about this Planter hall called her away from the launch, away from her daughter.

When I inspect the soil bed, nothing seems out of place. The earth falls through my fingers, rich and dark and aromatic, as

Eli's toneless voice wanders through my memory. *She slipped and fell, I think. . . .*

She fell . . .

I look up. A maze of catwalks is suspended from the ceiling. These walkways enable us to monitor the Seeders, multipurpose machines that hang over the soil beds. From the Seeders' silver bellies protrude the tips of spidery fingers, which will extend to till the earth before the seeds are planted.

My footsteps resonate off the hall's reaches as I climb into the catwalks. The height dizzies me, coupled with the thought of Commander Jefferson slipping out of place, grabbing for the railing—falling—her hair flickering behind her. My own hands are tight on the rail now. I position myself over the site of impact.

The nearest Seeder's controls are directly opposite me. I trace the line of buttons, feeling cold, realizing that actually I don't want to know what brought Commander Jefferson here. At the least, I want to delay it. I want to be told by someone else in a way that cushions the blow. I don't want this responsibility, but I guess if I have the chance to push it away, it's already mine.

I press a button emblazoned with the image of a claw. The spidery plow descends, uncurls, and flexes back together like a fist made of knives. Another push, and the blades retract.

Next I press an icon of a drawer sliding out from a curved surface. The seed trough glides open. Inside someone has written, in permanent marker, the name of the seed species for each compartment. The first tray has been designated for *Solanum tuberosum*. The next, *Ipomoea batatas*. The sight of that slapdash, grown-up handwriting surprises me so much—the uneven but perfectly replicated loops of the *A*s, the hurriedly crossed *Ts*—that it takes me a long moment to look down at the compartments, already knowing what I'll see.

They're empty. Where our seed bank is supposed to be housed, where I should see a guarantee of our future, we have nothing but the smooth gray interior of the machine, and words scribbled down like temptations.

CHAPTER 4

THE PILOT

I don't let myself run through the ship, but even at a brisk walk, I feel beads of sweat trickling down my back. I imagine a hand seizing my elbow and Lilly asking, "What's wrong? You look awful." She's bright and casual, and it's September, sophomore year.

"I feel sick," I told her, which was true. I threw up four times in the bathroom that day. The announcements were still a week away, but my parents had told me the news the night before. Knowing what was on the way, I floated through school like a ghost. I watched people fret about unsympathetic teachers and getting included in weekend plans, and it seemed unbelievable that anyone could feel so normal.

Now, three years later, I feel the same sick dread. I know so much I could burst from the internal pressure.

Entering the fifth floor of the Residential Wing, I try to reassure myself. Each ship is stocked with a cache of nonperishable food, meant to be used during the initial growing season and in case of emergency shortage. It's enough to last a thousand people four years, so with only fifty-three of us aboard, the supply should last our lifetimes.

But a voice like Irina Volkova's murmurs in the back of my mind. *They weren't ready. They hadn't loaded the seeds. They hadn't finished the Catalog . . .*

By the time I reach the canteen, I'm clammy, nauseated, a fear like the flu. At the far end of the deserted hall is the dispensary, a wall of screens that feed bars of vacuum-sealed food into trays below. In the corner is a white door.

I rush between gleaming lines of trestle tables and into the storeroom. The place is dimly lit, glimmering with metal architectural struts. One wall wears a maze of pneumatic tubes, which supply the dispensary. These tubes connect to a steel cage affixed to the ceiling—and inside that cage is a crate full of silver-wrapped meal bars.

I stop beneath the cage and peer upward. The word SAMPLE is stamped on the side of the crate in fat red capitals. A diagram painted on the wall nearby explains, in cartoon graphics, how to unload an empty crate from the cage and replace it with another.

And as I approach the metal struts along the walls, I realize they aren't architectural supports. They have catches. This is where the extra crates should be, stacked five high.

An automatic light flickers on. Strip lighting races down to my left, down a corridor that stretches a hundred feet. I drift toward its end in a horrified trance, scanning the number ranges inked between the struts: *116–120*, *171–175*, all the way to *246–250*.

I look back down the empty hallway. This time, I let myself run.

"Eli," I gasp as I break over the threshold of the bridge. "There's—"

I break off. The scene I left has transformed. Commander Jefferson's body has disappeared, but I can't ask to where, because Eli is no longer alone. Caro Omondi is on the lower level with her, lounging in one of the copilots' seats with her feet up on the dashboard, while Sergei and Francisco are leaning over the railing nearby. Eli is seated in the commander's seat, but rather than facing the others, she's picking at the ends of her long hair.

"Leigh," Sergei says with a smile that shows the millimeter's gap between his front teeth. "We were explaining our plan for—" He falters at the sight of me.

Eli looks up. When she sees my expression, her apparent discomfort vanishes. She's on her feet at once, blank and tense and alert, like a prey animal who's heard a sudden snap in the undergrowth. "What's wrong?"

I didn't want to tell anyone except Eli, but there's no point trying to keep this from the others now. I descend the steps to the bridge's lower level, Sergei and Francisco at my heels, and perch on the edge of a bunk. "The food. The seeds... They're not there."

As I describe the empty Seeders, Sergei drifts into the remaining copilot's seat like a leaf, and Caro's feet slip down from the dashboard. Francisco's cheeks take on the color-less tinge of ash. With his erect posture and his meticulously arranged hair, he looks like a wax statue.

Eli is the only one who doesn't exhibit signs of horror. She listens unflinchingly until I describe the slots in the dispensary where the crates were supposed to be. Then she reanimates. She snatches a tablet from a drawer and starts writing, circling figures as she goes. She's still writing long after I've finished speaking.

"One crate," Francisco says hollowly. "How long will that last?"

Eli answers without looking up. "Split among fifty-three people, with a two-thousand-calorie average per day—four months."

A sick silence settles into every crevice of the bridge.

Eventually I find myself saying, "So we're going to starve." It is unbelievable how normal my voice sounds, as if the words are like any other.

"This isn't happening," Sergei moans. "This can't be happening." His broad chest trembles. Despite his size, he looks as young and terrified as Fatima.

Caro closes her eyes, fingertips steepled against the bridge of her nose. Her shoulders quiver. I wait for her to start sobbing.

Instead, laughter peals through her delicate fingers. She laughs and laughs, the sound eventually petering out into a weak chortle. When she takes her face out of her hands, her eyes are bright and bitter.

"That was fast," she rasps. "For a whole three hours, I thought we had a chance."

I dig my fingers into my quads, but I feel nothing. I'm

thinking of the last message I sent to Marcus. He and L̲
had just watched a VR movie we'd been meaning to see, and
he had a lot of opinions on the immersion effects, but I'd said,
*Tell me tomorrow? The soldiers are calling curfew and they're
heavily armed.*

I should have stayed up in secret to hear what he thought. I
should have pressed the kill switch before takeoff, then gone
back for my earpiece. At least then I would have spoken to my
parents and my best friends one last time.

"Hey." A voice resounds through the bridge, as vibrant as a
bow drawn hard across a viola's strings. "This isn't over."

I open my eyes. Eli is standing before the commander's chair,
hair tied back, those electrically blue eyes glaring like head-
lamps out of her thin face. The change is startling. That braced
stance is her mother's, squared shoulders to steady feet. There's
no trace of the listless girl who balked at my help and mumbled
answers to my questions so I could barely hear. The girl behind
the visor is back, the one who strapped herself in to leave Earth
with no hesitation—the girl the end of the world built.

"We're not just going to lie down and die up here," she says.
"All we need is one seed."

Sergei is the first to recover, his head bobbing on his long
neck like a tulip in high wind. "Could there be seeds in the
dispensary?" he suggests. "In the meal bars, I mean?"

"I don't think so," I say slowly. "The tour guide said making
them nonperishable was the first priority, so they'll keep something like two hundred years if we leave them sealed, but . . ."

"Yeah," Eli finishes, "nothing organic in there. I'd know if
there were something on this ship that could work. Outside is
our only shot." She begins to pace the length of the dashboard.

ɔ repeats, gazing through the windshield.
a seed bank into space at some point, trying
ɹ with aliens? It had details about Earth, and
ɹr soil, and things like that."

exclaims, stopping in her tracks. "I remember reading ↵   that. It launched in 2045 or something."

I shake my head. "I read about it, too, but that's because the
tracking went dark when I was in middle school. We have no
idea where it is anymore."

Caro's face falls, but Eli seizes on a new possibility at once.
"Bases, then. Are there any active moon or Mars bases?"

"The US's were dismantled ages ago," I say.

"What about China's?" Sergei says. "There was a Chinese
moon base, wasn't there?"

"Yes, the *Tiangong 7*," says Francisco with a trace of his former briskness. "My father worked on it, but its components
were returned to Earth with the *Delta*'s."

I press the heels of my hands into my closed eyes, making dark masses of color migrate across my vision. The *Delta*,
the space station in operation since '64, was deorbited this
January during the atmospheric clearance sweeps, when every
nonessential satellite, spacecraft, and piece of space junk was
brought back to Earth in preparation for the launch of an
unprecedented number of ships. But do we have any other
manned projects? Where else have we been? Haven't we left
any other marks on the universe?

Then it comes to me. An image of a tall, slender rocket
sculpted like a chess queen, a name emblazoned on its side:

"Antaeus."

Everyone looks at me. I'm on my feet, though I don't remember standing from the bunk.

"The Antaeus colony," I say. "They were going to terraform the place. Which means..."

I don't need to finish the sentence. The others' faces are tense with breathless understanding. If there's anything left in the ruins of that expedition, even just a single seed, the would-be colonists might not have died for nothing.

Eli rushes back to the commander's seat. "This is it," she says, drumming something into the dashboard screen. "It's got a thin atmosphere, less mass than the moon. So we could make entry and exit without boosters, and—"

"Wait, wait," Francisco sputters. "What if the seeds were caught in the explosion? Can seeds even germinate after this long?"

"What other option is there?" I say.

Caro speaks up. "We could go back to Earth," she says, tracing the logo on her *Silverwing* T-shirt. "Sure, we can't reenter, but doesn't the ship have rovers we can send down to the surface?"

"What rovers?" Sergei asks.

"They're sampling devices," Eli says, tapping a sequence of shortcuts, *SYS > EXT > SUP > ROV*. A schematic unfolds on the screen, showing a bullet-shaped pod. "They deploy to potentially habitable planets and test for potable water, run soil tests, that kind of thing. But..." Eli zooms in on the schematic, then shakes her head. "Yeah, they're too simple for this. They're not designed for retrieval or advanced navigation."

"Maybe we don't need to send anything down," Caro says. "Maybe if we broadcast a message from orbit, someone on Earth could—"

"Yes!" Francisco wheels around to Caro with sudden excitement. "Yes. Maybe someone can put a craft together and launch a seed bank up to us!"

re empty," I say quietly. "I tried base after base

s answering."

.isco says. "You said it yourself, it's too soon to

.ould go back and try until someone *does* answer."

.ears his throat. I exchange an uncomfortable look

w.. ... We know what's happening on Earth. Even as we speak, tsunamis are building across the Pacific. Tomorrow they'll crash into the coastlines of Asia. By the end of August, you'll need a respirator to walk down the street in DC, and by the end of September, Shanghai and Mumbai and nearly all of Denmark will be underwater.

Still...if word spreads that the *Lazarus* made it out, what if someone decides to brave the climbing temperatures and staff one of the bases, in case we try to send word home? At the very least, they'll scramble to build other ships. Humanity won't just go out without a fight. Won't that mean workers at the stations?

Eli seems to have arrived at the same conclusion. "We'll do both," she says. "I'll set up a recurring radio blast to Earth every hour, and we'll go for Antaeus. If we hear something from Earth, and someone tells us they can build a craft in months that gets us a seed bank, we turn around."

Sergei's head is bobbing harder. "Two potential chances. That's not bad, not bad."

"Okay," Francisco says warily. "Let's say there are seeds on Antaeus. Isn't it eleven months away?"

Eli taps the screen a few more times. "Six. The *Lazarus* is faster than the colonists' ship. Obviously we'll have to ration hard, six months' travel plus three for the seeds to grow. But it's doable, as long as...the ship..."

Eli looks up from the dashboard screen. Her eyes move between the four of us as she rises to her feet.

"Software," she says, pointing at Caro.

"What?" Caro says.

"You said you know programming."

"Right, but—"

"So you can get familiar with the autosystems. Lead the software team."

"What software team?" Caro says, blinking rapidly.

Eli doesn't seem to hear. She's already rounding on Sergei and Francisco. "You two—since you're doing the checks . . . Social Architects."

Sergei and Francisco exchange a baffled look. Eli makes a grasping motion in midair, like the words have physically escaped her.

I clear my throat and say, "The Social Architects were supposed to map out the ship's life flow. They'd design school systems, job selection, that sort of thing."

"Oh." Sergei's brows rise. "You want us to lead the group?"

"Lead the crew," Eli says in a rush. "*Train* the crew. We're supposed to have doctors, engineers. I mean, one micrometeoroid hits the rotary frame in the wrong place, and if we can't spacewalk out to make repairs, we'll lose gravity. So, Caro, you're Head of Systems. And you two can design a training plan. And"—she turns to me and subjects me to the full force of her evaluation—"Chief of Personnel, obviously. You'll give the directions, run damage control, coordinate everyone. What you were doing tonight."

I bite my cheek. The prospect of more nights like tonight is exhausting. I couldn't keep Irina from spreading doubts, couldn't soothe Fatima's fears, couldn't even convince Anis that I was being reasonable. After two hours of this, I feel as hard and hollow as a suit of armor.

But it seems ridiculous to say no. Haven't I spent years developing this version of myself, the one who could pacify the crowd?

"Of course," I say. "Just tell me what to do."

But as we await more from Eli, she shifts her weight, swallows. Now that she's convinced us to join her, the framework of a plan in place, the restlessness is coming back to her surface. She seems to withdraw, as if she's only now realizing that we're watching her with rapt attention.

"It's late," I volunteer with a glance at the clock, which reads three in the morning. "How about we meet back here at nine to start planning?"

"Yeah," Eli says with obvious relief. "That's, yeah."

"Good idea," Sergei says, yawning. "I could use some—"

"No," Francisco warns, sticking the tablet under Sergei's nose. "You said you'd help." They retreat up the steps, Sergei complaining, Francisco insisting. Caro pauses halfway up the stairs, her eyes lingering on the windshield with something like mistrust, before she follows the boys.

I look at Eli. She's centered in the panoramic sweep of the windshield, a rigid figure snared in a funnel web of stars. I try to imagine what's happening inside her, the loss of her mother suddenly intermingled with the immense task of replacing her. And the whole process is happening in secret. The others clearly didn't know anything about the commander.

She must have heard my footsteps catch, because she glances back. I'm torn between asking if she wants to talk and giving her some privacy, but she speaks first:

"Um, I should thank you."

"You don't have to thank me. Anybody would have done the same thing."

"I don't think so," Eli says. She's my height, I realize, so exactly my size that when she fidgets, it's like watching my reflection move in a mirror across a room. "You don't have to act like it was easy," she adds. "I know it was hard, but waiting would've gotten us killed. You made the right decision."

Then I understand. She isn't thanking me for shouldering the checks, buying her time to stay with her mother's body. She's thinking about our last few seconds on Earth.

I look back at her, unable to tell her how wrong she is. With the kill switch trembling beneath my fingertip, I didn't make a decision at all. Presented with two terrible options, I somehow found a third that was worse. I did nothing.

But how can I admit that to anyone, let alone to Eli? When I froze, she made a choice. She thrashed and yelled to stop my interference. That's what's under her surface: conviction, momentum, the drive for survival. Sometimes I think there's nothing beneath my surface except dread, or a sense of resignation.

"Not many people would have done it," Eli goes on with a hint of hesitation. "You and me, we're the same."

I've been quiet too long, so I place a small, even smile on my lips and tell her, "I see it," but it's a lie. Instead I see the differences between us more and more vividly. I see that Eli's mother brought her up on a diet of direction when mine was feeding me temperance. I see that she became a pilot, while I became a mask. I see how lucky it is that she's here, leading in a way that I never could. I stand across from her and realize that I am the mirror, the surface that reflects her.

PART II

THE *LAZARUS*

CHAPTER 5

HOW TO FORGET A HOME

It's 1:47 a.m., Pacific Time, and I'm on mile three. After four days aboard the *Lazarus*, I still can't sleep. I keep falling awake, that feeling of being grabbed at the ankle and yanked downward, so I wind up circling the track every night.

The Exercise Hall stretches the length of the Residential Wing and occupies two floors. The vaulted ceiling, like a gymnasium's, bounces my footfalls back at me while I run. The sound is hypnotic. I detach little by little until I've left the ship, left the present. I'm running through clouds of memory, winding through the trails around the lake near my school, where stands of trees cast dark blue shade even in the highest, hottest sun. It's August, and the air is wet and soft like a wound, and the sound of cicadas quavers around me. I turn left at a tree with a red birdhouse, then run down a secret path to a log strung across a slow, flat creek. We hide here sometimes, Lilly and I, on the afternoons when our freshman year feels like an endurance test, when I'm so sick of people's scrutiny that I want to disappear. We settle in the middle of that log and let ourselves rest, me peeling whitish bark away in long threads, Lilly cracking jokes like a stand-up trying a new routine.

Coach Valdez will notice if we're gone too long, though, so we find our way back to the trails eventually, and I run alongside someone who knows me like the map of freckles on the back of her hand. I dip my chin so that my tied-up hair swings in time with hers, two black pendulums.

Tears prick my eyes. The sensation brings me back into my body. She isn't here. She never will be. I know that.

Still, I can see a world where she is, overlaid on top of reality like an annotation. I feel her at my side, the shape of her negative space—I see her heels snapping up in full gallop. I see Marcus waiting at the finish line at a race, never the type to cheer but always faithfully, steadfastly present, his enhancement glasses glinting in the late-afternoon sun. I can almost hear their voices in the monotone whirs of the humidity regulators. I'm waiting for that feeling like free fall to burst open in my body, the way it always used to.

Then I make a turn and feel myself hinged at the ankle, centripetal force whipping me along the hundred-meter sprinting track. There it is, that primordial shock of alertness, lightning up my spine. For a moment, the fantasy jars, and there's no part of me that's three years and a hundred million miles away. For a moment, I'm all here. But it's only a moment.

Eight hours later, I'm standing in the breakfast queue at the canteen, holding back a yawn. "Leigh," Francisco says with a curt nod when I reach the front of the line. "No sleep?"

"No sleep." I note the twitch just beneath his high cheekbone. "And you?"

"I'm fine," he says shortly, scrolling through his ration tracker, which contains the age, weight, height, and sex of everyone in the group, everything he needed to calculate our daily caloric requirements. "Size...B." He taps the selection on the dispensary screen. A vacuum-sealed meal bar clatters into the receiving tray.

I give him a tired salute with it and retreat, running a fingertip over the characters printed on the silver wrapper: 500 CAL. For now, we're allowed to eat 90 percent of the calories we need to maintain our weight, but in a month's time, we'll cut back to 70 percent. Five months after that, when we've reached Antaeus and started planting, we'll restrict down to 50 percent in staggered groups based on size and age.

The canteen has divided into these kinds of groups already. I pass the thirteen-year-olds at the long row of portholes, then the seventeen-year-olds closer to the dispensary. Everyone is dressed identically in ship's uniforms now. Even their faces look similar—the chapped lips and outcroppings of acne, the faraway looks. As my translator picks up snatches of conversation from passing tables, I feel as if I'm listening to a montage of thoughts, hearing the way our collective consciousness is still fixed on Earth.

"...be able to finish one of the other ships..."

"...mostly evacuated inland, so maybe..."

"...weren't supposed to be there..."

Some tables are silent except for the crinkling of silver

wrappers and the slick sounds of teeth sinking into meal bars. Most people are grimacing through them, which is fair. The things taste like curdled corn syrup and have the texture of wet tissue paper.

As I approach Sergei and Caro, who are seated at our usual table halfway down the hall, my mind is on the *Lazarus*. As much as this ship is a safe haven, it's also an intimidating burden. Over the past four days, we've finished hundreds of diagnostic checks without finding any major mechanical issues, and that's been relief after relief, but we've still seen just how unready this ship was for passengers. The missing seeds and crates of food are the worst problems by far, but they're not the only ones. In dozens of storerooms throughout the med bay and maintenance hall, hundreds of bins lie in mountains, waiting for unloading, sorting, and identification against inventory lists. In the Residential Wing, we've found huge rooms that contain all the ship's clothing, thousands of uniforms, athletic wear, and nightclothes stuffed into unmarked boxes. The books in the Catalog weren't the only stray artifacts, either. Deeper in the wing, towering stacks of crates are packed with priceless artworks that still need installation into their sterilized, acid-free cases.

I'm wondering if the most fragile artifacts survived the launch, when a sound jerks me out of my thoughts. Angry voices are rising behind me.

I'm already spinning around as the argument explodes into yelling. A boy and a girl are on their feet at the front of the canteen, screaming at each other from opposite sides of a table.

"—just stood back and let it happen to—"

"—were trying to stop it, but you had to come in and make everything worse—"

"Worse?" the boy yells, looking so hysterical that the girl takes a step back.

I'm already dashing between the tables to their side. "Hey! *Hey!* Y'all, what is this, what's going on?"

They spin to face me and start talking over each other again. I know both faces. Sahir Shafiq, whose patchy facial hair makes him look younger rather than older, helped me fix a mechanical problem with a Catalog case yesterday. Jayanti Chakraborty, the Indian girl whose curly black hair is cherry red at the ends, has hardly spoken since our first night aboard, except to thank Francisco at meals in a whispery little voice like an exhalation.

There's nothing small about her voice now. *"He's* saying," she snarls, "that India didn't do anything to stop what happened in Gujarat, as if—"

"You didn't!" Sahir yells. "Thousands of people died because your lottery lists were—"

"Sahir, Jayanti!" I say. "Please!"

They break off. The Pakistani boy's cheeks are flushed, and Jayanti's fists are balled at her side.

I know exactly what they're fighting about, of course. Everyone aboard does. This is where the fleet effort wound up at the end of the day: with tens of thousands dead, everyone in the world at each other's throats.

It didn't start out like this. Actually, when the announcements broke, the first thing that happened was a spate of cease-fires. Overnight, fleets of drones withdrew from war zones. Factions laid down arms on the outskirts of Tibet and in the Second Nigerian Civil War, and my mother pulled troops from bases in Iran and Mongolia. Every government on Earth turned their focus to the fleet and to organizing the passenger lottery.

But as the lottery date crept closer, the selection process

came under fire. The Global Fleet Planning Commission had given each country a quota of passengers based on population, but that meant millions of survivors from China, India, and the US, while countries like Liechtenstein and Seychelles wouldn't even scrape enough to fill a single ship. The UN spent weeks debating the Kurds, the Catalans, and half a dozen other stateless nations who'd been trying to have their declarations of independence recognized for decades.

Then, last fall, the GFPC released their draft list of Necessary Personnel. When the world saw that 95 percent of the NPs came from just sixteen countries—with the US at the top of the list—the agitation ratcheted up to fever pitch. Russia's president, Denis Komissarov, released a statement accusing the US of prioritizing our own survival. Thirty, then forty, then fifty countries called for a reevaluation of the list, then of the entire lottery process. The GFPC's plans began to stall as protests swept through hundreds of cities worldwide. I remember the signs that protestors in the streets hoisted up: WE WANT OUR SEATS and GFPC FLEET IS GENOCIDE.

But the situation didn't seem truly unfixable until the turn of this year. A week into January, reports broke that the lottery lists were being manipulated in dozens of countries. In some places, certain names mysteriously appeared in the entry lists thousands of times. In others, officials had apparently manipulated the lists to exclude ethnic minorities, or religious dissidents, or queer people, or homeless people. The uproar was immediate. The protests in Moscow turned to riots, and the others followed suit. Some prominent figures with duplicate names on the list were dragged out of their homes and bludgeoned in the streets. People began to take the odds into their own hands. If they couldn't guarantee their own spot aboard, they'd cull the competition—especially if they didn't think that competition deserved a chance to make it out alive. Fighting erupted on conflicted territory between Armenia and Azerbaijan, race riots broke out in the US Southeast, and—two months ago—the news reported widespread attacks on Muslims in Western India. Enraged, Pakistan sent thousands of troops over the border, and what followed has been a brutal array of military conflict and civilian casualties.

As I stand in front of Sahir and Jayanti, this chaos replaying in my memory, my thoughts are a scramble. "Damage control," Eli told me, but what do I do when the damage is already done? I can't turn back the clock and ask all the world's political leaders to stick to the plan. I can't stop anyone from remembering the past year, or the decades before that, or hundreds of years of history. All we have to hold us together is the present, and right now that feels thin and breakable.

I lift my hands as if in surrender. "Listen, please. We can't have this conversation right now."

"I'm not going to let him say whatever he wants," Jayanti seethes, "when he's acting like—"

"So it doesn't matter that *fourteen thousand* people died in—"

"Of course it matters," I cut in, "and I know you're angry, but think about where we are right now. We can't let anything distract us when we're running tests on our carbon dioxide scrubbers or the water treatment plant. One leak, one problem we don't catch, and then what?"

They consider the question, which feels like progress. But then a sharp laugh sounds behind me. "What a surprise."

I turn to face Irina Volkova, who sits nearby, leaning back against a trestle table. "Of course *she* doesn't want you to think about Earth," she says, her eyes playing coolly over me.

I nod. "You're right. I think it's the most important thing to focus on the ship."

"Oh, yes, yes," the blond girl says with mock seriousness. "It has nothing to do with how *you'd* look if we talked about what happened."

I glance to the table where Sergei and Caro sit. Caro looks as nonplussed as I feel. Sergei's cheeks have grown ruddy in that way they always do when his sister is involved.

Irina lets out a short sigh. "I'll make it simple." She looks to Jayanti and Sahir. "If you two care whose fault this is, there's one answer. Who discovered the eruption was going to happen? Who suggested half of those sloppy GFPC plans? Who sat back and watched the world fall apart after *centuries* of sticking their fingers into every global conflict they could?" She turns her steely eyes back on me. "Which president told us we had until next year? Who got that minor detail wrong?"

Furious heat floods through me. She can't be serious. The unfinished fleet isn't the US's fault, and it's not my mother's fault. It definitely isn't *my* fault.

And the GFPC's plans weren't sloppy, I want to snap. Working on those plans drained the life out of my mother and everyone around her. I watched white lines run through their hair; I watched their faces droop like melting wax. Between summits, Mom spent so much time in the GFPC's virtual forum that she might as well have slept in her VR headset.

Obviously now we'll never know, but maybe the plans would have worked if everyone had just done what they were supposed to do, if people had fallen into line and been more cooperative. But no. Instead we got selfishness. Instead we got *this.*

Barely able to keep my anger bottled, I fold my hands behind my back to hide my nails digging into my palms. My family used to get these stares on the street, in restaurants, in school, everywhere: *You're responsible.* Irina is just like the rest of them, looking for someone to blame.

Jayanti and Sahir are looking at me with new eyes now, no longer expectant, more accusatory. So are the rest of the canteen.

"No one could have predicted this would happen," I reply.

"Really?" Irina says, dripping derision. "No one? Not even the US research teams whose only job was to predict when this would happen?"

"Come on," Sergei calls from our table. "Those teams had scientists from dozens of—"

"Oh, sure, defend them," Irina shoots back. "Of course, *you* couldn't wait to move west, it's no wonder you're licking their boots."

For the first time, I see real anger in Sergei's face. "You—" he starts.

I cut him off. "Irina, say what you want about the US's research efforts. I'd be making the same point if I were from anywhere else: We're not out of the woods. We still have a life-threatening situation on our hands."

"Yeah," Irina says, rising to her feet, "and you've made sure that *you're* deciding how we deal with that situation." She casts a scornful look around the canteen. "I think it's unbelievable that it's wound up like this. A pair of Americans telling us what to do, like we already forgot how that turned out last time."

"They're not all Americans," someone points out. I glance around for the source and find a South African boy at the English speakers' table—Pieter van Zyl. He's tall for sixteen, golden-skinned and copper-haired, popular with the others. "I hear you," he goes on in quick, earnest tones, "but let's be fair, right? Your brother and Francisco are the ones making the assignments, and Caro's going to be the ship system overseer."

Irina glances from table to table. Others around the canteen are nodding. "Still," she insists, "two Americans out of five is forty percent. And the rest of us don't even get a say?"

"Clearly you do get a say," grumbles a Ugandan boy, Luke Nabwana, "or we wouldn't still be listening to you talk."

Laughter rings through the canteen, and Irina's cheeks flush red. I feel a rush of secret vindication. It serves her right. The whole argument is ridiculous, anyway. If we judge each other on the way our countries responded to the announcements, it's not like she'll come out looking spotless, when the only leadership Russia showed was being the first to dissolve into riots and conspiracy theories. Maybe if *they'd* just quieted down and stuck with the GFPC, the plan might have held, and we wouldn't be the only ship in the fleet.

I'm eyeing the laughing crowd with satisfaction when my eyes catch on Anis Ibrahim. He's sitting alone, tables away from the nearest group, without a trace of amusement on his face. His gaze is locked on me, as critical as it was that first day in the Planters. My feeling of smug pleasure shrivels into sudden embarrassment.

I look back to Irina and force several deep breaths, rattled. What am I doing, thinking about scoring points? We're supposed to be building a crew, a team who works together and keeps each other safe. We have to cooperate, exactly the way the GFPC couldn't, or the last year will repeat itself. I need to detach.

"Everyone," I call over the last remnants of the laughter. "Every second we spend thinking about what happened on Earth, we're distracting ourselves from the fact that we're the only thing we have anymore. We don't all need to be best friends, but our lives depend on each other."

I look from face to face, making fifty brief moments of eye contact. Their amusement has faded. "We have something in common," I go on. "Our parents put everything they had into designing this ship. They wanted to make sure the human race had a future. That's us. We've *got* to rebuild; we've got to trust each other. That means finishing these ship checks today, then getting ourselves trained for a medical or mechanical emergency. We don't have room to do anything else."

As my voice reverberates off every hard surface, I look to Irina, to Sahir, to Jayanti. "I'm not denying that what happened on Earth was terrible. But it wasn't us. No one on this ship had a say in anything that happened before. Now we do. Are we seriously going to throw away our second chance?"

Irina crosses her arms, scuffs her soft-soled shoe against the tiled floor. But eventually she twitches her head and lowers herself back into her seat.

"Come on," she says, beckoning to Jayanti and Sahir. "Sit."

Jayanti and Sahir look at Irina with raised eyebrows, then back at each other. I can practically feel waves of dislike rolling off them, but after a moment, they retreat to Irina's table and settle into seats beside her.

I'm not sure how to feel. Is this Irina's attempt at an olive branch? Is she trying to help smooth over the fight?

I survey the watching group, scanning steadily past Fatima Awad's round eyes, Luke Nabwana's bearded jawline, Anis Ibrahim's penetrating stare. They become a sea of uniforms, indistinct. "Okay," I say. "Let's finish up breakfast, then get these checks done."

My eyes catch on one of the dispensary screens, which Caro

has reprogrammed to serve as a countdown clock to our arrival at Antaeus. It reads: 5 *months, 21 days, 18 hours, 20 minutes, 45 seconds, 44, 43 . . .*

I allow myself five seconds to imagine a trail of silver canisters strewn among the wreckage of an old ship, half-buried in unusually colored soil. Then I walk to our table with the others' voices stirring back up like wind across a desert, surrounding me like an atmosphere.

"You're wasting your time, Leigh," Francisco says. "You can't stop every fight."

It's early evening, and the five of us are sitting at the round table in the bridge's upper level, finalizing the training schedule that Sergei and Francisco have assembled. I tug at the ribbed cuffs of my uniform, which are reflected in the table's dark screen-topped surface. Opposite me, Eli is manipulating a holographic joystick that hovers between the tabletop and her propped-up tablet. She mostly spends our nightly meetings submerged in her pilot courses, speaking only when someone asks her a question.

"I'm not just talking about Sahir and Jayanti," Francisco goes on. "Three of the younger kids were at one another's throats today in the Catalog. Some stupid thing about which artifacts were placed where." He shrugs. "No one wants to get along, for whatever reason."

"I mean, I know the reason." I rub my bleary eyes. "It seems insane to feel anything good right now, so people are looking for negative outlets wherever they can find them."

"Wow," says Caro, looking over our job list. "I'll mark you down as a psychologist."

Sergei laughs, and my mouth twitches in a smile. "I'm serious, though," I say. "I'm worried about Irina opposing what we're doing every step of the way."

"Why?" Caro tugs her feet up into her seat, sitting with legs crisscrossed. "Who cares if she hates us?"

I regard Caro with a light frown. The girl is so easygoing that she'd make Lilly look straitlaced and serious. In days of discussions over the crew plan, she's mostly contributed jokes and noncommittal shrugs, which I attributed to her being two years younger than the rest of us, intimidated to take the lead. But her father was the president of Kenya. She should know as well as I do that who hates you and why are the only things that matter.

"We should all care," I say, "because we need to get the group trained. It's important that they trust us to lead that process competently."

Caro tilts her head. "You really think that depends on whether Irina likes you?"

"It has nothing to do with who *likes* me. It's about us coming together. Our job is to make that happen."

"Actually, that sounds like your job." She picks at her thumbnail. "My job is to read a million thrilling manuals about humidity gauges."

I look at her, bewildered. She brushes her braids back and twirls one of the three glittering studs in her left ear—just some of the treasure trove stashed in the black canvas purse she brought aboard. There's something amused built into the structure of Caro's face, the indentations at the corners of her mouth like the promise of a smile.

"Is this some kind of a game to you?" I say.

Caro's shoulders bob. She hits START? on the tablet in her lap, where she's been playing a hologame on and off throughout the meeting. As her avatar emits a sound like a firecracker, I think I hear her say under her breath, "Might as well be."

Francisco lets out a short sigh. "Caro's right, Leigh. It's not our fault if Sergei's brat of a sister has a victim complex." He glances at Sergei and adds grudgingly, "Sorry."

Sergei gives a moody shrug. He lifts a hand through his hair, which stands on end an instant, as if electrified, before floating back down. "It's true. Irina thinks the worst of everybody. If you disagree with her, it can't be because you have a different opinion—it has to be because you're out to get her. It's exhausting." With a note of guilt he adds, "She has her reasons. She had a hard time in school, that's true, kids picking on her all the time. . . ."

"Lots of people have a hard time in school," Francisco says dismissively.

"You didn't," Sergei snorts.

Francisco blinks. "What? How do you know?"

"Because this is how your mind works." The Russian boy waves one big hand across the tabletop, over the meticulous scheduling charts that are organized into day, week, and month view. "Let me guess. Top of your class, perfect scores in everything, captain of some sports team for good measure. Am I right?"

Francisco looks flabbergasted. Caro glances up from her game and lets out her high, lilting laugh like wind chimes, and I can't help breaking into a grin. "Looks like a yes," I say to Sergei, who taps his temple twice and says:

"I'm never wrong."

My spirits have lifted. "Okay," I say, gesturing to the training plan, "is this ready for tomorrow morning? Eli, can you think of anything else?"

Eli lifts her pale eyes from the holographic joystick. "We're ready to go," she says, the first words she's spoken in an hour.

"Good." Francisco rises to his feet. "Let's get to bed, then."

"Bed," Sergei agrees. "You two look like you need it." Before Francisco and I can dodge, he rubs his palms vigorously over our hair.

"*Will you stop,*" Francisco sputters, slapping Sergei's hand away. Sergei hoots with laughter and dives in for another attack, chasing Francisco over the threshold. Protests in Spanish fade into the distance. A chortling Caro strolls after them, her game still emitting enthusiastic *hangs,* and leaves Eli and me alone at the table.

Eli has been quiet the past four days. After our initial meeting—when she outlined our responsibilities as officers, then described how the crew was supposed to operate—she sank down into pilot training and hasn't resurfaced for longer than thirty seconds. She's always first into the canteen and first to disappear, leaving before most of the group has arrived.

Caro is long gone, but I don't stand. "Hey," I say.

Eli looks up from a holographic projection of the ship that hovers before her, revolving like an ornament on a string.

"How have you been doing? I've been wondering."

"Doing?" she repeats.

"Yeah. With . . . about your mom."

She's regarding me more readily than usual. I sense her defenses lowering, although she seems to have to engage in the process actively, almost physically, like lowering a drawbridge to a medieval fortress. "I'm okay," she says. "Honest. We talked about this when we got to the complex."

"Talked about what?"

"What I'd do if she died."

I must have let some reaction show, because Eli lets loose a quick, strained laugh and says, "What, you didn't get the talk?"

"No." I run my hand through the tangles in my ponytail. "My parents are kind of chronic optimists."

"Weird."

I force my mouth into a weak smile.

"Anyway," Eli says, "part of my mom's job was running the test flights, and with the design and assembly this accelerated, there were, you know. Non-negligible risks. So we talked about it right after moving."

The conversation is almost too bleak to imagine, a fifteen-year-old Eli and her mother in a gray cell in the launch complex, discussing *non-negligible risks* as if conducting a business meeting. Somehow I know that Eli didn't cry. I imagine she went taut like stretched elastic, rearranging her future to allow room for yet another awful possibility.

I realize I'm angry with Commander Jefferson. She didn't have to drag Eli into the possibility of her death. She could have written a letter in case something happened. Just once, she could have let Eli believe that things might go right.

Of course, maybe if she'd tried to shield Eli from the possibilities, the girl sitting in front of me would be dissolving into tears rather than sitting upright, unruffled, as if she was born for this.

"You know," Eli mutters, averting her eyes, "I'm not the only person who lost someone. It's the same for everyone else. It's the same for you."

I lift my shoulders. "Not as concrete. I don't know what's happening to my family or my friends."

Eli hesitates, then says a bit too quickly, as if unable to stop herself, "I'm guessing you had tons of friends at home."

A laugh escapes me. "What? No."

She looks so taken aback that I laugh again. "Yeah, no, just . . . just two." My smile falters, and I realize I don't want to talk about Lilly and Marcus.

But before I can say anything else—before I can even figure out why the idea of talking about them makes me feel so apprehensive—Eli looks away and says, "You should get some rest."

The abrupt dismissal surprises me. "Oh," I say. "Right. You too."

But Eli has already twisted in a pair of earbuds and reopened her holographic controls. She's looking down at them with something like frustration, like she regrets asking me about my friends at all.

As I leave the bridge, I think about how Sergei looked at Francisco and could tell exactly who he used to be. I glance over my shoulder and try to imagine Eli in school back on Earth, not wearing this black-and-gray uniform but something that made a statement about how everyone should see her. I try to picture her in torn jeans or a boat-neck sweatshirt that slumped halfway down her shoulder. Maybe she was one of those hoverboard kids, cutting class to smoke PVG and do tricks a half-dozen feet off the ground out on the football field. Every possibility seems as unlikely as the next. I can't imagine her anywhere else but here, as much a part of the ship as the commander's seat or the windshield full of stars.

———

Tonight I dream of winter. A woman in rubber gloves is scattering chemical salts like bird seed onto an iced-over sidewalk while I watch from a hotel window. Radiant cold touches my cheeks as I lean close to the glass, and the falling snow is so fragile that it tricks gravity, suspended in the black air like particulate in tap water at night.

When I wake up, all this is still so vivid that when I look out the window at the stars I could swear to God they're snow. The idea of closing my eyes again is ridiculous. I'm wholly conscious, night-before-Christmas awake.

I throw my covers from the sweaty line of my body and propel myself out of bed into the main room of my cabin. It's small and bare, like every other in the Residential Wing. Each cabin was designed for a family of four, with a common room and two bedrooms. I've sealed the door to the second bedroom. I wish I could move something to obstruct it from view, stop my parents' absence from staring at me this way, but every piece of furniture is either built into the wall or bolted to the floor.

The only decoration is an observation window in the common room that frames the swirl of the galaxy. Outside, the Preservation Wing extends to the right, a pale aluminum arm puncturing the darkness, and past it, the glimmering Sato-Burkhalter radiation sail is spread delicately behind us like a peacock's fan. I picture a tear working its way into the mirrored material, snagging near the corner, and ripping apart the source of our power. I picture us stalling and freezing and falling upward.

With a shiver, I jog out into the halls. The balconies are deserted, the atrium vacant, but when I arrive at the track, I find someone else here for a night run. Anis Ibrahim is trudging along on the inside lane, slow and determined. He's wearing the same simple exercise gear that I am, pulled from the boxes in the Residential Wing, a plain black T-shirt and shorts that fall to mid-thigh. The fabric is lighter and more breathable than our day-to-day uniforms, though the clothes still have the stiff, slick texture that shows they're made to endure centuries of reuse.

If Anis sees me, he makes no sign. He and I both live on the eighth floor, where we've passed each other half a dozen times, and we've always looked studiously away from each other before.

I still haven't thanked him for helping me on Earth. Every time I consider it, I feel defensive. When I was tearing through the barracks, the only thought in my mind was getting to the *Lazarus*. I barely saw the strangers around me, let alone expending precious seconds to help them. So I owe Anis, but it's more than that. When I compare myself to him, I come up short.

I fall into the fifth lane and run one mile, then two. Mile three is when time usually slips away from me, when I settle into pace and the run becomes automatic, but tonight I'm distracted by Anis, whose form hurts to see. His shoulders are hunched, his fists clenched, his body a landscape of exertion. When I come up to lap him, I can hear his breathing from twenty meters back, the narrow sound of air being sucked into nostrils.

I slow to a jog alongside him and say, "Don't breathe through your nose."

He startles, then tilts his head, showing me his empty ear. No translator. I tap my lips and draw a deep, openmouthed breath.

He buckles forward into a tired run, lips parted now, and looks determinedly away. I sigh and leave him behind.

My imagination rises up around me again. This time Lilly and I are street running in the preseason, bouncing through Marcus's neighborhood. We make a left on Poplar Avenue.

We pass the house at the corner of Orange Lane, the colonial with the tire swing that Marcus and I both love. Lilly always says we're going to move there, the three of us; Marcus and I will have the master bedroom, because this will be after we've declared our undying love for each other, while Lilly will have the whole attic to herself. As we run, we argue for a few blocks about the fact that Marcus and I are not in undying love, and then we come up on Adison Street, Marcus's street, where we'll turn right and find him waiting on the steps for us.

My stride flags. I wipe sweat out of my eyes. That isn't right. *Poplar Avenue*, I recite to myself. *Orange Lane. Adison Street*... but there's something before Adison Street that I'm not remembering.

I try to shake it and move on to some other afternoon—running on the beach, the year Lilly and Marcus came with us to Goldport Island—but lap after lap, I return to the missing road. I fly ahead of pace and wear myself out. I fall back, gasping. The name swans over my head, out of my grasp, and suddenly I feel like I'm running toward something I'll never reach.

I veer off the track and run to the corner where water fountains are shaped into steep funnels to contain splashes. Anis turns oddly as if to watch me go, but I don't acknowledge him. I'm out the door, racing through the ship, dread falling over me like a shadow.

Someday time will destroy my memories of Earth. It's already happening. What will I still remember in ten years? Thirty? First I lose the name of a single street. Maybe the next to go will be the red notes in Lilly's hair or the oak-dark colors of Marcus's eyes, my mother's laugh, or the smell of winter. Maybe someday I'll sit across from a kid who was born aboard the *Lazarus* and try to explain the feeling of sunburn, and I'll find myself inventing something, rubbing my thumb over the back of my wrist, trying to evoke what used to come on its own in volumes, so much memory I can feel it in phantom sensation.

When I return to my cabin, I twist a dial near the door. A circle of light blooms to life on the low ceiling, tinted harvest-moon orange by a bedtime filter. I head for my bedside table and lift out my backpack.

I haven't touched this bag since that first night, when I folded my old clothes inside. The touch of soft cloth against my fingers makes my throat tighten. I hold the shirt to my nose and inhale. Beneath scents of sweat and smoke is the perfume of home: the lemon scent of cleaner that hovered over our sinks, the mild burn of detergent.

Blinking hard, I return the clothes to the bag and pull out the notebook and pencil case at the bottom. My bunk hushes me as I settle upon the mattress sealed in soft plastic, and I riffle past pages of my notes from the tour.

I land on a new page. *Winter*, I write at the top, and then I'm pouring out everything I have. I scribble so quickly that the pen smears against the side of my hand before each word is dry. The dream about snow exists, breathing, in this room with me. I write down how we ducked our heads and pressed through the wind chill, hands stuffed into pockets until we got through the next door. We'll never walk that way again—no seasons, no weather, no variation. I have to write down spring, with its pollen-sweet air and wet breezes, and the way it felt to run alongside my best friend. I have to write down everything I remember, in as much detail as I remember, for as long as I can remember.

CHAPTER 6

THE SHIP'S CREW

After breakfast the next day, the group percolates down into the atrium for our first training meeting. A hundred and fifty feet above our heads is the sunspot, which composes the ceiling over the atrium and balconies. Magnificently large, it gazes down at us like a pale eye, casting its light into each crevice of the atrium so everything takes on the cast of midmorning. It's been programmed to follow the sunrise and sunset patterns of a hypothetical San Francisco every day until the end of time.

Francisco and Sergei set up a display on the hearth, unrolling a four-foot softscreen over a metal easel while the group trickles in from the canteen. By a few minutes after ten, the last few people are jogging down from the elevator bay.

"Morning, everyone," I say once they've settled before us. "Today's the day. Now that we've finished the diagnostic checks, we need to start training ourselves into a crew."

An excited current runs through the crowd. I glance to Sergei, who steps up to the display and taps a brightly colored tab on the softscreen. A flowchart appears with four boxed titles at its head: AGRICULTURE, COMMAND, MAINTENANCE, and MEDICINE.

"The crew was meant to have a hundred members split among these four basic divisions," I say. "Our biggest change to that plan is putting the Agriculture track on hold. That'll eventually include jobs like crop harvesting and food prep, but we don't need to think about those until we reach Antaeus."

I glance back at the list. "The Command track will also be cut down, because it's mostly based around ship administration for a larger crew. So, the Maintenance and Medicine tracks are our priority right now. Maintenance means ship upkeep, which could be mechanical repairs, electrical engineering, sanitation, or anything in between. As for the Medicine track, we have a med bay in the Systems Wing, and that equipment's dead weight if no one learns how to use it."

Sergei has been tapping the flowchart while I speak, causing sub-branches to appear beneath the four training tracks. Now, with a double tap, the softscreen goes blank except for the word EDUCATION.

"Obviously," I say, "most of us haven't finished school. Eli wants everyone to move toward a training track right away, but we're going to try and strike a balance. So, the older you are, the more training-focused your schedule will be, while younger kids will have a few more general education classes. We think everyone should know the basics of physics, computer science, and biology, so those classes will be mandatory, and others like psychology will—"

"Wait, wait," interrupts Irina, who's standing in the heart of the group, arms folded. I realize that Sahir Shafiq and Jayanti Chakraborty are standing at her side. Apparently the friendship stuck, which I'll admit is a surprise, since Irina has the personality of a cat dumped in a bathtub.

"Mandatory?" Irina goes on. "You're deciding all our classes? Who put you in charge of this?"

"Eli's in charge," I say, "but since she's flying the ship—"

This time, Jayanti speaks up, projecting a bright, brassy voice like a little bell. "We didn't vote to let Eli decide our entire lives."

"Exactly," Irina says. "And I definitely don't remember electing *you* four to be our supreme council, or whatever you think you are."

As I look at Sahir, Jayanti, and Irina, I feel an unhappy squeeze. So this is why Irina asked them to sit with her yesterday morning. She saw two younger kids who were angry with me for failing to take either side. In the wake of that fight, it was probably easy for Irina to position herself as the reasonable one—the one who really cared about the injustices on Earth, the one who would take them seriously, unlike the American girl who told them to sit down and shut up.

"Eli has spent years around this ship," I reply. "She knows what life on the *Lazarus* was meant to look like. Everything we're saying is something she knows is necessary."

"So is there a reason she isn't here herself, if it's so vital?"

Francisco bristles. "Why is it always you, Irina?"

"Why do you mind when I ask questions?" she shoots back.

"We don't mind," I say, aiming a warning look at Francisco. "Ask all the questions you want, Irina. We're on the same team."

Irina addresses the kids around her now. "Do you hear that? *Team*. That's how you know they're getting ready to order you around."

Francisco lets out a derisive laugh. "Well done uncovering the conspiracy. We've been ordering you around for five—"

"To your question, Irina," I cut in, "Eli isn't here because she's already knee-deep in pilot training. As for this plan . . ." I gesture toward the softscreen. "If anyone has ideas, feel free to talk to one of us afterward, and we'll bring them to Eli to see what she thinks. All right?"

No answer. Irina folds her arms and waits. Francisco rubs one bloodshot eye, looking even more poorly rested than he did yesterday.

"Okay. Then here's step one." I nod to Sergei. At a tap of his finger, a list of forty-eight names unrolls down the softscreen, starting with *Awad, Fatima* and ending with *van Zyl, Pieter*.

"Everyone has three slots on their wish list," I say, indicating the blank spaces under Fatima's name. "Sometime today, stop by this screen and fill out three positions that you're interested in. You can write something specific, like 'pediatrician,' or something as vague as 'Maintenance track.' It's okay if you don't know exactly what you want to do."

Laughter breaks out near one of the sofas. Matteo Marini, a tall dark-haired boy from Italy, is miming something that looks like spacewalking, bouncing off a few other grinning boys.

"Step two," I call. "Today and tomorrow, we'll take a set of placement tests built into the EdSys, the ship's schooling pro-gram." Seeing signs of alarm in the crowd, I quickly add, "You don't need to study. It's best that we don't prepare so that the tests get a sense of our actual working knowledge. Then, based on the results, the EdSys will generate lists of courses we're qualified for, pulling from thousands of classes on the servers."

The others settle down as I describe the course bank. In the year after the announcements, the GFPC recorded lessons from legendary figures in everything from genetic engineering to cub-ist art. In some ways, the uniformity of the fleet would have been revolutionary, thousands of identical city-states where everybody would have been able to learn from the best, free of charge. As it is, there's more knowledge stored in the EdSys than the fifty-three of us could learn in a hundred lifetimes.

"Step three," I say finally, "tomorrow night, we'll make the crew assignments. Eli has to get final say, since she knows which roles are highest priority, but we'll try our hardest to give everyone their top choice. We'll begin our courses on Friday." I pause. "We also want to have language exchange lessons every evening. Based on the GFPC plans, the standardized fleet language was supposed to be English, so we'll start there."

"Are you kidding?" Irina says loudly.

"Did you notice you're wearing a translator?" Sahir says at her side. The kids around them think this is hilarious.

"Of course it's English," Irina goes on. "Caro, Sergei, Francisco—did you get a say in this?"

"Oh, for God's sake," Francisco says with exasperation. "Yes, we did. As we just told you, the GFPC decided on English. If it was good enough for our parents, it's good enough for us."

"It wasn't good enough for our parents," Irina shoots back. "They debated this, too, and they never got a good reason why there needed to be a standardized fleet language. Why couldn't each ship have its own language, or multiple languages? Although I shouldn't be surprised, since those communication plans came from the US delegation."

Hands clasped behind my back, I squeeze my anger into my knuckles. "Irina, the whole commission passed that proposal by a wide majority."

"Of course they passed it—five days after they picked the *Lazarus* as the prototype. No one was going to risk offending the US when the prototype was your design, meaning you'd have a huge head start on exporting ship parts."

Despite everything, I'm grudgingly impressed that Irina knows this much about the process. But I can sense the rest of the atrium growing impatient. "We're getting sidetracked," I say. "Translators are useful, but they can break. If there's an emergency, communication will be vital, and half of our group already knows enough English to scrape by, so it's the most convenient. English speakers will also be learning a second language, so it's not just one-way."

"But you didn't *ask* us."

"Ah, of course," Francisco says, rolling his eyes. "How could we have forgotten? We can't wipe our asses on this ship without getting Irina's clearance."

Snickers ripple through the atrium as Irina turns bright red. Sergei is gazing up at the sunspot, his cheeks a similar shade of crimson. Caro, on the other hand, is sitting casually on the edge of the hearth, surveying the proceedings with mild interest, like all this is a TV show she's only half watching. She's wearing bright lipstick today, a pop of magenta upon her full mouth, another prize from her purse that's earned her some envious looks from the other kids.

"Okay," Irina says, her voice unusually high and thin. "Okay. So, after everything we just went through, the five of you are going to shove us into this. Without asking any of us what we think or how we feel, you're going to send us to the classes you choose, then tell us to sit down and study conjugations? We won't have time to breathe! But I guess it doesn't matter, because obviously you don't think we need any time to process what happened. Have you forgotten that everyone we know is dying on Earth?"

The words land low in my gut like a well-placed elbow. Irina's nostrils are flaring. She's blinking hard to force back furious tears. Before I know what I'm doing, something unplanned is coming out of my mouth. "I never forget it."

The sentence hangs in the air. The words seem to replay at me, smaller and more pathetic with every repetition. I wait for Irina to smell weakness and tear into me, but she doesn't. She looks startled, as if it hadn't even occurred to her that I could feel something as normal as hurt.

I'm suddenly aware of the cavernous size of the atrium, the way the *Lazarus* dwarfs our group. Uncertain faces stand out to me, a Brazilian girl picking at the soft puff of her hair, a Syrian boy huddled in the corner of a sofa. No one meets my eyes, not even the others on the hearth. Caro is compulsively twisting the studs in her ear, while Francisco's teeth are clenched so tightly that the muscles stand out against his jaw.

In this moment, I imagine sitting down on the edge of the hearth and asking everyone what they're feeling. With one question I could force us to turn on our heels and face everything that's happened to us.

But even as I consider it, repulsion comes hard and immediate like a kick reflex, the same thing I felt last night with Eli in the bridge. I don't want to talk about home. I don't want to give that to anybody. I want to keep Lilly and Marcus and my parents inside, secret and whole, where no one can get at them, where I won't describe them in ways that feel shallow and inadequate. Right now it feels like the only way I have to keep them safe—alive in the way they'll always be to me.

I'm dimly aware of my mouth opening, my tongue shaping new words. "Again, we'd be happy to hear your suggestions on the schedule." I am composed again, everything about me smooth and untextured like lakewater on a still day. "For now, let's go over the list of tests we'll be taking today, Francisco?"

Francisco twitches at the sound of his name, then hurries up to the easel to finish out the meeting. When it ends, I step down from the hearth and walk toward the elevator bay as if nothing has happened. I am a suit of armor, my visor slammed shut.

"I think Fatima would be good in Medicine," I say, leaning over the round table and comparing Fatima's wish list to Eli's list of essential crew positions. "Why'd you put her in Maintenance, Francisco? She has Medical track as her top choice."

"Fatima Awad?" Francisco says. "You want the girl who's always halfway to hyperventilation to cut people open?"

"Be nice," Sergei says, frowning, as Caro chortles.

"She doesn't have to be a surgeon," I say. "She could be a physical therapist, or a psychologist. She's empathetic. That's important in a doctor."

Francisco sighs, flicking his fingertips against the tabletop to magnify the lists. "I suppose we could swap So Min-ji out of psychology. She had dentistry second. . . . Did we say another dentist was a maybe?" He glances up at Eli.

"Yeah," Eli says. She's put away her training for once, listening intently to our discussions on the crew positions. "Put Awad in Medicine," she says, and Francisco drags Fatima's name to land there.

It's nearly ten p.m. We've been fiddling with the assignments for hours, trying to arrange the group's top choices to match Eli's list. Luckily there's a decent spread of interests, not just forty-eight people who want to learn how to spacewalk.

I scan the preliminary list: twenty-two names in Maintenance, twenty in Medicine, six in Command. "I think this looks good," I say slowly. "As long as the second day of tests doesn't throw it out the window."

Sergei magnifies the Command track. "Are you sure people won't be jealous of Pieter? A dozen other people listed copilot as their top choice. If Pieter is the only one we pick . . ."

"We don't need two copilots," Eli says. "There are only fifty of us. I'd rather have an extra EMT or electrician."

Sergei chews his lower lip.

I sigh. "You're not actually considering Irina, are you?"

"Not because she's my sister," he says quickly. "I was thinking maybe she'd be more cooperative if we gave her the position she wanted."

"Hmm," Caro says, applying another layer of magenta lipstick. "Not that I have strong feelings one way or the other, but . . ."

Sergei sighs. "I know, it's a bad reason." He eyes her newly refreshed lip color. "Aren't you worried you'll run out of that?"

Caro laughs. "Am I supposed to save it for my wedding?"

"You could, you know." Sergei glances at the clock. "Also, didn't you have the VR room reserved for ten o'clock?"

"Ten fifteen," Caro says, bouncing to her feet and stretching.

"I should go, though. One of those heathens might take my spot if I don't get there on time."

She's obviously trying to sound casual, but I hear her excitement bubbling up beneath. The diagnostic checks were an all-consuming, twelve-hour-a-day process. Now that they're over, allowing us some unstructured time in the evenings, I've stationed reservation screens at every door in the video hall. The sign-up process at the VR room was a bloodbath.

"I couldn't get a slot until Thursday," Francisco says enviously. "Let me know if it has *Thunderhead Empire*."

"If it doesn't," Caro says, flipping her braids back, "I'm launching myself off the ship."

Sergei winces, but before he can tell Caro not to joke about that, a quiet voice says, "What's *Thunderhead Empire*?"

We turn to look at Eli with disbelief.

"*What is* the best-selling VRPG in history?" says Caro. Her faux-casual attitude has evaporated. She looks half-appalled, half-fascinated. "Eli. It's life-changing. You control one of the elements with magic, and there are three thousand quest routes, and the world is over fifty thousand cubic kilometers. Full development to the millimeter."

I smile. "My friends and I were always waterwalkers."

"I'm a lightning main," Caro rushes on. She only ever gets this animated when we talk about games, like she's opening a tap and letting herself pour out. "Lightning is the best, because once you're level forty, there's this cheat that takes you to—if you remember the ghost city, it's a time-travel code for that area. So you get to go back to when it was a massive imperial hub in the second century."

"You have to show us sometime," Sergei says.

I raise a brow in Caro's direction. "As long as we're in

noncompete. I get the feeling she'd outscore us in about twenty seconds."

Caro grins. "Ten, if you're lucky."

Francisco and Sergei laugh, and I feel myself smiling, too. It feels good, like unclenching a fist, to talk about something that doesn't matter.

I glance over at Eli. She hasn't joined in the laughter, but her mouth has tugged in a hesitant smile. There's something shy about it, even awkward.

Sergei is also watching Eli. "I can't believe you've never played. Didn't the other kids on the complex ever ask you to join?"

"There were no other kids on the complex."

Our smiles dim. "What about the locals?" I ask. "I thought the sanitation team and mechanics were from the area."

"Yeah." Eli shrugs. "They mostly commuted from Eureka and Arcata. It's a twenty-minute drive, no reason for them to uproot their families to live on-site. The complex wasn't exactly a relaxing place to live. I'm not complaining," she adds quickly. "As long as I stayed out of people's way, I had tons of access, even when I was fifteen. So. I liked it."

"You didn't miss home?" Francisco says with unusual strain. "Where were you before?"

Eli's pale eyes move between us. She seems puzzled by our interest. "We lived all over," she says eventually. "When I was little, my mom left NASA to fly for YouMoon, so basically playing chauffeur for billionaire space tourists. They have twenty-something locations, and demand was always up and down, so we never stayed anywhere longer than eight, ten months until the complex."

Unbidden, images appear to me of Eli as a little kid, scrawny and surly, sitting on a beige carpet and surrounded by moving boxes.

Eli adds, "You're going to be late for your slot, Caro."

"Right," Caro says with a twitch of her head. "Yeah. See you tomorrow."

A contagious yawn echoes between the four of us as we head out of the Command Wing. "My God," Francisco says grimly once we're nearly at the balconies, "I can't decide which part of that sounded lonelier."

"Yeah," Sergei agrees, his hazel eyes filled with sympathy. "On the bright side, if she hadn't spent the last three years shadowing the crew instead of having friends, we wouldn't have any idea what we're doing."

Francisco doesn't laugh. He seems lost in thought, nibbling at a split in his lip, picking at calluses on his fingertips. A guitarist's fingers.

We walk out onto the balconies. Overhead, the sunspot is a desaturated navy color, like a night sky washed with light pollution. It gives off enough illumination to show the rings of balconies, the white skeletons of the railings, the dark mouths of the hallways.

I sigh. I already know that if I return to my cabin, I'll lie awake for hours, looking out the window into the stars, imagining Lilly or Marcus or my parents underground somewhere.

"I'll see y'all tomorrow morning," I say. "I'm going to check that everything's strapped down for the gravity switch tomorrow."

"Don't stay up too late," Sergei says.

Francisco scoffs. "She will."

I smile, then glance at Caro, who hasn't yet moved toward the Preservation Wing, where the video hall and her VR slot are waiting. She's been quiet since Eli's description of her life on Earth. For an instant I think that Caro looks destabilized, even upset—that there's a kind of sadness in the way her eyes are passing over us. But then it's gone, and she's saying easily, "I'll try not to have too much fun without you." She strolls off, trailing one finger down the rails.

———

I pass through the lower levels of the Residential Wing, my hands folding around small items to make sure they're secure. I wander through the canteen, through the religious chambers. I walk the maintenance halls in the Systems Wing, ensuring that every object is locked, tied, or packed down so that tomorrow afternoon, when the *Lazarus* rotates in its frame, nothing floats out of place.

We'll perform this ship ritual at 2:30 p.m., like we do every second day. We'll strap ourselves into our bunks, and the acceleration drivers will shut down, and for fifty seconds, while our hair drifts weightlessly around us, that underwater look, the ship will turn slowly over. The rotations are adjusted by thousands of microthrusters meant to make the transition less jarring, but it still feels like the throb of a pressure headache at first, our blood and organs groaning with the weight of inertia. Then, once we're facing the correct direction, the drivers will come back to life, and with it, gravity. I'll stand up from my bunk with the queasy-kneed feeling of getting off a too-long flight.

Near midnight, I finish checking the last of the lids on the Planters' soil beds. Then I take to the track.

The door hisses open to reveal a hunched figure laboring his way around the inside lane. The person I become when

I'm alone retreats into me, my posture correcting, my muscles tensing, but Anis doesn't react to my arrival.

I take the middle lane. For half an hour, Anis and I circle in silence, and I try to relax into the workout.

Then a gruff voice calls, "Why are you here?"

I stop halfway around the curve, looking back. The white edge of a translator protrudes from Anis's ear. This time, he came prepared.

"To run," I answer.

He stops in front of me. "I know that, but why don't you run during the day?"

"I'm trying to tire myself out. I could use the sleep."

"Oh. Right." He rubs at one of the circles under his eyes with a knuckle. His shoulders ease down. I realize he looks like a boy who used to run track with me, who had the same expressive mouth, the same inky brows, like two calligraphic strokes.

I nearly do it then. I nearly force out a thank-you. Last night I spent hours writing in my notebook, remembering the way my father slipped it into my backpack and gushed about the benefits of non-virtual activities. As I wrote, I felt close to him. I owe Anis for that.

But before I can speak, he says, "Why didn't you listen to Irina this morning?"

I stiffen. "We did listen. We answered every question she had."

"No, you didn't. You *can* answer simple questions like 'Why don't we have an election?' You just choose not to. You make up different questions to answer, like 'What does Eli think is important?'"

This blindsides me so much that I can't even be annoyed.

That's exactly what I do: map out a network of questions I can answer that will satisfy but never provoke, guiding conversations down detour after detour. But no one's ever confronted me about it, not even Marcus or Lilly.

"You do it so quickly," Anis goes on. "Like another language only you speak. And every time, your so-called answers are close enough to make everybody happy."

"Not you."

For a moment I think he's going to laugh. Then he forces an even deeper scowl. "No," he agrees. "Not me."

Something about his thunderous expression leaves me with lingering amusement. Maybe it's the idea that, for the first time in my life, I might have met someone more serious than I am.

As one, we push back into a run. I lope easily alongside him. "Stop clenching your fists," I tell him. "It tightens the muscles in your chest."

He doesn't acknowledge the advice, but his fingers uncurl. "I didn't get to make my point."

"God, didn't you?"

"My point is, just because Irina's angry and obnoxious, it doesn't mean that she's wrong. She has a point about needing real elections, and about you five choosing English as the ship's language without asking anyone. She's right about the GFPC's plans, too. I'm sure you of all people read the summaries."

"Not exactly."

"What? Then how—"

"I read the plans in full. And the debate transcripts."

The look of disbelief he shoots me is gratifying. I must have spent hundreds of hours scribbling notes in the margins of 200-page PDFs while my parents' voices burbled away in other rooms at home. I read the GFPC's plans for building multiple launch sites in militarized complexes so that desperate people couldn't storm the ships; I read pages of counterpoint concerns about involving militaries in what would already be a tense boarding process. I read the proposals for monocultural ships, where each vessel's passengers would be drawn from a single country to preserve cultural heritage; I read the dissenters' clashes over the long-term effect this could have on tribalism and racism.

"Okay," Anis says as we round the edge of the oval. "If you read the proposals, then you can't actually think they were perfect."

"The point isn't whether they were perfect. They were workable plans, and they fell through because of infighting. The point is learning from our mistakes, which means establishing a plan and carrying it out together, no matter what we personally think of minor details."

"*Minor details?*" he says, his words coming unevenly between strides. "None of it was minor. The GFPC adds one clause about making English the official language of the fleet, and maybe five hundred years later, we only have one surviving language. Those plans would have determined everything. Who would live and die, *how* we'd live, *how* we'd die. That goes for what we're doing now, too. Are you really saying elections are a *minor detail?*"

I force my own fists not to tighten. "All I'm saying is that this is a bad time to toss our stability out the window. Eli isn't . . . She's not a people person, all right? She trusts me, Caro, Sergei, and Francisco, and that makes it easier for us to get the ship's crew to where it needs to be. We'll have an election in a few months, when we've made strides in training."

"A few months is a long time. Will it happen before we write the ship's laws? Before we form a judicial system?"

I have to hold back an exasperated sigh. Form a judicial system? To do what, punish people who show up late to lectures?

I realize he's panting hard and ease my pace. "Look," I say, "obviously I want to have an election before any of that, but right now nothing matters more than training. That doesn't mean I'm not thinking about these questions, though. I think about all this constantly. What happened on Earth, and—and why, and how we can do better. All right?"

Anis palms sweat off his forehead. For someone who claims to know everything that goes on in my head, he studies me with so much frustration, like someone in the dark trying to narrow in on a piece of faraway light.

"Fine," he says eventually. "It's good that . . . as long as you're not sleeping, you might as well lose sleep over something that's—" He cuts himself off. "Over something else."

With that, he speeds up and away from me. The effort he expends to do this is obvious. The boy loves his exits.

I frown after him. *Something else*, he said, as if he knows what keeps me awake.

"Why are *you* here?" I call.

He breaks out of his run. I do the same. Without the ricocheting sounds of our feet striking track, the exercise hall suddenly seems twice as large. Anis looks very small, hunched over twenty feet ahead, a black-clad avatar in a rain of white light.

Thoughts of elections and leadership fade from my mind. "Are you all right?" I ask.

"No, of course not," he says without straightening, without turning. The words are blunt and immediate, like even this kind of honesty costs him nothing. "Are you?"

A dozen deflections appear at the tip of my tongue, a hundred ways to diminish or transform his question. But I think he already knows the answer.

"No," I say quietly. "That's what I was trying to say this morning."

He faces me, as slow and reluctant as a turned screw buried deep. "I know," he says. "I was listening."

CHAPTER 7

AUGMENTED REALITY

Time seems to accelerate. The second day of testing passes the same way as the first, the fifty-two of us bowed over classrooms of screen-topped desks in the Command Wing. The Council—as we've started calling ourselves, first as a joking reference to Irina's insult, then unthinkingly—stays up most of the night coordinating every schedule in one go. The following morning, we post the assignments on the softscreen at the hearth.

Thankfully nearly everyone seems satisfied with their position, but the training schedules are a different question. All weekend, I field complaints from people who didn't get assigned the courses they wanted most, explaining to disgruntled kid after disgruntled kid what we've already told them: that even beyond their training track, we need to prioritize classes that will be useful aboard the ship. Math, programming, any kind of engineering, and physics—especially astrophysics—as well as plant biology, for when we have seeds for the Planters.

Slowly the group adjusts to rising earlier and going to bed later. Soon enough, walking through the halls of the ship, it's common to see groups of two or three kids from the Maintenance track watching lectures on-site. They sit on the mesh floors, screwdrivers or monitors in hand, and lift gray plates away from the walls, consulting tablets that show diagrams of the wiring. Others hover in the canteen, studying the observation window, while a scientist filmed in a lab in Germany explains the properties of ALON, the translucent ceramic that composes our glass. The kids in the Medical track file in and out of the med bay quizzing each other on gross anatomy. The group figures out quickly enough that Luke Nabwana is the one to ask about physics, and Noi Sarasin about calculus, and the two of them sometimes hold tutoring sessions after our hour of language exchange lessons in the evening.

Caro and I decided to pair up for the language exchange, since we already spend so much time together on the Council. She has a handful of English phrases in her back pocket, but I don't know any Swahili and have to learn from the bottom up. We guide each other through lessons on the EdSys, Caro chortling away as she corrects my pronunciation on small, useless sentences like "He is a horse" and "She sees twelve museums." I've tried to coax Eli into joining the language exchange, too, but she always sinks deeper into the commander's chair and insists she doesn't have time for anything except pilot training.

I understand the feeling. We could all use an extra hour

or two in our schedule. Caro, Francisco, Sergei, and I are taking fewer classes than the others, only three apiece, in order to make time for our other duties. To familiarize herself with the ship's software, Caro spends hours every day inside the codehome. This is a dark chamber in the Systems Wing, its walls composed of floor-to-ceiling screens. The sight is mesmerizing—the touchscreens glittering beneath Caro's fingertips, instantly responsive, tags bracketing columns of text feet upon feet long.

Meanwhile, as Social Architects, it's Francisco and Sergei's job to divide the ship's upkeep tasks between the crew. They split us into teams to sort the boxes of clothes in the Residential Wing, install artifacts in the Catalog, and organize floors' worth of equipment. They've also assigned us more routine chores, like the strapdowns for gravity switching and daily checks on the humidity regulators. The worst of the chores is probably laundry duty. That means carting sticky, pungent uniforms over to the Systems Wing, where we rinse them by hand in a long trough of bubbling water.

With the start of training, half the group has been either forgetting or willfully neglecting their chores. At the end of the first week, Francisco snaps at Annie Daly, the Irish girl who's the youngest aboard, for studying near the hearth when she's scheduled for inventory in the med bay. She dissolves into tears in the middle of the crowded atrium.

While Sergei soothes Annie, I steer Francisco away into a chapel room on the first floor of the Residential Wing. "Next time," I say with forced patience, "when you're angry at someone—"

"I know, I know," he says irritably.

"—just tell me. I'll handle it." Mediating arguments has

become most of my role. During our few spare hours in the evenings, I always wind up at the door to the VR chamber, sorting out fights about time slots, despite the reservation screen that was supposed to prevent exactly these types of situations. There's always someone arguing that they should be allowed to override the list because they were here first, or hadn't used it in three days, or only wanted to use it for ten minutes.

So I don't love the concept of taking over every time Francisco wants to vent at somebody. But it's better than more thirteen-year-olds reduced to tears because he can't keep his temper under control.

The stress must be taking more of a toll on him than he's admitted. After nearly two weeks aboard, I've almost forgotten how he looked back on Earth, collected and pristine, arrogant with perfection. Now he looks sleepless and drained. I can't help noticing the contrast with Sergei, who seems to look fresher and better-rested every day.

"You know," I say, "if you need Sergei to handle more of your duties, you can tell me. Or Eli."

This seems to surprise Francisco out of his irritation. "What? No, Sergei's very helpful. We're starting our plans for an elementary school system and he's very... he has a lot of good ideas."

"Right." I hesitate. "But then—"

"We should get back to that now." With that, Francisco strides away.

But ten minutes later, I find Sergei studying with Caro at our usual table in the corner of the atrium. When I ask Sergei where Francisco is, he asks, "Should I know?"

I don't have time to dwell on how Francisco's acting, though, because the next morning, my role aboard the ship takes a sharp left turn. In my political science class, I notice that So Min-ji is absent, so I slip out to the Residential Wing, worried that she might have come down with something. The last thing we need is a contagious disease aboard. My thoughts escalate, Irina's voice in the back of my head predicting disaster, and by the time I reach the elevator, I'm imagining wild scenarios where it turns out someone's tracked the bubonic plague onto the ship.

When I reach her cabin, though, she isn't sick. She's lying prone in her bunk, crying so hard that her face has turned the slick, oily red of a maraschino cherry.

"Min-ji?" I say, dropping to my knees beside her bunk. "Min-ji—are you . . . ? What's wrong?"

She sobs something, the syllables so fragmented that my translator doesn't even try.

"Okay," I say. "Okay, Min-ji, just turn over. Here."

It takes fifteen minutes to get her to talk to me. When she does, she tells me through hiccups that her little sister was still on the complex when we took off. The soldiers ordered her to go ahead.

"I should have gone back," she sobs. "I don't know why I didn't. How could I leave her there? Why do I get to be here when I'm the kind of person who would leave her sister behind?"

I don't try to make Min-ji go back to training. For another hour, I listen to her describing her sister, Min-seo, who wanted to be an artist, who always made Min-ji pose for drawings when they were in elementary school. For an hour, and then for hours afterward, I try not to think about the kill switch.

That night, I run so hard in the exercise hall that I nearly make myself sick, pushing myself faster and faster while Anis keeps a steady pace on the inside lane. There's an obvious, sloppy desperation in the way I'm taking the corners, but he doesn't say anything.

I expected to stop seeing Anis at the track once we settled into training, but instead our runs have become more regular, starting around midnight and finishing by one. At this point, it feels like an appointment. Two nights ago, when he didn't show up, I spent half my run wondering what he was doing, and last night, I considered asking him where he'd been. Then I remembered that our whole acquaintanceship consists of one unreturned favor, two unwanted debates, and exactly three sentences of public interaction. So I kept my mouth shut.

Anyway, I'm relieved that he doesn't break the silence tonight, because I promised Min-ji I wouldn't repeat a word of what she said. She asked me to say to her friends, if anyone asked, that her stomach was having trouble with the meal bars.

Min-ji is back in training the next day, but I start taking roll call at our meetings every morning. It's only then, over the second week of training, that I realize just how many people are in the same condition. One morning, I find a boy looking so close to comatose that I think for a terrifying moment he suffocated in the night. The next, I miss an entire political science lecture searching for Matteo Marini, whom I eventually find asleep in one of the Planters, his fingertips still sunk three inches in soil, where he apparently dozed off in the small hours of the morning.

Some of these kids get angry at me for coming after them, assuming that I'm trying to guilt-trip them for missing training. Most of them, though, wind up doing the same thing that Min-ji did: apologizing for wasting my time, looking ashamed or embarrassed, calling themselves pathetic or unworthy of being aboard, and pleading with me not to tell anyone.

So I don't tell anyone why I've started taking roll call. I don't repeat what they've told me about their lives, their homes, their feelings of emptiness or hopelessness. I hold it all at my core and it throbs like a bruise. And if Anis notices some nights that I'm doing sprints at a more brutal pace than normal, he never comments.

The end point of this doesn't really sink in until the third week of training. It's a Wednesday morning, and Francisco hasn't shown up for breakfast, leaving Sergei to fumble through the ration tracker.

"I need him for morning meeting," I say, holding back a yawn. "He's supposed to schedule people for upkeep in the water treatment plant—there's a whole list of maintenance tasks in there that are supposed to start this week."

"He probably overslept," Caro says with a shrug. "He looked like he needed it yesterday."

"I'm sure he'd love to hear that," I say, standing up. "I'll go get him."

But when I knock on the door to Francisco's cabin on the sixth floor, there's no response.

"Francisco?" I call. "Are you in there?"

I knock again, more loudly this time. When he doesn't answer, I feel a tingle of worry. Didn't I think to myself, a week and a half ago, how drained he looked? Haven't I noticed him coming later and later to breakfast, seeming withdrawn during conversations?

I try pressing my thumb to the control panel beside the door, which, of course, flashes red and tells me I'm denied. These panels are everywhere on the ship, catchall thermostats, light regulators, and electronic locks; they're outside every cabin door, keeping us safe and alone.

I step back, telling myself that maybe Francisco isn't in his cabin. Maybe he's gone to ask Eli about something—maybe there's nothing wrong.

I hurry up to the bridge and find Eli seated at the round table, a streamlined black headset over her eyes. Her dark kinesis gloves clack upon the tabletop where she touches it. From here, the motions look like pointless tapping, but I know that inside the headset, she's seeing some kind of equipment, the actions of her hands duplicated into virtual space by the sensors in the gloves.

"Eli, do you have a minute?" I say

Eli twitches and tugs up the headset. "Hey. Kind of. I'm in a jet simulation."

"Like a plane?"

"Yeah. You're supposed to have a thousand-plus hours of jet flights before you even touch a spaceship, so. Lots of catching up to do." She hesitates. "What's up?"

"Have you seen Francisco?"

Eli frowns. "No. Why?"

"He didn't come to breakfast, and he's not answering at his cabin. I'm worried about him."

Eli removes her headset, her frown deepening. "He . . . yeah, he has seemed sort of distracted. I didn't want to say anything." She stands. "Have you checked the VR room? Doesn't he usually have a slot there on Tuesday nights?"

"You're right. Maybe he just fell asleep in there."

We hasten across the ship to the Preservation Wing. Soon we're passing the screening theaters, then reaching the end of the video hall. We stop at the entrance to the VR chamber.

This door is a black screen panel nine feet tall and four feet wide. It needs to be slid gingerly into and out of place to seal the atmosphere, completing the full-immersion effect inside. There's no handle, no lock, but the panel is heavy. I hook my fingers into the shallow groove at its back, push it gently inward, and roll it away to reveal a blur of brilliant multicolored light.

We hurry inside. As I roll the door shut again, Eli whispers, "Leigh."

I spin. At the front of the chamber, a figure is sprawled out on the floor. Francisco is motionless, his ears engulfed by the bulbs of soft headphones.

Suddenly my heart is banging against my ribs. Eli and I dive toward Francisco and drop to our knees at his side. I seize him by the shoulder. "Francisco?" I say. *"Francisco!"*

He stirs.

Eli and I exchange a look of terrified relief. My skin prickles like I've just come in from freezing temperatures. "Jesus," Eli says hoarsely. "I thought . . ."

"Yeah." I swallow. "Francisco, what's— Did you fall asleep?"

He doesn't answer or even look at us. He shrugs my hand from his shoulder and sits up slowly, not removing his headphones, his once-sleek hair hanging lank over his forehead. I see something black coiled in his hand, but before I can identify it, he's pushing it into his pocket.

Gazing ahead, he goes limp with bliss. I take in the VR environment for the first time, and suddenly nothing else seems to exist.

An urban preset glows out from every concave inch of floor, walls, and ceiling. The dawn is as bright as an aurora over dark, geometric rooftops. We're looking down a clean, steep street lined with swaying trees, their clouds of lush leaves fluttering in the wind. Long lines of people, rendered in perfect realism down to each hair on their arms, are passing along the sidewalks. There's a woman with a cloud of an Afro dyed red-orange, and a man with a beard creeping into the lower regions of his cheeks, and a pair of toddler twins with salmon-pink hats pulled low over their eyebrows. Their mother is fussing. The screen's display is as crisp as sight, so high-resolution that it's hard to imagine that this is a collection of pixels—that I couldn't just reach out, touch, feel.

Then the image flattens into a white line and disappears into darkness. Eli has hit the reset button on the control panel.

Francisco jerks and looks around at us for the first time. The bliss is gone. He looks as disoriented as if he's been yanked out of a nightmare, and there's a split in his lip that hasn't healed. For weeks now I've seen him nibbling at that red line during classes, coaxing it open, wincing as he does it.

"Turn it back on," he rasps.

"No," Eli says.

"Give it back!" He staggers to his feet and sways, hands akimbo for balance. I realize with a lurch how gaunt he is. He's always been lean, but now he looks as if his skin were plastic wrap, tugged hard against the bone. I've seen him pocketing half-finished meal bars several days the last week, but I thought he was saving them to eat throughout the day.

He goes for the control panel, but I intercept him, catching him at the elbow. "Francisco," I say, but his attention is fixed on the glowing screen that asks, *Resume?*

"Francisco!" I give his arm a shake, until he looks at me. "What are you doing in here?"

"Doing?" he says.

"When did you get to sleep?"

"I don't know. Five, six?"

"Six a.m.?"

Eli and I trade a glance. Francisco doesn't seem to notice, staring again at *Resume?*

"So," I say, "when was the last time you ate? You put all that effort into the ration tracker. You know we've got to stick to it to stay healthy, to make it through this." He doesn't answer. I try again. "We can't afford for you to camp out in here when the real world needs you."

"This is real," he insists, staring right through me. "This *is* real."

Then Eli speaks sharply. "Francisco, what's that?"

She's pointing at his neck. At the base and sides of his throat are thin red abrasions.

His hand twitches toward the pocket where he stowed that black coil. A shock races through me as I realize it was some kind of cord. Wire, or rope.

"It's nothing," Francisco says. His voice is too high and too loud. He tugs at his uniform so the collar sits higher, hiding the redness.

We all just stand there for a moment. I search for something tactful to say, something correct and uninflammatory, but my mind has never felt emptier.

"Stop looking at me like that," Francisco bursts out. "The others do this, too."

My head spins. "You mean other people have tried to—"

"I mean they sleep in here, that's all I'm saying," he snaps. "Because I didn't do anything else, obviously—I didn't! So you can stop looking at me like I'm some stupid fucking child who didn't stick to his bedtime!"

I've never seen Francisco lose control like this, not even when I broke the news about the Seeders, when he was convinced we were going to die. Every ounce of poise or assurance has disappeared. He's running his fingers through his hair again and again, strand after strand coming free. "I'm sorry," he says. "I'm trying to—I'm just—"

"Francisco." Eli approaches. He doesn't shy away. He just stands there, hyperventilating, his fingers forming fists and loosening again.

Eli settles a hand on his shoulder. "This is gone," she says, her voice low and rough. "You're still here."

"But—I don't want—" The words are barely more than gasps. Francisco hunches forward. He's passing out.

No. He's crying. And now he's collapsing into Eli, balling his fists against her back so tightly that I hear the soft crackle of one of her vertebrae. Eli's eyes widen, but then her arms settle awkwardly around him. Francisco shakes, his split lip gaping, his eyes squinted into glistening paisley shapes. He sobs and sobs, big openmouthed noises near surprise, like someone burning himself over and over on the same hot surface.

"I thought," he forces out, "if I tried hard enough . . . I'm—I'm doing everything right . . . it isn't working. It's not the same. I wish I'd died on Earth."

"No." Eli draws back from him. "You can't say that."

He lets out a wild-sounding laugh. "Why not? It's true. Someone who knows something could have taken my spot. It could have been one of my family, or any of my friends—"

"Yeah, except we didn't get to pick." Eli grips his shoulders. "If you die, we don't get a replacement. You're it. And we need you. Leigh and me, and Sergei and Caro."

Francisco's face slackens. "Don't tell Sergei and Caro about this. You can't."

"We're not going to," Eli says. "Right, Leigh?"

"Of course not."

He lets out a long, slow exhalation. "Okay," he mutters, wiping his eyes. "Good. Because I didn't even really try. I was just being . . . stupid, I was just thinking about it, not seriously trying. It's a stupid way to do it," he adds. "Inefficient. If I'd *wanted* to do it, I would have chosen a better way. Give me some credit."

Some part of my brain recognizes that he's trying to make a joke. I can hardly manage a ghost of a smile, and Eli doesn't humor him at all. "I bet you're starving," she says.

He gives a reluctant nod.

"Okay. Let's get back to the bridge, I have today's rations there already." Eli slips her fingertips into the groove of the door and rolls it open. The halls outside, the cirrus-gray walls, the soft morning-tinted lights, look blindingly bright. As Francisco totters out into the glow, I make to follow, but Eli glances back at me. She's as bloodlessly pale as she was the first night aboard. Mingled with her alarm is that hardness that comes out of her in emergencies.

"Meet us in the bridge after the meeting?" she says, nodding toward the headphones on the ground, a can-you-take-care-of-that gesture, and I nod back.

I roll the door shut behind them. Then I'm alone beside the control panel. It's still resolutely asking, *Resume?*

I stand motionless for a while. A minute? Two? I don't know. Francisco's face hovers like a ghost before me. I feel shaken, but not by his tears—I've seen enough tears in the past few weeks. What struck me was his expression when he woke up to the sight of La Paz. Rapture.

Without thinking, I press *Yes.*

The control panel folds away, and La Paz billows out of the

pixels again, swallowing the dark. The balconies cast shadows on the pastel walls. The toddlers are still wearing their pink hats, bobbling away down the street.

The plush headphones Francisco left on the floor are still warm from his skin. It occurs to me that I should replace them in their cache and walk away, but the thought is separate from me, like something I've overheard. Instead I slip them over my ears.

At once, an ambiance as huge as life encloses me, the mixed voices of wind and tree branch and creaking plastic and flapping flag cloth and vocal cords producing Spanish. Someone passing by is complaining about a vactrain that took nearly three hours to get her to New York. Another person is exclaiming about a cousin he saw last weekend, whom he hadn't seen in years. I know the conversation is autogenerated, but it sounds impossibly real. A feeling of relief is penetrating past my skin as if I'm sinking into cool water after a strenuous workout.

I've never spent longer than a few moments in the VR chamber. The others demand too much of my time. Now I finally understand the arguments, why everyone is obsessed with coming back again and again. Out there in the halls, the *Lazarus* is smartly designed and accommodating, a lifeline. But this, in here, this is beautiful.

I'm moving before I can stop myself. I'm falling back to the curved wall and pressing my hand against the concealed catch so that the control panel springs free. I'm entering *Goldport Island*, the beach town my family used to visit in the summers, and hitting *Go*, and La Paz blinks off into black. My body fills with a buzz of anticipation.

New color accumulates around me. The dark pixels fill up, images assemble, blue crisscrosses over my head in glowing streaks, and then it all seals together into a seamless whole, and I'm back. I'm here. I'm standing in a gray-cobbled plaza in the middle of town, watching the fountain like I used to in those quiet summers, and the sun is glancing off the falling water, painfully brilliant. I know that storefront, that bronze memorial statue, that traffic light swaying on its wire. I know the taste of the mint ice cream from that corner store.

I listen hard. The whip of the sea air rubs against my ears. The calls of gulls are miles away in every direction.

Something in me is released from gravity, swimming in the well of my body. I drift trancelike onto the motion plate embedded in the center of the room, where the slopes of floor and wall converge to a flat point, and take steps in place. The world shifts forward around me, guiding me along.

I proceed down the street to the ocean and stop at a railing painted yellow, dimly aware that I am free of tension in a way I haven't been for months. Small, elegant sailboats cloud the harbor before me, floating up and subsiding in uncoordinated surges. Every ripple of the sea is perfectly convincing all the way up to the horizon, and above, the dawn stirs and rises like steam, lifting a divine light into the sky. When I lean forward, I can see down the long white beach to the edge of the island. There's the sun-bleached house where my family always stays, perched on a protruding tip of green, because security is easier to monitor when you're hugged by water on three sides.

An avalanche tips inside my head and begins to accelerate. Every detail in front of me resurrects something else, the images building upon each other. A couple's yellow-patterned towel makes me see my parents lying on the beach under an umbrella, two scars on my mother's abdomen, one from the appendectomy and the other from me. The horizon line conjures

Lilly standing on a mountaintop in Roanoke, squinting out at layers of peaks painted from earth into sky in a gradient of green to misty blue. I squint up at the blinding sun and see Marcus, not even two months ago, his cheeks sunburned after we spent the day walking down DC sidewalks and pretending like we had all the time in the world. That afternoon feels dangerous to remember, unrolling and unrolling, transforming into evening, melting into the moment he leaned toward me on the landing outside my room—I want it to stop, I don't want to relive it—the way I stopped him with a touch, not because I didn't want to, or because I hadn't wondered, but because it was too late. Because I knew the odds. When I told Lilly the next day, she put her face into my shoulder and cried, the kind of crying that swelled her eyes half-shut. Her hair was warm and soft and smelled like lilacs. "I'm so scared," she told me, "I don't want this to be over," and she could have been talking about a million things.

But it's not over. It's right here in front of me, the way it always was. I could walk to that house right now, then rinse myself off beneath the old showerhead out back, the fresh water slipping cold and resistant over the surface of my eyes like contact lenses. I could look up to see Lilly and Marcus leaning over the rail of the deck, and Warren and Jones suited and long-suffering in the sun, my father staining a paperback's pages with SPF 80, my mother inside taking a briefing. As I watch the sweep of color and motion, the soft play of reflection and shadow, I feel something welling up in me like a hemorrhage, because I'm home.

Then I strain a deep breath through my nose, and it shakes me loose. It's wrong. The salt scent that always hung in the Goldport air, rich and fresh, is missing.

I snatch off the cushioned headphones and tweak my hair

back into place behind my naked ears. My hands are quivering, and I'm breathing as if I've just finished a race.

Most VR experiences came equipped with scent cartridges on Earth, but something that exhaustible was never going to make it aboard the fleet, and they were never accurate enough to be convincing, anyway. When I was younger, I didn't understand why it was so hard to fool our sense of smell. Hadn't we figured out ways to simulate sight and sound and touch? But touch could be imitated by varying degrees of resistance—there were gloves for that, suits, pressure points—and sight and sound, they were only ever sequences of waves and patterned light. When I was little, I didn't understand that to create a scent, you have to take a part of the world into yourself, to let fractional pieces of the universe settle into your body. There is no way to do this without the real thing.

How long have I been standing here? Three minutes, half an hour? It isn't even real. Did I think it was real? Did I fool myself for a moment? The others are waiting for me outside.

I back away, push the headphones back into their bank, and teeter on the threshold. *Let me stay*, pleads something in me. *Please, don't go.*

I have to extinguish a part of myself to leave. I die a little when I place my thumb to screen and see my world go dark. I die a little when I walk out the door.

When I arrive in the bridge, Eli and Francisco are on the lower level. I watch them for a moment, the way Eli sits on the lip of the commander's seat as if ready to spring forward, the way Francisco is huddled in a copilot's seat with a meal bar held against his mouth. He's clearly forcing himself to eat.

"Leigh," Eli says, looking up as I seal the door to the bridge. "Was the meeting okay?"

"Fine," I say. It isn't a lie. I stood there and gave scheduling announcements to a group that didn't seem to notice anything different about me. When Sergei asked where Francisco was, I said that he needed to catch up on rest, and neither Sergei nor Caro questioned the answer.

"Sit, come on," Eli says.

I descend the steps and take the other copilot's seat. Eli adds, "Francisco was telling me about playing cello."

I look at Francisco's fingertips. He's pressing his bitten nails into his calluses, leaving shallow marks.

"I guessed guitar," I say.

"I picked up guitar in middle school, too." His voice is still scratchy but calmer than before. "It's easier because of the frets, and already knowing a string instrument helped, too."

"How long have you played cello?"

"Forever. Since I was three, four."

"The VR room has music programs, right? Can you play virtually with kinesis gloves?"

Francisco gives me an almost-pitying look. "It's not the same. When you play the cello, it's like you're . . ." He stretches one hand as if imagining strings beneath his fingertips. "It goes into your whole body. The sound and the vibrations. And you're holding it so close, it's . . . I can't describe it."

He takes another bite of the meal bar, chews slowly, swallows hard.

"So," I say, trying for lightness, "what you're saying is, Sergei was right about you being an overachiever."

"Mm." Francisco's mouth twitches in a painful almost-smile. "Well, I've told him already, my whole family was like that. My oldest sister Ana, she's twenty-six, she had sculptures show-cased in galleries in La Paz before she graduated from college. And Lucia, who's four years older than me, had universities all over the world recruiting her because of a project she was doing with plastic reduction. And I had grades like theirs, and I was the fastest swimmer in our school, and I was starting to win some pretty important cello competitions. So this was the sort of thing our family talked about. Checking in about competitions and scores and award applications and...and now I'm never going to play again, or swim again, and...I don't know." He pauses. "People at school, too—they used to think I was cool or impressive because of those things. I was an athlete, I was a musician, I was talented. And now everything that made me..." He lets out a shaky sigh, looking annoyed with himself. "*Special.* It's gone. Like that." He gives a dispassionate little wave. "And I thought I could just pretend I'm still the same person."

We all look out the windshield at the stars, our heads moving at once, like it's something we've agreed on. Francisco says distantly, "It felt so good. I took it for granted how good it felt. I think about that all the time."

"Me too," I say quietly.

We both glance at Eli. She shrugs. "I think about life before the announcements, but I don't miss it." She traces one fingertip around one of the keys on the dashboard. "I specifically remember sitting at the back of a classroom in Austin and thinking, none of this matters at all. I was learning how to solve an integral. My mom and I were living in our third city in two years, and I was getting ready to apply to the State Collegiate Panel, and I remember thinking, then what? Then I get my school placement and my job and I'll travel around the globe a couple times and then I'll die and what's the point, what does it matter?"

She shakes her head. "Every second I spent on Earth, I felt like I was . . . I guess, waiting for something. Every city we lived, I thought, the next place, that's where things will start to matter. But it never happened."

Francisco lets out a hard laugh.

"What?" Eli says, giving him a chagrined smile.

"That's how I feel now."

Eli's smile falls away. She turns toward Francisco and pushes that long shadow of dark hair behind her ear, her face revealed like an illuminated window. "But this does matter. Every day, every tiny thing we do. And I mean, that's not just some precious feeling I have, you know? We're the new seat of human civilization." She splays her hand on the dashboard. "Look, I don't want to sound like a fucking counselor, but everything that made you special *isn't* gone. You doing cello and swimming and all that stuff, that means you know how to multitask and put things in order. And we're going to need some order if we're going to make a real society where people can be happy. I know it feels like shit right now, but soon you're going to look back and you're going to think—what we were doing on Earth, that was just going through the motions. *This* is real life. You're going to feel that. Like I do."

The thundercloud that's hung over Francisco these past two weeks seems to part momentarily. His eyes are brightening, the color evening in his cheeks, like he's a photograph being retouched. I think I feel what he's feeling, too, like my skull has come open on a hinge, airing out its dark wet contents, exposing my thoughts to Eli's vision of the future.

"You promise?" he says.

She says, "I swear on my life."

When Francisco finishes eating, Eli and I walk him to his cabin, where he collapses into his bunk and sinks into sleep. I want to stay for a few minutes, but Eli is already backing into the hall, returning to the bridge.

"Are you okay?" I say as we reenter the Command Wing.

"I don't know." She looks pale and disturbed in a way I haven't seen since our first night aboard. "Do you believe what he said in there? That he didn't actually try?"

"I think so. If he'd reached the point of passing out, the . . . the cord would have been around his neck when we found him, right?"

"I guess." The lines between her brows deepen. "But I had no idea he was feeling like that. Completely went over my head."

"None of us knew it was that bad. If we'd known, we would have done something."

"Yeah. It just feels like I wasn't paying close enough attention." As we round one of the hallway's gentle curves, Eli looks up at the ceiling. "But I guess I wouldn't have known what to do anyway, like even if I'd noticed, since you four are basically my first real friends."

Her hands are in her pockets, a defensive hunch in her shoulders, like she's bracing for me to tease her. I can't tell her that the four of us already guessed we were her first friends, after the way she spoke about her life on Earth.

"Even really close friends need privacy," I say evenly, "and Francisco didn't want us to know."

"But we *should* know about this stuff. He said there are

other people doing that same thing, sleeping in that room. I thought everyone felt lucky to make it out. Like, I thought we all knew how important it is that someone survived, and we've got this chance to rebuild. And now there are people wishing they were still on Earth, even if it means they'd die? How does that make sense? Their families would want them to be here. Their friends would want them to stay alive."

I think of Min-ji's swollen eyes, of Matteo's fingers sunk in soil, of the rush through my own body as I stood at the Goldport Island harbor. Color seems to drop like a veil over my vision, blue sky, golden sand, my parents' sunburned shoulders, and my pulse begins to thrum like a snare roll. If Eli doesn't understand, I don't think I can explain.

We stop on the threshold of the bridge, and she looks at me with real fear in her eyes. "You're chief of personnel; have you been seeing this with other people? Is he right?"

"I wish he wasn't. But yeah."

"Fuck." Eli touches her hand to her forehead like she's felt the sudden onset of a headache. "I'm just . . . If Francisco had actually, or if anyone else winds up . . . I can't do this again." She makes a jerky motion toward a door in the wall that I've never paid much attention to—an airlock leading to the ship's exterior.

Her meaning sinks into me like a needle. I see the scene as perfectly as if it were recorded in full immersion. Eli is carrying her mother's body into the airlock, our first night aboard. She staggers under the weight as she kneels, letting the commander slide to the ground. Her quick, competent fingers arrange the commander's hair around her face and wipe blood from the corner of her forehead.

Then Eli seals the door, presses *Unlock* on the control panel, and watches as the hatch beyond snaps open. Commander Jefferson falls through, bathed in distant sunlight.

"No," Eli says. "I *won't* do it again." Her face hardens like fired clay as she steps over the threshold into the bridge. "I'm not going to let it happen. We're not losing anyone else out here."

CHAPTER 8

THE CONSERVATION OF ENERGY

"Leigh's sleeping in class," a voice crows.

"Her battery probably ran out," someone else says. "Wake up, robot."

Something hits the back of my neck, and I flinch upright. We're in the darkness of one of the screening theaters, and when I twist around, I see Irina and a few other psychology students grinning, their teeth reflecting the light of the projector. Sahir and Jayanti are chortling at Irina's robot comment, and she keeps glancing at them with obvious pleasure.

"I'm awake," I say. "Stop talking over the video, please."

This triggers a fresh wave of snickering. My eyes slide to the end of the row where Anis sits, wearing an unfamiliar hesitant expression. The instant I meet his eyes, he looks back down at his notes, as expected. It's been three weeks since we started running at the same hours, three weeks of panting in each other's peripheral vision every night, and still we don't acknowledge each other in public.

I turn back to the screen and look down at my notes, furious with myself. There's a blotch on my tablet where the side of my hand met the screen, leaving digital ink all over my careful bullet points. I revert to a legible version, hitting the screen with more force than necessary.

"I think you missed about twenty minutes," Caro says idly at my side.

"I'm aware." My irritation expands to include her. If she realized I was asleep, why didn't she wake me up? Would it kill her, just once, to tell the others to focus on the lesson so I don't have to? I'm not a teacher.

"Mm." She glances over at me, brows raised. "What's going on with you?"

"Nothing," I tell her curtly. Nothing, except that this psychology video showed a sequence of Rorschach blots, and one splattered shape made me picture the swoop of a seagull in the VR chamber. My mind filled with brilliant images, rebuilding everything I saw three days ago. Balcony shadows, early light, rippling ocean. Then I was there again, gone from my body, the daydream lifting me out of this reality.

Maybe I should have predicted this. When I was eleven, my parents let me join my first MMOVR: massively multiplayer online virtual reality. I was instantly obsessed with the Movers. I joined the steampunk *Gaslite 1850*, then the epic fantasy *Dragonet Volcanis.* I loved the magic, the landscapes, the story lines—but mostly I loved my avatar. Her name was

RealGirl2054, and she could walk around without whispers trailing her, never pretending, never hiding. And if I ever did anything wrong, I could wipe my history, and RealGirl never had to suffer any consequences. Eventually my parents had to lock up my headset to keep me in the real world. I guess I'm susceptible.

So I haven't let myself return to the VR chamber. I keep telling myself what I told Francisco: *We can't afford for you to camp out in here when the real world needs you.* I have to stay present.

My worries about Francisco, at least, have eased. What Eli said about the *Lazarus's* significance seems to have made a serious impact on him. He's spent every free moment of the past two days in the bridge, still looking sleepless, but moving and speaking with an obsessive new energy. Whenever I arrive for our evening meetings, he's already deep in discussion with Sergei or Eli, walking around a spread of glowing documents that occupy the whole tabletop. Under headings like Repopulation, Physical Health, Artistic Fulfillment, and Holidays are dozens of pages of his meticulously cited ideas for the *Lazarus's* future.

I've tried to steer our private conversations toward how he's doing, but whenever I make any reference to what happened in the VR chamber, or anything he mentioned from Earth, he brushes it away and asks my opinion on one of his new plans. Last night, when we were studying in his cabin's common room, I suggested the possibility of a virtual orchestra as a group enrichment activity. He huffed a sigh and said outright, "Leigh, I need you to stop this."

"Stop what?"

"Please." He unrolled a softscreen over the square table, one foot tapping at the juncture where its legs were soldered to the

floor. "Eli's right. We've got a real future here and it's important. I . . . I don't want to get distracted anymore, all right?" He
hunched lower over the softscreen. "Don't bring those things
up. It makes it harder."

I let him change the subject. So he doesn't want to talk about
it—that's okay. I just don't know if *I'm* okay. I'm back to waking
up at night every two hours. The daydreams turn into periods
of fitful sleep. And now I'll have to rewatch this Rorschach
lecture some other time, because I've absorbed maybe eight
seconds of it.

The video finishes, and everyone lines up for the door, tablets under their arms. "Hey, Caro," Irina says from behind us.
"Does the Robot drool when she sleeps?"

Caro's delicate shoulders hunch by an inch. She doesn't turn.

Irina laughs, overtaking us. "You know," she goes on in a
mock whisper to Caro, "you don't have to pretend you're really
friends with her."

Caro looks up at Irina, her lips—blood orange today—
downturned. For a second I think she'll stand up for me, or
even for herself, but then she turns away without a word.

Disappointment makes my face burn. It takes everything in
me not to shove Irina as I stalk past her, down the hall, toward
our physics class. But halfway there, I change my mind and
duck into a storeroom. I stand in the dark, listening to the
sounds of people moving down the halls beyond the door.

There's a pang through my teeth. My jaw is clenched so tight
it hurts. Caro could have said something to defend me—but
of course, that would remind people that she's part of the
Council's decisions, and she only shows up to Council meetings to quip her way through them like nothing we do matters.

Why can't she take anything seriously, besides games and TV and things that aren't even real? It must be so peaceful, getting to disconnect from everything around her and hide away in walls of code.

As for Sergei, maybe if he stood up to his little sister instead of pretending they have nothing to do with each other, she'd be less insufferable, but no. He's too worried about being on everyone's side, never making waves, winning some popularity award that doesn't exist. With Francisco focused on recovery, I can't lean on him, either, so I guess this is just it. I have no one at my back except some vague idea of Eli's authority.

I've been thinking of the Council as my friends, but even after weeks of learning each other's languages, Caro can't muster one word to defend me. Lilly and Marcus would never have let anybody speak to me the way Irina does.

The wave of longing that crests over me is too much. The boundaries between the ship and my memories have felt thinner and thinner the past three days. Right now I can almost smell the intermingled scents of bagged lunches and soft plastic, hear the talk at Lilly and Marcus's table in sixth grade, where I'd exiled myself.

I'd sat at that table for weeks before we spoke. They hardly looked at me until the day a few intimidatingly tall eighth graders approached my corner of the table and started asking the usual questions. Was it true that there were secret rooms in the White House, was it true I wasn't allowed to roll down the windows in the car. I gave them my bland smile and recited my answers, but the older kids didn't leave. They wanted to know more. Did I know my mom's administration was actually involved in a conspiracy to control people's brains. Was it true my mom was crazy. Did I know everyone thought she was crazy, and also probably a Chinese asset, how did she even get elected?

"Hey," Lilly snapped from across the table, "I have an idea. What if you shut up and leave her alone?"

"She has Secret Service," Marcus added. "I'll get them if she won't."

Once they were gone, Lilly said to me, "You *can* just tell people to go away, you know."

Marcus laughed in his low, nervous way. "Lilly, not everyone is fine with people thinking they're mean." He added to me, "Sorry about them."

"It's okay," I said warily.

"Here, sit," Lilly said, pointing to the seat next to her. "You don't have to talk or anything, but I'll punch the next person who tries that crap."

At first not much changed. I read or did homework through lunch while they talked with each other. But eventually, almost despite myself, I started listening to their conversations. Then they'd ask me occasional questions about homework or classes, which I answered. The longer I sat beside them, the less I understood why people were mean about them. Okay, Marcus rambled on about everything and could be kind of condescending, but he also described movies in ways that made me rethink every detail, and he helped Lilly with her homework without being a jerk about it. And no, Lilly wasn't exactly *nice*, but she was exciting, always gibing, always one-upping, obsessively competitive; she had fast hands that could draw with uncanny attention to light and play oboe third-best in the state. Soon they were asking me actual questions, normal questions, did I like *Thunderhead Empire* and wasn't that quiz unfair and what was I doing that weekend, and I was giving them the answers. A year later I had them over for dinner. Nothing bad happened.

By high school, I knew them better than I knew myself. I knew how Marcus wound his shaggy hair around his first two fingers, how Lilly doodled unflattering caricatures in the margins of her history notes. I took risks with them, even. We nearly got in trouble in September of sophomore year, the last normal month of our lives, when Lilly dragged Marcus and me to a house party and insisted on mixing martinis for us in the bathroom. She sat on the toilet seat and drenched her wrists with stolen perfume, and Marcus and I wound up lying in the bathtub, laughing helplessly but not meeting each other's eyes, our forearms touching in a way that felt vaguely dangerous. After half an hour, someone hammered at the door—the host, probably—and Lilly dived for the window and threw it open. We escaped up the dark slope of the yard, yelping with laughter, to the place Secret Service had parked. Safe.

I could go there right now. I could be there, safe again. The VR room is so close, hidden by the *Lazarus*'s gentle twists and turns, at the end of this hallway. It would be so easy to disappear into it, to make all this go away.

The sounds of changing classes have faded. I slip out into the hall. The closer I come to the VR room, the more I remember Francisco's face, screwed up, tear-smeared, but desire overwhelms the shame, powering me forward. I shouldn't even have to be ashamed. The engineers knew better than any of us, and they put the VR equipment here for us to use. Us means me.

I turn the final corner and stop, swaying with inertia. I was walking more quickly than I realized, nearly running.

Pieter van Zyl is standing at the end of the hallway beside the door. The South African boy's coppery hair has grown quickly in our time aboard, a fringe the color of autumn leaves, and multicolored stubble has come in on his pointy chin. His arms are folded, but when he sees me, he smiles.

"Leigh," he says. "Hi, is everything all right?" He speaks English with an airy accent, his vowels long and breathy.

I recover quickly. "Yeah, everything's fine, Pieter. What are you reading?"

"Jet piloting manual," he says, showing me a wall of minuscule text. Then he adds, "Don't worry, I'm paying attention, I put it down when anyone shows up."

Perplexed, I glance to the sign-up screen beside the door. Pieter's name isn't listed. I realize most of the sign-ups have been erased, the time slots replaced with black bars. The only active slots read *Training Simulation*.

Pieter isn't waiting to use the room. He's here to make sure no one gets in.

I bite down hard on the inside of my cheek. Eli did this. So, she made a unilateral decision about closing the VR chamber? The Council is supposed to be a team. She didn't even ask me, when I'm the one who'll have to field everyone's complaints. I can already picture them squabbling at morning meeting tomorrow, turning on one another and then on me. The thought makes me want to retreat to my cabin and lock the door.

"I'm glad you came by, actually," Pieter says, tucking his tablet away. "I've got a question about this."

"I . . . Right, sure. What is it?"

"Eli and I had our first copilot simulation in here this morning," he says, smiling, "and that's when she asked me to recruit the others, and everything. But she didn't mention why we're doing it in the first place." He leans toward me, face earnest.

"Everyone gets angry when I say they can't go in. I could be a lot more useful if I had a reason."

Guilt begins to churn in my stomach. Pieter's always been fair to the Council, ever since the first day in the canteen when he told Irina to be reasonable. I remember his look of pride when he saw we'd chosen him for copilot training. He looks up to us.

And he's right to look up to Eli. What happened to Francisco could happen to anyone, and Eli said we weren't losing anyone else, and this is her first step to make that happen. Meanwhile, here I am, selfishly thinking about the sky above the sailboats and the sound of the breeze.

I blink hard, feeling dizzy, and take half a step back from the door. Francisco must have been thinking the way I am now when he shut himself inside. Just one minute's distraction, just one more, until it becomes a day, until you've lost all sense of reality, until you think, *If I just drifted away in here forever, it wouldn't be so bad.* If Eli hadn't assigned Pieter to stand guard, I'd be back in there right now.

"Can I trust you not to repeat something?" I ask.

"Of course," Pieter says before I've even finished the question.

Without giving any clue to Francisco's identity, I recount how Eli and I found him in the VR room. As Pieter listens, the cajoling smile playing around his lips melts away. "Is this person okay?"

I nod. "But we don't want to spread word around about it. They deserve space, and we don't want other people thinking about hurting themselves."

Pieter's thin brows cinch together. "You're right. Of course. I'll think of something to tell them. Maybe— Could we say the room is broken?"

"No," I say quickly, "we don't want to lie. We can generalize it. Just tell the others we're worried it's too addictive."

"Great. I will. Definitely." A smile turns Pieter's elfin features into an array of acute angles, dimples in his cheeks like the tips of arrowheads. "Thanks for telling me. I won't let you down, promise."

I give him a tired smile back. His keenness to impress is so palpable that it makes me want to stand taller, to be better, to be the person he thinks I am. But as I return down the hall, every step still feels labored, a battle against the gravitational pull of the room and its infinite contents.

When I come down to the atrium after training, I find Sergei at our usual table near the hearth. "Leigh," he says. "You look..."

"Awful," I finish. "I know." To be fair, nobody looks too glamorous these days. The recycled air has made us all dry-skinned and spotty. The worst part, though, is the smell. My perpetually greasy hair is slowly adjusting to life without shampoo, but the lack of soap is torture. We were supposed to have soapweed yucca to grow in the Planters, but somehow I doubt we'll scavenge that from the ashes of Antaeus.

As I scan the atrium, it strikes me how different we look from the group who gathered at the launch complex weeks ago. The decorations I remember from our tour—moussed hair, floral dresses, dark eyeliner—have been erased. We're a wash of neutral tones on a sepia scale, bare skinned and unaltered.

The exception, of course, is Caro. I spot her at a table with her programming class, where she stands out like a beacon, golden shadow dusted over her eyelids, earrings shimmering, mouth a red-orange curve. I keep expecting her to cut back on the makeup so she'll have some for the future, but every day is a new palette, every evening a fresh application, like we're still on Earth and she has an unlimited supply. I guess it's probably a kind of denial, but I almost admire the recklessness of it.

As I watch Caro type something into So Min-ji's tablet, which displays a wall of text and pictograph shortcuts, I wonder if she's avoiding me. We both know Irina only put Caro on the spot because we were sitting together. Maybe she's decided I'm not worth the effort. I don't even know if I'd blame her.

I tie my hair into a ponytail so tight that it stretches my cheeks backward. "Where's Francisco?"

"In the bridge, of course." Sergei hunches over his tablet, looking moody. "It doesn't really seem like he needs me anymore."

"What do you mean?"

He bobs his big shoulders. "Eli's been a lot more involved with our planning the past couple of days. She and Francisco seem to agree about everything."

"That's exactly why they need you," I say. "If they have all the same priorities, then your perspective is twice as valu—"

"Leigh," says someone across the atrium.

Sergei groans under his breath, and I steel myself. I knew this would happen, but that doesn't make the prospect any more pleasant. Irina is bearing down on me, Sahir and Jayanti close behind her.

"Hi, Irina," I reply.

"I had an hour booked at the VR room just now," she says so loudly that a dozen people studying nearby look up. "But Sahir's telling me that Eli ordered him, Pieter, Luke, and Pilar to stop anyone going inside."

"Really?" Sergei says. "Why?"

Sahir's lip curls. "What, she didn't even tell you two?"

"I can explain," I say. "It's a safety precaution."

Sergei's head turns toward me too quickly, and at once I wish I'd phrased it another way. Didn't he just confide in me that he was feeling excluded from the Council? He'll think Eli and I planned this together without him, and there's no time to clarify, because now Irina is demanding:

"A safety precaution for who? For people who want to play a game with our friends? What a terrible crime."

"For people who are getting addicted to virtual reality. We're planning to reopen it once we reach Antaeus, when we've had more time to adapt. Right now, the room has become a problem for some people."

Jayanti shakes back her long hair. "Just because some people have no self-control, it doesn't mean the room is bad for everyone."

"Not to mention that we're supposed to be training," Sahir grouses. "For weeks you've been saying that's the most important thing, protecting the ship, so on, so on. Now I have to spend six hours a day sitting outside that door? The pilot wants me to stay up until three thirty tonight doing this!"

"Also, Antaeus is five months away," Jayanti adds. "That's forever."

Irina has been making emphatic sounds of agreement at her friends' points. Now she declares, "I want to know something. When did you five decide the VR room was something you could take away? We've gone along with all your plans, and now, as a reward, you've decided to give yourself the right to set guards, like this is a prison?"

They wait for me to respond, but the barrage of words is confusing me, ricocheting around in my skull. It must be true that the room has different effects on everyone, and training *is* our top priority. Isn't it extreme to shut down the VR room without consulting the group, or even the Council?

Maybe Eli thought involving the Council would put Francisco on the spot, but if that was her reasoning, why didn't she tell me in private?

With the sudden, cloistering feeling of being watched, I wonder if she's realized I've been thinking about the VR room. I replay our meetings in the days since. I made sure not to mention anything, not to seem too fixated. Was she trying to protect me, maybe? Or was she testing me?

"Hello?" Irina is looking at me with disbelief now. "Do *you* even want them there?"

At this point, the whole atrium is watching. I scan from Annie Daly to Matteo Marini to So Min-ji, then to Anis Ibrahim, sitting alone near the door to the Catalog, wearing that hesitant expression again.

I rise to my feet, stamping my own instincts away until only Eli's clarity remains. "It's not a permanent situation," I announce, making myself a megaphone. "We can't take chances. The most important thing is that we don't put one another at risk."

"You're so predictable." There's an unexpected note of pity in Irina's voice that digs deep under my skin. "I watched clips of you doing interviews, you know. It's all on the web archive. Every single video is the same: You get on-screen and you recite your piece and you stick to the family script. No wonder you can't think critically about any of Eli's plans, when you've never said anything for yourself your whole life."

In this moment I look into Irina Volkova's face and I hate everything about her. I hate the tilt of her mouth and her pointy chin and the way she flicks her bangs out of her eyes. I hate the wounded, righteous way she speaks, like she thinks she's some tragic hero.

Most of all, though, I hate her for the shade of truth in her accusation. Of course I didn't speak freely in public back home. Maybe it's even true that I never questioned my parents' judgment. There were times that I read about my mother's policies, or her team's proposals to the GFPC, and felt the beginnings of doubt, but I never probed into those feelings and let them develop into disagreement.

That was the choice I made. I wasn't going to be the nick in the varnish of my family's reputation, the soft brick in the fortress wall that made our defenses vulnerable. I chose our safety, our happiness. I chose the party line.

And is that so awful? Isn't it enough to fulfill the role I was assigned, First Daughter, chief of personnel, member of the team, megaphone for the people with actual expertise? My cooperation is moving us toward our long-term survival. I'm sacrificing my own desires for that. I won't apologize for it.

"I'd like to use the room sometimes, too," I say. "I'm giving it up just like everyone else. Why can't you give us the benefit of the doubt, that we're trying to help?"

Irina considers the question without sneering or scoffing. "It's a matter of principle," she says finally. "Not that I'd expect you to understand."

She walks away, Sahir and Jayanti flanking her. Irina leads her stride with her shoulders, every step a miniature punch, clearing an imaginary crowd. It takes a moment to realize that the feeling simmering inside me is no longer anger or dislike. It's envy. I wish I could spit my feelings out like a killing blow and disappear, leaving behind only an aura of moral triumph.

But this is what I choose. Every eye in the atrium is still on me, so I calmly lower myself back into my seat and watch the countdown clock on the message board: *4 months, 24 days, 10 hours, 32 minutes, 9 seconds, 8, 7, 6...*

———

Tonight, as usual, I meet Anis at the track. And as usual, we keep our silence. I run hard, pouring my argument with Irina into every stride until I ease through that barrier into a runner's high, my body suddenly weightless, and I realize I'm imagining the VR chamber forming in front of me, clearer with every step.

I blink away the sight, but it seeps back. The light of dawn and the cobblestone plaza. The pale walls of the exercise hall seem to shrink around me, every anathylene fixture an echo of the doorframe and the struts that curve up over the ceiling. Every part of the ship identical.

I push myself faster. I lap Anis once, then twice. Every night, he walks less often. He'll be fast once he's trained. Coach Valdez used to tell me I was built to run. It wasn't so much my height or weight as the way my muscles clung to the bone, and my skin to the muscle, layer to efficient layer, the shape of me as hard and brutal as a torpedo. During stretches, I used to look at the bulges of my calves and picture anatomy diagrams, pink and red bands, the skin peeled away to reveal what I was made of. Anis is the same way, his muscles visible in topographic slumps and juts, as if his skin were a size too small. He'll probably be faster than me someday.

Not yet, though. For now, with the cheetahs and gazelles reduced to strands of DNA, I'm still the fastest thing aboard. I should be fast enough to outrun my imagination.

I begin to gasp. The Goldport Island harbor is fracturing,

giving way to La Paz, then to vignette after glowing vignette. I'm running myself into suffocation, smothered by pictures of jungle canopies, of sherbet-orange sand arcing in dunes against a blue sky, of my high school's brick south face reflecting the late-afternoon sun. Places I've been and places I'll never go.

"You're fast," Anis says as I come up to pass him a third time. I stumble to a stop. My hands find my knees, and I hunch, my shoulders heaving. I stare at the porous texture of the floor, negatives of brilliant images floating against my eyes.

Anis has stopped beside me. I glance up reluctantly, exhausted. After Francisco, after Irina, I don't want to field whatever Anis has to throw at me tonight. I wish he were gone and I were alone on the track, circling by myself.

But he just says, "I guess you were on a running team on Earth."

I scour his words for discontentment or judgment but find none.

"Yeah," I answer.

"How much did you run? How far?"

"It varied. I think I maxed out at thirty-five miles a week, but I would've liked to work up to a marathon at some point, which would have taken a lot more."

"Did you want to do it professionally?"

"You have to be beyond fast for that." I hesitate, suspicious. This is the first thing approaching a normal conversation we've ever had. Why is he doing this now?

"What about you?" I ask.

"I wanted to be a neurosurgeon."

Crouching to tighten my shoelaces, I mumble, "Not an interrogator?"

There's a weird sound from above me, somewhere between

a choking sound and a cough. When I glance up, Anis looks as off guard as I feel.

"You just laughed," I accuse. "You laughed at my joke."

He sticks his hands deep in his pockets. "Someone has to."

I straighten up, scrutinizing him. Suddenly I remember the look on his face during our psychology class, and in the corner of the atrium as Irina berated me. Only now do I realize it was sympathy.

This is why he stopped to speak to me. He saw that I had a bad day. He was trying to make it better, asking me about my favorite thing to do. It's such a small thing, I'm embarrassed to feel grateful. But maybe I shouldn't be surprised. This has happened before. I have been stuck in place, wrenching at unsolvable problems, and that night, too, Anis stopped midstride to ease up some of the weight.

With this quiet offer of distraction, it feels like he's making a habit of helping me. But maybe these are things he'd do for anyone.

Anis looks away from me, flicks away a trickle of sweat from his heavy brows. "Want to run?"

"Sure."

We kick off again, this time falling into step. "Neurology," I muse as we round the curve. "What part of the brain controls sleep?"

"It's a network of areas. The hypothalamus is important."

"Right. Hypothalamus. Do you know how to trick your hypothalamus into letting you sleep?"

"If I did, would I still come here every night?"

"I don't know. Would you?"

It's a moment before he says, "I might."

I let him set the pace. I stop trying to outrun anything. I don't have the energy, or, I guess, the willpower. At last there's nothing to distract me from the glow of the city that rebuilds itself again and again before me, as if I'm running into it and out through the other side in an instant, every step taking me into what we had and then away again into a bare, circular future.

The protests from Irina, Sahir, and Jayanti aren't the last. Conversation after conversation, the only thing I hear about is the VR room, but the Council still hasn't spoken about the guards in detail. Eli has made a few passing references to asking Pieter to do her a "favor," but when this happens, Sergei starts speaking in sullen monosyllables and Francisco makes aggressive moves to change the subject.

But Caro, who spent the most time in the VR room of anyone on the Council, hasn't seemed bothered by its closure. This only heightens my feeling that I'm going insane. Wasn't Caro the one who couldn't restrain her excitement about returning to *Thunderhead Empire*? Isn't she the one who talks about logging dozens of hours a week in competitive VRaces on Earth? So how can she brush off Eli's guards with nothing more than careless looks, when the place is consuming every second of my consciousness? I spend hours every night buried in the pages of my memory diary, trying to build anything as real as that place felt, but I can't make the words feel big enough. I've been using progressively smaller handwriting, jamming two lines into one, dreading the day I run out of space. I'm falling asleep in class after class.

Five days after my visit to Goldport Island, I'm trying to focus on Swahili numbers, sitting beside Caro in an empty screening room while she types a list of English verbs into her tablet. *Ishirini,* I think. Twenty. *Ishirini na moja, ishirini na mbili . . .*

Some video from a previous class is replaying, muted, on the screen. A wizened Korean man points to a diagram of the forces exacted on a wooden block, bouncing on the tips of his toes and smiling to the camera. My eyelids droop as I watch him gesticulate.

Then I'm jerking awake as Caro says, "Enough." She's on her feet, stretching.

I check the time and frown. "We still have half an hour."

"You think you'll learn anything like this?" Her eyes dart from my most recent stress-breakout to the twitch in my cheek. "Get some sleep. Actually, will you do me a favor and skip classes tomorrow, too? You make me want to fall asleep, snoring all over me."

I stand, feeling an embarrassed heat rising in my neck. "I can't skip classes. What kind of example is that?"

Caro sighs. "No one cares, Leigh."

Irritation lances through me, and it takes a massive effort to repress the feeling. I tell myself I'm not angry, I'm just hungry, I'm just tired, and these things are magnifying glasses for every irritant.

I must have let something show, though, because for once, Caro's amusement falters. "Showing up for class looking like a zombie isn't a great example, either."

My exhaustion makes me sloppy. "I thought you said no one cares," I say.

She lifts her hands, rolls her eyes, her whole body rising with exasperation. "I meant that nobody will notice if you skip—"

"Really?" I say before the translator's finished. "It isn't that *you* don't care? Just like you don't care about the way people treat me right in front of you, and apparently about whether any of us survive? I didn't forget you said this might as well be a game. What does that even mean?"

We stand at an impasse. Doubt flits across Caro's face in the way her emotions always do—there one moment, then flattened away into that nonchalant blankness.

But she doesn't give me some glib answer. She doesn't leave, either. She bobs on the balls of her feet, two fluffy ornaments on her earlobes bouncing.

"Well?" I push. "What did you mean?"

Caro turns the tablet in her hands over and over. Eventually she says, "Let's call it open-world."

I frown.

"An open-world game," she adds. "You can take on the main quest, or you can ignore it." She flutters her fingers at me. "You're all working on the main quest, but I don't want to. I want to go around and talk to all the autogenerated people and maybe read some of the lore they put into the scroll repository. If there's some enemy I need to beat, some assignment I get, I'll do it. But that's it."

"Yes, but you *are* part of the—the 'main quest,'" I say, drawing quotation marks with my fingers. "Once we reach Antaeus, the Council is going to need your help with the Planters. The autosystems in there are really important, and Eli said she doesn't know as much ab—"

"You're assuming we find anything on Antaeus."

"What?"

Caro makes a whole production of storing her tablet in a holster. Finally, with an air of letting something out that she's held in for weeks, she says, "Why are we supposed to believe there are seeds on that planet? I know it makes people feel better, but there's no proof. You're really going to get your hopes up again?"

The glow from the video reflects off her glossed lips, her sunshine-yellow eyeliner. There's not a drop of humor in her features now. Piece by piece, everything she's done clicks together in my mind: her detachment, her flippancy, even the careless way she rolls on a new layer of lipstick. If she thinks we're still doomed, why should she save anything for the future? Why take anything seriously, when she can laugh and joke and have a decent enough time instead? As for engaging with the Council—isn't it masochistic to get attached to a group of people if you're expecting them starve to death in front of you?

I want to insist that the seeds are out there, but I can't form the words. Caro could be right. I remember the self-doubt that wracked me the night we left Earth, when Eli told me we were the same, and I felt that I could identify her but not myself. It's the same with Caro. She has real beliefs, she has a strategy, and I am a crystal ball: outside, a smooth, glassy shell; inside, a swirling fog of uncertainty. Am I the only one who feels lost all the time, like I could be convinced of anything if someone tried hard enough?

Five feet to our left, the Korean physicist slides the block across the table while an equation for frictional force writes itself across the screen. Caro laces her fingers together in a pattern I can't trace. "I learned my lesson on Earth, okay?" she says. "When you can't do anything that matters, you stay on the outskirts. You don't get so invested that it'll hurt when everything goes wrong."

"But we are doing things that matter. We're training, we're preparing for emergencies."

She lets out that flutish little laugh. "*This* is the emergency, Leigh. What we're doing is like toddlers playing with toy fire-trucks while our house is burning down. There's no point, and it was the same back home." She flops into a seat in the front row. "I know your parents dragged you into the middle of everything, but my parents never cared what I thought, they just wanted me to stay out of their way. My father's party voted to weight the passenger lottery so people with more money or influence would have more entries. You'll know something about that," she adds.

I stiffen, feeling the old knee-jerk defensiveness at anything near criticism of my mother, but she's right. In some places, like Kenya, the rich were publicly allowed to buy additional lottery entries, with the money put toward the manufacturing process. In the US, though, the scales were weighted behind closed doors. Networks of businesspeople rubbed elbows at extravagant mixers, coaxing members of my mother's administration to classify them as Necessary Personnel. After all, why try for better odds when you could transcend the lottery draw entirely?

The truth came out at the turn of this year, our scandal just one more piece of the worldwide outcry. My mother made a lot of oblique references to "regrettable incidents" and brought reform proposals to the GFPC, but she never spoke about the extent of the corruption. That didn't surprise me. Since the day she took office, she was forbidden to admit that anything might be beyond her control. Tell one person "I made a mistake," and the whole world takes it as a cue to paint you as a hopeless incompetent.

She brought that home, too. My mother could never admit she was wrong, or even that she was hurt. I think she wanted me, and the rest of the world, to believe she was invincible. I remember cuts and winces brushed away as nothing, only to reappear later as Band-Aids and prescriptions, every accident bandaged in silence.

Caro is watching me shrewdly. "Yeah," I force out. "I know something about it."

It's all the acknowledgment I can manage. I don't know how to talk about failure. I guess I never learned the language.

Caro sinks lower in her seat. "Well, I don't know about you, but I tried to change my father's mind, and he wouldn't listen at all." She bobs her shoulders. "Pointless, see? And meanwhile my friends were begging me to get them and their families spots aboard the fleet, and I couldn't do that, either. The only time I could actually accomplish anything . . ." She tugs her tablet out of its holster and gives it an absentminded flip.

"Was in other worlds," I say. My defensiveness has faded. I feel a pulse of sympathy, looking at her defeated expression.

Caro nods. "I knew it wasn't real, but at least it didn't hurt. It hurts to care about this stupid reality; it hurts to try. And if something's going to hurt, I want to do it for a reason. When we get to Antaeus and nothing's there, we won't be able to save anyone. Then we're going to look back at everything we're doing now and see how meaningless it all was."

I watch Caro twine her braids between her fingers, making more patterns. I choose my words carefully.

"So," I say, "you don't think these ten months mean anything?"

Her hands still. "What?"

"I'm saying, even if you're right, and there's nothing on Antaeus, and we're all dead in a year, we have ten months left. You really think it's pointless, trying to make these last months a little better for everyone?"

Frissons of movement in Caro's mouth and nose, a flutter of her eyelashes. A rare notch between her eyebrows: consideration.

In a different voice, small and muted, she says, "I don't know."

I tap the control panel, shutting off the projector. The lights come up, low and warm, illuminating the depths of Caro's eyes like sunbeams into dark rum.

I take the seat beside her. We both regard the blank projection screen for a while.

"You think we can do that?" Caro says. "You actually believe we can make any of this better for anyone?"

I give her a tired smile. "Don't I have to believe it?"

———

It's 2:48 a.m., Pacific Time, and I am standing in the bathroom, swaying. I've just stepped out of one of the showers, sealed tubes that rain water for a two-minute interval, then strain every speck of moisture back off the skin with a blast of vacuumed air. The toilets are just as loud and efficient, like an airplane's, steeply angled and deafening.

I hope no one interrupts me, but even in the daytime, that would be unlikely. The Residential Wing has fifty communal bathrooms, ten per cabin floor. Each was meant to serve twenty passengers, but with our numbers, each is basically private now.

I pass my hand beneath the tap. With the palmful of cold

water that burbles out, I splash my face, avoiding the tender heads of acne on my cheeks and chin. I prod the blue shadows under my eyes. This is the type of exhaustion that feels like abject misery, borderline insanity.

The only respite I've had all day was my nighttime run with Anis. He's been in a strange mood the past few nights, initiating conversations that tug me out of my visions of the VR room. He always sounds weirdly formal when he starts talking, and I wonder if he's only doing it out of a sense of obligation. The silence does feel different now that we're running side by side.

Tonight he asked me how I'd done on our psychology review, which turned into talk about which classes we'd take if we didn't have training, and we both wanted marine biology, so we wound up talking about how the deepest trenches of the ocean are as good as the deepest reaches of outer space. Eventually I asked him if he thinks alien life exists, and he panted, with ironclad dismissal, "There's nothing else out here."

"Seriously? Nothing? Not one single-celled organism flopping around on one of the trillions of planets in the universe?"

"No." He hesitated. "What, you're saying *you* believe in aliens?"

I considered this for a while, then said, "I believe in the possibility of aliens."

"Of course," he said, looking away, and I heard a smile in his voice, although the translator didn't catch it.

I spy an odd half smile on my lips now, thinking about it, but as soon as I see my mouth move in the mirror, I'm back inside my body, inside the exhaustion. Clutching to the rim of the sink, I miss bathtubs and swimming pools. I wish I could submerge myself in something, hear the low, hollow drone of water pressing in on my ears.

I wonder if there's an underwater setting in the VR room. Maybe I could close the headphones over my ears and hear it again.

As I tug my ship-issued sleep shirt back over my head—a dark gray gown, soft and plasticky like something out of a hospital—I think of Francisco's enraptured face bathed in light.

Before I know what I'm doing, I'm striding out of the bathroom and down the hall to the balconies. I stop at the rails, staring across the intersection of the ship's wings. The *Lazarus* is dim at night. The dark passage to the VR room stares back at me from the Preservation Wing like a pupil.

I can still turn around, I tell myself, even as I take a step toward the elevator bay. I can still change my mind. But my heart rate is picking up and up, pulsing beneath my tongue, and I am helpless to stop myself. Desire is coursing through me, pure enough to override every cautionary instinct.

I'm in the elevator, emerging on the seventh floor of the Preservation Wing. I'm careening down the hall toward Earth, going home. I'll tell the guard that I need to get in for a simulation. I'm one of the Council; they'll believe me. And then I'll load DC, and the Virginia backroads that we used to coast through in the nights, and then I'll go everywhere else, to rippling savannas, to moors blasting wind across the heather, to forests as deep and black as oceans. Everyone has their hideaways. I need a refuge. I need a place where I won't feel like my foot is plummeting through the air at the top of a staircase, forever, anticipating a solid surface that doesn't arrive to support me. I need some fucking relief.

I round the final corner and stop. My breath forms a needle in my throat.

The door to the VR chamber is open. Sahir is sprawled face-down at the threshold, his eyes closed, a dark line of blood drawn from his nose to his chin.

CHAPTER 9

RED TAPE

Eli is pacing back and forth in front of the bunk where Sahir lies. His chest rises and sinks slowly, his eyes still shut. Laid limply on the mattress, rather than standing by his friends, Sahir looks shorter and stockier than usual, clearly still growing into his big feet.

I rise from my knees, holding a cloth damp with blood. I've dabbed his lips and chin clean, but the bridge of his nose is swollen, clearly fractured. Two black eyes are coming in beneath the fans of his closed lashes like the color of a slowly developing photograph.

"I don't get what's wrong with him," Eli says, collapsing into the commander's seat. There are circles under her eyes, too, and her hair is thin and deflated, like a doll's polyester threads combed to death by a too-attentive child. "Do people seriously pass out from getting hit in the head? He can breathe fine, shouldn't he be awake?"

"I don't know," I say quietly, setting the bloodied cloth at the end of the bunk.

"Lucky you found him before someone else did." As a ghost of confusion passes across Eli's face, I realize that I never gave her a good reason for why I was wandering down the VR hall in the middle of the night.

"Not really luck," I say. "In the atrium the other day he said he was feeling overwhelmed with the night shift. I couldn't sleep, so I figured I'd check on him, see how he was holding up."

"Oh, right," Eli says, brow unfurrowing. "God, you're good at your job."

I force a smile and turn toward the steps. "I'll get someone who's taking the EMT course. Jayanti—she's friends with him, she should know about this."

But I've hardly reached the stairs when Eli says, "Leigh."

I look back. Sahir's eyelids are flickering.

We're both at his side in an instant. "Sahir?" I say. "Can you hear me?"

His eyes slide over me and Eli, unfocused.

"Can you hear us," Eli repeats more loudly.

Sahir winces. "Yes."

"Are you okay?" I ask.

"I don't know," he mumbles. "Someone . . . My arm . . ."

He makes an uncoordinated motion with his left hand. I roll up the sleeve. Just below his elbow is a single puncture mark.

I feel a cold rush of disbelief, and Eli's face contorts with anger. The anesthetic shots in the med bay are invaluable. They're meant to be used for major surgery, in life-threatening situations.

"You saw who did this?" Eli says.

Sahir tries to sit up. I brace his back, helping him upright. "No, I . . ." He tugs at the dark hair that hangs over his forehead, unable to hide his guilty look. "I was just . . ."

"You fell asleep?" I say quietly. "It's okay, it was really late."

"Yeah. I woke up when a bag went over my head, and then someone hit me through it. . . . I was trying to get out of the bag when the needle went in."

"How do you feel?" I ask.

"Achy." He tries to stand. "Tired."

"You need to sleep it off," Eli says, stooping to slip his arm around her shoulders. "Come on." I take her cue and do the same, and we lift him to his feet.

We navigate the ship unspeaking. Standing in the elevator and padding through the pale arteries of the Residential Wing, I can't think of anything besides the weight of Sahir's uncoordinated body. The truth is just as heavy as it settles onto me. This is my fault. If I'd solved the VR problem myself, like a real chief of personnel would, if I'd set my obsession aside for even an hour, Eli wouldn't have had to implement her own plan. I'm supposed to put myself last, and now, because of my failure, Sahir is taking in wet-sounding breaths through a broken nose, listing from side to side like a drunk person.

"Don't worry about training tomorrow," Eli says as we stop outside his cabin door.

"I'll bring your breakfast here, okay?" I add.

"No, you don't have to. I'll be there." Sahir's shoulders are slumped. "I'm sorry. I thought you were overreacting with the guards. I didn't realize—"

"Stop," Eli says. "You've got nothing to apologize for. Whoever did this, we'll find them. *They're* going to be sorry."

I see gratitude in Sahir's face, then a shadow of intimidation. It comes together into something like respect.

"You don't think it was Francisco, do you?" Eli says quietly as we head back down the hall.

I try to imagine it. For the last five days, Francisco has been so devoted to the ship's future that it's hard to get a sentence out of him that doesn't have to do with lifecycle maps or pedagogical methods.

"No, I don't think so," I say.

"Me neither. But if it's someone else, the place is a bigger problem than we thought."

As we rise in the elevator, the atrium shrinks beneath us, the fire waving and fluttering like hands in goodbye. Eli is watching it, too. There's a ghostly version of her face in the curved glass wall. Her reflected eyes meet mine, and she says, "We should double the guards. The attacker won't be able to sneak up on two people in secret."

I make a noncommittal noise as we walk the balconies toward the Command Wing. I can't help considering every argument I've heard over the past few days, every resentful mutter at morning meetings when I mention the VR room.

"Listen," I say when we're halfway down the hall to the bridge, "why didn't you tell me before you assigned the guards?"

Eli glances over with obvious confusion. "So that you could be on their side."

"I— What?"

"I thought the crew would hate it, so it'd be better if I just did it. And then you could tell people, you know, 'Oh, I'm annoyed by it, too, and I'm on your side.' I thought it'd make it easier. They could hate me for it instead of you."

I process this for a moment. Then I say slowly, "You thought they'd hate it."

"Yeah. Obviously."

"But you did it anyway."

Eli shrugs. "And? We've been leading the crew for a month, making our own decisions, and things were going well until all this happened with the VR room." She tugs at a tangle in her hair as we head into the bridge. "What, you don't think so?"

"I think this is a different kind of decision," I say, choosing my words carefully as we jog down the steps. "We've been designing all the training plans because you know more about the ship and its protocols than everyone else. Putting guards at the VR room is a matter of opinion."

Eli stops at the bottom of the steps. "Opinion?" she repeats. "No, hang on. We're way beyond opinion. This is two people hurt now because of that place. If everybody keeps torturing themselves with it, we're never going to get through training, let alone get to a point where things feel normal."

"But it's one of the central features of the ship. Can we really close the whole thing down without asking them?"

"Yeah. This VR shit is obviously poison to them, and all they want to do is drink it. So we throw away the bottle. Problem solved."

I look back at her, so tired that my thoughts seem to be orbiting my skull, just out of reach.

"Leigh, come on. Francisco said there were other people doing the same thing. Maybe they're not hurting themselves yet, but it's messing people up to go in there and see all that." She paces along the length of the dashboard. "And no wonder. I mean, think about it. You go back to this version of Earth that isn't even what Earth was like, this version that's *better* than Earth, and then you're resenting the ship. You're thinking, well, the *Lazarus* can never be like that. But of course it can't. Earth wasn't like that, either."

"Wasn't it?" The words slip out before I can catch them.

"What?" Eli stops pacing.

"I mean, they're stereoscopic simulations," I say quickly. "Those rooms have the most realistic images ever recorded."

"Oh, right." Her look of alarm fades. "I'm not talking about image quality. I'm saying that those presets are idealized versions of whatever they show you. They're not supposed to be accurate—they're supposed to make you want to stay there. Remember that whole blowup when they released the Beijing preset, and it came out that the CCP had gone in and made all these generous edits to get rid of the pollution, make everything pretty and shiny?" She shakes her head. "They're all like that. That's not what the actual world was like."

For the first time, when I think back to the Goldport plaza, the memory seems overbright, artificial. I feel shaken. Eli's right that the real world was polluted and dangerous, violent and judgmental. Haven't I been telling myself almost since takeoff that we had to do better than Earth, that we couldn't rip ourselves apart the way they did back home?

Maybe I've been pining after something that isn't even real. Maybe it's just postcard images in that room, glossy and flat, beautiful and ideal, revealing nothing.

Eli studies me. Eventually she says, "I know what you're thinking, all right?"

"You do?"

"Yeah. It feels weird to make unilateral decisions like this because you're..." She waves a hand at me. "You're *you*. The First Daughter. Obviously you want everyone to get a say, your mom was the president, I get it." She approaches me. "But come on. You're the one who's had to deal with the fallout. Those fights about countries, and who's to blame, all that stuff that doesn't even matter anymore—" Her face is filling slowly with evangelical certainty, gaze fevered, cheeks flushed. "Irina going after you because you're American, these kids you're playing therapist for, don't you see it? This is all because they can't let go of Earth and focus on the present. And the VR room is making it a hundred times harder for them to think logically."

My disorientation intensifies as I think of my memory diary. It suddenly seems embarrassing. Hundreds upon hundreds of pages of disorganized memories...it *is* illogical. I don't even know if it's helped me feel better. Have I been gouging myself into a deeper and deeper rut?

"I don't know, Eli." My voice is feeble, unlike itself. "I just don't know if we can expect them to let go all at once."

"They've got to. We can't do this halfway, Leigh. We've all got to choose: Hold on or let go. I mean—" Eli's face twists, full of pain and conviction like she's running through a stress fracture. "I could've held on to my mom, you know? And the crew would've found me here, crying over her, and they would've been twice as terrified. But I wasn't going to let that happen. She died to give us a future, and I'm not going to waste that. I am not going to walk backward through my life, staring into everything I left behind."

She comes right up to me, eyes on an exact level with mine.

"You made the choice when we took off," she says, low and intent. "I did, too. We're going to Antaeus, we're going to Juventas, and everyone on this ship is coming with us. We're going to keep them alive. That's why we're here. That's the reason we made it."

Perspiration gleams like rhinestones at her temples. Looking at her, I feel the momentum of the whole ship, like I am the *Lazarus* itself, accelerating down this dark, empty highway toward our destination, steered by her hand. For the first time in five days, since I stood by the ocean and saw the sky, the weight of Earth eases off my shoulders, and I feel something like emptiness or freedom—some light, hollow feeling that at this moment is such a relief I could cry.

"We've got to keep that door shut," she says.

"I know."

As the words fall from my lips, I know I will never go back to that place again. It's a promise. I choose the future. I choose to face forward, to follow her.

At morning meeting the next day, Sahir joins us atop the hearth. Overnight, the swelling around his nose has darkened, the bruising pooled beneath his eyes. As clusters of kids notice his battered face, conversations die, until all that's left is the usually inaudible hum of the ship's power. Sahir glares out at the group as if daring us to think less of him for his injury.

"This happened to Sahir," I say, "during his shift at the VR room last night."

Francisco peruses the crowd gimlet-eyed, as if he'll be able to identify the attacker on sight, and Sergei moves closer to Sahir, already whispering questions about whether the EMTs have checked on him. Everyone else goggles—none more so than Caro. Sitting on the edge of the hearth, she's leaning back like the scene before her is an onslaught she longs to escape, but her gold-lined eyes are locked on Sahir's injuries.

This is what I meant, I think, seeing realization fall across Caro's face. This is exactly what we were talking about yesterday. Maybe in eleven months, everyone aboard the *Lazarus* will be gone, but right now, Sahir is hurt, and maybe we could prevent this from happening again.

"This is serious," I say. "If anyone thinks they have any information about who's responsible, please let us know. As for the VR room, our plan is to double the guards so that nobody has to keep watch alone."

My eyes stray to Irina and Jayanti in anticipation of an argument, but they're gawking at Sahir along with everyone else. Jayanti is twisting the ends of her hair, which have faded from red to maroon, and Irina's usually hard features are stricken, the way they were in the Menagerie our first night aboard.

A timid voice on the other side of the group is the first to speak. "We're stationing more guards?" Fatima asks. "Don't people need time for training?"

"Yeah," says Xu Jie, a plump Chinese boy with an open, guileless face, "and besides, what if the guards just go into the VR room themselves? Who's going to stop them?"

I realize with a lurch that I've heard this argument before. It's the same counterpoint I read to the GFPC's militarized launch plan. *Stationing a military to protect the fleet sounds like a reasonable enough idea,* said a representative from Cameroon, *until you ask yourself why those troops wouldn't just take over the ships themselves.*

"It's a good point," Sergei says. Under his breath, he adds to me, "When did you and Eli talk about this?"

I don't have time to answer. Someone asks from the back of the crowd, "Are you going to take away TV, too?"

"Of course not," I say, unsettled by the phrasing, like the Council is a strict parent sticking a toy on the top shelf. "We're not . . . We don't want to take anything away. We just want to make sure we're all safe."

"*Safe?*" Jayanti says from Irina's shoulder, her stupor breaking. "Sahir only got hurt because Eli made him guard that room."

"Hold on," says Pieter indignantly. "I'm helping guard the room, and no one made me do anything. Of course we should close the place when someone nearly killed themselves over it."

The second the words are out, Pieter seems to realize what he's said. His hand jerks toward his mouth as if to grab the words back, but the damage is done. Chatter rises through the atrium.

"It's making—"

"Someone tried to—"

"Who?"

"What are you talking about?"

Pieter looks at me, face drawn with guilt. I sigh. "Everyone," I call. "Everyone! Please." The chatter falls to a simmer, and I go on, "Pieter's right. That's why we've tried to keep the place shut. The person who tried to . . . to hurt themselves is recovering okay, but it's still a safety issue."

My words don't seem to reassure anyone. I see Moses Nabwana looking at his friend Kwasi with concern lining his face; Kwasi catches him doing it and starts speaking under his breath with visible annoyance. Fatima Awad is studying

Sahir's injuries with fresh, breathless fear, her fingers moving absentmindedly over her own cheek as if imagining how it would feel to be struck there. And Matteo Marini is eyeing everyone around him with suspicion, shifting away from his usual group toward the outskirts.

Francisco's voice slices through the murmurs. "All of this is irrelevant. We should be focusing on catching the person who hurt Sahir."

There are spots of color in his cheeks. As he busies himself with his tablet, scrolling, flipping, and adjusting, Sergei's eyes fix on the side of his face. Caro's restless gaze flits from Francisco to me, and I can see the quick gears of her mind grinding into the question, too. I see them both putting it together—Sergei understanding why Francisco and Eli suddenly seem so much closer, Caro understanding the way I've been acting this week.

Pieter sticks his hand into the air. "I have an idea," he says, looking determined to make up for his slip.

"Go ahead," I say.

"There must be a way to tell when somebody's door opens or closes. Control panels operate the doors. Shouldn't that send a signal? Can't we tell who left their room yesterday night?"

Uneasy voices mix into one another. "That's so creepy," says Irina, looking unnerved. "You want to track who goes where every hour of every day?"

Pieter fires back. "No, I want to find out who hurt Sahir, even if *you* don't care that one of your best friends was assaulted."

Irina's face screws up in anger. She and Jayanti make retorts, lost in a flare-up of laughs. I don't miss the raw edge to the laughter, like the nervous bleating in a theater after the scare in a horror movie. "Hey," I call. "Enough! Enough. We'll talk it over with Eli and see what she thinks, all right? For now, let's get back to training, and again, if you know anything about what happened, come talk to us."

The group disperses toward the elevator bay, preparing tablets and equipment for their courses, the unsettled notes of their voices making a discordant clash. As I climb down from the hearth, someone is waiting for me on one of the sofas.

"Anis," I say, feeling flustered. We haven't said a word in public since our first night aboard. Speaking in front of other people shatters the unofficial rules.

I collect myself. "Do you know something about Sahir?"

"No, I have a question."

I glance at the clock. "We have a Council meeting in a few minutes. Walk with me?"

Anis nods at a nearby stairwell, I follow him in, and the door shuts behind us. "I forgot what you looked like without the sweat," I say as we begin to climb.

"I forgot what you sounded like when you weren't wheezing for breath."

"Only one of us wheezes, and I hate to tell you, but it's not me."

That coaxes out a bark of a laugh, and I grin at him as we jog up past the second-floor landing. It's another couple of flights before I remember: "What did you want to ask?"

"It's not really a question." He scrubs his hand through his curly hair. "You can't let the Council look for those door records. You've already closed that room without a vote, doubled the guards without a vote. And I know you don't agree with any of it."

"Why would you say that?" I reply, half a second too quickly.

Anis gives me a look that's half amusement and half exasperation. "Don't try this with me."

"Try what?"

He sighs. "In the atrium, Irina asked if you wanted the guards at the room, and you said, 'It's not a permanent situation.' I know what that means. I wish you'd just say it." We climb another few steps, and then he adds, "I'm learning your language."

I don't answer. Every defensive instinct is telling me to deflect, to deny, but there's a bizarre tingle over my skin, like the touch of sunlight. I feel exposed, and for some reason, I don't dislike the feeling.

When I next glance at Anis, his cheeks are dark, although he doesn't seem out of breath from the climbing. He meets my eyes and looks away at once. "Anyway, I was going to say... the door records. My point is, Irina's right. Watching people's movements is creepy. This might be a good reason to track someone down, but not every reason will be."

I bite the inside of my cheek. "I get that, but we've got to take steps to eliminate the threat."

Anis stops on the steps. "Kill the threat? What's that supposed to mean?"

"What? I didn't say kill. I said eliminate."

He lifts a hand to his translator. "It's coming through the same."

"*Prevent.* We have to prevent another attack. People are scared."

Anis's brow eases. "I know," he says, leaning against the railing. "And I'm not pretending that I know what to do. All I know is that this isn't the way to do it."

I join him at the rail. We look down at the steps folding into themselves, concentric rectangles disappearing into lines. "I feel that way all the time," I admit.

"You do?" he says with obvious surprise.

"Yeah." I don't look at him. The feeling of exposure has intensified. "But I...That feeling's not enough. Anyone can feel dissatisfied. Anyone can ask a question. At the end of the day, someone has to give an answer."

"A plan," he says slowly.

"A plan," I agree.

But we climb flight after flight, and neither of us has an epiphany. As we near the top floor, he grumbles, "You still haven't said it."

"What am I supposed to be saying?"

"That you don't agree with stationing the guards. I all but said it for you, and you still won't admit it."

"I don't see why that matters."

"Are you joking?" There's real frustration in his voice again. "Okay. Ask Irina. She'll tell you why it matters."

I climb faster. So, he's reminding me he's on Irina's side, that he thinks Irina is a better person than me. I shouldn't be hurt by that, or even surprised, but I reply more sharply than I meant to. "If you like Irina so much, why aren't you trailing after her, too?"

"What would the point be? She can't ever get any answers out of you."

"Yeah, because even Irina isn't as pedantic as you are."

We reach the tenth-floor landing. Anis stops, not moving for the door. "I'm not pedantic," he says hotly. "I'm—unsatisfied. And I want to hear it from you."

"Fine," I say, stopping, too. "I don't adore the guards. Is that what you wanted?"

"Yes. It is."

"*Why?* What difference does it make if I agree with the

guards? What does it matter what I think about school scheduling or a bunch of scattered books?"

"Because we're doing everything you say, Leigh! We should
know what you think and what you stand for!" Anis takes half
a step toward me. As I lift my chin to hold his gaze, I realize
with a strange heat in my palms how little distance there is
between us. "Well?" he demands. "I can't figure it out. What
do you stand for?"

My throat tightens. I feel as if he already knows, somehow,
that I caved to what Eli wanted last night. I feel as if he's asking, *Why didn't you stand your ground?*

The obvious answer is fear. If I'd kept arguing about the VR
room, Eli might have seen through my mask to my obsession.
Then she'd look at me and think, *Illogical, overemotional, sen-
timental, incapable.* Sergei and Caro would think I'm a faker;
Francisco would think I'm a hypocrite. I'm afraid of what's in
everybody's head, all the time, I think.

But it wasn't only fear that kept me quiet. Eli has her reasons
for wanting the VR room closed, and they're good reasons.
Why prioritize my own judgment? Why argue for the sake of
argument? All my life I've learned to accept what I don't want.

"I stand for compromise," I say.

"No," Anis says, "that's not what I'm saying. I mean, *what do
you stand for?*"

The question sounds different. He's chosen other words,
translated identically by the bud in my ear, and I feel a mad-
dening itch to know the change. What is he really asking?
What have I stood for? What would I fight for? What do I care
about the most?

I realize I don't know the answer to any of those questions. I
feel as if I should be able to summon something up as easily as

I'd retrieve my own name, a cause I believe in, some value I'll never disavow. And I'm sure that if I turned the question back on Anis, he could answer easily. I try to reassemble my life story in a way that might show me an answer, but all my highlights, all my lowlights, seem to include flight or fear or both.

I watch myself do it again. I watch myself say, in a cool, impersonal voice, "I have to go," then brush past him, shove through the door, and leave him alone, still waiting for an answer. Maybe I don't stand for anything at all. Maybe I run.

———

Halfway through the Council meeting, I find myself staring into the black disk of the tabletop, tracing the obscure shapes that are our reflected bodies. Sergei is gesticulating, his motions fluid and generous. Parts of his sentences reach me, muffled as if from beyond a windowpane. "...that you and Leigh decided on this guard by yourself... changing it in the middle of the night..."

Eli's response wanders through, her silhouette unmoving in the seat that has somehow come to feel like the head of the round table. "...had to make a quick decision..."

"...should all be included," Sergei is insisting. "We don't know how the others feel... haven't asked them..."

Francisco breaks in, rapid-fire as always. I register him saying, "...in the interest of efficiency... other tasks we need to prioritize..."

Their voices recede until it's only Anis's question I hear. *What do you stand for?* I gaze into the Council's outlines—at Eli, who never doubts where she's going next, whose entire world exists in the future tense. Sergei, who held the elevator, always concerned with others' comfort and happiness. Francisco, the image of correctness, who tried so hard to bring order to our broken situation that he put a fracture in himself. Caro, the cypher, glossing cheer over a well of nihilism—quietly putting pragmatism over optimism.

I look into the dark hole of my own reflection, too close to see my own shape.

"Leigh," Eli says.

I jump. "What was that?"

Eli looks puzzled. "We were trying to think of nominations for the new guards."

"Right. Yes." I straighten in my seat. "I . . . Maybe Pieter could help with that?"

Eli's eyes linger on me, but she says, "Good idea. Francisco, Sergei, work with Pieter to draw up a list. He knows everything about everyone. He'll have a good sense."

As Sergei nods and Francisco makes a note, it occurs to me how different Eli's voice is now than it used to be, clear and assured. There's something familiar about the cadence. I frown down at the table, trying to pinpoint it.

"More guards won't help us catch the attacker, though," Eli goes on. "I promised Sahir we'd figure out who did it."

"Pieter had an idea about that," Francisco says. He's been terse during the meeting, and he keeps giving Caro and Sergei furtive looks, although they haven't said anything about what might or might not have happened in the VR room. Now he describes the idea of tracking who's gone through the ship's doors, finishing by saying, "I think it's an excellent idea. We find the records, we pull this one record, the whole thing's finished."

Eli has been listening with interest. "Yeah, that could be

perfect, if it's possible. Caro, do you think you'd be able to find threshold signals in the codehome?"

Caro tugs at one of her cartilage piercings. She's sitting up straight in her seat, more serious than I've ever seen her during a meeting. "I doubt the ship would store that kind of information."

"Even if it does," Sergei says, sounding uncomfortable, "I don't think it's a good plan."

"Why not?" Eli asks.

"It's only two days until we cut back our meals. Hungry people start trouble. Adding this tracking thing on top is a bad idea."

I knead my temples. Amid all this, I'd forgotten about the restricted diets. How has the first month skipped by so quickly?

Eli drums her fingers on the table. "Okay, but how else are we supposed to catch them?"

"And," Francisco adds, "after we catch them, what do we do with them?"

No one answers right away. I feel a slow twisting sensation in my stomach. I didn't think about what sort of punishment we'd be doling out.

"We could cut back their meals," Sergei suggests.

"No," Eli says at once. "Not with the tighter rations about to kick in. We don't want to risk anyone getting malnourished. What if . . ." She hesitates. "Caro, could you program external locks on a few of the empty cabins?"

Caro wets her blue-painted lips with the tip of her tongue. "External locks?" she repeats.

"You want to make cells?" Sergei says, his feathery brows lifting high.

Eli grimaces and says, "Yeah, I know, but what else could we really do to them?"

"I think it's a good idea," Francisco says. "Irina and Jayanti nearly started a fight with Matteo Marini when I was on the way here. They think he's the attacker."

"Matteo?" I ask, distracted. "Why him?"

Francisco shrugs. "He spent a lot of time in the VR room before it closed, and he and Sahir are both in the water treatment division in Maintenance. Apparently Sahir's been outscoring him in their fluid dynamics class, even though he's three years younger, and they argued a few days ago because Sahir wouldn't stop being smug about it." He sighs, waves a hand. "It's beside the point. I'm not saying Matteo hurt Sahir, but whoever did won't be popular. If they're separated from everybody, then we all have time to cool down. Better a few days alone in a cabin than a broken nose. And . . ." His clipped tones waver. He folds his hands. "And it would help them to stay away from the place."

I feel the truth settling between us in the center of the table. Francisco's cheeks darken.

"Francisco," Sergei begins, "are you . . . ?"

"I'm fine," Francisco says curtly.

Sergei sits forward in his seat. It's obvious that he's been holding this in the whole meeting. "You always say that. You were saying that two weeks ago, so clearly it's not true. And I'm not trying to make you feel bad," he adds, "I'm just saying you don't have to pretend to be fine if—"

"Leave it," Eli cuts in. "He doesn't want to talk about it."

Sergei frowns. "I'm talking to him, not you."

Francisco doesn't look up from his interlaced fingers. "She's right, Sergei. I feel better when I'm focusing on other things."

"Yeah," Sergei says with barely concealed exasperation, "but you can't focus on other things all the—"

"Just stop, all right?" Francisco snaps. "This isn't why I brought it up. I don't need this."

Sergei wilts. His shoulders come down, and he closes his mouth.

Francisco slumps forward to rest his elbows on the table, rubbing his hands over his face. I can tell that this was exactly what he wanted to avoid.

I clear my throat. "Caro, do you think you can make the external locks?"

Caro considers. The doubt on her heart-shaped face reminds me she's the youngest in the room. I feel a pang of regret, because I know what she's weighing. Her plan to stay on the outskirts, to float above ship life like cream floating at the top of milk, is about to fall apart. If the group felt uneasy about the threshold signals, they'll be twice as vocal about us making cells, and Caro will be at the forefront. She'll have to stand with us and defend herself, and I'm realizing I don't want that for her. I wish I could take all the scrutiny and she could stay in the shadows, protected.

But she also wished she could help her friends on Earth survive. She wished she could help everyone in Kenya get an equal shot at the lottery. She wanted to *do* something, to act in a way that really mattered, and this does matter. Confining the attacker could keep anyone else from getting hurt.

"Okay," she says finally. "If it's the best option."

"It *is* the best option," Eli says. "Honestly, it's the only option. The ship would have needed something like containment cells eventually. People aren't perfect. Of course there's going to be an actual, serious offense over eleven hundred years."

Again I feel that tug of familiarity, a bell rung in the back of my mind. What is it, that cadence in Eli's voice, the matter-of-fact tone? Where have I heard it before?

Eli tightens her ponytail, makes a note on her tablet, and says, "We should start writing laws. It's just a matter of time."

And as she says it, as her high, tight ponytail swings and gleams at the top of her head, I recognize the similarity. The sentences are smooth. They sound predetermined and inarguable. She sounds like a politician. She sounds like me.

Several days pass without another attack, but life aboard the *Lazarus* still feels off-kilter. Pieter and the rest of the guards sit together in the canteen now, debating who gets the night shift, everyone looking to Pieter—as the copilot-in-training—for a final call.

I wouldn't have expected anyone to want the job, after what happened to Sahir, but taking the late shifts seems like it's become a badge of status among the eight guards. "Try me," it says, the eagerness to stay up half the night waiting, maybe hoping, that somebody will try to break in. But nobody has crawled out of the woodwork to take them up on the challenge.

By day, I field everyone who thinks they have information about the attack. Fatima Awad tells me in a whisper that So Min-ji was complaining for a whole day about the VR room being closed, and saying she'd beat up the guards to get in—but that seems like it was pretty obviously a joke, with Min-ji being thirteen and the size of a matchstick. Pieter comes to me with an elaborate theory that it was Jayanti, suggesting that she's been stewing in resentment since her fight with Sahir, and that she only signed up for EMT training to get intimate knowledge of the sedatives.

Jayanti and Irina, for their part, keep insisting that Matteo Marini had it in for Sahir. So one evening after our language exchange lessons, I take Matteo aside to ask him if he knows anything. I try to do it without outright accusing him, but he still thunders at me that if he'd wanted to break into the VR room, he could have just beat Sahir's scrawny ass to a pulp instead of sneaking around with needles.

Pieter, seeing trouble, sidles up to help me defuse the situation. The next morning, I notice that Matteo has joined the guards' table at breakfast, the blue stripe that we use to signify guard duty on the sleeve of his uniform. He's sitting tall, apparently pleased to be included. Pieter sneaks me a thumbs-up, and Matteo stops giving me dirty looks in the hallways, and this is a relief, but it doesn't bring us any closer to identifying the attacker. The more suggestions I hear, the more I feel as if it could be anyone. Everyone who mentions the VR room's closure sounds either resentful or wistful. Everyone wanted to get back into that place.

The only progress we make is with the confinement cells, which Caro spends an afternoon setting up on the ninth floor. I don't publicize their existence. This isn't the time, given the new cutbacks on our diets, which have dealt another major blow to the mood aboard. The instant we switched to partitioned bars at meals, I noticed an uptick in pointless arguments, in glum expressions, in restlessness during training.

I feel it, too. My mind wanders during lectures. Hunger cramps hit between eleven and noon, then again in the evening, when Caro and I are trading phrases in English and

Swahili by the hearth. I'm always suppressing a feeling of irritation, like trying to ignore a constant, low-grade itch.

But no one has been more affected than Sergei. I guess it makes sense—at six foot four, he needs more sustenance than anyone aboard—but he's spending more and more time ruminating to Caro and me about Francisco. "Of course he didn't have to tell me what happened," Sergei says, "but it's like he replaced me with Eli. He always talked about how we were a good team. So much for that. Now he's just decided he wants to be exactly like her. Have you listened to him lately? Eli this, Eli that, Eli thinks, Eli's priorities . . ."

And I never know what to say, because Sergei's right. At first I was glad that Francisco had something other than the VR room to focus on, to bring himself back to reality, but it's starting to seem extreme. He's all but moved into the bridge, and he never talks to anyone except the Council and, occasionally, Pieter. Once, sitting at the Council table, I saw a page he and Eli were working on titled "Reproduction." It was filled with flowcharts and forking trees. The group was listed with ages in parentheses and bracketed together, boy to girl, like a tournament. Crammed into the margins were notes in their handwriting. In Francisco's, *Multiple pairings beneficial or detrimental to gene pool?* And in Eli's, *Peak fertility happens in our 20s. Should prob start soon to minimize genetic deformity.*

When I asked about it, they both waved it away. "That was just a hypothetical," Eli said. "We weren't actually pairing people off. It'd only be useful if we knew which people's genes were most different, and we don't have that kind of equipment."

"Still," Francisco added, "if we can have children or plan families in a way that helps the ship seven hundred years from now, we should do it."

"You don't think that seems controlling?"

"Of course it's controlling," he said shortly. "As a group, we need self-control. We don't have the time or resources to— This isn't Earth." Avoiding my eyes, he minimized the reproduction sheet back into one of his many subfolders.

I don't think he seems happy, but sometimes I envy his obsession. My mind is still slipping back to the VR room, and to break myself free, I have to cycle through the same litany of thoughts every time. I think of Eli's drive and Pieter's dedication. I think about the colors blooming around Sahir's eyes, his pain and embarrassment after the attack. I've shoved my memory diary into the back of a drawer.

When I run, I force myself not to think about the places I've left behind, either. I focus on keeping pace with Anis instead, watching the now-familiar jog of his elbows at his sides, always too close to his torso, his biceps flexed taut under the short sleeves of our exercise gear. I'm starting to think he just wasn't programmed to make anything look effortless.

We haven't acknowledged our conversation in the stairwell since I told him the Council had decided not to search for the door records—to which he gave a single nod and said, "I'm glad." Still, something has shifted between us. A thickening of the air like humidity. Sometimes, halfway through one of our panted talks, I remember his question, "What do you stand for?" and it gives me that tingling feeling of exposure again, and I get stuck on the fact that he asked, that he seems to care so much. I wonder if he's still waiting for my answer.

Then, one night, Anis breaks out of his run, swaying slightly. "You okay?" I ask, stopping beside him.

For a moment he doesn't answer. I wonder with a lurch if this is it—if he's finally going to bring up everything we spoke about in the stairwell. I remember how he stepped toward me on the tenth-floor landing. Suddenly there's heat in my face that has nothing to do with the exercise, and I'm wondering, absurdly, what I look like right now—how my hair might be falling, whether my skin is flushed or blotchy.

Then Anis pants, "I need to stop running. I'm too tired. I can't do it anymore."

The heat in my face fades. "Oh," I manage to say, a slow sinking feeling in my chest.

It's about the running, I tell myself. I've come to rely on our workouts. No matter what happens during the day, the track is always here, and so is Anis, as reliable as clockwork, waiting for me to begin. I like that. I like our conversations, which wander off in unusual directions. I like having a running partner.

But that doesn't account for the cold pulse of rejection I'm feeling. This is a reminder that we're not actually friends. Once he stops showing up, we'll be strangers again, like we always have been in public. That's what everyone sees. That's reality. "I'm learning your language," he told me, but clearly that meant nothing to him except that he was overcoming a challenge.

"Okay," I manage to say. "Yeah, we probably shouldn't, with the new rations."

He wipes his forehead, and I think I catch him sneaking a glance at me beneath his hand as he does it.

"Do you want to walk instead?" he says, a bit too fast and too loud. "Or sit?"

Surprise spreads through me. Right on its heels is relief, erasing the pulse of cold. I'm aware of the warmth in every inch of my skin again, flushing up my chest to my collarbones. "Yeah," I say, unable to keep down a smile. "Sure."

So, by night, Anis and I meander around the track or lie side by side in the center of the oval, wandering between topics. One night we're up for hours talking about semi-real governments—how different countries around the world were trying to govern virtual-reality worlds. Anis listens with intent focus as I describe all the approaches I can remember, Sweden's laws against psychic violation, China's teams of monitors to regulate all multi-person interaction. As for the US, we spent years in court with VR companies who claimed that placing limits on avatar behavior was an infringement on free speech.

Even with Marcus and Lilly I'd never have been able to get two sentences into a conversation like this, not without Lilly calling me pretentious or Marcus going off on a tangent about how all old people are VR alarmists. But Anis has more opinions about semi-real government than I knew it was possible to have, all expressed while making a lot of emphatic hand motions, like he's practicing a martial art.

By day, my eyes start straying to him in the canteen, and it begins to feel strange that we still don't talk in front of people. I even feel self-conscious about it. Is it because people dislike me so much that he doesn't want to be associated with me? But then, I guess, I never make any move to talk to him, either. We pass in the halls, and I'm aware of the space that stretches, compresses, and stretches between us again. I feel it physically when he looks at me; I find myself wanting to watch when he pushes his hand through his hair.

But I try not to let these thoughts linger, with so much else to worry about. Francisco and Sergei have assigned the entire crew additional duties, trying to cover the gaps in ship upkeep left by the eight guards, so I spend most of my free time doing hatch, valve, and seal checks, making sure that no micrometeoroids have compromised the ship's entrances and exits.

It's becoming clearer and clearer how overtaxed we are, the size of the *Lazarus* demanding everything from our skeleton crew. On the sixth day after Sahir's attack, we run out of time to finish strapdowns before the gravity switch, and one of the storerooms in the med bay is reduced to a scattered mess of supplies. The day after that, minor alerts begin to flash on Eli's screen in the bridge. Two dozen filters are late for cleaning in the Catalog. The reclamation and dehydration stations in the water treatment plant aren't being checked twice a day. As fast as we complete a task, something else pops up in its place.

Finally, one night, I jolt awake to a voice. I stare through the dark. According to the glowing digits on the wall, it's 4:32 a.m.

"Leigh."

The voice is coming from the corner of the ceiling closest to the bathroom, where a speaker perforates the metal.

"It's me," Eli says. "Come to the bridge."

I look around for a way to respond, but nothing here resembles a microphone. Picking sleep from the corners of my eyes, I emerge into the sterile brightness of the hall. When I reach the balconies, an elevator's already moving, bringing Sergei, Francisco, and Caro upward.

I slip in. "What's happening?"

They shrug. Sergei's sandy hair is pointing in several directions. The elevator light draws white crescents over Caro's high forehead. We're all clumsy as we enter the bridge, tumbling after one another, halfway to sleepwalking.

"What is it?" Sergei says, dropping into a copilot's seat.

Eli, sitting tall in the commander's chair, doesn't speak. She opens a blueprint on the dashboard's main screen, then drags the image up into 3-D: one of the silos in the water treatment plant. As it revolves, one of the pipes feeding into the top of the silo pulses red, like an artery.

"There's a breach," she says.

Adrenaline wipes out my grogginess. All at once I'm imagining dry tongues, hallucinations from dehydration, the ship a graveyard moving into infinity, the autosystems operating without us.

"There's a nick on the top side of that pipe," Eli says. "The second the alert woke me up, I climbed up there and wrapped it with duct tape, but the blueprint hasn't stopped blinking."

"I don't get it," Sergei whispers. "How?"

"We reassigned all the upkeep tasks in the treatment plant," Francisco says, already pulling a tablet out of his pocket. "Eli, I promise, we did everything on the list you gave us." His dark brows knit. "Someone was careless, that's what it was. I'll go through the whole list and find out who forgot tomorrow."

Eli doesn't answer. She's obviously sleepless and looks worse than all of us. Sweat has collected into grease in the corners of her nose, in the crease of her chin. Her lips are chapped, split from licking and drying, and her eyes are like glacier ice, the irritated capillaries make her irises look so blue.

I feel the sudden urge to tell her to go to sleep, to let us handle this. She's been shouldering the bulk of this voyage since we took off, handling her mother's death alone, teaching herself to fly the ship alone, carrying the weight of being the only person aboard who was really ready for any of this. If she were anyone else, I'd sit down beside her and speak in soothing tones, but this is Eli. She'd make an impatient gesture. She'd ignore any attempts to placate her.

"What do you need us to do?" I ask.

The question seems to penetrate through to Eli in a way nothing has so far. She regards me with an expression that's difficult to read.

Then she rises from the commander's seat. "Sergei," she says, "go through the Residential Wing and test one of the sinks, showers, and water fountains on every floor, make sure the leak hasn't affected their operations. Francisco, you do the same thing with the canteen and the watering systems in the Planters. Caro, you and I are going to look through manuals and see if we can figure out the cause of the breach, and, Leigh—"

She looks back to me. This time the corners of her mouth tug, and with the smile, I recognize the expression. It's a mixture of gratitude and trust for knowing what she'd want, for knowing what she needs. For knowing her.

"I want you to go up to the breach," she says. "Stay there and watch. See if you can find any hints of what might've happened. If you take the sixth-floor entrance and go up the main ramp, it's the second silo from the back of the wing."

Sergei, Francisco, and I don't speak as we hurry through the Command Wing, then split up at the balconies. I glide through the Systems Wing into the water treatment plant, up the maze of dark, thundering walkways, until I reach the silo. I climb the rungs that lead up its titanium plating, clamber across its angled top, and stop before the red band of tape hidden away in the darkest corner of this place, warm to the touch, this minuscule fastening that holds us together.

CHAPTER 10

THE *HERMES*

"Can you hear me?" I ask, planting myself before the hearth to look up at Eli, who's displayed on the four-foot softscreen.

"Yeah." As she leans closer to the tablet broadcasting her image from the bridge, her face grows to three feet tall, the dark wispy hairs at the ends of her eyebrows several inches long. "Am I loud enough?"

"Speak up and you'll be all right," Sergei calls from fifteen feet behind us.

I sat in the thrumming darkness of the treatment plant for hours last night, but with no breakthroughs on what might have caused the breach, we've decided to tell the group, hoping that one of the training courses might have mentioned something like this. Still, it feels bizarre to see Eli here on the hearth, looking out over the place where I've been speaking on her behalf for a month.

Eli must feel it, too. She's shifting in her seat, her eyes scanning every inch of the atrium. The ease she's found with the Council over the last weeks is nowhere to be seen.

"Hey," I say quietly, "it'll be fine. The group's been following your lead for more than a month. They trust you."

"No, you're the one they trust. This is a terrible idea."

"We need you here," I say firmly. "They might have questions about systems that Caro and I can't answer. It'll be faster and easier to solve the problem if we're all talking it over togeth—"

I break off. The first group of kids is coming down from breakfast, nudging each other and pointing to the softscreen, whispering to one another. When Eli meets my eye, she looks nearly frantic.

"You've got this," I tell her.

Ten minutes later, the whole Council has assembled atop the hearth, and the group has settled before us. They can obviously tell we have bad news. Their murmurs sound restless, the way they did the morning after Sahir was attacked, and I see some people scanning the crowd as if looking for other injuries in the group. Surveying their drawn, unhappy faces, Eli is as pale as the sunspot overhead.

"Everyone," I announce, "for those of you who haven't met her yet, this is Eli, our pilot."

"Hey," Eli manages to say, looking determinedly away from the group. "I'm, yeah. What she said." Her cheeks redden. A hint of surly defiance shows on her face, as if she's waiting for them to laugh at her.

No one does, but most of them look back to me, waiting for me to take over again. Eli's eyes dart to me, too.

I mask my disappointment. I wanted this to go well, wanted Eli to feel at home talking to the group—but I pick up the thread without pausing. "Last night," I say, "we found a breach about the size of a nail head in the water treatment plant. There's no immediate danger, because we've contained it, so the important thing is finding the cause so that it doesn't happen again."

I don't give them time to panic. I move methodically through the steps we took last night to ensure there was no ripple effect from the breach, and as I speak, I can see the others digesting it all: not just the news itself, but the fact that the five of us stayed up through the night formulating a response. I'm reminding them that the Council is a team, one who got handed a potential crisis and came out with a plan.

I feel Eli watching. Wondering if she wants to add something, I glance at the screen, but she doesn't move to speak. Instead I glimpse admiration in her eyes, like I've done something.

It feels ridiculous, the idea that I could be impressive to Eli in some way, but it makes me stand taller as I look back to the group. "So," I finish, "our first question is whether anyone in the Maintenance track has any other theories. What could have caused the problem?"

Heads turn, angling toward Sahir and Matteo, who have spent the most time with the water treatment system. "It could be a bad part," says Matteo, the Italian boy's hair sticking up at the back from bed head. "Maybe it was manufactured that way, too thin at one point, and it eroded."

"We've only been aboard a month," says one of his fellow guards. "Metal can't erode that fast."

"More likely," says Luke Nabwana, "someone forgot to do one of their maintenance jobs, and something nearby impacted it." The bearded boy shoots a disgruntled look around the group.

"Or," says his younger brother, Moses, pushing his glasses up his nose, "maybe someone dropped something during maintenance. Let a wrench slip from a story up . . . It could have been an accident."

Dubious murmurs spread. Then Sahir calls out, "Where is the breach located?"

I find his trio near the front of the group. Sahir is studying a glowing blueprint of the treatment plant on a tablet, his face still bruised but no longer swollen. Jayanti and Irina are examining the tablet over his shoulder.

"The pipe is about halfway up the wing," I tell him.

"Did you say it's near one of the input valves?"

"Yeah, that's right."

Sahir looks up from the blueprint. "Then it might have been damaged when we filled the treatment plant with water after takeoff."

"How?" I ask.

"It would have been easy. Say there was a spare nut or screw in the payload on the *Hermes* station. . . . The autopumps filled our plant at a really high velocity. Even a tiny object could have done a lot of harm. So the object impacts the pipes. Then the water wears on the impact over the last month until it's detectable."

"So, it could circulate again and do more damage?" says Fatima Awad's tremulous voice.

Someone else blurts out, "How can we even find something that small?"

"The *Hermes* station . . ." Eli says, then falters as the group's eyes turn up to her. Fidgeting, she starts again. "The *Hermes* station is supposed to have output filters to catch anything bigger than a grain of rice."

"Eventually, yeah," Sahir says. "But they might not have installed all of them yet."

"What?" says Jayanti. "Why not?"

Matteo clears his throat, maybe feeling that the younger boy is upstaging him. "The *Hermes* was built last year. But they were going to adapt the station to connect to a space elevator sometime this year, and install some of the finer mechanics during that mission. So some of the output filters might not have been in place yet."

"Well," Francisco says impatiently, "do we know if this filter installation thing happened before we took off?"

"Wait, wait, I'm looking it up," Matteo says, typing again.

But before Matteo can say anything else, Sahir makes a bizarre sound like he's being strangled. At the same time, Jayanti and Irina, reading the tablet over his shoulder, let out sharp cries.

Everyone in the atrium turns toward them. "What?" Sergei says. "What happened?"

For a long moment, the three of them seem unable to move or speak. Irina is the first to look up from the tablet. Her blond bangs have grown. She moves them out of her eyes with clumsy fingers, her lips slightly parted.

"July," she says.

"What?" I say.

Irina reads aloud from the tablet, gaining strength as she goes. "'Step four: Lead astronaut Kshipra Anand will conduct a final inspection of the *Hermes* for elevator prep. . . . The one-week mission is due for launch in July 2072.'"

Silence lands hard on the atrium. No one moves or reacts. I feel dizzy, but I can't take in any air.

I look down the hearth. Caro, Sergei, and Francisco are pole-axed, their eyes transfixed on the tablet in Sahir's hands. I hear something like a buzzing, a ringing, like the absence of sound I felt deep in my head after takeoff. Then, as if to match, a hum begins to build through the crowd. It pushes higher and louder, spiraling toward chaos.

I know I have to speak, but I can't get past the single thought: There could be someone aboard the *Hermes* station. Kshipra Anand, lead astronaut, could have been in orbit when we took off.

She could be in orbit right now.

Eli breaks through the noise. "What date in July?" On-screen, that familiar change is coming over her. She's growing rigid in the commander's chair, taking on her mother's posture.

"It doesn't say a date," Sahir says hoarsely.

"Which means," Irina says, her voice half an octave higher than usual, "the astronaut could be there."

Eli shakes her head. "No one answered when we called. I sent signals out for hours after launch, and we've been sending new dispatches out every hour."

"Well," Jayanti says impatiently, "maybe the *Hermes* isn't listening to whatever frequency we're transmitting on."

Irina glances to her friend, still pale. "Exactly. Or our communications could be faulty. The library, the seeds, all this unpacking—why should our contact equipment be ready, when nothing else was?" She looks up at the hearth, her resolve igniting again. "We have to go back for her."

Eli considers. "You're Irina, right?"

"Yeah." The one syllable is filled with belligerence. "So?"

Eli looks from face to face as if trying to delay an answer. Eventually she replies, "We've been out here for over a month."

"And?" Irina says.

As I realize what Eli means, a leaden weight settles in my chest. "It was a one-week mission," I say. "We're over a month away. Even if this astronaut took off for the *Hermes* on the same day we launched, she'd only have one week of food. By the time we get back…"

I don't—can't—finish the sentence. A hush falls over the atrium. If that's true, we left her behind when we could have saved her. We let her starve.

"Then we have to turn around right now," says a small, firm voice. We all hunt a moment before our eyes land on Moses Nabwana.

"No, we don't," says his older brother in rapid-fire Swahili. Luke rubs his beard as he speaks, which makes his words feel indisputable somehow, like Socrates has spoken. "We need to get to Antaeus. The eruption might have happened before this mission was even scheduled. There might never have been anyone there."

"It says July," Irina says, "and we launched on the nineteenth. The odds are better that she took off before we did."

"But with a one-week mission," says Luke, with the forced patience of someone explaining simple math to a child, "she'll only be on that station if she took off between the thirteenth and the nineteenth. There are thirty-one days in July, so the probability is less than one in four."

Someone else calls out from across the group, "What if she brought fresh food up to the *Hermes* with her? We're looking for seeds!"

"Be smart," Pieter says. "We're not going to find seeds on

that station. It's been a month. She'll have eaten any part of anything edible."

Voices rise. "You don't know—"

"*We're* rationing, why can't—"

"There's a chance—"

"Look," Eli says, "we don't have time for this. We're stretching our time too thin as it is. By the time the Antaeus seeds grow, we'll all be living on one meal a day."

"So you're going to let an astronaut starve to death?" Irina says in disbelief.

"There's— Would you just—" Eli lets out a growl of irritation. "We don't know if there *is* an astronaut! We can't turn the ship around on some shred of a possibility that someone was up there at the right time, and *also* survived on a fraction of the food they'd need, and *also* can't reply to our messages for some reason."

The group fills with whispers so inaudible that my translator can't operate on the syllables. Irina's voice breaks through, defiant. "You just don't want to go back."

Anger flits unmasked across Eli's face. "Yeah? You're basing this on what?"

Irina lets out a humorless laugh. "Oh, I don't know. Everything the five of you do? You're keeping us out of the VR room because we have the nerve to want a glimpse of Earth. You put together all the schedules and didn't assign anyone a single history course, like if we don't think about home, we'll forget it."

"This *is* home," Eli says with the instinctive force of a kick reflex. The murmurs crescendo, all eyes glued on her. I open my mouth to come to her aid—we didn't assign history classes because we need technicians and we live on a spaceship, for

God's sake—but didn't I try to tell her that we couldn't expect everyone to let go of Earth all at once? Wasn't this exactly my point?

Now Irina is standing taller, eyes bright, a victorious flush coming into her cheeks. "Maybe you think the *Lazarus* is your home, but mine is Earth, and I can't just forget about it."

Framed in the center of the screen, Eli looks so alone up there, and I feel a pang, because this *is* her home. She's never had another one, and she wants to share it with us, to make it ours. But I can see her searching for words, unable to find the right ones. "We're trying— We just want everybody to be okay."

"Really?" Irina says. "Then open up the VR room so we can work through everything in our own way. Maybe no one else will get beat up at three in the morning if you let them get some sleep, and let us do what the ship is built for. The engineers put that room here for a reason. My dad worked on it for a reason! Do you trust the engineers or not?" The chatter is in full-blown life now, and Irina shouts over them, "And I want to vote on whether we go back! You don't get to choose that for us!"

The atrium is a wall of sound barraging the hearth. My translator can't take any of it, and Eli is so frozen on-screen that she looks like a glitch.

"Everybody," I call out. "Let's talk about this, please." But the noise doesn't even quaver. The balance I worked for weeks to strike has fallen apart. I shoot a desperate glance back at Eli and see her lips move the tiniest fraction, a word mouthed to herself. A frown is knitting her forehead. Finally she says something, but the group is so loud that I can't hear it.

I yell, "Everybody, *shut up!*"

A surprised lull spreads through the crowd. I look back at Eli, praying she's about to offer some perfect consensus. "Eli, what did you say?"

Her eyes are still trained on Irina, her irises glowing out of the softscreen like blue planets. "I said, how did you know what time Sahir got attacked?"

The current of debate dims. Then the last whispers die. Every head turns toward Irina as the color drains out of her face.

"Sahir told me," she says, too brash, too fast, turning toward him. "The day after you got attacked. You said—"

"No," Sahir says. "I didn't."

People are craning their necks to get a glimpse of them. Sahir's cheeks are flushing dark red, and both he and Jayanti are looking at Irina with betrayal spreading across their faces.

Even my thoughts of the *Hermes* are overridden by disbelief. I remember how happy Irina looked when Sahir and Jayanti laughed at her jokes—how they've backed one another up on every tiny, silly point of every tiny, silly argument since the day they sat down together in the canteen.

"No," murmurs Sergei by my side. For once, he doesn't look embarrassed by the fact that everyone's attention is on his sister. He's twitching his head as if to dislodge a stubborn gnat, apparently unable to process the information.

But Irina doesn't deny it. She crosses her arms, her body folding in as if to protect her core. "Fine. I—I broke into the room, but I didn't mean to hit you. I was just trying to make sure you didn't see—"

"Are you serious?" Sahir says, shoulders trembling with anger. "Are you actually trying to make excuses?"

Jayanti swells in outrage. "And you've just been lying to our faces about it? Trying to help us think of who might have done it?"

"I didn't mean to; I wasn't myself!" Irina insists, high and wild, and I feel a sting of doubt. I remember the impulse that guided me to the VR chamber in the middle of the night, like a starving animal who scented blood, my body moving without my agreement. I know exactly what she means.

Then Eli says, "What are you talking about, you *didn't mean to*?" Her voice resounds around the atrium, projected through the softscreen's speakers. "You brought a pillowcase to put over his head. You stole from the medical wing. You wasted anesthetic that could've been used for someone who actually needs it. You planned all this shit out!"

My doubt drains away. Eli's right. Why am I wasting my sympathy on Irina, who—from her first second aboard—has done nothing but pick fights and show how self-obsessed she is? This girl insults me for trying to help people, while secretly she's attacking her own friends. Maybe she even planned it for that night because she knew Sahir would be on duty, knew he might fall asleep. I remember her standing beside Jayanti and lying to my face, trying to pin it on Matteo, and I feel a wrench of disgust.

She *was* herself. This is who she is. And I felt it, too, I wanted to go in so badly, but I didn't hurt anybody. As Irina makes another frantic protest, I feel pride and shame and triumph warring inside me. I beat it when she didn't. This girl who's claimed over and over to be morally superior to me—here's the proof that she was wrong.

A harsh laugh cuts through the air as Matteo shoves closer to Irina, through the crowd. "And you tried to say it was me? You lying bitch."

"*Oh, it's a matter of principle,*" someone else mimics across the atrium as disbelieving laughter fills the air. "You're such a hypocrite."

"Hit her back, Sahir," another kid yells.

"No." Eli stands from the commander's seat, and the camera tracks up to her. From that angle, she looks down at us like a giant considering ants. Satisfaction tightens her features as she zeroes in on Irina, who made her look incompetent and selfish, who was about to win the argument.

"Pieter," Eli says. "Pilar. Bring her up here."

Pieter and Pilar square their shoulders and forge through the crowd. Pieter gets there first. He grabs Irina by the elbow. "Get off," she snaps, struggling. "Sahir—" A note of desperation enters her voice. "I promise, I wasn't trying— I didn't mean—"

"Move," Pieter says loudly.

"Get *off me*!" Irina wrests her arm free and lashes out. The blow clips his temple. Pieter reels back. For a moment everything is still.

Then color fills Pieter's face, and righteous determination, and he swings back. His palm meets her face with a sound like flat stone smacking raw meat.

There's a roar of sound. I leap off the hearth. "Stop," I cry out. "Stop!" But I'm not loud enough, not fast enough, and the crowd clamps in around the fight like a bear trap. From the periphery, I can make out two faceless bodies grappling with each other.

I cast a wild look around. Sergei is also trying to force his way into the crowd, but Francisco is standing stiff as a statue on the hearth, and Caro's eyes are perfectly round. Eli's mouth moves, but the softscreen's speakers are too quiet, the audio lost in yells and laughs and vocalizations, an "OHHH" growing within the crowd like a jet turbine beginning to roar.

Then Eli's voice booms throughout the entire ship, through the PA system, electronically amplified, dark and huge and metallic: *ENOUGH.*

In a mass of shuffling, the group pulls away from Pieter and Irina, opening like an oyster to offer them up. Irina's hair is disheveled, Pieter's nose bleeding. He's panting, looking down at the red smear on his hand with disbelief.

As one, every face turns to Irina in accusation. She's clutching a red mark on her cheek where Pieter struck her, her mouth hanging open.

The light is harsher in the bridge than the atrium. Eli's nose and chin are like knives, cleaving shadows down her mouth and throat; the stripes on her uniform stand out red. "That's enough," she repeats, her audio coming through the softscreen's small speakers again. "Irina, you'll stay under confinement in the Residential Wing until you're not dependent on the VR room anymore, and you're not a danger to everyone else." Eli glances through the crowd. "Luke, Matteo, get the elevator. Pieter..."

Pieter's already gesturing for Pilar to help him pinion Irina's arms. The guards drag her out of the crowd toward the elevator bay, Irina's shoulder blades jutting out from her shirt as she struggles. They push her between the glass doors, and everyone watches them rise overhead, toward the shimmering eye of the sunspot.

It all seems like it's happening so fast, too fast—but isn't this the best option? If Irina really didn't mean to attack Sahir, then this is good for her as well as for everyone else. With time to herself, maybe Irina can focus on beating her dependency. As for the rest of us, we need to focus on the treatment plant, on the short-scheduling, on the question of the *Hermes*.

I back away from the periphery of the crowd and clamber onto the hearth, cold waves still rolling through my body, adrenaline or fear or dopamine, I'm not sure which. As I survey the group, the crew, my eyes are drawn first to Sahir and Jayanti. Jayanti is touching Sahir's elbow, while Sahir swallows over and over, looking torn.

Then my eyes stray to Anis, who stands at the side, separated as always from the others. The crowd's murmurs sound satisfied, but there's no satisfaction in Anis's face. I remember how I wanted to scoff when he asked about a judicial system that first week aboard. Now he looks away from the elevator, and when he meets my eyes, I can almost hear him saying, *So this is the system, then?*

Sergei is still watching his sister go, motionless. As the silhouettes slip out of the elevator and disappear into the ninth floor of the Residential Wing, I realize something. Why does Pieter know what to do, or even where to go? I glance over at Caro, wondering if she showed him the confinement cells at some point, but she looks as taken aback as I feel.

Slowly, the group reorients back toward the hearth. On the softscreen, Eli is retaking the commander's seat.

There's a long, anticipatory pause. Then she says with a shaky laugh, "Okay. That was dramatic."

Laughter starts in the corner of the crowd, and soon the atrium is ringing with it. Eli breaks into a smile, pushing her hair out of her eyes, and the final traces of reluctance melt away. Her cheeks are tinged with color, and I know what she's feeling, this girl who grew up in the shadows, lost in the cracks of the world we had back on Earth. She's come out into the light—and it feels right. Eli has waited her whole life to be here. She's caught the attacker, she's keeping us safe, she's opening the door and saying, welcome home.

———————

When I arrive at the track that night, there's Anis, his hair bouncing as he runs. It's been a week since we ran, but I join him.

We go a mile without speaking, keeping pace. With every strike of my shoe to red rubber, I think, *Forward or back? Forward or back?*

In some ways, the crew is already moving forward. A dozen of the Maintenance-track kids have put their training courses on hold to pin down the source of the water treatment breach. Some are helping Caro in the codehome, hunting for anything in the autosystems that could detect a spare nut or bolt swirling around in the bowels of the plant. The rest are manually examining every pipe in the plant in case there are other, smaller breaches that may not have been detected.

At dinner, though, I heard other kinds of talk. I heard scornful comments about Irina. I heard worries about the containment cells. "When did the Council do that?" I heard Fatima whispering to Annie Daly, but they shut their mouths when they saw me passing, looking almost afraid.

And underneath everything, I heard questions about the *Hermes* circulating through every conversation.

Do you think the astronaut is there? Do you think she's alive? Do you think we could save her?

Now I picture that silver tube spinning through the atmosphere. I've been distracted all day, trying to weigh the chances that we could ration our way to Antaeus if we reverse our course now. I've turned Irina's arguments over and over in my head until they've grown smooth and clear, like gemstones in a tumbler. Caro said it the other day—we don't even know that there *are* seeds clinging to the surface of Antaeus. Maybe we're hurtling into the biggest emptiness of all, and there's nothing out there, and we're moving farther and farther from someone who needs us.

But Eli's right, too, that the astronaut could be dead. The only thing we know for certain is that *we're* here. Maybe to turn around would kill us all, and maybe it would be for nothing.

Forward or back?

We didn't speak much about the *Hermes* at our Council meeting tonight. We were busy consoling Sergei, who was still shaken by Irina's confession. "It's not like her," he kept saying. "She argues, but she's loyal, you know? If you even say something bad about a movie she likes, she'll go for your throat, and these are her friends."

"They *were* her friends," Eli corrected, stony-faced. "I wouldn't stay friends with someone who did that to me."

Francisco studied the boy slumped beside him, then reached out and gave Sergei a rare pat on the shoulder. "Sergei, I know you're probably thinking this is because you weren't forgiving enough, or something, but that's just not true. Irina made this decision herself."

"Good thing, too," Eli said, flicking through one of Sergei and Francisco's social architecture plans. She drew a finger under the Holidays section, underlining *Independence Day/Launch Anniversary Celebration: July 19.*

"How is it good?" Caro asked.

Eli shrugged. "I think this whole thing with the attack helped everyone see where this kind of thinking gets you," she said with confidence, even a hint of smugness. "That whole fight about the *Hermes*? Irina didn't want to go back because she thought someone miraculously survived, come on. She wanted to go back for the same reason she attacked Sahir, because she's got this obsessive attachment. And the way to get over that isn't by humoring it, it's by actually making moves to distance yourself from it. Francisco did it. There's no reason everybody else can't, too."

Francisco straightened up in his seat, looking self-conscious but proud. Sergei watched this exchange from across the table, then blew his hair out of his eyes.

We didn't talk about the *Hermes* again, but the station hasn't left my mind for more than a minute since. I've been shuffling mental images of lead astronaut Kshipra Anand, first tall, then short, then burly, then slender, always kind-eyed. Always moving with the sort of confidence that comes from decades of expertise. I keep thinking over the decisions the Council has made, wondering if a real astronaut would have acted differently. Maybe Kshipra Anand would have known immediately what to do about something like the seeds or the water treatment breach. At the very least, if we'd had an actual adult aboard, I doubt I'd be the one standing on the hearth every morning, trying to convince everybody to listen to us.

As Anis and I run a second mile, then a third, I know he's thinking about the *Hermes*, too. I'm not sure how I know, but I do. It's in his expression, both troubled and distant, like a storm cloud on the horizon line.

We slow to a walk, then head to the drinking fountain. I take a long draw from it, and finally he asks, "Do you think someone's there?"

As I straighten and turn to him, I wonder about his motives. Is he trying to figure out what Eli or the rest of the Council have decided about the *Hermes*? Is this a veiled attempt to pry out my opinions on what happened to Irina?

But as I look into his stubborn, honest face, my calculations fade away. If Anis wanted those things from me, he would ask for them. He's so blunt, so unsubtle—I've never needed to dissect his intentions. It's because he's always so difficult that things have started, somehow, to feel simple.

My nerves settle, and I look at him with surprise loosening my muscles. I've only ever had this feeling of simplicity with Lilly and Marcus. Before the announcements, I used to fantasize about the three of us moving into the wilderness when we grew up, living alone in some meadow sizzling with honeybees. Nothing would need analysis, and I'd make careless choices, say whatever I wanted, break every rule I'd ever made for myself.

Words come out before I can stop them. "I don't know what I think. I . . . I went to the VR room a week and a half ago, just for fifteen minutes or something, and I couldn't stop thinking about it. I don't feel like I can trust myself with this stuff." As my throat tightens, I force out, "I want someone to be aboard the *Hermes*, but maybe I just don't want us to be the only ones left."

Anis stares. I avert my gaze, the hum of the ventilators overhead suddenly seeming twice as loud. A chill wanders over my skin, the cooldown from so much adrenaline, and the usual doubts rush through me: *You said too much, you showed too much, you sounded stupid and embarrassing, you did something wrong, they'll never forgive you.*

But when I force myself to look at Anis again, he's smiling.

It's more than a change. It's a complete metamorphosis. A layer of fear and anxiety has been stripped away from him. His eyes are warm, his forehead and brow unlined. He looks like a different person in a different time.

"So you can do it," he says.

"What?"

"Answer a question."

I laugh. "Just this one time. Special occasion."

I step back so he can drink from the fountain. Then, with a pang of anxiety, I add, "Please don't tell anyone."

He lets out a quiet huff, wiping a bead of water from the corner of his mouth with a knuckle. "Who would I tell?"

It's a fair point. Five weeks in, Anis still sits alone in the canteen. He never chats with a group before morning meetings, never does homework in the atrium at a table of friends. I realize that for more than a month, I've never actually seen him speak to anybody except me.

"Why don't you . . ." I clear my throat. "You know. Have friends?"

He looks bemused. "You ask me that after it took us three weeks to have a conversation?"

"I thought that was because you didn't like me, not because you're bad at conversations."

"That's exactly why I'm bad at conversations. Everyone thinks I don't like them."

I laugh. Smiling, too, he seems to consider. Then he asks, "Do you spend much time in the Catalog?"

"No, why?"

"I want to show you something."

I follow him through the ship and into the spiral of artifacts. As we walk through the dim light, looking up at walls of scrolls and beaded masks and Delft pottery, we don't speak. I remember what I overheard Anis saying our first night aboard—that his father designed these cases. I wonder if he looks at these artworks and sees his father reflected in the glass.

Anis leads me past a tower of paintings to a back corner. We stop in front of a case that looks like all the others at first. As I approach, though, I see the difference. Rather than a single artifact, there's a little shrine inside. I see a woven lanyard looped around an old Spanish cent, oxidized copper patching its edges like lichen. There are two watches, one leather and one plastic, and a used stick of concealer, and a bottle of water crumpled by a too-hard grip, and a knotted pair of shoelaces, filthy with wear, and a pewter ring and a stick of gum and a card in French for a discount from a sandwich shop. Ten percent, valid through December last year, a cheerful, curved font, easy to read.

Anis doesn't need to explain. This is what we brought with us that night. It's our exhibit.

"How long has this been here?" I ask.

"It started the first night. I put this inside just after we talked in the Planters." He presses his palm to the glass, and it clicks open. He nudges one of the coins, gentle, as if reaching into a terrarium and touching a living thing. Then he plucks a brass key from the cushion in the center of the case. It's small and tarnished in his palm.

"Your house key?"

"Apartment." He turns it over and over. "I came back two nights later, and someone had put in one of the watches. The water bottle appeared a few nights after that. I don't know who did any of it. Nobody talks about it."

We lean against the wall in the shadowed space beside the

case. I watch him moving one fingernail over the teeth of the key, tracing the jagged shape, like a mountain range.

"I've been thinking about home all day," he says. "Where I'd be if none of this had happened."

I half smile. "I used to do that after the announcements. Before bed I'd close my eyes and give myself a minute to just imagine life like it was supposed to be."

"I still do that."

"What's it like?"

He lets his eyes slide shut. "I'd be at university starting pre-med, but living at home, since most of the housing at schools in Cairo is too in demand for city students to stay there. My mother would complain a lot about how lonely she thinks I am, and she'd drag me out to shop with her at this street market she likes. It's Ramadan, so she'd be trying to decide what decorations to buy, and she'd bring them all home to our apartment and regret buying them within five minutes and say she should have gotten different colors because they clashed with the art."

"Is she a conservator, too?"

"An artist," Anis says. "A painter. I must have the only parents in the world who were disappointed when I told them I want to be a doctor."

I laugh. "What is it about brain surgery, anyway? Why do you want to do that?"

"I'm interested in what's inside there." He lifts his shoulders. "That's probably not surprising."

"No. Not at all." Looking at his still-closed eyes, the dark wisps of his lashes, I feel a warm pulse travel down into my hands. "Keep going."

He obliges. "Lanterns on all the street corners. Some cousin would visit and have a glass of karkaday with my mother and complain about fasting or traffic. I'd sit on the sofa and read, and my sister, Sadaf, would be in the other room making beat tracks and singing the same phrase over and over.... She always sang to our dog during thunderstorms. He used to get scared and hide in my bed."

He's smiling again, that transformative smile. Then our eyes meet and his smile fades. "I want to believe the astronaut could be alive, too. But maybe I just want a reason to go back."

"Yeah. It's hard to tell."

As one, we slide to the ground beside the case, sitting against the wall. Then he flips his apartment key to me. I catch it.

"Your turn," he says.

I close my eyes. In the dark red place behind my eyelids, I see my life as it should have happened. I describe it to him as best I can. I'm coming home from a trip with my parents in the last summer of my mother's presidency. She's walking down the steps of Air Force One, drawing ripples in the air with a waving hand. Dad has a hand on my back, smiling so hard that his cheeks press up into his eyes. We'll pick up our dogs from the kennel, Nate and Lyla, two floppy beagles, and head home, talking about our plans for next year, since it's all nearly over, the primaries for the next presidency past us. Maybe my dad will go back to teaching. Mom will do a public speaking circuit. As for me, I'm getting ready to go to college, worrying about a whole new set of people who will gape and point and whisper. So although I'm trying to pack my room into boxes, it's taking a while. I want to hold on to how things are. Marcus and Lilly are messaging me through dinner, and my wristpiece is a constant buzz. There's a new immersion flick at the VR cinema that Marcus wants to see, as always.

And the nights are my favorite part. We drive out into

Virginia for hours, Lilly at the wheel, me in the passenger seat, and Marcus lounging in the back, Secret Service following at just enough distance for us to pretend we're alone out there. The electric engine takes us coasting over hills, like the three of us are driving over the ocean, and the sound of insects blossoms around us when we crack the windows. Everything is normal and I appreciate none of it. In an alternate reality, I never think about alternate realities. I am sleepwalking through every blissful, quiet day. I am happy in a way that I will never realize.

———

I startle awake. Anis is touching my shoulder, but when my eyes open, his hand darts away.

"What time is it?" I say, squinting around the Catalog in its perpetual twilight.

"It's okay." He speaks in English, accommodating my translator, which ran out of charge in the night. My eyes stray to his mouth as he says, "It's not morning yet."

The absence of the translator's voice in my ear makes more of a difference than I could have imagined. It's as if I'm hearing him speak for the first time, suddenly aware of the interaction of his tongue and teeth and vocal folds, the melodic rise and fall of the sound they create together.

"I'm sorry," I say. "I didn't mean to fall asleep. You should have woken me up."

He waves my words away. "You look tired." He rubs the back of his neck, looking sheepish. "But I am tired, too."

"Of course, yeah." I get to my feet. "What time is it?"

"We can see in the . . ." He points downward. So we pad down the Catalog's spiral and out into the atrium. High overhead, the sunspot is still dark, and the luminous clock above the digital fire proclaims an hour to go before first light: five thirty a.m. Anis and I ride the elevator to the eighth floor and head down the hall in the Residential Wing toward our cabins.

At my door, we slow and then stop, almost in unison. The silence is distinctly weird. I'm always careful to look into people's faces when I speak to them. I want to show them that I'm invested, that I'm focused, that I care what they have to say. And Anis, of course, places his attention like a sledgehammer. In this moment, though, our eyes are wandering, sliding from the door over each other, dislodged from our usual habits.

"Good night," he says, finally looking at me.

I reply, "Tisbah ala khair."

There's surprise in his smile. "It's not too bad."

I smile, too. "Thanks. It's all I know how to say."

"Try it again. More slow, like this."

He repeats the phrase, *Tisbah ala khair*, richer and smoother than my own pronunciation, and as the syllables flow from his lips, I remember the first words I heard him speak.

"I never thanked you," I say quietly. "For helping me the first night."

His lips part. He looks embarrassed. "You knew it was me?"

"Yeah. I wanted to say something, but I felt weird owing you. And I wasn't sure you knew that you'd helped me."

"I knew."

I let myself remember that night for the first time in weeks. The bitter air, the ribbon of urgent syllables flying loose amid the roar. My fingers move at my side, and as if I'm wearing a kinesis glove, I feel a phantom push against the skin, like I'm still tugging at that strap even now.

"You yelled something," I say. "Right before you lifted the bed, you said something in Arabic. What was it?"

"I said, there's no time."

"But you still stopped to help me."

"Of course." There's a slow easement in Anis's expression, as if—for the first time—he feels relaxed. "I could tell you weren't going to let go."

CHAPTER 11

CRAWL SPACE

4 *months, 17 days, 8 hours, 49 minutes, 8 seconds, 7, 6 . . .*
A voice across the atrium interrupts my watching of the message board. "Not me."

Sergei, Caro, and I, studying at the same table, look toward the disruption. Sahir and Jayanti are near the hearth, standing over a sofa where the guards are surveying a large schematic of the water treatment plant. "No," says Luke to Jayanti, swatting away the tablet they've been waving in front of his face, but Moses reaches out to take it instead of his brother.

"This doesn't look good," I say with a sigh. "What do you think they're doing?"

"Maybe it's about Irina," Caro says. "She's been locked up in the ninth floor for four days. That's a long time." She's picking at her painted nails, leaving glittery black curls on the tabletop.

"I don't think it's about Irina," Sergei says. "They haven't even gone to see her."

"You visited her, then?" I ask.

"Yeah, yesterday evening."

"And she talked to you?" Caro says.

Sergei lets out an unhappy laugh. "Yes. So she must be really bored."

"What did she say?"

He shrugs. "Nothing friendly at first. 'It was an accident,' 'I guess you're here to lecture me,' and so on . . . but . . ." He perches his chin on the heel of one hand, gazing into the atrium with a slight frown. "It wasn't all like that. I asked where she was going when she used the VR room, and she told me she was mostly just walking around our neighborhood or sitting in our backyard." He lets out a wistful hum. "I liked our house. It was old, you know, had all sorts of hidden corners. We used to find things in drawers when we were kids from the people who lived there before us."

Sergei's eyes follow Sahir and Jayanti as they approach a table of younger kids, who lean in around the tablet with some interest.

"I don't know." Sergei sighs, rubbing his forehead. "I'd been there an hour, and Irina said, 'Why are you being nice to me?' Like it offended her. Or like I'd never been nice to her before. So I said that, I said, 'What are you talking about, I'm a nice person.' And she said, 'Well, it's always been obvious I embarrass you.'"

Caro and I exchange a look. "Is she wrong?" Caro says.

"Well, no," Sergei admits with a grimace. "That's why I feel bad. She *is* embarrassing. She takes everything so seriously, always spouting off her opinions. She can't ever keep quiet, and I didn't like people paying too much attention to me in Nizhnekamsk."

"Why not?" I ask.

He pauses, then says, "It's a traditional place. My family is very traditional, and I'm not a traditional person. I'm sure you heard about the Russian lottery officials purging gay people from the passenger lists. That could have been me if I'd been more open." He shrugs. "Honestly, the GFPC's plans were so vague, they made that sort of alteration easy."

Caro meets my eyes. Somehow I know she's remembering our conversation in that deserted screening room, when she spoke so freely about her father's party and I struggled even to acknowledge the flaws of the process in the US, let alone any issues with the GFPC.

I feel a pang of discomfort. Just like Caro, Sergei speaks about these problems as if it's only natural to see them.

The plans weren't good enough, I think slowly, as if testing the words. Of course, I never felt they were perfect. I told Anis that much ages ago. But the thought still clashes against what I've always known: that above all, we needed to make compromises, to choose a single unwavering course; that if we'd just adhered to the plans, everything would have been okay.

But the GFPC's plans could have left Sergei to die. They weighted the system against Caro's friends and allowed the US to write the names of rich charlatans onto free passes. And if the lottery plan, the most well-publicized part of the process, had that many flaws, what about the rest?

What about the English-language mandate—the one we've adopted? Suddenly I'm running through Irina's old arguments with a kind of fear, trying to figure out whether we've done the right thing.

We need to be able to communicate in an emergency, I remind myself. That's still true. I cling to the reasoning.

Caro chips another fragment of polish from her nail. I look back to Sergei as if just registering his words. "Is that what Irina was talking about the first day, when she said you wanted to move west?"

"Yeah. She's known about me for years. She doesn't care, though. That's the thing—I never thought she cared about my opinion of her. She certainly never seemed to care about any other part of my life." Sergei rolls his eyes and powers his tablet off. "Anyway, I don't think it was an accident, what she did to Sahir. But I don't know if she needs to be in there for a whole week."

I sigh. "Honestly, Sergei, it's for her own good."

Sergei's brow crinkles the way it does when he's battling a difficult homework problem, and Caro says, "You really think that?"

"I voted for the full week, didn't I?"

Sergei shrugs. "I thought that was just to keep Eli happy."

"Well, it wasn't," I say, remembering the miserable week after I followed Francisco into the VR room. I would have welcomed being shut in my room, free of training and responsibilities, able to fight my thoughts in peace.

A shadow falls over our table. Sahir and Jayanti have finished circling the atrium. We've hardly even looked up when Jayanti is thrusting the tablet out proudly, saying, "We have something for the pilot. It's a petition. We want to turn the ship around to the *Hermes.*"

I take the tablet, not entirely surprised. The talk about the

Hermes hasn't settled over the last few days, but whenever one of us tries to bring the subject up at Council meetings, Eli shuts it down. "We've got bigger things to worry about, Leigh," she told me last night. "We still haven't found the breach in the treatment plant. We don't have the time to worry about some imaginary person."

Something has gotten into Eli since Irina's arrest. In some ways, the change feels positive, like the fact that she seems more confident with the group. Sometimes she lingers in the canteen at breakfast, now, sitting with the Council or stopping by the guards' table to talk with Pieter and the others. She smiles more easily. She's even brought up the idea of running a morning meeting every week. "Not to step on your toes," she said, "but it's good, right? The group feeling like they've got more access to me?"

But she also seems more dismissive during Council meetings. It was Eli's suggestion that Irina be kept in confinement a full week, and even though Francisco, Sergei, and Caro thought a shorter term would be better, she argued until Francisco switched his vote, Sergei looking sulky. And maybe if Eli had listened to my concerns yesterday that the *Hermes* was becoming a real issue among the crew, we wouldn't have wound up with a petition.

So I have my doubts about the change in Eli, but I think I understand it, too. I keep seeing her smiling face on the soft-screen as the crew laughed at her joke, everyone basking in the fact that she'd solved the case. That kind of approval must feel intoxicating for someone who was a complete recluse until five weeks ago. They chose her. Of course it's gone to her head a bit.

I slide the petition onto the table so Sergei and Caro can see.

The list is longer than I expected—twenty-one names. Anis's signature is in the middle of the pack, his writing cramped and messy.

Sergei looks over the screen with interest. "This is a lot of people."

"So, you'll talk about it?" Sahir asks. "You'll make sure it gets to the pilot?"

"Of course," Sergei says. "Why wouldn't we?"

Sahir and Jayanti trade dubious looks. "After that meeting," Jayanti says, "we didn't think the pilot was all that interested in what other people wanted. Dragging Irina off like that."

"I would have thought you'd be fine with it," I say. "You were both angry with her, too."

"Of course I was angry," Sahir splutters, scratching at the scraggly tufts of hair on his chin and jaw, "but I didn't want to throw her into solitary confinement for an entire week."

"No one even asked Sahir what he thought should happen," Jayanti says, "when he should get more of a say than anyone."

We eye the faint map of bruises that linger around Sahir's nose and eyes. "You have a point," Sergei says slowly.

"And what about those secret cells?" Jayanti presses on. "Most people didn't even know they existed until that morning." She rounds on Caro. "I suppose *you* designed them?"

Caro shies back. "I was trying to help. I didn't think . . . I didn't vote for her to be in there this long."

"Oh, that fixes everything, then," Jayanti says, oozing disdain. "Clearly your vote really matters."

Heat prickles in my neck and cheeks, and I stand up. Caro doesn't need to hear this. She's spent enough time holding her own life at arm's length, feeling like she couldn't make an impact even if she tried. I'm not going to let Jayanti tell her that the *Lazarus* is the same as Earth, just another place to feel helpless.

"Caro's opinion matters as much as anyone aboard," I say, scooping up the tablet. "Yours included. We're going to take this petition to the meeting right now and talk it over. Okay?"

Jayanti, several inches shorter than me, still somehow manages to look down her nose at me. She exchanges another suspicious glance with Sahir. Then he says, "Okay."

"I've wanted to talk about the *Hermes* since the meeting, too," Sergei reassures. "This is a good reason." He and Caro stand, too, Caro hardly coming up to his shoulder. "Listen, you two," Sergei adds. "I don't know if my sister . . . That is, she doesn't like to apologize, but I know she feels bad about what she did. Maybe you could go and talk to her?"

Their eyebrows lift. Sahir says, "*You're* giving us advice on talking to Irina?"

Sergei returns a troubled smile. "Just think about it."

As we wind through the atrium, I whisper to Caro, "She was just trying to make you angry. Ignore her."

"But she's right," Caro says with a bob of her shoulders. "My vote didn't change anything. It never does."

This is exactly what I was afraid of. "Caro, no, that's not true." I glance to Sergei for reinforcements as we start up the ramp toward the elevators.

Sergei pats Caro on the back. "I know how you feel. We just need to take a stronger stance from now on. Maybe we've both been giving up too easily, you know?"

But when Sergei turns away to tap the call button, I see his brow furrowed, his face conflicted. We slip inside the elevator, and I lift the *Hermes* petition so we can all scan the list of names again.

Eyeing it, Caro sighs. "Eli's going to love hearing about this."

———

Eli, as it turns out, does not love hearing about this.

"Why did you even bring this up here?" she says, pushing the tablet toward Sergei. "You should have told them it was never going to happen."

"Why?" Sergei says.

Francisco sighs, leaning back in his seat. "Because it's a minority, obviously. And it's very nice that you want to stick up for the minority, Sergei, but if they wanted to be useful to the ship, they'd focus on the breach, ship upkeep, and training, not trying to force this *Hermes* thing onto everyone."

"Thank you," Eli says.

Sergei frowns at them. "They're not forcing it onto anyone. I don't remember us deciding that no one else gets to have an opinion." He holds up the tablet. "Besides, it isn't that small a minority. If we added the five of us, that's essentially a tie."

"We're not going to add the five of us," Eli says. "We're not going back to the *Hermes*."

"Why not, though?" Sergei leans over the table. "I've been thinking about this. We've been traveling for five weeks. If we turn back now, we add two and a half months to our trip to Antaeus. Why don't we make a ration plan, then set it to a vote? Maybe we could survive on our supplies."

"Survive on our supplies?" Francisco repeats with disbelief. "Sergei, the other kids are only saying we should turn around because they have no idea of the logistics involved. You made that ration plan with me. You know how hard it's already going to be, stretching four months of food to nine. You want to push that to nearly a year? As it is, we'll be dealing with exhaustion, probably sickness—the younger kids' growth might be permanently stunted."

"And," Eli says, "if we waste time going back, that's two and a half more months that any seeds left on Antaeus have to rot. That's our only lifeline. We're not risking everything on a ghost of a possibility."

A stubborn look has settled on Sergei's face that makes him look like his sister. He turns in his seat to me and Caro. "What do you two think?"

Caro has been quiet throughout the meeting. Now she straightens in her chair, darting cautious looks at Eli and me. At an encouraging nod from Sergei, she says, "Yes. We could make a plan. To see if it's possible."

"Yes. Exactly," Sergei says, jubilant. "And you, Leigh?"

All eyes fix on me. Suddenly I feel clamped in a vise. I can't be the tiebreaker. I can see both angles. *You gave Anis your opinion,* says an unfamiliar voice in my mind—but I reject it, because all I said was that I *wanted* someone to be aboard the *Hermes.* That doesn't mean I think it's true, or that it's necessarily safe to go back.

Turning around gets riskier every day, though. Every second I delay, we're a million meters farther from the *Hermes.* I vowed that I'd follow Eli, that I'd focus on our future, but if there's even the slightest chance that there's someone back there, shouldn't we try to help them? Couldn't that be part of our future, too?

Before I can answer, Eli says, "This isn't a debate. I fly the ship. We're not going back."

Four faces turn to her. Eli's face is steel, eyes moving between each of us as if waiting for a challenge.

"Leigh," she says, "tell Jayanti and Sahir we talked over the petition. You can say that Sergei and Caro were on their side. But we don't have to follow orders from a minority."

"We haven't voted," Caro points out, her voice small. "Leigh hasn't decided. We could still have a majority."

"Even assuming Leigh doesn't see reason," Francisco says, "that makes you three plus the twenty-one people on that list. Twenty-four to twenty-nine, you're going to call that a majority?"

Sergei is staring at Eli with amazement, as if she's transformed into someone else before his eyes. "Eli," he says, "come on, now. Picture being aboard the *Hermes*. Just imagine being there, alone, starving to—"

"I don't have to imagine it," Eli says. "That's us if we turn back. We're halfway to starving already."

Francisco nods. "We can't get distracted. Eli's—"

"Oh, here we go," Sergei interrupts, the resentment of the past weeks glowing in his pink cheeks. "*Eli's right.* Of course! Eli's always right! Because if someone's in charge, they have to be right. And that's why you're going to copy everything she says and does until you don't have any opinions of your own anymore."

Francisco recoils. "Sergei," I say, giving him a reproving look, but Eli breaks in.

"What's your problem?" she snaps at Sergei. "Where is this even coming from? What, did you and your sister just spend the whole night complaining about it together? Pieter told me you visited her. I guess you forgot she attacked one of her best friends because of this exact kind of thing, because she wanted to play pretend for a few hours."

Now anger contorts Sergei's friendly features. "I'm not pretending anything," he says, rising to his feet. "Unlike you, *I'm* thinking about a human being. Do you not care that we could get somebody else aboard? You can't seriously be that selfish."

Eli flinches like he's slapped her. *"Selfish?"*

"Yes, selfish. What else do you call it when half the ship wants to turn back to save someone's life, but you won't even listen, just because *you* had such a bad time on Earth?"

"Are you fucking serious? I tell you one thing about myself and you're going to throw it in my face?" Eli lets out a harsh laugh. "Fine! Go ahead. It doesn't change anything. Yeah, I've been getting ready for this for three years, so maybe that's why I'm putting our future first. Is that what you're trying to say? Write off her attitude, it's *baggage*? Write off her priorities, they're *personal*?" She shoots to her feet, too. "Of course they are. We all think we know what's best, and I know *I'm* going to keep us alive, even if every other person here would throw our lives away for nothing. I know that if there was anybody aboard that thing, they're dead."

"No, you don't," Sergei shouts. "You don't know, you just decided! So why are the four of us even here, if you're going to make this kind of decision by yourself?"

"I don't know," Eli yells back. "Why *are* you here? To talk about your fucking feelings? We're in the middle of an extinction!"

"Eli!" I yell, on my feet, too. "Sergei! Stop it!"

Silence rings through the bridge, so sudden and absolute that I become hyperaware of my body. My fingertips tingle. My tongue is pressed hard to the roof of my mouth. This is just what it was like on Earth when we left. It's happening all over again.

I stretch out one hand to each of them. "Sergei," I say, "the petition is short in numbers. You don't have the votes, okay? It might be different if you did. Right, Eli?"

They glare at each other a moment longer, their faces still twisted with hurt and rage.

Then Eli jerks her head. "Yeah," she says. "It's . . . That's what I said in the first place; it's the numbers."

Sergei's face is stony. I know he doesn't believe her. Caro is watching Eli, eyes so round that her silver eyeliner has disappeared, and Francisco is staring at the back of Sergei's head, clearly still processing what Sergei shot at him—but Sergei doesn't turn.

Eventually Caro says, "Are . . . are we done? I'm supposed to do gravity strapdowns with some of the younger kids. . . ."

"Yeah." Eli sits back down in her seat, hard. "Go ahead."

"You want a majority," Sergei says, "I'll get one." He turns on his heel, the tablet still clutched in one big hand, and beats Caro down the hallway. She veers out of his warpath. Watching him go, I wonder what Eli will do if he finds the votes.

Francisco must wonder the same thing, because he stands abruptly, looking flustered. "I'll try—I'll try to talk some sense into him. You know how he is; he'd follow his feelings off a cliff. But he always sees reason eventually."

Eli softens. "Thanks, Francisco . . . Want to come back later? We can talk over—"

"Athletic programs?"

"Exactly." She manages a strained smile. Francisco hurries after Sergei, but I stay where I am, standing at the table, trying to pick apart what's swirling inside me.

"This isn't a debate," Eli said. "I fly the ship." Suddenly I'm tallying up all the decisions she's made on her own and realizing how long the list is. She appointed the Council. She picked the crew's positions, closed the VR room, sent Irina to the ninth floor. She told the guards about the confinement cells—I still don't know when—and Pieter somehow knew that last night Sergei visited Irina in the ninth floor. He reported it to Eli. Why?

"So?" Eli says to me. I can hear her defenses rising back up. "Are—are you going, too, or what?"

She tugs her fingers through a tangle in her hair, and somehow I know she's thinking about Sergei calling her selfish. I know she's wondering if I agree.

No, I think. Eli is rigid and defensive and sometimes tactless, but she isn't selfish. Sergei didn't see her fear when we found Francisco in the VR room, her alarm and determination when Sahir got attacked. Sergei has no idea that Eli passed up a burial for her mother's body because she didn't want to scare the other kids.

She doesn't make these choices just because she wants to get her way. It's because she's dead set on our survival, no matter the cost to comfort or conscience. That's her purpose, and it's still mine, too.

I lower myself back into my seat. "I'm going to stay, if it's okay."

I catch the look Eli sneaks at me. Again she's the girl standing over her mother's body, surprised that I would come back for her.

"Yeah," she says. She can't quite hide her relief. "Okay."

———

Anis is waiting for me at the starting line, hands deep in his pockets. "Hey," he says in English.

"Ahlan," I reply with a smile. In the several nights since our visit to the Catalog, he's spent a few hours teaching me bits and pieces of Arabic, not so much the structure of the language as useful phrases. I like the way he tilts his head to listen to my pronunciation.

"How was the test?" I ask as we fall into step around the track.

"Eighty-three percent," Anis grumbles.

"Could be worse. It's hard to focus on training right now." Eli's and Sergei's shouts reverberate inside my head, mingled with thoughts of some destructive object rattling around in the water treatment plant, images of an astronaut wasting away in orbit. It's no wonder my class scores have been dipping, too.

Anis doesn't look convinced. "I wouldn't let an eighty-three percent neurologist operate on my brain."

"I'm not letting you operate on my brain no matter what grades you get."

Anis laughs, actually laughs like a normal person. For a moment my thoughts calm, and we both grin down at our feet, moving along the parallel lines framing lane three. Then his stomach lets out a deep yowl, like a territorial cat. "Sorry," he says, looking embarrassed.

"Don't be. I'm starving, too."

He grunts in agreement. "I wish I hadn't skipped our last dinner on Earth."

"You did? Why?"

"I don't know. I walked into the cafeteria and saw everyone sitting and talking, and I didn't want to sit and talk. I only made the flight over to see the work my dad was doing." He pushes his hands deeper into his pockets. "He was hardly home the past two years. After designing those cases, he and the other Catalog consultants started flying around to museums, trying to choose artifacts for each ship."

"When was the last time you saw him?" I ask.

"February. He came back for Sadaf's birthday."

This has started to happen in the past few nights, too. It's as if our conversation in the Catalog pushed a door open, and now we're on the other side, out in some large, dark space, where we can speak about anything at all. Whenever Anis mentions something from his life on Earth, a physical weight seems to settle onto him. He looks down at his feet or into the near distance, and I feel like I'm watching him press a thumb into a bruise, hurting himself a little bit, exploring the damage.

My hand leaps to the back of my neck as pain shoots through the muscle there. Anis's eyes linger on my hand as I massage the sore spot. "What happened?" he asks.

I sigh. "Nothing, just a crick in my neck. I've been monitoring the breach in the treatment plant during the day, so I lie up there for hours when I'm doing assignments."

"Sounds exciting. Have you seen anything yet?"

I shake my head. "But there are lots of gaps when I can't monitor it. I think I'll ask Francisco and Sergei if they can find . . ." I frown, trailing off as my eyes find the clock. It's ten to midnight.

"What?"

"I'm wondering . . . A lot of the autosystems make checks and resets at midnight. If the breach has something to do with the surrounding machinery, like Luke said, then maybe we haven't been monitoring it at the right time."

We exchange a glance, then hurry for the door.

Anis follows me through the deserted ship to the water

treatment plant. Inside, the machinery's hum pulses through my skin like boosted bass. Azure light laces the black air, outlining us in blue. The dark makes every movement look graceful. I admire the lines of my hands as I reach from rung to rung, up and up the silo. With half a minute to spare, we crawl across its angled cap and stop at the pipe with its stripe of red tape.

Anis has a tablet out in front of him, and we watch the second hand of the clock glide forward. It passes over the number twelve, zeroing out the time, pushing us forward into a new day.

Around us, throughout the reverberant space of the treatment plant, echo distant whirs and whines. I hear low, faraway thuds like bass drums.

I keep my eyes fixed on the pipe. Nothing happens.

I sigh. "I guess it's—"

A mechanical click interrupts. A metal device swings down from a wall panel overhead, impacting the red tape before latching on to the pipe's elbow. I identify it as an automatic pressure gauge, poorly calibrated by a matter of centimeters—a gauge that's been biting into the pipe with every check.

As its small dark screen flashes green, then detaches and withdraws, Anis and I break into grins as one. "Nothing got into the system," I say with a laugh, the first time I've laughed in days. "Caro can probably recalibrate this in thirty seconds."

Anis exhales, closing his eyes. "And everyone in Maintenance can stop searching for another breach."

"Do you want to go tell Eli?"

The second the words are out of my mouth, I realize what I'm asking. If we tell Eli we found the breach together, it might lead to admitting that we've seen each other every night for weeks.

Eli will want to tell the Council how we solved it, so I'll need to tell them, too. Then it'll seem ridiculous that Anis and I don't speak in public. Maybe I could ask him to sit with us in the canteen. We could talk in the halls, study for training together. This could be as close to normal as we have aboard the ship.

All this flies through my mind in an instant, but Anis doesn't seem to register what I'm asking. He just says, "Eli. That reminds me. What did she say about the *Hermes* petition?"

My tentative feeling of hope shrivels up. Watching the Council get into a screaming match was bad enough. I don't want to relive the whole thing, especially since I have a good idea of how Anis will react.

Pick and choose, whispers my old instinct. It would be easy to tell Anis a sanitized version of the truth: that Eli decided to go with the majority. But if Sergei decides to tell the group everything Eli said—that she made the decision for everyone, even when the Council was undecided—then Anis will know I lied.

I'm not just afraid of being caught in a lie. I don't want to lie to him in the first place. I don't want to lose his trust.

I'm not even sure *when* he started trusting me. How did that happen? Why has Anis trusted me, of all people, with his mother's habits and his sister's music, with the sounds of his home? From the beginning, he's seen through all my evasive, indecisive bullshit, and somehow we've wound up here.

What's even more startling is that I trust him. I'm looking at his face in the blue darkness and realizing how valuable that feels. This stubborn, grumpy boy who never gives me a break—I trust him more than anyone else here. More than the Council, maybe even more than Eli.

Maybe I do want to talk about this with him.

"She didn't take it well," I say quietly.

I describe the Council meeting. Sentence by sentence, Anis's face grows alert, his jaw setting, his brows cinching. Soon the boy who laughed fifteen minutes ago has disappeared.

"This is bad," he says. "What are you going to tell the others?"

"The . . . the others?"

Anis lets out a quick, disbelieving breath, as if he's been elbowed in the stomach. "Yes, the others! You have to tell them this happened. We might have had enough Council votes to go back, but the pilot isn't even listening to you four anymore; she's just doing whatever she wants."

"But it's true that the petition didn't have enough people." I instantly feel pathetic for holding the fact up like a shield. "Look, I'd say something if she overrode a majority, but why rope everybody into this? What would telling people actually accomplish?"

"Transparency," he says without even stopping to think. "You have to know how this looks. The five of you keeping it a secret what goes on in there, because you think the rest of us are too weak or hysterical to handle it. Or maybe it's because you know Eli's out of control."

"She's not out of control," I say sharply, "and that isn't why I don't want to tell people."

"But you realize that it looks that way, don't you?"

I dig my fingernails into my palms. He's right. It seems ridiculous that I could have failed to consider this angle, like the Council only exists as a cover for Eli's decisions.

"Why did you even tell me this?" He's staring at me almost despairingly. "Why didn't you just lie, like you're doing to everyone else?"

I feel a rush of hurt and anger. "I'm not a liar!"

"You're not? Then what is this? What are you?"

My heart is beating so hard that it feels as if somebody is prodding my collarbone with a screwdriver. I don't know. I only know what I used to be, and we aren't allowed to be now what we were before. Maybe Anis was awkward and overearnest before the airlock hissed shut, that person I see in glimpses, but it doesn't matter, because now his mouth seems built to shut away a smile, his body formed from tension down to the molecule. This version of him was chiseled in the threshold and polished on takeoff, and whatever other iteration there might have been, it's been overridden.

I try to imagine the person the others might all see in me. I feel like the same Leigh as before, who dreamed about disappearance, who dodged decisions because at the end of the day she never had to make a choice. I still feel like that's my genuine core, and everything I've done here is decoration, a thin mantle I'll be able to shrug off someday. But maybe that's delusional. Maybe how we act under duress isn't a shell that hardens into place to keep us safe, but a core we tear away our skin to reveal, which has been there since the beginning, ready for the day that we wake up to find the world has shattered around us.

Tears sting my eyes. I blink and blink, but they don't retreat, rising instead to blur my vision. I thought I was used to this. I thought I could withstand any challenge by now, but somehow his words find new places to destabilize me, new ways to make me question myself. Maybe I miscalculated, and Anis doesn't trust me at all, and I shouldn't have trusted him. Maybe I should leave now, shut off and never say another word.

Two hot tears spill over. When Anis sees them running down my cheeks, the frustration disappears from his face. He looks stunned. Of course he does. He's never seen me cry, never seen me delighted, never seen me laugh so hard that my sides ache—he's never seen me lose control. No one ever has besides Lilly and Marcus. To everyone else in the world, I'm not a real person, just a mannequin for target practice. I don't know why I thought this was different.

"Leigh," Anis says, reaching for me.

"Don't touch me," I choke, jerking away. He pulls back.

It happens in an instant. His body lurches as his foot slips from the edge of the silo. His torso twists, trying to reclaim his weight from where it's poised over the edge, but then his arm is swinging, and his knee has slipped into empty air.

I grab for him too late. A scream rips out from me as he plummets, and I lunge forward to see him toppling through the space between the silo and the wall, curled and fetal. One arm lashes like a whip. There's a shrill squeak, the sound of cloth sliding against metal, and then a muffled thud.

"Anis!" I yell. "Anis?"

For a moment there's only the hum and churn of the treatment plant. Then: "I'm okay." His voice swims up from far below. "I braced myself against the wall."

"Can you get back up?" I call.

"I can't see a ladder."

"Hold on. I'll come down, I'll find you."

"There's a passage," he says, sounding sluggish. "It might lead to one of the ramps."

"Okay, try that," I call, descending the rungs on the silo's other side. I run a labyrinth of ramps to the bottom of the treatment plant, but the walkways down here, winding through the legs of silos and walled in by massive pipes, offer no glimpse of him.

"Where are you?" I call.

"The passage is a dead end," he says from somewhere above me. "I think I'm on a platform, or behind a wall." I follow his voice back up the walkways. We echo back and forth for several long minutes—"Where?"—"Here"— a game of Marco Polo through the shadowy avenues, forking left, then sloping down to the right, then climbing left again.

I stop at the intersection of a pair of ramps. "You sound closer."

"You do, too."

The side of a massive turbine faces me, but his voice is issuing from below, from a dark fissure between the turbine and the walkway. I crouch and maneuver myself between the ramp's safety railings. Gripping the poles, I lower myself through the fissure, check downward—there's a gleam of metal several feet below—and drop.

My feet impact a massive pipe, its diameter like a redwood's, so wide that its surface is hardly curved. "Anis?" I call.

"I'm here," says his voice, more distinct than before.

"Okay. Keep talking."

I follow his descriptions of the light and the metal across the surface of the pipe. I duck systems of hanging mechanisms and feel intense heat radiating from a series of curved basins. Water churns somewhere out of sight. The world is a wash of deep blue. I clamber over the pipe's nearly invisible ridges, and finally, his voice regains shape.

I slow and scan the passage ahead, but his voice is coming from above.

There: At eye level, tucked away, is a gridded ledge against a wall. Searching for a foothold to hoist myself up, I realize I have no idea where I am, how high I've climbed in the plant, or which direction I'm pointed. It's as if I've climbed through a seal into a stranger's ship.

"Anis?" I call, pulling myself onto the ledge. It's hardly large enough for me to crouch. I squint among the indistinct shapes for another path upward, sorting through fuzzy bulges of light from hidden sources.

"I'm here," says his voice, so close that I nearly fall off the ledge. I turn. One eye looks out at me from behind what I thought was a wall. The plate of metal, notched with keyhole apertures, covers the space between two pipes.

"Hold on," I say, feeling around the edges of the metal plate. "There's— Yeah, I think I can unscrew this."

It takes twenty minutes to find the way out of the treatment plant's underbelly, run to the Command Wing, and return with screwdriver in hand. At last, I unscrew the metal plate so it swings outward, revealing Anis on his knees.

"Are you okay?" I ask.

He shows me one forearm, rubbed raw and shiny.

"We should put disinfectant on that. Let's go to the med bay."

"Wait. You have to see this first." He maneuvers himself around and crawls back toward the place he fell.

After a moment's consideration, I follow. The passage is as dark and narrow as the hollow of a bone. I've never been claustrophobic, but the slight aliveness of the surrounding machines makes me feel as if they might decide to lean in and crush me.

Then the crawl chute opens up into a space like a cave, tucked between the water silo and the wall. I thought everything on the *Lazarus* was mapped, everything blueprinted, but this doesn't look meant for access. It was walled up and meant to be forgotten. Nothing here to see except curves of reinforced titanium, reflecting infinitely off one another.

As we rise to our feet, I understand why he wanted to show this to me. It feels private in a way that nowhere else aboard this ship ever has.

I wish I could turn back time to the night in the Catalog. That night, I would have been able to tell him, *home*—this dark corner makes me remember home. The polygons of light that flew up the backseat as the car slid down a city highway. This secret space makes me remember the way it felt to have everything: to be able to disappear in a crowd, to be miniature and forgettable in the grand scheme of things. Maybe that terrified Eli. To me it was comforting.

But I can't speak. I'm still raw from the conversation we left fifty feet overhead. I look up at the gap where he tumbled, the thin cobalt line of light above. Anis leans against the wall beside me.

"I can tell the others about the petition," he says. "I can pretend I eavesdropped on the meeting and found everything out on my own."

I'm looking down at my feet, but I feel him watching me; I feel his attention like the atmospheric stir of air before a storm.

Words build in my chest, clotting up my lungs until I give up—I let it all out. "I know you think I should have taken Sergei's side. And I wish I could take a stand, I wish I could be like you and Eli and Sergei and even Irina, but that's never who I'm supposed to be. If someone doesn't keep the peace, everything breaks. I mean, come on, you watched the news at home. We spent the last six months fighting and killing one another because everybody was on their own side first. We can't let that happen." I swallow hard. "My thoughts and feelings—I've been telling you this forever, Anis! What does any of that matter? I have to think of the big picture and what's good for everybody and all these concepts that have nothing to do with me at all. The world needs people who put themselves last."

I expect him to return a finely tuned argument, but he just says, "I know."

"What?"

"I know why you do it." He gives his head a little shake. "I'm sorry for yelling at you."

I don't understand. Why is this the time he apologizes? He's always been a living critique—and maybe I should hate him for it. Maybe I'm too used to criticism. Maybe I should walk away and find someone who will tell me, all the time, that I'm doing the right thing, someone who will always reassure and validate me. But even the thought feels like I'm losing something that I can't afford to give up.

"I just don't know why you're still here, if—" I start, but he says at the same time:

"I hate watching you compromise yourself into nothing when I know you're more than that."

My face grows hot. His words beat in my ears like a pulse.

A small part of me feels galvanized by the way he said it—with faith, like I'm something brave and good underneath everything. Most of me is terrified that he's wrong.

The machines' gentle vocalizations nearly swallow my words: "I'm scared I'll never stop letting you down."

His perpetual frown eases. He looks almost sad. "You don't let me down," he says. "That's not what I feel."

I tilt my face up to see him, the crooked arrow of his nose and the stubble that he, like most of the boys aboard, has beaten back with a dry shave, leaving red dashes against his neck, the corner of his jaw. His black hair is long enough now that a defined curl reaches for his eyes like a shepherd's crook.

As his gaze moves over my face, something pulls tight in my abdomen.

"What do you feel," I say quietly, but it's not really a question, and he doesn't answer. Instead his knuckles brush mine and stay there.

Something happens in my vision like a curtain drawing back, removing a layer of shadow. I realize how close we're standing, how every time he exhales I feel the touch of air on my cheek. I'm startling awake in a way I thought I'd forgotten.

He waits, quiet but not expectant. I remember how nervous I was when Marcus stopped me outside my room a lifetime ago, when he set his hand on the wall above my shoulder, as if he'd read somewhere that this was the stance you took to make your declarations. I was filled with dread for the moment I would have to push him away, for the disappointment that would—and did—crumple his expression.

I spend so much time afraid. But as I look up into Anis's face, I feel my fear draining away instead. There's only the realization that for once in my life, I know what I want. I want him to keep looking at me this way, like he understands me, like he trusts me, like he even wants me. Like I'm someone worth wanting.

I rise toward him as he tilts down into me. When our lips touch, it's not what I expect it to be. It's not strident or forceful. His mouth is soft, settling gently against mine, one of his hands brushing my cheek as the other slides into my hair. A shiver runs through me. My nerves reverberate like chimes. I link my arms around his waist to pull him closer.

The murmur of the machines. The soft, frustrated sound he makes against me when I press him back against the wall. The line of blue light that drapes across his dark features in dramatic chiaroscuro. I've heard a hundred stories about first kisses, about their awkwardness, their upsetting taste, the way that tongues or teeth or noses or hands become unfortunate main characters. Marcus used to tell and retell the story of his lip getting caught in his eighth-grade girlfriend's mouth guard. I always wondered why I never heard anything positive or reassuring, nothing except comedy and humiliation. Now I think I understand. I think maybe when it's beautiful, people want to keep it to themselves.

———

The next morning, when I wake up, my cabin feels quieter than usual. I stand from my bunk, unable to keep a small smile from my lips as I tug my uniform on. The world seems tinted, slightly different than it looked yesterday. I'm picturing Anis rolling out of bed, splashing water on his cheeks, working his fingers through his hair. I don't know how I'll keep myself from glancing toward his usual seat at breakfast, how I'll act normal.

But when I arrive in the canteen with Caro, there's no sleepy breakfast chatter, no usual divide of groups at tables. We find the group clustered around the dispensary screens, their discontented rumbles traveling the length of the hall.

My thoughts of Anis, the secret, giddy feeling—it all fades. I trade a glance with Caro before hurrying forward.

As they part to let us through, I catch glimpses of Sergei and Francisco at the front, and worries begin to circulate. Sergei was livid last night. Has he relayed the story about the petition to the group? Did he get enough signatures for a majority? Did he and Francisco get into a public fight?

But when we reach the boys, neither one looks angry. They're facing the dispensary screens.

"What is it?" I ask, hurrying up with Caro.

"We don't know," Francisco says while Sergei points to one of the red messages blinking at the top of every screen. ERROR 318.01, they read, unhelpfully.

"Okay," I say. "Caro, can you check if something's wrong with the displays? I'll check the storeroom—there are some diagrams of the dispensary in there. Francisco, Sergei, just keep people . . ."

"Calm," they say together.

"Yeah. Thanks."

I hurry down the line of screens and slip into the storeroom, but I don't need to consult the diagrams. Positioning myself below the sample crate in its steel fixture, I see the issue right away. A catch at one corner of the cage isn't quite secure. It's been opened.

"No," I whisper, rushing to the wall and hitting LOWER FIXTURE on the control panel. "No, no, please . . ." The moment the cage slides to the ground, I'm pulling a dozen other catches, tugging open the steel gridding to reveal its contents. The cube's packaging has been peeled back, displaying long grooves where columns of food have been removed.

My knees threaten to buckle. I grip the raided crate to stabilize myself, questions pelting through my mind. Who did this? Who could have been selfish enough? And what can I tell the others? Someone's a thief, and if we can't get the food back, we'll have to cut our rations even further.

I close my eyes. Eli will know what to do. She'll have a contingency plan for this.

Before returning out into the canteen, I clench my fists, close my eyes, and picture myself stepping out of my weak, frightened skin, but it only half works. When I emerge, the lights feel too bright, and Caro, Francisco, and Sergei seem to hover too close.

"Caro," I say quietly, "can you call Eli with that?" I wave to the one dispensary screen that still lists the Antaeus count-down: *4 months, 16 days, 18 hours . . .*

"Sure." She turns to it at once, navigating to the screen's call function.

"What happened?" someone calls from the group.

"What's wrong?" says Jayanti, slipping up to the front.

For the first time, I notice how skinny they've all become, how their cheekbones press out from their faces like knuckles. My eyes meet Anis's. He looks as tired and hungry as every-body else, but when a smile touches his stubborn mouth, soft-ening his eyes, some of the unrest inside me quiets.

"Everyone," I call, "I have good news and bad news. The good news is that we found the cause of the water treatment breach last night. One of the pressure gauges was miscalibrated, but it'll be easy to fix. There's nothing in the treatment plant that we need to find. That means we can stop studying the auto-systems and checking pipes."

Relieved chatter breaks through the crowd. "Finally," says Luke to laughs from his friends.

"Wait," Sahir calls out, "what about the bad news?"

"These error messages aren't because of a glitch. Someone broke into the dispensary last night and stole some of our food supply."

The smiles disappear. A low moan issues from someone in the crowd, and in the front row, Fatima's hands come up to clutch her midsection, her mouth distorting like she might cry. *Eli,* I think, but Caro hasn't reached her yet. She's gaping over her shoulder at me. Sergei and Francisco look just as horrified.

"How?" Sergei says.

"How *much*?" Francisco says.

"Dozens of bars. We'll need to do a recount, and depending on whether we can recover the missing food, we might need to cut back our diets ahead of schedule. Caro—we need to tell Eli, now."

"Yes. Right." Under her shaking finger, the screen offers up call locations—Planter floors, the Menagerie, the Catalog— until she presses *Bridge*. A gentle tone hums rhythmically through the speakers, once, twice, three times. It goes on and on, sending signals out through the ship, rippling over the heads of the hushed crowd.

It goes on until I realize Eli isn't going to answer.

CHAPTER 12

THE LOCK AND THE CELL

I pelt down the hall toward the bridge. When I round a bend, I see the door open far ahead, a white curve like a tooth. "Eli?" I call as I near the threshold. "Eli!"

I break into the bridge and scan the area. The Council's table is empty, the commander's seat empty. One of the bunks is unmade, but there's no trace of her. It's the first time I've seen the room without Eli inside since we were still nestled in Earth's atmosphere. What is this? What happened?

My eyes are drawn unwillingly toward the airlock. The fine hair on my arms lifts. Inside me is a slow twisting sensation, like someone has gripped everything in my abdomen and wrung it like a rag. I take a step toward the door.

Then a noise comes from the other direction. I spin to face the curved section of wall beside the nearest bunk. There's a notched handle there, a door to the bathroom. I run for it and throw it wide.

Eli is sprawled on the bathroom floor, stirring feebly. Her long hair is a straggly mess, strands caught in the pool of vomit that's congealed around the base of the toilet. The smell hits me in a putrid blast—evaporated bile and something sickly bittersweet.

"Eli," I choke out. Covering my nose, I kneel by her. "Eli, can you hear me?"

Her eyelids and mouth are both sagging. Again she makes the sound that I heard through the door, an incoherent moan.

I slip one arm beneath her knees, the other under her back, and manage to carry her to the nearest bunk. As her arm flops over the edge of the mattress, I spot a puncture mark in the crook of her elbow, surrounded by a greenish spot of bruising.

Her eyelids flutter, neither open nor fully shut. I want to sprint back to the canteen and get the rest of the Council, but whoever did this could still be roaming the ship. Could they pose a threat to Eli if I leave her by herself?

My eyes land on the dashboard. I run to the navigation screen and scroll back through the contact history, through our hourly unanswered transmissions, until I find access to every screen connected to the network. Moments after I dial in to the canteen, Caro's face swims up on the other end. In the background, the group is watching the screen noiselessly.

I focus on their faces. The sight of their uncertainty composes me.

"Everybody," I say, "what I need from you right now is to listen, all right?"

No answer.

"Someone hurt Eli. It looks like the same sort of sedative that was used on Sahir, but she had a reaction to it. She still isn't really awake. So everyone in Medical track, raise your hand."

I'm already looking toward the back of the group as Anis lifts his hand. "Great," I say, my throat tight. "Let's say Jayanti and Anis, come to the bridge with Francisco, Sergei, and Caro. Then—" My eyes fix on the group of guards. "Pieter, make sure everyone gets breakfast as normal, then take a headcount. We need to make sure nobody else is hurt or missing. With seven in the bridge, there should be forty-seven—" I break off, remembering Irina. "Forty-six in the canteen. After the count, Annie and Pilar, go make sure Irina's all right in the ninth floor and bring her breakfast, too. Then everyone needs to stay put in the canteen until we figure out a strategy. Eli should be able to tell us more soon—we'll keep in touch this way. Got it?"

Pieter nods, striding to the front of the group. "Got it. I'll call you when I've got the count."

"Thanks. Talk then."

I end the call. Eli lets out another mumbled sound across the bridge. As I hurry to her side and wipe the vomit from across her chin, I remember being eleven years old and seeing my mother with an indigo bruise across her forehead. She'd knocked into the edge of a door, nothing dramatic, but the sight was still deeply wrong. The idea that anything could hurt her felt like a personal threat to me.

"Maybe four thirty," Eli rasps. Her breath is foul, and we have to huddle close to hear. "Five? Don't know . . . not sure."

My throat tightens. Anis and I got back to the eighth floor

last night around 4:30 a.m. If the attacker left the Residential Wing then, we could have been only minutes away from seeing them, stopping them.

Jayanti studies the puncture mark in Eli's arm. The younger girl looks perturbed, restless. "We . . . we haven't learned much about anesthesia yet, but she probably overdosed on whatever they gave her, if she's like this."

"Overdosed?" Caro says, her voice brittle.

Anis, crouching at Jayanti's side, stands up. "None of us are anesthesiologists," he says gruffly. "Dosage is delicate."

"You didn't see who it was, Eli?" Francisco asks, feeding her more water from a cup.

She twitches her head no. "Pillow over my face," she croaks.

"Here." Francisco draws a damp towel across her chin, wiping away the last of the residue. It comes away the dark, treacly color of our meal bars. "I don't see why someone would do this," he says with rising agitation. "What would they get out of it? What's the point?"

"And the food," Sergei adds from one of the copilots' seats, sounding numb. "What does this have to do with the food?"

Beeping from the dashboard signals an incoming call. I jog over to the screen and hit *Accept*. Pieter is standing so close to the camera that I can count every freckle on his pointy nose. "We did the headcount," he says. "Everyone's here."

"Okay. Thanks, Pieter." I lower my voice. "Irina's door wasn't open, was it?"

He gives me a knowing look. "No. She was locked in like usual." His eyes stray over my shoulder. "Is Eli okay? Can I do anything, bring her anything?"

"No, it's—"

"Yes," Eli scrapes out. "Come to the bridge."

Pieter nods. "I'll leave Matteo and Luke in charge. I'm coming. Be there right away."

He disconnects. When I turn back to Eli, she's levering herself upright, one hand clamped to her head with such force that I can practically feel the splitting headache. She pushes away Jayanti's and Anis's attempts to make her lie down again. "I'm fine," she grinds out. "Fine. Thanks . . . Go back to the canteen."

Anis glances to me for confirmation. Again the world seems to slip like a poorly fit garment. Not even six hours ago, I was resting my head on his chest in that hidden blue-lit space. Now his face is unreadable.

"Go ahead," I say.

"Okay." He looks back to Eli. "Get plenty of sleep."

"Drink as much water as you can," Jayanti adds, "but be careful with food. Don't nauseate yourself."

As they leave, I watch Anis shrink down the hall, his fists held tight at his sides. He doesn't look back at me. With a feeling of compression in my stomach, I begin to wonder.

Anis and I left the treatment plant last night near 4:30. He was awake.

My mouth is suddenly paper dry. Anis couldn't have done that to Eli. The same hands that held me so gently, they couldn't have stabbed a needle into her arm, forced down the plunger, clasped the pillow over her face while she thrashed, making muffled cries, and eventually went limp.

When I come back to myself, Francisco is saying, "Of course someone wants to steal food, Sergei. You were just complaining about how hungry you were yesterday."

Sergei shakes his head. "But why all this? Attacking Eli, wasting more of the anesthetic—what's the point?"

"Whoever stole the food," Eli rasps, "isn't going to eat it. They want to send it to the *Hermes*."

"What?" says Sergei at the same time as Francisco says, "How?"

But Caro has closed her eyes in understanding. "You think they want one of the rovers."

"Yeah. Someone knocked me out," she goes on with more strength, "because they needed time in here. Wanted to figure out how the rovers work... Send our food to some imaginary astronaut."

I frown. "Could the rovers deliver food to the *Hermes*?"

"No. They don't have the communication or the navigation.... And if they try to do it, they'll waste... Here, help me...."

Francisco and I lever her up and help her totter toward the dashboard. As she collapses into the commander's seat, footsteps clamor out in the hallway. A moment later, Pieter is jogging down the stairs to join us. "I'm here."

"Good," Eli pants, pushing her hair back with a shaking hand. "We'll need you."

Pieter's chest swells as Eli looks at the dashboard screen. Her hand gives the occasional involuntary twitch as she taps through the menus. *SYS > EXT > SUP > ROV.*

She examines a series of charts. Then her wan face sags. "Yes," she breathes. "Thank God, they're all still there." She leans back so we can see the list of seven rover pods. "The food's still aboard."

"How do we find it?" Pieter says at once.

"Need to search... every inch of this ship." She grips the arms of the commander's seat and slowly, excruciatingly, lifts herself upright. "Besides us, who do we know didn't do this?"

No one speaks. I half expect Sergei to say Irina's name—after all, she was locked in the ninth floor—but he doesn't answer, worrying at his knuckles until they pop.

And me? Who do I trust? *Anis*, I think, but my doubts redouble. Not even a week ago, he and I spoke about our hopes that someone might be aboard the *Hermes*. Last night, Eli's reaction to the petition sent him into panic mode. What if, after walking me back to my cabin, he went to the canteen, and then to the bridge, and took matters into his own hands?

"I trust Matteo Marini," Pieter says. "And Luke Nabwana. They're watching the canteen right now."

"All right," Eli says. "That's eight of us for a search party."

"Seven," I correct. "You need to rest."

A mulish glint lights in her eye, and I think she'll protest, but then she sighs. "Yeah, guess I'd slow down the effort." Some of the color is returning to her face. "Does everyone know how to set your tablets to video capture?"

"Why?" Sergei says, frowning.

"If we're inspecting the whole ship, it's going to take . . . don't know. Could take weeks. We need to make sure whoever took the food doesn't just move it from hiding place to hiding place. Live video is the only way. We can't be everywhere at once." She nods to Pieter. "Get a box of tablets from the first storeroom down the hall. We'll make a plan for stationing them."

Pieter gives a thumbs-up and dashes off.

"Wait, slow down," Sergei says, holding up his big hands. "We should start by talking to everyone. Maybe we can convince whoever it was to return it. We'll remind them of the risks, we'll explain that—"

"They know the risks, Sergei!" Eli winces, fingers darting to her temple, and as her bloodshot eyes glare out at him, their fight last night seems to resurface, drawing battle lines across the bridge again. "They're already starving, which is probably why they did this in the first place. You said it yourself. Hungry people start trouble." She glances to Francisco. "That reminds me. We need to recount the remaining food."

Francisco makes a note. Sergei still looks dissatisfied, but as he opens his mouth, I cut in. "Sergei, whoever did this is never going to confess. That would be a confession to poisoning Eli, too. If she'd... If it'd been worse..."

I can't finish the sentence. I'm imagining a world where I pulled open the bathroom door and found Eli dead, her face not ashen but alabaster, the angles of her limbs held in permanent, unnatural positions. Her body indescribably different from a living thing, in the way her mother's was.

Footfalls sound behind us. Pieter's voice rings out from the bridge's upper level. "Eli!"

We turn to see him panting in the threshold. "The tablets are gone. Every box. They must have known you'd want to do this."

"Shit." Eli closes her eyes. "We still have the fifty-three that we're using for training. . . . We shouldn't put training on hold, though."

Francisco snaps his fingers. "The desks on the second floor. People can use them for their training assignments instead."

"Not all of them," I say. "Maintenance needs something portable to learn on-site, and a lot of the medical simulations revolve around being in the med bay, too."

"Okay," Eli says. "Then we'll take the tablets from the Command track, which gives us—"

"Six," Francisco says.

"Right. Station them at the entrances to the cabin floors,

plus one in the atrium. Try and hide them. Maybe we'll spot the thief trying to move the food."

"But—" Sergei starts.

Eli talks over him. "They'll also want to get back into the bridge to launch the rover. We have to guard this door day and night."

"I'll do it," Pieter says immediately.

This coaxes a smile out of Eli. "Good. That only leaves six of us for the search, though." She pulls up a holographic diagram of the ship to revolve above the dashboard, then pinches the Command Wing and turns the glimmering display. She zooms in through the ship's internal canals and back out again, light sliding over her knuckles.

"After we check the rover bay," she says, "we should start with the Residential Wing. It'll be the simplest to search, since all the cabins are uniform. I don't really think they'd hide the food in their own cabin, but one of the empty rooms, maybe—"

Sergei interrupts. "And how exactly are we planning on checking people's rooms?"

"Well, we tell them to leave," Francisco says with exaggerated patience, "and then we go inside."

"It hasn't occurred to any of you that the others might not love the idea of us barging into their cabins and overturning everything?"

For a long moment, the rest of us just look at him. Then Caro, Pieter, and Francisco all start talking at once.

"Sergei, that's not the most important—"

"We're doing it to keep them safe—"

"If it makes them uncomfortable, let them be uncomfortable—"

"Are you listening to yourselves?" Sergei demands, the angry flush in his cheeks creeping up to his forehead. "Those are their private spaces, the only thing that actually belongs to them!"

"There's nothing *there*," Francisco says. "There's nothing left."

"There's the way people feel about it," Sergei shoots back, eyes burning. I'm vividly reminded of Irina's "It's a matter of principle."

"Enough," Eli says roughly. We all look back to her. She's steadying herself on the dashboard, one hand at her temple again. "This is ridiculous. Sergei, you don't have to do the inspections if they're so offensive to you. Everyone else—"

"You can't," Sergei all but yells.

A cold sensation trickles down my back. The look Eli gives him is venomous. Her eyes flare like dilating camera lenses. A muscle hikes alongside her nose.

"Why not?" she says.

"Because as long as the food is still aboard, we can find it. We have months to figure out who stole it and convince them to turn themselves in, without invading everyone's privacy!"

"You're making a lot of excuses."

Sergei's hands ball up into fists the size of small melons. "Hold on. I didn't do this. You think I'd do this to you?"

"Why not?" Eli says through gritted teeth. "You were halfway to calling me a murderer last night because of the *Hermes*. What if you decided you didn't care about the petition numbers and wanted to make the choice yourself?"

"I didn't touch you, I just don't want you turning this ship into a surveillance state at the slightest complication!"

"The slightest complication?" Eli's voice rises to a shout. "I could have died tonight! I was drugged in the middle of the night, I could be in a coma, you could be burying my body right

now, and whoever did it is still wandering around out there. You don't know what they'll do next. Do you want to *be* next?"

"We can find them," says Caro.

Everyone looks to her. She's been sitting in one of the bunks, arms crossed over her midsection, but now she's on her feet, determination in every inch of her slender frame. "I'll find the door records. If it's possible, that's the fastest way. We figure out who opened the dispensary last night. Then it's over."

Something settles heavily in my chest. I remember Anis's objections in the stairwell, the first day we mentioned those records—but I can't intervene. The seeds on Antaeus could be slow to grow, or maybe we won't find enough seeds to sustain us until a second harvest. If anything goes wrong, those dozens of bars could be the difference between someone's death or survival, and if Caro can find a cache of data that solves everything, we have no choice. I have no choice.

"Caro," Sergei croaks, dismay spreading across his face. "No, come on, don't do this."

"I'm sorry." Caro is as resolved as I've ever seen, eyes glinting like the studs in her ears, her lips pursed into a crimson whorl. The girl who shrank under Jayanti's barbs yesterday has been replaced with someone who's realized exactly what her vote is worth.

At first her resolve surprises me. After all, before any of this happened—before the cells, before the *Hermes* question, before the first attack on Sahir—she'd resigned herself to our starvation. Part of me would have expected her to sit back and give up, to say a few extra meal bars won't make a real difference. But maybe I do understand. Caro thought we had ten months. It's a grim outlook, but maybe this is her last stand: refusing to settle for even a day less.

"Thanks, Caro, great," Eli says vaguely. Her outburst seems to have sucked the life out of her again. Her skin is pallid, her brow pearled with sweat. "So . . . the inspections. While we're swee—"

Her hands fly to her stomach. For a moment I think she'll be sick. Pieter makes a sudden motion toward her.

"Eli?" I say.

She pushes on. "While we're . . . conducting inspections," she says, but the words are sloppy. *Inspesshens.* "We can't tell anyone too much. Give away too much. We don't want the thief to know our movements. Good thing is, they have to pretend everything's normal. While they're in training . . . we have all the, all that time to stay a step ahead of . . ."

Eli lists like a ship on choppy water. We watch, waiting for her to recover.

Then she gropes for the edge of the dashboard and misses. Her body topples sideways. I dive forward, arms outstretched, and catch her. Pieter's hot on my heels, and he helps me bring her backward, her heels squeaking on the tile. Her speech is completely slurred now. It isn't until she's lying limp on the bunk that I can lean close enough to understand what she's saying: "Leigh . . . Help me. . . . Leigh."

I rise to my feet. As we all stand over Eli's huddled body, watching the sweat bead on her clammy skin, I feel a wave of fear. I round on the others. "Caro, get to the codehome. Pieter, go station those tablets, and Francisco, organize the inspection schedule."

"Leigh—" Sergei says.

My voice comes out like ice. "We'll start now."

The magnitude of the task becomes clear almost instantly. Luke and I start our search on the sixth floor of the Residential Wing, while Francisco and Matteo take the ninth. We've decided to check the rooms out of order so that the thief won't know where it's safe to move the food. In each cabin, we pat down every pillow, scour every cabinet, and overturn every mattress. The only blessing is that the rooms are all but empty, even the ones that are occupied, since none of us owns enough possessions to fill a cabinet, let alone a whole cabin.

Still, among the four of us, clearing the pair of floors takes until dinnertime. When I think about the rest of the ship, every poorly lit cranny of the Catalog with its hoard of treasures, all the unmarked hollows of the water treatment plant, it seems impossible that we'll ever find one small cache of food bars.

"It's useful that the wrappings are silver," Francisco says over dinner. "It'll be easier to spot reflective material." He turns his half-eaten bar over and over in his hands. He's been nibbling at it intermittently in an apparent attempt to make it last longer.

Matteo, always twitchy and suspicious and a little bit aggressive, has been pushed into full-blown paranoia by the theft. He looks over each shoulder before saying anything, no matter how unimportant, and mutters it in a dark stream of Italian that no one at a neighboring table could possibly overhear. "I have a theory," he says, hunching his broad shoulders as he leans toward the rest of us. "I think Irina broke out of her cell, stole the food, attacked Eli, and locked herself inside again."

"There's no evidence of that," I say, although I've been thinking through that possibility all day. After Irina's humiliation in the atrium, I could see her wanting to pay Eli back—and didn't Sergei just tell Sahir and Jayanti to make amends with Irina last night?

"Think about it," Matteo insists in a harsh whisper. "She and Sahir and Jayanti are the ones obsessed with going back to the *Hermes*. They have to be behind this."

Luke looks skeptical, tugging on his beard. "Yes, but since when do they come up with secret, elaborate plans instead of making a lot of noise where everyone can hear them?"

"My money's still on Sergei," says Pieter, his green eyes as hard as chips of jade. "Eli told me everything he said to her last night. He obviously doesn't understand what she's trying to do at all. . . . And you two should have heard him in the meeting, Luke, Matteo. He was trying to stop us from finding the door records, from looking around the ship too hard. He's not even being subtle about it."

"I don't know." Luke shakes his head. "Sergei's still going around with that petition, trying to convince people to sign. Would he bother if he had the food?"

This line of thought seems to disturb Francisco. "Sergei wouldn't do this, petition or not," he cuts in. "Besides, maybe the two things are unrelated. Maybe someone just stole the food because they were hungry, and what happened to Eli is separate."

"Who cares?" Matteo crumples his empty meal bar wrapper in a knobby fist. "All I know is, when we catch the thief, we should give everyone else their food. They obviously didn't mind letting the rest of us starve."

"We'll think about consequences later," I say quickly. "Come on—we should get back to it."

We return to the Residential Wing and divide up again. With each cabin I search, I feel more and more dejected. Last night, as Anis and I returned to the eighth floor from the water treatment plant, I imagined how every night was about to change. I pictured us exploring the ship in our secret hours. Now that's off the table. I need sleep, and then I need to wake up at seven a.m. to resume inspections, and more than ever, I feel guilty about the time I've spent with him. If Anis really is the thief, if our conversations somehow encouraged him to steal the food and attack Eli, this is my fault.

Then, as I move down the eighth-floor hallway, I hear his voice ahead.

"I didn't agree to this."

"You don't have to agree."

The voices are coming from the end of the wing, from his cabin. I accelerate through the tunnel's gentle twists, then round the last bend to see Francisco and Anis ahead. Arms folded, Anis guards the control panel beside his door. Francisco, several inches taller, is advancing on him.

Anis sees me. Francisco follows his sightline and loses momentum. "Leigh."

"What is this?" I stride forward. "What's happening?"

"I'm trying to inspect Anis's cabin," Francisco says impatiently. "I told him this would take ten minutes."

"I don't care," Anis says, gruff and unmoving.

Francisco rounds on him. "If you don't have anything in there, why do you mind if I go in?"

"Because it's my cabin. Even the fingerprint reader knows that. If you people can't catch up with a computer chip, you shouldn't be flying the ship."

"This is a waste of time. I'm not asking. Get out of the way."

"Are you giving orders now?" Anis demands. "Is this an army? Are you a general?"

I step forward. "Hey. Stop. Let's calm down, okay? We can make this work; we can—"

"I doubt it," Anis says, not taking his eyes off Francisco.

Francisco fastens his hands over his head, mumbling a string of what I can only assume are Quechuan curse words, since my translator stays silent. "Forget it," he says. "You take care of this, Leigh. I'm going to bed."

We both watch Francisco stalk back toward the balconies. When he's gone, I turn to Anis with a tired smile. "So, do you want to let me take a look?"

He kneads his forehead with his fingertips.

My smile fades. "Anis?"

"I don't want anyone searching my room. Not even you."

The lights of the hallway suddenly feel too bright. *Just ask him*, I tell myself. *Just ask if he did it.* But I can't make myself speak, because I know he'll tell me the truth, and maybe I can't handle the truth this time. What will I do if he's guilty? How could I sit back and pretend I don't know who the thief is while the rest of the group is theorizing, searching, starving?

But how could I hand Anis to the Council, either? At the very least, he'll be locked in confinement for God knows how long. At worst... didn't Matteo just suggest starving whoever stole the food? I've never seen Eli this angry. I remember her satisfaction when she ordered Irina stripped out of the group. Part of me thinks she'd want more than confinement. She'd want revenge.

Anis still hasn't spoken. As I look into his stubborn face, I can feel the warmth of his skin under my fingertips, how he shivered when I drew one hand down his back. I feel how he cradled my face delicately, carefully, like he couldn't believe what was happening.

My eyes prickle with sudden, angry tears. If he could do this—attack Eli and steal food from the group—then he's not the person I thought he was, and he's more a liar than I've ever been. And if I've been wrong about him the whole time, he could reveal everything I've told him. My secret objections to the guards. My reliance on the VR room. The way I tattled on Eli last night, like a little kid who couldn't keep her fucking mouth shut.

My fault, I think. *My fault, my fault, my fault.*

When I take a step back from him, disappointment settles onto his face. His silence seems to dare me to ask, but I refuse. I think of the tarnished brass key he showed me that night in the Catalog, the night we first opened ourselves to each other. But maybe some doors should stay locked. He can keep the key this time.

CHAPTER 13

FORWARD

Three days have passed since Eli was attacked, but nothing has returned to normal among the Council, and I'm beginning to doubt it ever will, even if we find the stolen food. It feels unbelievable that we're the same group who designed the training plan during our first weeks aboard, joking together, reassuring one another, always ready to give one another the benefit of the doubt.

Now, as much as I try to smooth the mood, our meetings feel steeped in stress and hostility. Although Eli is healthy again, the attack took something out of her. The confidence and easy dismissiveness I'd begun to see after Irina's arrest have been siphoned out. She sits very straight in her chair at meetings, less talkative and less flexible, listening to every word with rapt attention. And she's back to staying in the bridge, isolated all the time. When I reminded her that she'd wanted to run a meeting with the group every week, mistrust flashed in her eyes, and she said, "No. Not a good idea." She seems to have aged several years in the space of three days.

The attack has clearly shocked Caro, too. I'd give anything for one of her easy jokes to lighten the atmosphere, but she's unrecognizable as the idly cheerful girl of two weeks ago. Gone are the vibrant lip shades and colorful patterns of eye shadow. A twitch has developed in her eyelid from so much time in the codehome; between her search and my inspection rounds, we can no longer spare the time for our language exchange lessons. Every day at our meetings, she delivers long, detailed rundowns of the sections of code she reviewed, which none of us understand.

Sergei, meanwhile, sits in silence at meetings with his arms crossed, glaring as Francisco delivers reports of our inspections. He's stopped sitting with us in the canteen, instead joining a group of Medicine-track kids he knows from Child Psychology. The petition never leaves his hands, although he hasn't managed to get the numbers high enough for a majority. In fact, after the attack on Eli, several people have asked him to take their names off the list. I often see him coming in and out of the ninth floor.

On the day Irina is released, she and Sergei start sitting together in the canteen, just the two of them, whispered about by most of the other tables. Irina seems fidgety but quiet. She keeps her head down during morning meeting and doesn't try to talk to Sahir or Jayanti, although I see them sneaking glances at her during our psychology lecture. When I ask Sergei how Irina is doing before the evening's meeting, he gives me a cold, suspicious look and a vague nonanswer. He's giving Caro and Francisco the cold shoulder, too, although with Francisco it seems to be a matter of betrayal rather than judgment.

Still, as much as Sergei might loathe the inspections and Caro's hunt for the door records, he attends every Council meeting at the end of each day. Maybe he doesn't want us to forget his disapproval.

Unfortunately, there's no end to the inspections in sight. The rover bay is still untouched, so the food must still be aboard, but we've checked not only the cabin floors at this point but the entire Residential Wing, plus the Menagerie and half the Catalog. We haven't found the boxes of tablets, any sign of the food, or any evidence of who the thief might be.

The only semi-newsworthy event during inspections has been Anis's refusal, which resolved itself quickly, in the end. Francisco went back to Anis's cabin the morning after their confrontation, and he brought Pieter and Matteo along. At this point, according to Francisco, Anis rolled his eyes and let them in without a fight. Then he stood in the corner, arms folded, staring mutinously at them until they left. They found nothing.

I didn't react to the story in front of the Council, but my body suffused with heat. I knew exactly what Anis was thinking, watching them root around in his room: *In most countries, this would be illegal, and also you should be embarrassed about your lack of a social conscience.*

But we haven't spoken about it, because I haven't been to the track since our non-conversation outside his door. During morning meetings I make sure never to look his way. In the canteen, I pass on the other side of the room to avoid the spot where he sits alone. Sometimes, though, seated several tables over, I think I feel him looking toward me. I wonder if he goes to the track at nights, waiting to see if I'll show. Or maybe he's so angry about the inspections that he's finally given up on me. I know I'm the one who's avoiding him, but the thought still makes something in my chest hurt.

Then, five days into the inspections, Caro shows up for our evening meeting at a run.

"I found something," she says, taking her seat.

We all sit up straighter. "What is it?" Eli asks.

"I've been going through the code for our identity profiles. It turns out that whole system is actually localized." She taps one finger on the table. "It's based here, in the bridge, so the pilot and command chain can access the census. If there had been a thousand people aboard, a directory would have been really useful to the pilots." She pauses. "If I'm right, when the ship's control panels connect to the census, they create access records in this system. So, somewhere in the bridge, there's a list of pings describing who's been where and when."

For the first time since before the attack, a grin breaks across Eli's face. "Amazing," she says as Francisco claps Caro on the back. "How long will it take to find the pings? Maybe I can help—I know some basic TRP."

Caro's excitement flags. "The code's in TRP up here? That isn't my best language. It could take a while." She grimaces. "I still can't be sure these pings are accessible, either. They could be temporary, deleted right away."

"It's a lead, though," Eli says.

I glance at Sergei. A trace of foreboding remains through the rest of the meeting, but he doesn't say a word. When we finish, he's the first out of his seat, heading down the hall before the rest of us have even stood up.

I hurry after him, wanting to talk, but by the time I reach the balconies, he's already across the atrium. I slow, watching the tall glass elevator shaft. Sergei exits the car on the sixth floor, glances around, and disappears into the Residential Wing.

I bite my tongue, torn. I don't want Pieter to be right about him. I'm even less eager to pry into Sergei's private life. But I've never seen that nervous look on his face before, and his lack of reaction to Caro's news feels too loaded to ignore. If he is the thief, I'd rather know as soon as possible so that I can start planning damage control right away.

I hurry to the elevator bay, then slip into the sixth-floor hallway. At first it sounds quiet, but about halfway to the end of the wing, I hear muffled voices.

I approach the first door in sight with a name ID on the control panel: *Irina Volkova.*

I lean close and hear Sergei saying, "This isn't the same. They could find out. They could know by tomorrow."

"Sergei, would you trust me for once?"

"That's what I'm doing. I'm telling you I don't care, I don't mind. I can help. . . ."

"And I told you I don't need your help!" Irina says hotly. "This is exactly why I didn't tell you about the VR room. I thought about it, you know? When it got really bad, I thought about it. But I knew you'd get this idea in your head that I need to be fixed, that you need to be the hero, that you need to save me. I don't want you to save me, I want you to listen to me." Her brashness gives way to something more vulnerable. "I want you to care about me the way I actually am. That's all I wanted from anyone."

The sound of footsteps pads toward me on the soft mesh of the floor. I sprint away without looking back.

As the evening wears on, as I inspect the cases in the fifth floor of the Catalog, the fragment of conversation replays in my mind over and over. If I'm understanding, then Sergei wasn't trying to slow the investigation to save himself—he was trying to hide Irina. Unless . . . what did he mean by saying he'd help? Was he offering to return the food anonymously, to lie for his sister? Or was he offering to help with the launch of the rover?

Maybe he was part of it from the beginning. That was the night he stormed out of our meeting. What if he pretended to calm down for Francisco's sake, then returned to the ninth floor and planned this with Irina for the same night? He was there when we decided on the passcode for the locks. He could have let his sister out of confinement, then gone to steal the food while she went to the bridge to pay Eli back in person.

It fits, but my thoughts keep returning to Anis and the conflict on his face as he blocked his door. Was that just a matter of principle, then? Was Anis testing me, taking a stand to see what choice I'd make?

I don't know, but even now, Irina and Sergei could be preparing to try and launch the rover somehow. By ten p.m., I've decided this is too much for me to hold alone. Eli needs to know what I overheard.

Pieter is standing guard when I arrive at the bridge. His broad shoulders relax when he sees me. "Leigh. What do you need?" His eyes brighten. "Did you find something?"

"No, I need a word with Eli."

"Of course, go ahead." He hastens away from the threshold, allowing me through. The bridge is empty, and as I jog down the stairs, I hear the patter of the shower from the bathroom.

While I wait, I pace from one end of the dashboard to the

other. Irina's insistences, which have been buzzing in me like a hornet all evening, have gone quiet. Now that I'm here, I'm dreading the moment I'll have to mention Irina's name to Eli. After all, the last time the two of them clashed, Pieter got a bloody nose and Irina got dragged into the ninth floor kicking and thrashing, and that was when Eli felt like she'd come out on top.

If Sergei really did spring Irina from confinement, and if Irina really is the one who gave Eli an overdose, it's a repeat offense. She wasted more anesthetic, endangered another life, and all this after she'd supposedly repented the first time. What will Eli want to do? With Francisco and now Caro backing up pretty much everything Eli says, with Pieter and his guards on their side—our side—who could stop her from doing it? I want to believe that Eli would never really hurt anyone. Everything she's done has been to ensure the whole crew stays alive and healthy.

Except—after she sent Irina to confinement, she said, "You'll stay there until you're not a danger to the rest of the ship." That was her priority then. Not Irina's safety, but removing the danger to everyone else.

The noise of the shower turns into the sucking sound of the water reclamation system. I move for one of the copilots' seats, then hesitate. A plastic bin is sitting in the commander's seat, something glimmering inside.

I turn the chair toward myself and jerk my hand back. Inside the bin are half a dozen foot-long metal pipes, threading exposed at their ends. A scattering of blades are sifted in among the pipes, eight inches long and razor-fine, with blunt cylindrical ends. I recognize them from the Planters, sections of the metal hands that were designed to plow our soil.

I stare at them, motionless, until the bathroom door opens.

"Leigh," Eli says with surprise that turns at once to alertness. "What happened?"

"Nothing happened," I say automatically. "I just wanted to ask...I...What are these?" I point to the bin.

She relaxes. "A new precaution. I was thinking about you four wandering around the Residential Wing, and it doesn't feel safe. We did an inventory recount, and the thief took a whole case of anesthetic, so they've still got eleven doses. If you do find the food, or if you get close enough that they think you're a threat, they'll probably do the same thing to you that they did to me." She approaches the chair. "So I had Matteo collect these."

"We're supposed to carry these around during inspections?"

"Yeah. I need you to stay safe." Eli hefts one of the pipes from the bin. "Also, now that I've got some protection, I can watch the bridge by myself so Pieter can join the inspections during the day." She pauses. "What did you want to ask?"

I open my mouth, but nothing comes out. Looking at Eli with the section of pipe in her hand, I feel a rush of disorientation, and confessing what I overheard is suddenly the last thing I want to do. What *did* I hear, anyway? The conversation proved nothing. Irina never admitted she'd stolen the food. She only told Sergei to trust her, and that was why I didn't come to Eli immediately, wasn't it? Because the whole thing is imprecise, circumstantial.

I should be trying to patch things up between the Council, not widen the rift. I can't accuse Sergei's sister without any evidence. If I mention anything, I'll do it tomorrow, after the Council discusses these weapons.

"I just wanted to see how you're feeling," I say.

"Oh." Her shoulders relax. "Thanks. I'm . . . yeah, I'm okay. Better now that we have these." She slides the pipe back into the bin. "I can't believe I didn't think of it before. We can finally stop doubling up the guards, and everyone can get more rest. Which reminds me—we should cut down on calorie deficit by sleeping longer nights. I need to talk to Francisco about our hours."

"Yes. Right. Let's discuss that tomorrow." I glance back to the door.

"Are you still doing rounds? Here." She proffers the bin.

I don't move. The knives glint up at me like gemstones.

"I don't really think I need one," I say.

"If anyone needs one, it's you. Matteo and Luke and Francisco could fight off most people on this ship. You can't."

I still don't reach out.

Eli lowers the bin. The point of her tongue wets her thin lips. "Leigh, when I passed out the other day, I thought I was going to die. Halfway through falling, I was sort of semiconscious, and I had the actual thought, *I'm dying. This is the last thought I'm ever going to have.*"

It strikes me again how much older she seems than before her attack. She's still quiet and serious, but the hints of furtiveness and awkwardness have gone.

"It made me see everything more clearly." Eli sets the bin back into the pilot's seat. "When I lived at the complex, I used to think the crew took me seriously, but now I'm realizing I was probably more like this precocious pet teenager to them. To my mom, even. And before that I was the weird kid in the corner at all my schools. Before I got here, no one actually knew or cared who I was, or what I thought, or who I want to be. But you do."

"Of course I do," I say, caught off guard. "So do Francisco and Caro and—and Pieter."

"Right. So you see my point."

I shake my head, at a loss.

Eli steps so close that I can see each spoke of color in her blue irises, each delicately overlapping thread. "Leigh, I want to keep everyone safe. But apparently that's not an option, and if we have to choose who to keep safe, then I'm choosing us. You and me, and the people who actually care about . . . not just us, but everyone on this ship. Those people are my priority now. So—please, okay?" Eli draws a pipe from the bin. "I'm not letting you wind up where I was two days ago. I can't watch someone bring you in here passed out, or worse, all right?" She holds the pipe toward me, its threads brushing the lapel of my uniform. "My mom was right. We have to save who we can."

At first I think there's a ringing in my ears left behind by her words, the realization of what she means. But then Eli's head twitches toward the sound, too.

In the distance, someone is screaming.

"What—" Eli starts, but I'm already sprinting for the steps, up, then out.

At the door, Pieter is poised as if to run. "Stay here!" I tell him as I fly past, down the hall, back toward the ship's center.

By the time I reach the balconies, others are leaning over the rails below, craning their necks to see. I run half the circumference of the balconies, but nothing is visible. The scream percolates up from somewhere in the Residential Wing.

I take the stairs three at a time, stepping out on each floor, training my ears the way I did to find Anis in the treatment plant. On the seventh floor, the scream clarifies. The torn-open vowel sound has separated into words that my translator can wrangle: "STOP IT! HELP!"

I hurtle through the hall. Twenty doors down, I jerk to a halt. Sahir stands over Jayanti, whose body is hideously contorted. Sahir is the one screaming, hunched in an arc over Jayanti, hand flung up toward Matteo. Jayanti moves slowly, curling into fetal position.

"What did you do?" I yell, running toward them. "What are you doing?"

"She went for me!" Matteo shouts back.

"Give me that, you—" I grab for the pipe in his hand. He holds it higher, backward, out of my reach, and the movement is so much like a windup for a swing that I instinctively duck out of the way. Then Jayanti's head lifts, and I choke. A violet stripe mottles the side of her face. One cheek has swollen upward like a tumorous fruit.

I drop beside her. "Jayanti, are you okay?"

No answer. For a moment I think she's too concussed to speak, but then I see her ears are empty. She must have been asleep. She didn't even have time to put in her translator before Matteo did this.

"What is wrong with you?" I yell, standing. I feel completely outside my body. I've squared up to Matteo and risen to my tiptoes, trying to reach his height, like my anger wants me to become him. I can't stop my words, can't shape them; they blast out from me like vented steam. "You think this is what you were supposed to do? Did you even find anything?"

"No, but she could have hidden—"

I whirl away from him, forcing myself back down from my toes to the flats of my feet. I crouch by Jayanti again. "Jayanti. Can you hear me? Can you stand up?"

But her eyes have closed, and when I take her by the shoulder, she doesn't stir.

The med bay occupies two floors in the Systems Wing, each room a sterilized pod. There are a hundred beds, as if the ship's architects were planning for an epidemic.

Jayanti is stirring again by the time we get off the elevator. Sahir and I carry her to the nearest room and place her upon a pristine white cot. "Jayanti?" Sahir says gently, brushing her hair back from her face. "Are you all right?"

"Light," Jayanti slurs, squinting through watering eyes.

I hurry to the door and dim the bulbs until her facial muscles unclench. But when I take a step toward the bed, Sahir turns toward me, his stare so filled with hatred that I stop.

"Get out," he snarls. "Now."

I don't argue. I need to get to the bridge.

I return to the tenth floor to find Matteo, Pieter, and Luke congregated around Eli's seat at the head of the table. The rumble of discussion cuts off when they see me. Matteo wears a defiant scowl.

"Go, you three," Eli says.

As the guards make for the door, more footfalls echo down the hall. Seconds later, Sergei rounds the corner, closely followed by Francisco and Caro, who both look shell-shocked.

No sooner are they inside, the door sealed between us and the guards, than Sergei is yelling at Eli. "You gave them *weapons*?" He storms up to the table where she sits, stone-faced, in front of the pile of pipes and blades. "What the fuck were you thinking? And what are these?" He snatches up one of the blades.

Eli leans back as it cuts the air before her. "We need to move faster. When Pieter suggested—"

"Oh, Pieter! Okay." Sergei laughs. "Since when did Pieter start making these decisions?"

"Since no one else had any better ideas to keep us safe."

Sergei is shaking his head. "No, no, no, no. Armed guards never make a situation better."

"Oh? How do you know?"

"Because I've read a history book! When has it ever been a good sign when a country has to resort to military rule?"

"This isn't 'military rule,'" Eli snaps. "You can't just apply what countries did on Earth to our situation. They're two different things. None of them were living on a spaceship without any access to food production. Whatever they did on Earth, that's behind us."

Sergei's eyelids flutter as if he's trying to blink out a foreign body. "Behind us? You think you can just ignore all of human history? What do you think, you think you're different?"

"Yes! Obviously! How can you compare this to that? I'm trying to keep us from getting attacked, and you—"

I pick up the empty bin from the opposite end of the table and let it land with a bang on the tabletop. Sergei and Eli jump and twist toward me, seeming to remember that I'm here.

"Please," I say. "We have to calm down. We need to think. We'll already have to explain to the others what happened to Jayanti. Whatever we decide, we need to be united on this. We can't risk more upheaval right now."

Sergei has never looked so disgusted. "I guess I shouldn't be surprised that you're more worried about smoothing the surface than fixing what's happening."

I grit my teeth. "What's happening is we can't get anything done anymore without fighting. That's not just the surface. We have to solve this."

"I agree, and here's the solution: Get these out of people's hands," Sergei says, snatching the Seeder blade off the table again. "If we don't, I'm not going to pretend that decision represents me."

"He's right," Caro says. She sits down hard in her chair. "This is a mistake. Someone just got seriously hurt."

"Hang on," Francisco says, looking between Caro and Sergei. "Why are you ignoring the fact that people were already *being* hurt?" He points to Eli. "How many innocent people need to be attacked before we start looking for a proactive solution? If Eli or Sahir had something to defend themselves with, maybe none of this would have happened in the first place!"

"Do you even believe what you're saying?" Sergei says, turning on Francisco. "Or are you just parroting—"

"No, I'm *not* just parroting Eli," Francisco snaps, "and yes, I do believe what I'm saying, and I'm getting sick of you assuming I can't have my own opinions, just because I agree with someone other than you."

"Sergei," Eli says, "I'm lucky whoever gave me that shot didn't kill me. If something like this happens and you don't do anything, you're asking for it to happen again."

"Maybe it should happen again."

Eli blanches. Then she rises to her feet. "Excuse me?"

Sergei pushes on. "It's no wonder someone's trying to take matters into their own hands. You're so far gone you can't even see what you're doing anymore. Of course they stole the food instead of asking, when you've decided you can just do whatever you want, whenever you want!" He thrusts the blade toward the commander's seat. "You're not the only one who can learn how to fly this ship."

Eli and Sergei are staring at each other with an ugly look of realization.

"So," she says, "that's what you're trying to do. You and your petition. Just because you want to go back to the *Hermes*, you're going to throw away everything we've worked for to put someone else in the commander's seat."

"You're delusional. This has nothing to do with—"

"This is all part of it," Eli breaks in. "You know who took the food. You know who it is."

A ghost of dread flits across Sergei's face. "No," he starts, but she's already saying, "Tell me who. Tell me. Now." Her voice skews into a snarl as she advances on him. *"Tell me now!"*

I can see Sergei casting around for an answer. I can pinpoint Eli's moment of epiphany, the instant her face wipes blank.

"Irina." She turns to the door and calls, "Pieter!"

"No," Sergei yells. As the door slides open, he lunges for Eli, the blade still in his hand. Her eyes fix on it and widen.

Pieter, Matteo, and Luke absorb the sight in a split instant. They move as a perfectly coordinated unit. Pieter dives forward and crashes into Eli, knocking her out of the way. Matteo and Luke hurtle into Sergei. The blade flies out of his hand and clatters across the table, sliding to a stop in front of Caro, who leans back, her mouth hanging open.

It's over in seconds. The tangle of limbs becomes comprehensible again. Matteo and Luke have pinned Sergei's arms behind his back, and Sergei's nose is cracked, blood crawling across the bridge of his upper lip. Red streaks form sloppy webs across Matteo's forearm, marking where his skin met Sergei's bloodied face.

"Ninth floor," Eli pants, getting back to her feet, Pieter steadying her. "Get him to the ninth floor, n-now." She's not looking at Sergei but at the blade that lies, still quivering, on the table. Her eyes are glazed with fear and disbelief.

"No," Sergei yells as they force him through the door. "She was trying to do the right thing! I can talk to her. Just let me talk to—"

He's still yelling as they drag him around the corner and out of sight. Caro, Francisco, and I are frozen as we watch him disappear. "Are you all right?" Pieter says to Eli, grabbing the blade from the table and looking it over as if searching for bloodstains. "He didn't hurt you? We were listening, but I didn't see—"

"I'm all right. He didn't get to me." Eli is blinking hard, her face twisting. I see mistrust in her darting eyes, rage in her contorted mouth. "Pieter, Francisco, find Irina and bring her back here."

Francisco's first few steps are shaky, but soon he finds his stride, and he sets off down the hall with Pieter. I watch them slip out of sight, my sweating hands balled into fists.

Eli collapses into her seat at the table. As she ties back her hair, then splays her hands on the tabletop, I notice that her fingers are trembling. "Okay," she forces out. "I think we can end this tonight. Let's talk about what's next."

Sentences come from Eli's mouth, none of which sound real. She's talking about indefinite confinement for Sergei, saying that if he'd go for her with a knife, there's no way she can ever trust him again. She's suggesting Pieter as his obvious replacement on the Council. She's talking about bringing Sergei and Irina before the group for a talk, to ask them some questions, and I know she means interrogation. I hear these plans as Irina must have heard all our decisions from the beginning, through a sheet of doubt like rushing water, distorting everything.

But I don't know why I'm surprised. Of course Eli will do whatever it takes to recover the food. From the first words she spoke to me—the grim, clipped "Suit up"—I've known she is the consummate survivor. Isn't that why I've trumpeted her plans so confidently, believing in them the way I believed in the GFPC's directives, the way I believed in my own mother? Isn't that why, when she said we were the same, I wished it were true?

Eli has asked me a question, I think, but I can't speak. I still haven't moved. I picture Francisco and Pieter in the elevator, Sergei wrenched down the hall, and something is building up inside me. I try to imagine what Anis would do. I want to sit in the center of the track with him and talk for hours until I know what I think and feel. What would my parents do? The astronaut who could be aboard the *Hermes*? Would they chase after Luke, Matteo, and Sergei to make sure no one gets hurt? Would they stay here and talk with Eli, try and get through to her, make her see that all this has spun out of control?

Make up your mind, I think to myself, hating every instant I stand here immobilized, my body rigid with anxiety. A memory flashes through my mind from the year I turned thirteen. That October, I was finally tall enough to ride the Viper, a fuchsia-and-lime-green roller coaster at an amusement park two hours' drive from DC. My father came with Lilly and Marcus and me to the park, and we waited forty-five minutes in line, the whole apparatus twisting overhead like a problematic spine. We waited so long, but the closer we inched to the Viper, the steeper the painted curlicues looked, and the louder the screams of the people rocketing along in the shuttles sounded, and when the sunburned boy manning the line finally reached to scan me in, I ducked the marquee, and my friends were bulled ahead by the people in line, and I stood with my hands sweating against my bare thighs, refusing to look at my father and reveal that I was terrified. I was terrified that my skull might crack open on that brightly painted ride, or that my panic would ruin the day for my friends, or that I'd get sick in a way that someone would record, and everyone would see and remember forever. I was terrified, as always, of pain and judgment and ridicule, of letting everybody down.

Five years later, I've found new ways to paralyze myself. Now I'm afraid that I'll always regret ducking out from that line, that soon the fairgrounds will recede behind the shades of memory with everything else, lost to me forever. I'm afraid that I saw so much color in eighteen years on Earth that the rest of my life can only be a funnel toward a monochromatic point. I'm afraid that we will fail to find the seeds, or fail to keep the *Lazarus*'s thousands of parts working, and we'll collapse into disorder, and our parents' last efforts will go to waste. I'm afraid that we will all die alone out here.

But even more than these things, I'm afraid of what I see us all becoming in the name of survival. The ghosts of memory flicker and die. It's a vision of the future that comes to me now. Eli is hardened into a relentless commander, Caro into a keen-eyed tracker. There's Francisco, directing guards into every space that might have held a secret life, while I stand upon the hearth, mind empty and mouth open, echoing each directive. And this vision doesn't paralyze me. It makes me need to act.

I step toward the door.

"Leigh?" Eli says.

I take another step. I have to place my body between the present and that future. I have to stop the Council before we go an inch further, and I know who can help me.

"I have to talk to Irina," I say, and then I'm over the threshold. I'm gone.

———

When I reach the sixth floor, and Irina's cabin, her door is open. I find Francisco searching one of the bedrooms. "Irina ran," he says, sounding disgusted. "She's fast. Pieter went after her, I don't know where. . . . Maybe she's running to the place she hid the food."

But I know that's not right. Irina's been accused. Somehow I know she's fleeing to the one place she feels safe, the place she longed for beyond any other. It's where I would go, too.

I tear back down the hallway and out onto the balconies, hoping Irina has managed to lose Pieter on the way. I can't let him drag her back to the bridge in disgrace. I need to speak to her alone, not while standing alongside the Council.

The elevator doors have hardly cracked open before I'm forcing myself through. As I run the circumference of the balconies, approaching the video hall, I hear voices.

"Let go of that," comes the order. "I'm not going to say it again."

Shit, I think, kicking my heels up in a sprint. She hasn't shaken Pieter off, and all the friendly energy has leached out of his voice. He sounds all but unrecognizable. I only know it's him because he's speaking my language.

I race past door after door, and rounding a bend, I nearly collide with two of the VR guards. One is clutching a red mark on her neck, wheezing, eyes watery. The other is helping her down the hall, casting a terrified look over his shoulder. Just before I turn the corner, I hear something blunt whooshing through the air, emitting a hollow whistle.

I round the corner. The sight makes the bottom drop out of my stomach. Irina is twenty paces ahead, swinging the pipe that was hanging at Pieter's side earlier. Pieter dodges the blow, but he's blocking the door from Irina, refusing to step aside. Irina's face is stretched with panic.

"Stop," I yell, accelerating toward them. "You two, stop it!"

Irina is already lashing down again with the pipe. Pieter lifts an arm to block the blow. The pipe hits beneath Pieter's elbow with a sickening crack, and he yells, huddling over his arm.

Irina lunges for the door, and Pieter's other hand scythes out, gripping the blade that was supposed to plow furrows for seeds in the earth. I've seen the move a thousand times in games and movies: a sweeping plunge that cuts air, because the other person darts out of the way just in time. Sometimes half a dozen glittering strands of hair are caught in slow motion, sometimes a shallow cut is drawn onto the cheek or jaw. Except this time there's no careful choreography, no elegant evasion. Irina doesn't dodge. The knife sinks into the center of her chest.

I can't even cry out. There is no air to take. I stagger to a halt feet from them. Pieter looks to me, and we share an instant of eye contact before he looks back to Irina. I watch emotions revolve across Pieter's face, a spinning carousel. The anger wipes into shock, and then into denial, each with a sideways jerk of his head, as if he's trying to dislodge water from his ear. "No," Pieter says. He sounds confused, afraid.

A dreamy look has come over Irina. Her knees give way, and she falls forward. Pieter half catches her with his good hand before she can land on the knife hilt. "Wait," Pieter gasps. My pounding head, this unreal sight ahead of me—I feel bile rising in my throat like magma.

Pieter turns Irina onto her back. The silver column in her chest shivers with the motion.

When Pieter meets my eyes again, the denial is gone. In its place is conviction. He shoots to his feet, cradling his shattered arm. "I had to," he says. "You saw her, you saw what she was doing!"

I have nothing to say to Pieter. I can only look at him. There's an acne spot on his chin, near his mouth, and it reminds me of a kid I knew in sophomore year who had medicated putty he would dab onto his breakouts. He was sixteen, too.

"Eli," Pieter says, sounding like he might be sick, "I have to get Eli," and he lurches down the hall and around the bend.

In his absence, everything is suddenly so still. The only motion is my own body, still heaving for breath, and Irina's face tilting incrementally toward me. Her eyes transfix, lids batting lazily over the irises. *The med bay,* I think, but we have no doctors, no surgeons, no time. We have a handful of mostly untrained EMTs who would have no idea what to do.

"Please," she manages to say. Her eyes fix on the black arc of the door to the VR chamber.

Facing the entrance, I can't remember why I promised Eli I would never go in again. A feeling of absence comes into me, like when we gave this up, we sealed something of ourselves inside, something important, and we'll never get it back until we open the door.

I hook my fingers into the screen panel and roll it open. Inside it's as dark as a starless night.

The instant I lift Irina beneath the elbows, she lets out an agonized noise that doesn't subside. I back over the threshold as quickly as I can and tug her to the center of the room. "Where?" I whisper as I lower her to the floor. "Where do you want to go?"

She makes another painful sound, a tiny sob.

"I'll find it. Hang on." I dive for the control panel and start the system with clumsy fingers. The last preset somebody used is still loaded in: rain thrumming on a cobblestone road, Germanic gables crosshatching the streets. I tap through to the system's history. Everything that everyone's asked to see since we came aboard is displayed to me.

As I scroll upward, I see a record that doesn't match the long list of maintenance sims. It's a piloting simulation.

In the back of my mind, pieces are starting to assemble. But my brain feels split into parts, unable to communicate with itself, because Irina is letting out little noises, choking sounds, and my ankles feel like water, and my body seems to weigh a thousand pounds. I tap through the system's history and scroll back into the memory until I find the name—*Nizhnekamsk*. I twist the dial so the sound blooms all around us. The remote hush of wind in a forest. Birdsong in the morning.

A garden unfolds across the pixels, dark soft flower beds lined in front of a yellow-painted porch, a long road unwinding into a flat green distance. As the preset seals around us, I pant, "Hold on. I'm going to get Sergei. I'm going to—"

"No," Irina chokes, her voice thick. "I don't want," she manages to say, but that's all. I don't know what she means. Maybe she's saying she doesn't want him to see. Maybe she's saying she doesn't want to be alone when it happens.

"Okay," I whisper. My eyes and nose are burning. I sink to my knees at her side. When I was dashing through the ship, I had so many ideas of what I would say to her. I thought about how I'd apologize for every dodged question and evasive answer, then for the way we threw her in confinement. I imagined confessing that the VR room had sucked me in, too, and we had that in common. Then I'd ask her to visit Sahir and Jayanti, and the four of us would talk everything out; they could lash out at me and I'd sit there, I'd take it, I'd really listen. I'd try to connect to the girl Sergei described, the girl I overheard in her cabin—wounded by taunts in school halls, but loyal to anyone who saw her the way she wanted to be seen. I had a thousand words in mind to fix things. Now I'm looking down into her face and I can't find any of them.

"Hold . . ." she manages.

I maneuver her head into my lap with shaking hands. Her hair is soft under my fingers, her face contorted. "Like this?" I say.

She doesn't answer, just cracks her eyes open, two wet crescents reflecting the light that surrounds us. Her gaze travels across the scene. It's a beautiful day in early spring. The last patches of snow are melting in the distance, and wintry sun is falling onto us from a blue-white sky, lighting Irina's features, turning her flickering eyelashes to silver brushstrokes.

"It was all I wanted," she says.

I feel the muscles at the back of her neck go limp. The weight of her head rests fully in my cupped hands. Suddenly

I'm crying, shuddering, sobbing, but the people passing on the side of the road don't stop to look. That's the difference. Someone would have stopped in reality, yelled for help, knelt down and told us everything would be all right. That was the way things were back home.

———

When I enter the bridge, Francisco hasn't returned yet. Eli and Pieter are sitting at the table, Pieter's arm in a sling, his hands clean. He's staring out the windshield, catatonic. Down on the lower level of the bridge, Caro is working on the door records. I wonder if she knows.

Eli looks at the blood on my hands, then into my eyes. "Irina . . . she's . . ."

"Yeah." My voice has never felt more separate from me. I'm hearing all this like a recording, millions of miles away. "In the VR room."

Any trace of anger has gone from Eli's face. She balls her fists, pushing her knuckles against her closed eyes. I can see her neck between her wrists, see her swallow again and again. "This is my fault," she whispers. "It's my fault."

Yes, I want to say. And it's Pieter's for striking the blow. And it's mine for seeing that bin full of weapons and thinking it could be bumped onto a docket of discussion topics like a bureaucratic blip. I should have reacted the way Sergei did, yelled the way I yelled when I saw Matteo standing over Jayanti, wrenched my mouth open and let the outrage come. Every second I refused to act, I let us take a step closer to this.

"If I'd done this right," Eli says, "she wouldn't have gone there in the first place."

I can't speak. I can't argue that that was not the problem at all. I keep seeing the arc of Pieter's arm, the glittering blade, so false-looking, like some foil prop that should have crumpled on impact. I want to scrub the blood from my skin, then peel my skin away, too.

I told myself I'd do better after Sahir got hurt. I told myself that I'd move forward, that I would be selfless. But I have been, haven't I? Didn't I make what I thought were the right choices? Didn't I shove that book of memories into the drawer and resist the VR room? Didn't I hide even my feelings for Anis as if they were a selfish distraction? Didn't I banish every part of myself into shadowed corners in pursuit of a clear, well-lit path down the middle of the road? Didn't I follow Eli's lead?

I look into her face and feel my faith in her splinter.

She warned me the very first night. *You and me*, she said, *we're the same.*

She was right the whole time. We are identical. We're both unqualified kids who have no idea what we're doing, and as long as we continue to stand here in this command center and make our mistakes, people will continue to suffer.

My skin feels very cold. I can't remember ever feeling so small or so weak. I want my mom. I want my dad. I want someone to tell me it's going to be okay. I want someone to give me a procedure to follow, and I want that procedure to be based in centuries of human knowledge, and when everything goes wrong, I want to know, at least, that we did the best we could. Let the world end. I want to go home.

Home. As I think it, a candle lights inside me.

Weeks ago, I told Anis that I didn't want us to be alone, which feels right now like the only completely true thing I have ever said. Somewhere in the universe I want there to be someone who has the answers, someone who will take the pilot's seat and show us the right way, the way forward. A path lit by truth and decency and decades' expertise. That could all be out there, in sight of the planet Irina wanted to see one more time.

My mind is made up. *Go home, go home, go home*, it beats in me like a second heart.

"Please," I say to Eli, "take her out of there."

Eli nods. Seeming to draw strength from some painful well-spring in her body, she stands. Our first night, as her mother lay in the threshold of this room, I was strong for her. I see her resolving to be the same for me now.

"You stay here, okay, Leigh?" She takes me by the elbow and guides me toward the water fountain set into the bridge's wall. "Wash your hands off. We'll be back in ten minutes." She beckons to Pieter, and then they're gone, retreating down the hall.

When my hands are clean, I approach the rail and look into the lower level of the bridge.

"Are you ready?" I ask.

Hunched over the dashboard, Caro goes still. "Ready for what?"

"I saw a piloting simulation in the VR room's history, but Eli and Pieter haven't been in there since she got attacked. You saw that Eli was never going to turn the ship around, so you decided to teach yourself how instead. And all our ideas about someone wanting to steal a rover . . . none of that was true. You sedated Eli so you could practice at the dashboard that night." I hesitate. "There are no records of anyone's movements up here, are there? You stole the food so you could barricade yourself in here and fly the ship, and now that you've learned how, all you needed was Eli gone."

Caro looks up at me. There are tear tracks down her cheeks. "I didn't mean for any of this to happen," she whispers. "I didn't mean to give her an overdose. I didn't know Matteo would do that to Jayanti. I didn't know Pieter would . . . I didn't know . . ."

I nod, wordless.

She wipes her face with her wrist. "We could get someone aboard. We could give them more time, even if we don't make it in the end. I just wanted to do one thing that matters."

"I know." I glance over my shoulder at the door, then look back to Caro. "She's gone. Here's your chance."

CHAPTER 14

BACK

"Y̎ou have to act like this for over a month," Caro says, her fingers flying across the map of screens. "Can you?"

"Yes."

"Okay." She approaches me. "Get ready."

I close my eyes and brace myself.

She punches me in the temple, in the jaw, in the nose, three quick shots that break me open. Blood falls down my lip. I reel back but straighten up quickly. "All right?" she says as I cross my wrists behind my back. She wraps them in yellow cables, pulling until the skin of my fingers turns purple. She winces as if she can feel it, too.

"It's okay," I say, licking the blood from the seam of my mouth. "It's good."

Caro opens one of the service doors under the dashboard, rummages arm-deep in its innards, and extracts three plastic-wrapped columns of food. Then she returns to the pilot's screen. She writes in a mixture of pictographs—a shortcut language I've seen her using before—and characters drummed into the command prompt.

"Can we seal the door?" I ask.

"I have to revoke Eli's ID permissions first so she can't get in. Here."

I open my mouth, and she inserts a balled-up cloth until it presses up at my soft palate. Then I jog up the steps, move over the threshold, and lie prone in the hall as if she's struck me down.

The seconds creep by as Caro works. Soon a minute has passed. Three. Five. I hear her muttering to herself at the lower level.

My head twitches up from the floor, my ears trained. I pray to God those aren't voices I'm hearing down the hall, but soon they're too clear to deny. I want to warn Caro, but when I test a sound through the gag, it's unintelligible.

Then the ship begins to turn. It's a fraction of a fractional degree, so as not to send us all rocketing off our feet. I feel it instead like nausea, deep in my stomach. Caro has overridden Eli's course, complete with a passcode only she knows. We're going back.

The voices down the hall are turning to shouts, clearer every second. For an instant that seems to last an hour, there's no sign of the final, vital step—the locking of the bridge.

Then the nearby control panel lets out a monotone beep, and the huge, heavy doors begin to whir shut behind me. But they're moving so slowly—too slowly?—and with my hands tied behind my back, face horizontal, I see Pieter and Eli angled around the corner of the hall as if they're falling sideways through space. I begin to scream through my gag.

The door is halfway shut. Pieter and Eli tear toward me, pain twisting Pieter's face as his broken arm bounces in its sling. *Close, close, close,* I think, even as I'm forcing raw, panicked noises as if to galvanize them onward.

I look back and dare to hope. The crack in the door is small— too small for a body to fit through?

But even as I think it, Pieter shoves his good arm through the crack, and the instant the door touches his skin, it freezes. Like an elevator door, it knows he's there. It wants to keep him safe.

The door reverses direction. Slowly, agonizingly, it glides open again, and my nausea is increasing, because they're going to find Caro inside—they're going to hurt her, to interrogate her the way Eli was describing, anything to get that passcode out of her and regain control of the ship.

Then Eli is inside. I watch her move at a diagonal, my head craned up from the floor. I wait for her to snarl something at Caro, but she just pants, "Where is she?"

I hear the clattering of footsteps as Pieter descends into the lower bridge. A click and whine as he tugs open the bathroom door. "Not here," Pieter yells.

"Come back, come here. Help me with Leigh."

Their footsteps pad at my side. Pieter kneels to work at the cables around my wrists with his good hand while Eli teases the gag out of my mouth.

"You okay?" she says as I gasp for breath. Pieter tugs the cables away and lets out a sympathetic hiss. I've been twisting my wrists to leave red stripes of friction burn behind.

"What happened?" he asks. "What did she do?"

"She was waiting for me when I came out of the bathroom," I say wetly, allowing a drop of blood to slide out from my lips. I let my eyes wander as if I'm delirious, but I don't miss the look they exchange, their concern hardening into anger.

"Here." Eli helps me to my feet, and we reenter the bridge. My head is properly aching now. I don't understand how Caro did it. The upper and lower levels are deserted, and where the five weeks of food were stacked on the dashboard before, there's now only a green message reading *New flight path confirmed.* None of the cabinets are large enough to hold her. Did she somehow fit into one of the ventilation shafts?

Pieter breaks the silence. "This is her fault." There's something fanatical in the way he says it, like he desperately needs to believe it's true. "The whole thing is Caro's fault. If she'd come clean after Jayanti got hurt, none of this would have happened."

"You're right," Eli says, quiet and hoarse. When my mother was angry, she became a storm, her words thunder, her glare electricity. But Eli's anger has whittled away something vital from her, and now something lean and predatory wears her face.

"But where is she?" I let the question tremble. "And where's Irina?"

"Irina's in the Menagerie," Eli says. "To keep her body preserved until we can give her a burial. . . . I don't know about Caro." As she regards the empty bridge, her mouth flattens to a slash. "But we're going to find out."

I'm in the elevator when Eli's voice comes over the PA: *Attention, all crew. Gather in the atrium in ten minutes for an urgent meeting. Thank you.*

I check the messages on my tablet. Still nothing.

When I reach the eighth floor, I find Anis halfway down the hall. We both stop in our tracks, like the avoidance of the past few days is a physical barrier. He's bleary, his black hair tufted out in every direction, eyes glued into slits with recent sleep. But with one look at my injured face, he seems to awaken all at once. "Leigh?" he whispers, horror spreading across his face. "What happened to you?"

I feel light-headed, on the verge of breaking down again. On top of every idiotic thing I've done in the last week, I shut him out for nothing; it was never him. I want to tell him everything, need to let all this out of me, but there's no time.

"I need your help," I whisper.

He doesn't question. He just strides into a nearby vacant cabin, beckons me in, and shuts the door behind us.

"Caro turned the ship around," I tell him.

As his mouth falls open, I explain how she's changed the flight path, how she's locked Eli out of the system. My words are slow and labored, but he asks small, coaxing questions, and finally I reach the end. "We tried to close off the bridge, lock Caro in to fly the ship, but Eli and Pieter arrived too quickly. Now she's . . ."

I check my tablet's messages again. This time, a new chat from Caro has appeared. I hasten to show him. *In ninth floor Systems Wing. Storeroom in Scrubber 6.*

"You heard Eli call a meeting," I say. "I have to be there, but I need you to get Caro from here to somewhere safe, before

Eli starts deploying everyone to search the ship. Somewhere she won't be found."

"That spot in the water treatment plant."

I close my eyes, a knot untying in me. "Yes. Perfect. It's close. . . . You might be able to get her there before the meeting even starts."

When I open my eyes again, Anis is looking at me with something like admiration. "You planned this with Caro?"

Shame creeps through me. "No. I'm just helping. It doesn't matter."

"It does," he says with a smile, moving to touch my arm, but I shrink back. He doesn't understand yet. He thinks I acted out of nobility or morality, that my actions mean anything. When he finds out about Irina, he won't be able to look at me, let alone want to touch me.

Anis's smile falters. He redirects the motion as if he never meant to reach for me, his fingers tugging at the shoulder of his uniform instead. But as I watch his steady hands, I wish I hadn't moved away. Selfishly, I want him to hold my reddened wrists, to trace the sensitive bands of skin torqued crimson, to make some part of this recede.

The images come back to me, the feeling of Irina's body in my arms, the moment her face went still, sunlight playing across her features.

"Leigh?" Anis says, and I realize I've been staring at the wall with my eyes so wide that they've begun to burn.

"Irina's dead," I say hoarsely.

Confusion ripples across Anis's face, his brows drawing into a tight line. "What?" he whispers.

"There was a fight at the VR room. It was Pieter. He . . ." I lose my way in the sentence, blinking hard, fists curling. No—I can't do this now. Ten minutes, Eli said, and I've spent five of those explaining...and I don't want him to know. I study Anis's honest face. When he finds out the part I played in all this, I don't think he'll ever forgive me. I don't think I deserve forgiveness. All I'll have is the memory of the way he's looking at me right now, his concern and trust, the way he believes I'm better than I really am.

"Okay," I say, sealing the moment into the past. "Let's go."

———

As I slink through the atrium, people turn and watch. Some offer sympathy or ask questions, but nothing penetrates. I'm moving toward the hearth, where the digital fire flickers on and on. Overhead the sunspot is dark. Everyone looks gray.

For the first time, I don't climb up onto the hearth. Eli is already standing there, flanked by Pieter and Francisco, but she climbs down when she sees me. "You okay?" she says.

"Okay," I say weakly. Caro didn't pull her punches. My face feels full, achy, downward drooping. The bridge of my nose is throbbing.

"Sit down," Eli says. "We'll handle it."

I settle into a chair on the outskirts. More people join the group, hissing to one another, a sound like the brush of long grass in night wind.

Francisco is the first to speak. "Everyone. Quiet, please," he says, his face waxen. "We called this meeting to give you bad news." He works hard to jerk each syllable out, as if his voice is a disobedient animal he's yanking along on a leash. "It's about Irina Volkova. She...She died earlier tonight. She'd attacked Pieter with a pipe, and he had to defend himself."

The group is so still that they look suddenly smaller, fifty bodies huddled in a space that could have held half a thousand. My eyes search out Sahir and Jayanti before I realize they must still be in the med bay. It seems unbelievable that Jayanti's concussion happened only hours ago.

Eli steps up to Francisco's side. Compared to her larger-than-life image on the softscreen, she looks fragile. "This didn't need to happen," she says in a low voice that still carries through the hush. "Everyone's felt the ship turning by now. Caro Omondi changed our course to head back to the *Hermes*. She let us believe Irina was the thief, and chase after her, and get into a fight with her, all so we'd be distracted while she hijacked the ship. She stole food and wasted medicine, knowing everyone here could starve. We're already starving. And if we don't turn the ship around soon, things are going to get even worse."

The control in Eli's voice intensifies. "It's my fault. I should have known this could happen after the first attack at the VR room. Caro got obsessed with going back, and this is what happens. I've been saying this in Council meetings for weeks, but we should have been having this conversation as a crew, especially after that petition some of you signed. The problem is that we're still hanging on to Earth. Even me. It's everywhere."

She points to the softscreen, to the countdown clock to Antaeus. "Monday," she reads off the screen. "Our last day on Earth was a Monday. Every Monday morning, I think of how it was raining at sunrise, and around eight p.m., I think of the last sunset. My mom and I were in our rooms in the complex, and she said, 'After dinner, let's go aboard, and I'll teach you how to scan for asteroids.'" She takes a shaky breath. "So we went aboard, and I was asking her all these questions. We were there until the eruptions started. She launched the ship, but at the last second before liftoff, she realized the Planters were empty. That was where I found her. She'd fallen off the catwalk and died here."

The *Lazarus*'s ambient hum is all around us. It sounds almost mournful.

With the firelight playing behind her, Eli's features are invisible. "I told myself we wouldn't lose anyone else. I failed. Now I am going to figure out how to correct our course if it's the last thing I do. I'm not letting the rest of us starve." She steps to the edge of the hearth. "And we've got to move on, starting now. I want us to make this Year Zero on a new calendar, with new days and new months. I want us to close off the Catalog; it's too much of a reminder. I want us to make our future our entire priority, because the end of the world means the beginning of the world, and we've got to get it right, because we don't get another chance." She looks around the dim atrium. "I want to take a vote."

There's no contest. Soon so many arms have risen, shimmering like icicles in the firelight, that I can no longer see the gaps between them. I don't want to join them, but I have to be Caro's ticket into the bridge when it comes time to dock with the *Hermes*. When the astronaut comes aboard, when we have a new pilot, none of this will last. Until then, I have to blend in.

So I raise my hand. I watch as they plan the calendar. The new year will have two hundred days, divided into forty weeks of five days apiece. I watch them rename Sunday to Starday, Monday to Moonday. The week's other three days take a bit more time, but eventually they're decided. Luday, after the ship's chief engineer, without whom we'd be choking to death back on Earth. Saraday, after Eli's mother, who should have been the one at the helm. And Newday, after the thing we're chasing.

I watch them set new rules. "Until we find Caro," Francisco says, "we'll have a roll call twice a day to make sure everybody else is accounted for. Curfew is effective at nine p.m. through eight a.m., and we're putting training on hold. Except for ship upkeep, every hour will be devoted to searching the ship for Caro and the food she stole."

"I'm sorry we have to do this," Eli says. "But we have to find her and fix this. Everything will be normal again soon. I promise." Like an afterthought, she says, "I wish everything were different."

I think of Irina's pixel-bright eyes sinking shut, and I wish the same thing. I wish this were all a dream, and if anybody were hurt, even as lightly as a pinch, we would all rise up from our beds in the sweaty summer air, jolted awake, and look outside to see a stand of pines or a city street.

———

The walk to the end of the ninth floor feels interminable. When Francisco and I reach Sergei's cell, we stand perfectly still and watch the closed door. For minutes, we do nothing.

"What do we say?" Francisco whispers.

I shake my head.

"I don't know if I can do this." Francisco backs away from the door. His lips are parted, eyes glazed. "This is all wrong. None of this should have happened."

I hesitate. "He would want you to be there."

"What? Of course he wouldn't. He—he hates me now."

"He doesn't hate you," I say, but at the same time I think of Sergei's disgust when he looked at us in the bridge.

"After this, he will." Francisco turns away, speaking under

his breath. "He'll want me to say it was all Eli's fault, our fault, but it's not. Caro could have stopped it. We were just taking precautions. . . . We were trying to help everyone." He buries one hand in his hair. "I've been trying to help this whole time, I've been trying to get all this under control. I needed his help, so why wasn't he helping us?" His eyes stray to the door. "I can't do this, I can't watch him blame us for this."

"Francisco—"

He takes another step away from the door, tugging at his sleeves. "It should just be you. You saw it happen. I'll—I'll wait here and make sure no one disturbs you. Or—no, I'll go back to the bridge, we need to plan the hunt for Caro. We can't waste any time. I need—"

"*Francisco.*"

His eyes lock on to mine, and I see the shame and fear and residual horror there.

"If you don't come," I say quietly, "he'll think you don't care."

He swallows. I can see his pulse going in his throat.

"You don't have to say anything. I'll do the talking."

Francisco closes his eyes. His hands move unconsciously, straightening his appearance, creating order. Then I tap in the access code, and the door slides open. Sergei leaps up from the sofa as we enter. He opens his mouth as if he's planned out what he wants to say, but then he sees my face.

"What happened to you?" he says, staring.

I touch my swollen nose. "I got punched."

He takes this in stride and discards it. "The ship turned around. I felt it."

We nod.

"What's happening? Who did this?"

"Caro," I say.

Whatever he was expecting, it wasn't that. "Caro? She—she convinced Eli?"

"No. She disappeared after locking in our new course. Eli is focusing everyone's efforts on finding her."

Sergei's mouth hangs open for a moment. Then he closes his eyes, and comprehension washes over his face. "She stole the food."

I see the beginnings of guilt and regret in his face, the need to apologize to his sister for accusing her. That look breaks something in me. I try to let some vital part of me issue out and away so that I can say what I need to say, but it's all building up like steam.

"I'm so sorry" is what comes out of me. I told myself I wouldn't cry, it would be too self-indulgent, but everything is in my voice anyway.

Sergei looks at Francisco's ashen face, then at me, clearly unable to speak.

"Eli thought it was Irina," I whisper. "Irina got scared and went for the VR room. Pieter chased her down. I went after them. I tried to . . . It . . ." I stop talking. I don't want to defend myself. Some part of me hopes he'll rage at me, even that he'll hurt me, that he'll storm over to me and shatter something that deserves to be shattered.

There's nothing like that. Something is extinguishing in Sergei's face. He sinks to the sofa, his big shoulders shuddering, and covers his face with his hands. Francisco and I watch him for several minutes as, little by little, he stills. His shaking hands come down from his face and clasp in his lap. His complexion is blotchy, his eyes red, his lips moving wordlessly.

Francisco seems to have been mustering the strength to speak. Finally he says, "Do you want..."

"Leave," Sergei says, not looking up at us. "Get out."

I return to the eighth floor. I wish I could run, but I'm so tired, my brain filled with fog. My night miles with Anis feel as long ago as if they were part of Earth. I drift berth by berth down the hall, looking over every threshold at every empty bed. With each doorway, I imagine a different person standing beyond, a different potential astronaut.

I walk all the way to the end of the wing and find Anis waiting for me outside his door, which is closed as always. "Is Caro safe?" I whisper, hurrying up to him.

"Yeah. We'll need to get her some supplies. Water, obviously, and a way to charge her tablet. She mentioned writing a docking program."

"How did she get out of the bridge?"

"She went out through the airlock and climbed to the nearest exit."

I let loose a slow breath. Of course—the bridge's airlock is stocked with extravehicular activity suits. "Quick thinking."

"She's safe," Anis says. "We're safe."

I don't feel safe. I hold on to my elbows, my fingertips pressing hard against bone, as though my body might fall to pieces if I let go.

Anis studies me. I know he wants to ask about Irina. The thought of her shudders through me over and over again. I see her stricken face in the Menagerie. I see her flushing red during our arguments, sticking stubbornly to her principles even when everybody laughed at her for it. I hear her telling Sergei she just wanted him to care about her. I see her motionless features and feel the weight of her head in my hands. I see everything that led us here, and laid out in the past, it feels so inevitable, but if it was inevitable, shouldn't I have predicted it? And if I could have predicted it, how could I have let it happen?

"Here," Anis says softly. "Come inside."

He presses his thumb to the entry pad. The door to his cabin slides open, and for the first time in hours, my mind goes blissfully blank.

The room seems to vibrate with color and texture. Anis's cabinets are packed with books, their spines rainbowed outward. A painting stands on the desk, smeary and modern and taller than me, and on the bedside table is a bowl filled with porcelain beads of blue and black and white, like koi eyes. There's a woven rug and a small oaken chest and a scattering of neon cushions.

"Anis," I say faintly, walking inside. It's like walking back in time. There's another row of books on the windowsill, cast-iron bookends at each side, twin sculptures of Atlas holding the firmament upon his shoulders. Another painting, its frame leafed in gold, the dotted faces of dandelions upturned toward a blast of blue sky. Scattered across his sofa are plastic cases that hold cassette tapes and glimmering digital discs and tar-black records. They're in meticulous stacks; he's been categorizing them. A portable planetarium sits in the corner, aimed upward so Cassiopeia revolves dreamily across his ceiling.

"So this is why you didn't let me in."

He nods. "I should have told you I didn't take the food, but I wanted you to trust me."

"I do trust you," I murmur. "But I also know you."

His lips curve in an unhappy smile, and I know he under-stands. This is what conviction does. It makes you into some-one who could care so much that they'd strike a blow. It fills empty space with passionate color.

"I moved them the first week," he says, "when I couldn't sleep. I walked through the Catalog for hours every night. I thought this would help me get some rest—if the cabin felt more like home. Even though my dad would be furious."

"Where did you put it all when they inspected you?"

"Halfway up the hall," he said.

"They could have caught you moving it."

"I know."

The thought occurs to me that the Catalog cases are moisture-controlled and acid-free, that the artifacts need safety and preservation, that this is shortsighted and even selfish. But then I stop in front of the abstract, and I feel as if I'm looking out a window into rain. I see veils of water flapping with the wind, shattering in long waves against the streets. I remember how a room used to be a piece of lifelong installa-tion art, how the places we lived were a little bit alive, too. In my childhood room in Richmond, I used to stick glue dots to the corners of posters and press them to my walls, and when I was tired of them, I peeled them away carefully to spare the paint. I had a running trophy in glittering gold and purple atop my dresser, beside hand-built bowls I'd pinched together in pottery workshops, which came out so parched from the kiln that their edges were separated like an old man's teeth. There's something empty in me, a kind of deprivation as acute and familiar as hunger.

"I should have listened to you," I say numbly.

"Leigh . . ."

"You were telling me this whole time. Irina was, too. You were warning me."

"No, we weren't," Anis says. "I didn't know this would happen. None of us could have known."

"You would never have *let* it happen."

He lets out a soft, disbelieving laugh. "But I did."

I look at him, not understanding. "What?"

"Everything we talked about. I never said any of it in public, did I? Easier to stay quiet so no one would judge me or even think about me, and then run off to complain to someone who's too kind to tell me to shut my mouth." He looks tired, faintly disgusted. "If I weren't such a coward, I would have said something about the guards or the cells. Maybe other people would have agreed."

I shake my head. "It might not have done anything."

"That's what I'm saying. You could have done things differently, too, and it might not have fixed anything, either."

"No, you—" I blink hard, burning spreading through my eyes, through the top of my nose. "You don't understand."

"What don't I understand?"

I don't want to say it. I don't want him to have the mental image. I don't want him to hate me. But I can't hold it in myself anymore. "I was there," I choke out. "I was running...came around the corner right as he—Pieter—" My face is too warm, my shoulders shaking. I can't stop it anymore. There is no control left. "I keep seeing it happen. The knife just went into her."

Looking stricken, Anis reaches for me, but I feel a surge of self-loathing and back away. I don't want to contaminate him. I spread one hand across my face, crying properly now. "If I'd just r-run a little faster, if I'd left thirty seconds ea-earlier...I could've said s-something else, I could have—"

"Leigh." He curls his hands around my wrists. "Don't do this to yourself. You have to stop."

"I can't," I gasp, spots popping in my eyes. My legs tremble violently. I am falling open like a sandcastle under a hard swell. "I hate this place. I didn't want to know any of this. I want to go home."

Anis enfolds me in his arms, and I close my eyes and feel as if I'm falling into a dark and quiet place. No thoughts, no memories. He runs one hand up into my hair and down again, brushing the back of my neck. He kisses my forehead, my mouth, making reassurances that can't penetrate. I don't think, except about the repetitive motion of his hand, except about how he is warm and sturdy and tastes like nothing, like my own hunger. I want to go home, but I'm scared we're already there.

PART III

NEWDAY

CHAPTER 15

THE ORDER OF
THE REPUBLIC

38 DAYS TO THE *HERMES*

We bury Irina in a plot of what should have been coriander. Her uniform has to be cleaned, stitched, and repurposed for future generations, so she's placed naked in the soil before the ceremony, her body covered by the earth except for her arms, neck, and head, as if a dark blanket has been drawn up over her. Pieter doesn't attend the interment.

Sergei stands at the front, flanked by Luke and Francisco. He doesn't speak, or even move, but deep in the deadened expression is an ember of rage.

I accompany them back to the ninth floor. Francisco keeps glancing over at Sergei, who doesn't meet his eyes.

Once Sergei is back in his cell and Luke and Francisco have disappeared around the corner, I slip inside. Sergei, standing at the observation window, turns around.

"What do you want?" he says.

"To tell you the truth."

He lets out a scathing laugh. "That'd be a first for you." He rubs hard at his five o'clock shadow. "If you three had taken anything I'd said seriously, this wouldn't have happened. This didn't come out of nowhere. Irina was right about what we were doing the whole time, but you won't even admit that. Caro's the only one who came to her senses, and now you're pretending that this search for her is because you care so much that Irina died? You hated my sister! I bet you're glad she's gone!"

I let the words pierce into me. My eyes burn, but the rage and hatred are satisfying, too. Of course he feels this way.

"Well?" he demands. "You aren't going to say anything? No perfect answer to make me calm down? No telling me I'm being irrational?"

"No."

Sergei's hands curl into fists. "What's the *truth*, then? Say it."

"I did come to my senses." My voice isn't much more than a whisper. "I know it doesn't fix anything. But Caro and I are working together to make sure the ship connects to the *Hermes*. I know you wanted to go back for the astronaut, so I thought I'd ask if you wanted to help."

Sergei's mouth is still slightly open, his fists balled. He's looking at me as if he hasn't understood a word I've said.

"I'll give you some time to think about it." I swallow hard. "And I'm really sorry, Sergei. For everything I didn't do."

I turn and go.

37 DAYS TO THE *HERMES*

It's eighty steps from Anis's cabin to the stairwell. Six flights of steps from the eighth floor to the fifth, where we can come out onto the balconies without the cameras catching us. Sixty steps to skirt the balconies, and then we reach the entrance to the Catalog, and I can stop holding my breath. Maybe we're not entirely safe in the Catalog, but it's easier to hide among the artifacts.

Anis lifts the abstract painting back into its case but can't seem to make himself lock it away. I do it for him, pressing the glass gently into place. It clicks, then whirs, flattening itself into its frame to create a tight seal. The hunt will cycle back to the eighth floor soon enough, and if anyone saw Anis's room full of stolen artifacts, he'd be locked in confinement within the hour.

So we creep through the Catalog, returning everything we've bundled into pillowcases: a wicker basket, the portable planetarium, a ceramic vase, a small beaded pillow, and the last of his books. Then we sneak back to the eighth floor, moving like ants through the *Lazarus's* tunnels.

Anis comes to a stop outside my cabin, eyeing the closed door curiously. "Is anything hidden in here?"

"What do you think?" I try to smile. "No. It's nothing."

"I still want to see."

I open the door, and he steps inside. I shouldn't feel ashamed about my bare walls, my lifeless surfaces, my barren living room, offering no evidence I was ever here, but I do. I open my bedroom door. The wrinkled bedcovers are the only proof of me.

"Like I said, it's nothing," I start, turning on my bedroom light, but when I look back, Anis has my notebook in his hands.

One of my hands lifts instinctively toward it. I haven't touched that book since I found Sahir outside the VR chamber. I tried too hard to forget about it.

"This was in your bag that night?" Anis asks.

I nod.

"Is it a diary?"

"Sort of. It's hard to explain."

He slips his thumb beneath the cover, asking a question, waiting for permission. And part of me wants to tell him no, to snatch the book away. At the same time, I want him to read my memories and feel something. The desires for privacy and intimacy war inside me, these contradictory hopes for secrecy and connection. I don't want him to know, but I want him to understand. I want to hide. I want to be seen.

I climb onto my bunk. As I lie back, my tired body seems to melt, losing form into the mattress. Anis settles on the bed beside me, legs outstretched.

"Read it," I say.

When he opens the cover, I look away, into the window. Laid atop the stars, there is a smaller, skewed version of him sitting in the window's gleaming ceramic. I watch him reading me. I watch time pass upon his face, a line forming and then smoothing away between his eyebrows, and his mouth pulling into and relaxing out of a smile, and that tingle of exposure I felt weeks ago in the stairwell returns, all over my body now, making me feel naked.

"Your friends," he says after a few minutes. "You didn't tell me their names before."

"Lilly." It's the first time I've said her name in nearly a month and a half.

"And this boy. Marcus."

Anis's voice is a bit too casual. Surprised, I say, "What, are you jealous?" I realize I'm close to smiling. My mouth has to work to hold the shape.

"No. I don't know." He clears his throat. "Obviously you were very close."

"Didn't you have friends who were girls?"

"Not this kind of friend." He runs the tip of his thumb over a paragraph about Lilly and Marcus and me at an aquarium. I read a sentence and feel a sharp pang. I have to look away.

For once, Anis doesn't press me. He turns the page, and I slip under my bedsheets. I lift my tablet from the bedside table and try to focus on the bullet points of the plan that we've been developing with Caro, but my eyes keep straying to Anis's figure in the window.

He reads another dozen pages before speaking again. "It's strange to read about your mother."

"Why, because she seems different than she does on TV?"

"No. Because she seems the same."

I lower my tablet, biting the inside of my cheek. I still feel the defensive instinct to tell Anis he doesn't really know her, that he can't understand, but there's something else there, too.

"I'm angry with her," I whisper, sinking down into the pillow. "And all our parents. I trusted the GFPC so much on Earth. I used to feel so sure that those plans were the best we could do, and if everybody just kept quiet and cooperated, everything would work perfectly. My parents really seemed to believe that. They let me believe it, too. And now I keep thinking, maybe if it hadn't taken me so long to . . . maybe . . ."

I can't make myself say Irina's name. Anis settles his hand on my wrist. I tangle my fingers with his and squeeze until the burn has faded from my eyes.

"Anyway," I manage to say, "I'm sure your dad was more of a skeptic."

He lets out a quiet scoff. "Not at all. He voted yes on every single proposal the GFPC put on the table. Some of the plans he hadn't even bothered to read. He thought we should get it over with."

"Did you talk to him about it?"

"Of course."

"You couldn't change his mind?"

"No."

I sink down against Anis's side, head resting on his shoulder. We both study the open page of my memory diary, a description of my parents basking on the coast at Goldport Island, my father's feet submerged in wet sand.

"Honestly," I murmur, "it seems like we all felt the same way on Earth. Like none of us had any control over anything."

"Except Eli."

"No. Especially Eli. She was miserable. She might've felt more powerless than any of us."

"Well, now she has all the control she wants." Anis traces a pattern on the back of my hand. "It's depressing, isn't it? There are only fifty of us in this place. We can finally do what we want, and what we say goes. But it doesn't feel like we've said anything new."

I focus on the motions of his fingertips over my hand, my mouth growing dry. I know he's talking about how our cooperation has splintered in all the ways our parents' did. And maybe that's just the way it is. Maybe we've all inherited a little too much to break out of our cycles; maybe, even if I'd lived out my old daydreams of escaping into the wild, I would never have been able to set down all the things my parents handed me. On the grand scale, I know that what we've done to each other within the walls of this ship is nothing new. But on the small scale it's a different story.

"What I'm saying is new," I tell him, my voice quiet. "Even to Lilly or Marcus, I don't—I've never been like this with anyone."

Anis's hand stills on mine. I glance up at him. The softness in his expression is almost painful to see, but I make myself hold his gaze and ask, "Have you?"

"I think you know the answer to that question."

"Maybe I want to hear it from you."

And he tells me.

35 DAYS TO THE *HERMES*

Every day, when I bite into the halved meal bar I'm eating for dinner, I think of the Old Planet. That's what we're supposed to call it now. Earth will be the name of our next home planet, the Pilot says, whereas the Old Planet is historical, no longer relevant to our lives. When I made this announcement at the start of the week, there was some uncertain giggling, but since then, every time I've heard the words "Old Planet," they've sounded a little bit less like a joke.

As for the actual history of the planet, those records have been locked away, where they'll stay locked for twenty years. After that, our only world will be this world, and the Catalog will reopen, and educating ourselves about the Old Planet won't be about yearning but about archaeology.

For now, though, I'm still yearning. It's a hungry feeling, or maybe I'm confusing it with my hunger. On Earth, my favorite foods were the ones that swam, dumplings or eggs that bobbed in translucent broth. I liked fishing in smooth curries for chunks of soft meat. I was always adventurous with food, eating salmon by age eight, downloading restaurant reviews I found online so I could hunt for those words in whatever I ate next. "This is a subtle and piquant dish," I declared over dinner when I was nine, and my mother traded a glance with my father and choked out, "Yep, sure is."

So I've been having dreams about variety. Whenever I sleep, there are banquets fit for Valhalla, and I work through them in a slow, systematic way. Nothing is divided into courses. It's all there for me at once. Steamed pastries wrapped in bamboo leaves release flowers of steam when I peel them open. Nuggets of vegetable form conga lines on wooden skewers, and when I affix my front teeth and slide them free, I look down at the new strip of revealed wood, pale beside the sections of the skewer that were tanned over a flame and made golden with crisped juices.

And the meat. Some of these flanks and wings and chests are so tender that I hardly believe they're lab-grown; they seem so soft, so vulnerable, that I hate to bite in; I hate to stop biting; it makes me feel savage. There are slips of salami as thin and desiccated as paper, which I crisscross on tough briquettes of bread topped with a swipe of fleshy cheese. Greasy pods of duck meat burst against my tongue, and the sense memory is so flavorful that I realize new complexities, ones I never appreciated when I was there. No matter how much I eat, I'm never more than comfortably full. No matter how much I take in, there's always something new. I wake up and try to cling to the feeling of excess. I've forgotten how it felt to have that much of anything, to walk into a supermarket and see aisles exploding with color.

By day, I don't speak about the dreams. That kind of conversation would hurt the Pilot's plans for the *Lazarus*. She's
outlined three major goals: Reorientation, Fortification, and
Unification. The first obviously refers to reorienting the ship,
but the new calendar, the closure of the Catalog, the burying of the histories, and our new terminology are all part of
Reorientation, too.

Fortification is a more ambitious goal. Having a well-armed
guard and a well-trained crew is the first step, but that's not all
Eli wants. Along with our minds, we need to fortify our bodies
and our numbers. To that end, we've designed a new physical education course, and Eli and Francisco have gone back
to work on their plans for reproduction aboard the *Lazarus*.
They've chosen twenty-three as the optimum age for a first
pregnancy, with a child every two years after that, ideally with
the same partner, until menopause. To help everyone adjust to
the idea, Eli's also approved programs that focus on childrearing and early education.

We haven't implemented any of these programs yet, of
course. The world is on hold while we starve.

In the meantime, we can focus on goal three: Unification.
The crew congregates every evening in the atrium, gathered
before the hearth like a family. Eli asked Fatima to design
a flag for the Republic, and she returned with a small circle
of green encapsulated by a rectangle of white, a seed of life
pulsing in negative space. The next day, we strung up the
largest softscreen we had, and a 3-D rendering of the flag
ripples there above the hearth, overlooking the atrium, finely
pixelated, drawing us together. There is no more dissent, not
even the slightest disagreement. I deliver announcements to

blissful, obedient silence. After curfew, the body of the ship is deserted. Sahir patrols dutifully; Jayanti is still recovering out of sight. We are unified. We have something to hunt.

---

32 DAYS TO THE *HERMES*

I've visited Sergei every other day since Irina's burial. I've convinced Eli that it's inhumane for him not to have social contact, and she thinks it's better that it's me than someone else. So far, he hasn't made any mention of my confession. He's barely spoken, choosing instead to sit on his bunk, staring at notes for his training courses on his tablet screen. I stay for an hour, perched on the sofa, occupying myself with my own training materials, before leaving.

But halfway through my fourth visit, he says:

"So, you have a plan with Caro."

He hasn't stood from his bunk, or even looked up from his tablet.

"Yes," I reply. "We're working on it."

"And?"

"When she turned the ship around, she set us onto a flight path that'll bring the *Lazarus* back to the *Hermes*. But we still need to find a way to connect the two when we get there. Caro is working on writing a program that'll get us into synchronous orbit with the station, but the actual docking process will have to be manual."

He's quiet for so long that I assume he's gone back to ignoring me. I return to my own tablet, but then there's motion in the corner of my eye, and I startle as I realize he's standing over the sofa, arms folded.

"How am I supposed to do anything from in here?"

"I can get you out."

"I thought I had 'an indefinite sentence for attempted murder,'" he says.

"You do. I mean I can secretly smuggle you out. The question is when. If I did it now, they'd know it was me, and—"

"I still don't understand why you're doing this." The telltale angry red is rising into his cheeks. "This whole time, you only cared about not offending anybody, and now this? Is it just because you feel so guilty?"

I look past him, out the observation window, at the opalescent ripple of the radiation sail. "No. I'm just ... It's like Irina said. I'm not used to acting for myself. I got used to the way my life was on Earth. Four hundred million people watching everything I did."

Sergei paces from one end of the cabin to the other for several minutes, scrubbing at his sleepless eyes. I don't push him to answer.

Eventually he lowers himself onto the opposite end of the sofa. "So, if we want to connect to the *Hermes*, you'll need to get into the bridge."

"Yes, and get Caro into the commander's seat. She's spending this time learning how to dock the ship."

A shadow passes over Sergei's features. "Does Francisco ... ?"

"He doesn't know about this."

Sergei looks down at his hands folded in his lap, bitter disappointment in his face. "He really thinks Caro is some crazed hijacker?"

"Maybe. I don't know." I sigh. "I think it just doesn't make sense to him, that we could want to do something good for everyone, and take these steps that seemed logical and controlled in his head, and this could happen. So he has to make himself believe Caro is a thief and a liar and responsible for everything, or—or it means he's guilty. And I don't think he could handle that."

Sergei twitches his head, palms the back of his neck. "Okay," he mutters. "I'll . . . I'll think about this plan, all right?"

I nod, standing. "I'll come back in another few days."

But before I've taken a step, he says, "Leigh."

"Yeah?"

"You were there. What happened?" The stubborn hardness of his face seems to crack, showing a sliver of the Sergei he was before, sensitive and earnest. "What did Irina say? What did she do?" He brushes the back of his hand to his eye. His skin comes away wet. "I don't want what they said at the ceremony. I want the truth."

A lump rises in my throat. "What do you want to know?"

"Everything you can remember."

So I give it to him. It's the one thing I can give.

---

31 DAYS TO THE *HERMES*

"What about this way?" Matteo says, pointing toward a purplish glow.

"We've been that way a dozen times," Min-ji grumbles.

"And," adds Xu Jie, "you have to go up that ladder with the heated rungs. I burned myself last time." Still, the younger boy looks at me for a final decision, and so do the other two.

"Let's keep going this way," I say, pointing down the grated walkway. Following the purplish glow would take us closer to Caro. Not by much, but enough to make me uneasy.

Min-ji releases a heavy sigh, traipsing after me. "If we haven't found the hijacker by now, do you really think we're ever going to find her?"

"We will," Matteo says in a murderous growl. His face is gaunt and hollow in the half-light. "And when we do, I have some ideas for what the Pilot should do to her."

As the days go by, the hunger has taken more and more of us. It's carved away curves, shrunk us to lines. We're sleeping eleven hours a day. It's too much, and we're groggy all the time, but it suppresses the cramps that slice through our bellies otherwise. After the persistent gnawing stripped away the fat, it took our sense of humor, and then our energy, and now, apparently, our sense of mercy. What's left is a crew of hard skeletons, driven to a single objective.

Our routine is simple. We wake up late, form patrols, and search the ship for Caro. After lunch, we take a siesta and search again. At first, Francisco scheduled patrols to follow patterns, but he switched tactics after five days—a week, in our new calendar. "We need to outsmart her," he said at a Council meeting, red-eyed and restless. "She must be moving from place to place."

"If she has a passageway," I said with a frown, "avoiding us would be easy. We'd have to cover both places at once to find her."

"Could she be in the walls?" Pieter said. "We could start looking in ducts and pulling up panels."

"Careful," Eli said. "The only people who touch the infrastructure should be the Maintenance teams, who know what they're doing. We can't endanger the ship. But the random searches are a good idea, Francisco. I'm guessing someone helped her escape, someone who can bring her water without being noticed. So the less information the group has about our plans, the better."

Before, steering the hunting parties away was simple. I made sure that any group scheduled to the water treatment plant included Anis or me. If we found ourselves too close to Caro's hideout, we directed the others away, or distracted them during the small window that the entry panel was visible. Francisco's randomized approach has been harder to control, but days have passed since then, and she's still safe.

Matteo is tapping on the walls of the treatment plant, looking for hollow places. Deep tones emanate through the air. Min-ji, seeming to think this is a good tactic, joins in.

"What we really need to do is find the person helping her," says Xu Jie. As he passes beneath a blinking red bulb, his eyes flash crimson.

"I can't believe someone could do that," Min-ji mutters.

"I say throw them off the ship," says Matteo. "One less person to feed. It's their fault we're starving."

"Hey," I say sharply. "Nobody's getting thrown off the ship."

But the others don't reply. Min-ji and Xu Jie are clearly biting their tongues.

I forge ahead, feeling shaken. *We were starving already,* I tell myself. *We're doing the right thing.*

Last night, Anis and I were scouring the internet archives for any details about Kshipra Anand, and we found the flight records for two previous *Hermes* missions. She led both of those missions. She's forty-two years old and works for the Indian Space Research Organization, and in the live shot buried in the ISRO site, she's turning, laughing in loop, her eyes crinkling up over and over as she grins for the camera.

When we reach the *Hermes,* she'll still be alive, and when she walks through the airlock, everyone will realize how important this was. Eli will understand why Caro did what she did, and Francisco will stop blaming Caro for Irina's death. Kshipra Anand will fly us to the Antaeus colony, and it'll all be hard, but it won't be for nothing. I tell myself this story every night.

---

28 DAYS TO THE *HERMES*

"Here's an idea," Caro whispers. "We let Sergei out of his cell the night before. Then he breaks into the bridge, grabs Eli, and takes her back here. We make a fake threat or a ransom note or—" She waves a hand. "Something like that. That leaves everyone else searching the ship to save her the night we reach the *Hermes*. What do you think?"

Caro speaks differently these days. The tap is always open, now, new ideas always flowing up and bubbling into monologues. She speaks about real life now the way she used to describe *Thunderhead Empire*: as if there aren't enough words to contain her thoughts.

I mull this latest idea over, lying back on the warm, humming floor of the treatment plant. "Sergei would still have to get past the guards in the hall. There are half a dozen people stationed there all the time."

She shrugs. "He's the size of a horse, he can handle a bit of kidnapping."

Anis and I have to suppress our laughter. Francisco and Pieter have added night patrols into the mix, and we don't know who could be roaming around the treatment plant on a nearby walkway.

Caro leans back, allowing the blue light to fall more fully onto her hair. She's taking down her last few braids, snipping off the ends of the extensions, then pushing her fingernails into the grooves where the shining black lengths cross. As the last of each braid unravels into a diffuse bundle, she tugs it gently away from her natural hair, which springs back toward her scalp, each tendril fine and soft and twisted.

"How is Sergei?" she asks quietly, her usual sanguine smile fading.

I lift my shoulders. "Talking more. Still having a lot of breakdowns. I don't think he likes that I'm the only person he has to talk to, but it's better than nothing. And he's all in to help us, if we can just figure out how."

I tap a rhythm on the tablet in my lap. Only two things are really nonnegotiable for our plan. First, before we pass the moon, we need to plug this tablet into the dashboard, bringing us into synchronous orbit with the *Hermes* and unlocking the seventy-two-character passcode that Caro set on the manual controls. Second, Caro needs to get her hands on those manual controls. No matter what Eli wants, she'll never risk hurting an active pilot who could crash the *Lazarus* into the *Hermes*, or risk an accidental reentry.

Caro reaches into a recess under the silo and tugs out a plastic bin that we've borrowed from the med bay. She cracks its lid and scoops out a palmful of water. "I miss conditioner," she grumbles before soaking the water into her hair to detangle the knots. "Okay, another idea. We have a month, right?"

"Yes, an 'Old Planet' month," Anis says, his nose wrinkling as if he's caught a whiff of something rancid.

"Right," Caro says. "I forgot you two were on a new calendar. I was thinking about this yesterday, though. If the years are that much shorter, how old are you supposed to be?"

"I'm thirty-three," I say. "Anis is thirty-four."

Caro looks between us and grins. "Yeah, that makes sense."
We both scowl. "You're very funny," Anis says.

"I know. And you're old." Smile widening, she teases out a stubborn knot. "How do you say 'you're old' in Arabic? Did you get that far in your private lessons, Leigh?"

"Anta misan," Anis mumbles, while I stare off into space, refusing to meet Caro's eyes. It didn't take Caro long to notice that Anis and I are—whatever we are. Involved. Together. Yet another thing that I've realized I don't have the words for.

Once Caro is done enjoying my embarrassment, she says, "Anyway. We have a month, so what if we spend that time sabotaging their plans? Could we make so much go wrong that they just give up?"

"I don't think so." Anis scratches at the shadow of stubble on his jaw. "The safest choice is to do everything the night we reach Earth. The longer the process is, the more we leave things to chance, with fifty other people looking for you."

"Yeah," I say, the heat finally fading from my face. "I still think you should go in the same way you came out, Caro. Think about it. If you come through the airlock, you won't have to worry about bypassing the guards. I can wait in the bridge with the tablet to plug it in."

Anis nods. "That does get Caro close to the dashboard without being noticed. But we'll we need a huge diversion to draw the guards away, or they'll pile into the bridge the second they realize she's entered the airlock."

"Diversion. Okay. Diversion . . ." Caro pushes the water bin back under the silo, and I hear the rustle of fabric from the EVA suit she used to escape the bridge. She settles onto her back and elevates her feet against the wall, detangling the hair above her ears. It's coming loose into delicate coiled curls.

"Whatever it is, the diversion needs to be something that takes time," she whispers, the waves of blue light washing over her. "I think the program to sync up our orbit will take minutes to run."

"Okay," I say. "Then we need pandemonium out in the body of the ship. Anis, what if you said you spotted Caro in the atrium, or something?"

"I could," he says slowly, "but why should Eli care? If she's out in the atrium, she has no way to get control of the ship and dock us to the *Hermes*. There's no reason Eli should send guards away from the bridge."

After a few minutes, I settle onto my back beside Caro, looking up into the blue light, too. Anis follows suit, lying on my other side. I wish we could fall asleep here, the one place on the ship that feels really safe.

Caro says sleepily, "Leigh, tell Sergei about the kidnapping idea. I think he'll like it."

Our stifled chuckles are lost in the sounds of water rushing along above us.

---

24 DAYS TO THE *HERMES*

When I enter Jayanti's pod in the med bay, Sahir is seated at the end of the bed, looking out a porthole. The left side of Jayanti's face is a calamity of watercolors, red blended into purple into green, but she's sitting up and looks alert.

"Hi," I say.

They look back at me. Jayanti's eyes are as blank as paint chips. She doesn't answer.

"Are . . . are you feeling all right?" I ask.

"Oh, now you care," Sahir shoots back.

Jayanti puts a hand on Sahir's wrist. Some unspoken debate passes between them, and Sahir leans back, arms crossed.

"What do you want?" Jayanti asks.

I perch on the stool affixed in front of the desk. I don't know what my chances are here. All I know is that if Sahir, Jayanti, and Sergei all join us, if we double our numbers, we could double our chances of taking control of the bridge.

Sahir speaks first. "If you're looking for an alibi, we were here when the ship turned around."

"No. I know you didn't help Caro."

"Don't you mean *the hijacker*?" Jayanti says with a ghost of her old disdain.

"Right."

She sighs, and the scorn slides off her expression as if she doesn't have the energy to keep it pinned up. She picks at the edge of her blanket. "Sahir told me what happened to Irina."

I wait for one of them to say it. *We told you so.* I wait for them to remind me that they and Irina fought every choice that led to this, every step of the way. I wait for some vestige of the fight to show itself.

They don't say anything. Outside the pod door, other kids in the Medical track are audible in the hall. The whir of the humidity regulators seems to grow around us.

If they don't broach the topic, I can't see a way in. Anything that gives them the truth outright is too dangerous. They have too much reason to expose me.

"We'll reach the *Hermes* in a little over three weeks," I say carefully.

"We know you want to catch her before that," Jayanti says. "I'll help with the patrols once I can stand up without feeling dizzy."

"That's not what I'm trying to say. I'm saying...you wanted us to turn back. We've turned back, but the hijacker still has to dock the ship to the satellite."

"We don't want that anymore," Sahir says.

"What?"

"We're not going to do anything to help her, all right? We're done. It's over. We got your message: Be quiet and do what we're told. We're not going to offend your precious Pilot." Sahir regains some of his old bravado, but he can't hide the strain completely.

Jayanti says hoarsely, "We're not going to die to get the last word."

The skin on the back of my neck prickles. Even that first night aboard the ship, they've never sounded this afraid. I imagine Jayanti lying in this bed the night Matteo hit her, Sahir hovering anxiously at her bedside, not knowing if she was hemorrhaging or brain damaged, not knowing if she would wake up the next day. When they look at me, I realize, they see a threat that's just as real as an eruption or a blade lifted high.

I won't ask them to risk their survival again.

Sahir sighs. "Why did you come, Leigh?"

I rise from the seat. "I guess I just came to say you were right."

Jayanti looks up at me with something like pity. "So what?"

---

17 DAYS TO THE *HERMES*

This version of the Council has a new formation in the bridge. Eli sits in the commander's chair with me at her right hand and Pieter in the copilot's seat to her left. Matteo stands at the threshold of the bridge, manning the door, while Francisco hovers at the rails on the upper floor, ready to turn back to the tabletop, where the circular screen is filled with his checklists for the hunt.

"It's been three weeks," Eli says. "We need to be realistic. We should start talking about what we'll do if we don't catch the hijacker before we reach the *Hermes*."

"Hang on," Matteo says, sounding outraged. "Before we reach the *Hermes*? Are you saying we're going to give up when we get there? We're just going to let her dock to the station?"

"No, of course not," Eli says. "I'm talking about how we can make sure the rest of the ship stays focused. That petition that went around—do you still have those twenty-one names somewhere, Francisco?"

"Yes," he calls from the table, his fingers clicking against the screen. "Yes, I have them here." He pulls them onto a tablet and jogs down to the dashboard, where he hands the list to Eli.

"Moses Nabwana . . . no surprise," she says, glancing up at Matteo. "Luke's been keeping an eye on his brother, right?"

Matteo nods. "He hasn't seen Moses do anything unusual."

"All right." Eli scrolls down the list. "Anis Ibrahim." She glances over at me. "Is that the guy who didn't let you inspect his room?"

"Yes," I say, trying for a look of vague recognition, "but he changed his mind the next morning. He was just being stubborn, I think."

"Mm. Still." Eli keeps looking down the list. "These are the ones we'll want to keep a closer eye on as we get near the *Hermes*. We should listen for any theories about docking to the station, or searching for seeds there, or finding some astronaut who could somehow survive nearly three months on a week of food."

"A lot of these people have come around," Matteo says dismissively, looking at a copy of the list on the tabletop. "Min-ji was out for blood when I talked to her the other day. Even Sahir and Jayanti have finally shut their mouths."

"Still," Pieter says, "what do we do if we hear that kind of thing, Eli?"

Eli taps her fingers on the arms of the commander's seat. "Don't get angry. And don't make fun of them or act condescending, either. If people have actually deluded themselves into believing this stuff, it'll alienate them to brush it off. Just take them aside and talk, remind them of our goals. Maybe ask them if they want to go on patrol together, or if it's their free hour, you could do something fun together, working on one of the ship sports, maybe. Remind them we're their friends. We're the ones who care about them." She lets out a hollow laugh. "And make sure to remind them that we can't take on another mouth to feed."

We glance around at each other. All the luster has been stripped away from our bodies, our skin like ash, our hair and nails dull. I look into the reflective surface of the windshield and see five skulls.

"I have an idea," Matteo says. His eyes, always protuberant, have turned bulbous in his sunken face, twitching, darting, like security cameras hunting for something in the dark. "I've talked to a dozen people about this, and they all agree with me. Once we find the hijacker and whoever's helping her, we should eject them from the ship. Out. Finished. Make up for the food we wasted on them."

I fold my hands. They're cold and clammy. "That seems extreme," I say in the most neutral tone I can manage. "We're the ones who care about the ship's safety and longevity. I think capital punishment seems sort of off message."

"Yes," says Francisco, looking at me with slight relief. "Yes, I agree with Leigh. What happened to Irina was...We don't want to associate ourselves with that. It would also hurt our plans for genetic diversity."

Pieter stiffens at the mention of Irina's name. "That's noble of you," he says to Francisco, "but Matteo's right about making up for the wasted food. We can't think hundreds of years ahead if we're dying ourselves. If we get rid of the people who sentenced *us* to starvation, maybe that would cancel out the risk of what they did."

I look to Eli. Her chin is high. She deliberates with the same satisfaction I saw when she sent Irina into confinement. Now, though, I understand it wasn't a look of triumph. It was the look of someone feeling powerful for the first time and realizing the way it sets you free.

She almost smiles then, a flex of the cheek muscles that draws her mouth into a grim horizontal line. "Matteo," she says, "I think you've got a point."

13 DAYS TO THE *HERMES*

Word has spread throughout the ship. When the hijacker and her accomplice are caught, they'll be ejected from the *Lazarus*, their food reapportioned among the crew.

I didn't want to believe Matteo when he said the group was on his side, but not one person has spoken up against the executions. And if I'm honest with myself, I'm starting to see why. Three days ago, Annie Daly had such a serious dizzy spell that she slipped off a ladder in the water treatment plant and cracked a rib. The day after that, Kwase Asare cut a gash into his palm with a screwdriver, and the wound has been seeping ever since, his body too deprived to heal properly. Everyone is asking the same question, including Caro, Anis, and me: If it's this bad right now, how bad will it be in ten months?

Two people, ten months, three meals a day, I hear people whispering in the canteen. *That's six hundred meals.*

That could be the difference.

That could save people who are actually innocent. Good people. People who deserve to survive.

"She can't throw me off the ship," Caro whispers when Anis and I tell her about the threat. "No. She needs the passkey to get control of the systems again. . . . Also, she knows we just want to dock the ship to the *Hermes.* She knows we're not going to do anything after that."

Anis stiffens, then sits bolt upright. "That's it."

Caro and I exchange a mystified look.

"The diversion," he whispers. "Docking the ship! Eli needs to believe there's another way to dock the ship, a way she overlooked." He takes the tablet from the floor and waves it like a preacher brandishing a Bible. "You're the programmer, Caro. Eli doesn't know what you can and can't do. I can pretend I saw you lock yourself into the codehome, that you figured out a way to dock the ship from there—but Sergei will be the one who's locked inside. We can record your voice onto something for him to play back bits of audio."

Caro and I sit up, too. "That could actually work," I whisper. "We don't have guards scheduled at the codehome."

"So I'll run down the hall toward the bridge," Anis says, "yelling that I saw you with some kind of equipment, Caro.

That'll shake the guards, and, Leigh, you'll have to make sure the bridge door opens so that the message gets to the Council."

"Easy," I say. "We'll also need enough noise to cover the sound of Caro coming through the airlock. If people don't start panicking the second you tell them about the codehome, you can start yelling or picking a fight. That'll set everyone off."

"We'll have to time this out precisely," Caro says. "I won't be able to tell what's going on from outside the ship, so we'll have to schedule it down to the second."

I nod. "Not a problem. Everyone knows you'll want to make your move once the ship reaches the *Hermes*. We'll make the commotion when we're only a few minutes away, so there's no time for a reasonable discussion." I chew my lip. "That gets us close. I can do my best to empty the bridge. At the very least, Eli will send the guards to the codehome, and hopefully Pieter and Matteo, too. Once they're gone, I'll plug in the passkey."

"Right," Caro says, an excited shine in her eyes. "And once we start matching up to the *Hermes*'s orbit, we'll lose our acceleration, and the gravity will ease up little by little. They still haven't accounted for that?"

I shake my head. "No one's mentioned it."

"That'll give us another advantage. I'll come into the bridge after we start losing gravity."

"And then..." I tug the plastic box of vials out from the shadow of the water silo, the remainder of the stolen anesthesia. "Anis and I will try to subdue whoever's left. At least, we can hold them back long enough for you to get your hands on the controls."

We spend a while longer talking through the details, through potential problems, until we look down at a tablet and realize it's nearly three in the morning.

"You two should go," Caro whispers. "Anis, you first?"

As Anis crawls down the passageway, I settle beside Caro to wait. We always leave the treatment plant one at a time. A single pair of footsteps on the echoing walkways might be mistaken for the clanks and taps of the autosystems. Two pairs are noticeable.

"When can you tell Sergei the whole plan?" Caro asks after a few minutes.

"I should be able to get in there early next week."

"Good," Caro says, but the shine has gone from her eyes. The excitement of planning has faded into the nervous prickle that never leaves me these days. I wake up from dreams about clinging to the edge of the airlock while Eli hisses, *I trusted you.* Looking into Caro's face, I see the fear there, too.

She whispers, "I think they've been sending more patrols this way. I keep waking up and hearing people here."

"They're not going to find you." I clasp her shoulder. "I promise, all right? And if they do, Anis and I won't let—"

The sound of raised voices ricochets down from high in the treatment plant.

My mind empties except for one thought. *Anis.*

"Go," Caro hisses. "Go!"

I crawl as quickly as I can down the tunnel, wriggle out through the exit, and fasten it shut. Then I sprint through the pipes. As I dodge between silos and glittering machinery, my heart doesn't seem to race so much as grow, swelling to the point of pain. I clamber up the rails and hit the walkway, already concocting excuses. Maybe I can claim that Anis and I were night-patrolling together. If Francisco, Pieter, or Matteo is up there, though, someone who'd know the schedule, what do I say?

I try not to think about Pieter hefting one of those pipes, his knobby knuckles forming a ridge over the unforgiving edge. These days I can't think about Pieter any other way. At one point I found him reassuring. The idea is hard to imagine now.

Pieter's never spoken about what happened, but I can tell the experience of killing has honed something in him to a perilously thin, taut line, like a razor taken to silver wire. He's convinced himself it had to happen. He could convince himself of anything now.

I fly up the ramp, my feet clattering, but I haven't made it far when something moves in the corner of my eye. A hand seizes my shoulder. I spin around, clamping my hand over my mouth to stifle the start of a scream.

I drop my hand. "Anis," I gasp out.

"Hurry," he whispers. We creep backward, down the maze of walkways, out the third-floor entrance and onto the balconies.

Ten flights of stairs later, we're back in his cabin, gasping for breath. The door whirs shut, and in an instant, my arms are around him. His muscles slowly loosen. He moves one of his hands to my hair, gently working his fingers through the tangles as stings of reaction light up across my scalp.

When I pull back, a tendon is flexing in Anis's wrist, and he looks vulnerable, unprotected. I used to think of his body clocking miles beside mine, both of us banded collections of muscle. But our bodies are no longer machines to me. His clavicle holds a thimbleful of light, his hair looks like black down. He is made out of soft tissue.

His face, too, looks different. Always so steady and stubborn, he looks destabilized, his eyes darting from my mouth to my nose to my hairline.

"What is it?" I whisper.

"I thought they caught you. I was going to tell them the truth." The words seem to rattle him further, like he's just realizing the truth as he speaks it. "I would have told them everything. Our plans. Everything."

If I'd ever seen him lie, I'd wonder if he was making this up. It seems ridiculous. Anis, who makes every tiny choice into an ideological sticking point, cave to the Council? Anis, throw away our last chance at making a stand?

"No," I say. "No, you wouldn't."

"I would. I was already picturing it." He paces to the observation window, hand buried in his hair. "Everything they'd do. They'd want to get the passkey out of you, and where Caro is. They'd torture you. They'd—"

"Don't think about it. It didn't happen, okay? Just focus on the astronaut. We've got a plan."

"Leigh, don't talk around this. Please."

Looking into the fear and defiance on Anis's face, I can no longer ignore the threat. I see wires, pipes, and knives. I see the airlock opening. I see my body rising out into the dark.

I swallow hard. "Yes, I know what they'd do. But the *Hermes* is the most important thing."

"No," he says. "Not to me."

I feel as if I'm onstage, missing a line and unsure what to do with my hands, every inch of me lit up by a focused spot. He approaches me again, his gaze almost painful to hold.

"I don't understand," I say quietly. "You wanted me to do this from the beginning. You wanted me to stand up for what I cared about. I'm finally here. Now you want me to stop?"

"No," he says, although his face is contorted. "I don't know. Maybe." He closes his eyes, leans his forehead against mine.

I close my eyes too as he says, "Maybe I didn't know what I wanted either."

When he kisses me, there's something new behind it, heat and urgency. I press against him, winding one hand in his hair as he catches my lip between his teeth. I tug his head back and kiss his neck, tasting salt, and we move unsteadily toward one of the cabin's bedrooms, stepping like we're drunk.

But what if they'd caught you? I think as we tumble back into his bunk, clumsy, hands everywhere. I focus on the careful press of his mouth, on the scorch of his skin, the way he runs as hot as one of the old combustion engines, and I try to resist the question. I don't want to ask myself what I'd do if they caught him.

But the circles beneath his eyes are darker than ever with the sleep we've been losing, and around four a.m., he drifts off beside me, tousled and huddled in his sleepwear, leaving me alone with my thoughts. After a moment's debate, I sneak back down the hall to my cabin, bring my notebook to his room, and page through, looking for one of my older entries, the one about a summer's night three years ago, July, crickets, the morning after, sunlight. . . . *That's Lilly, that's Marcus, that's us. That's what I'd save.*

I run my hand over the page with a wistful pang. Then I tear it out and fold it into a small square. I pause, my cheeks warm, then scribble on the inch of free space, *If someone asked me now—it'd be you.*

I slip it into an inner pocket of Anis's day-to-day uniform, folded neatly on a nearby table. Then I slip beneath the covers. He murmurs something and turns toward me, and I watch his solemn face, his skin like brushed copper. I study every part of him, heavy brow and stubborn chin, cataloging him, committing him—fragment after fragment—to memory.

3 DAYS TO THE *HERMES*

"We're not going to find her," Eli says. "Fifty of us, one of her, and she's going to make it through this still hidden."

There's a periodic clicking sound from Pieter as his teeth snap through the edge of his thumbnail. The cast came off his forearm this morning, the fracture healed. He keeps running his fingertips over the arm as if reminding the skin how to feel.

"Maybe it would be easiest to call a truce with the hijacker," I say cautiously. "We could promise not to hurt her if she comes out now."

"I can't promise that," Matteo seethes.

Click. Pieter's teeth break into his index nail. "It doesn't have to be a true promise," he says.

Matteo glances at Pieter with a hard smile. "Here's one good thing. She's going to run out of stolen food soon. She only took five weeks' rations."

"Seven," says Francisco.

"What?"

"Five weeks would be by the old calendar. She has seven weeks' food by the new system."

"Oh. Right." Matteo glances at Eli, fidgeting, suddenly cowed. "Sorry."

Eli gives a curt nod. "What's your point?"

Matteo looks relieved. "I'm saying, if we block the dispensary door, she can't get in. She'll have to come out eventually if she doesn't want to starve to death."

Eli drums her fingers on the arm of the commander's seat. "We can't let her starve to death in hiding, or we'll be stuck in orbit. And every day we wait, we'll waste more rations. She needs to unlock the ship's controls so we can get ourselves back on course."

"What about the person who helped her?" Pieter says, taking his teeth to his middle fingernail. Click. "We don't need them. We could redistribute their food to the rest of us."

"Except," Francisco says crisply, "for the small problem that we still have no idea who that is and no way of figuring it out."

"How about the prisoner?" Matteo says. "We could cut his rations. He's in that cabin all day, he's not moving around, he doesn't need it like the rest of us do."

"No," Francisco blurts out. When Matteo and Pieter look to him, he adds quickly, "I—I've calculated very exactly how much everyone needs. You can't change my tracker. Besides, Sergei is the biggest person aboard. He's just as hungry as everyone else. Right?" he says to me, not quite meeting my eyes.

"Right," I say, and it's true. I made my last visit to Sergei several days ago. We spent an hour discussing the diversion plan until he could recite every detail, every contingency plan that we'd prepared. Sergei's once-round cheeks had sunken in like mounds of soil tapped by a spade, making his hazel eyes look large and plaintive.

I was returning down the ninth floor when I ran into Francisco, hurrying down the hall as if he didn't want to be seen. He froze at the sight of me. "Leigh. You're still here."

"Yes, Eli thinks it's best if I try to stay a full hour on visiting days. Make sure he's staying socialized."

"Oh. Well, in that case, there's no need for me to . . . Right. I was going to . . . Never mind." Before I could say anything else, Francisco was hurrying back down the hall, his gait jerky.

Now Francisco's head turns sharply toward Eli, and I realize that her fingers have stopped their incessant drumming. Her eyes are blazing in their hollowed sockets.

"What is it?" I say.

She smiles. It gives her a hungry look, all teeth in her gaunt face. "We don't know who's helping the hijacker," Eli says, "but she doesn't know that. She has no idea what we have or haven't figured out—and we're not going to give her time to check."

Eli turns the commander's seat to the dashboard and stands. "This is it," she whispers. "This is how we get you out of your hiding place. Come and play."

She hits the broadcast button with one skeletal finger and leans down to the microphone.

Caro, say all the speakers in Eli's massive, amplified voice. *The game's over. We have your accomplice. You have ten minutes to come to the bridge, or I'm opening the airlock, and we'll have one less mouth to feed.*

Eli lowers herself back into the commander's seat and turns it around. "Now we wait." She nods to Pieter and Matteo. "Get ready."

They jog up the stairs and flank the doorway. As one, we all face the open threshold. I sit very still, telling myself Caro won't believe it. Will she? Won't she notice how Eli avoided mentioning a name or even a gender?

I could run for the PA and tell her it's not true, but I'd never be able to break free afterward, not with the others here, and then they really would have a bargaining chip. I could flee the bridge, but I'd give myself away, and without my place on the Council, our plan is shot. Even if Anis can get to the treatment plant in time to show her that he's safe, that doesn't prove I'm safe.

Minutes pass. Feeling sick, I jog up the steps to pace in front of the door, my hands a knot behind my back. Caro's smart, she's skeptical, she can spot a lie when she hears one.

Then I hear footfalls down the hall. Pieter and Matteo go rigid. Eli and Francisco rise to their feet, hungry looks on their faces. *No*, I think as a figure bursts into view at the end of the hall.

Caro didn't believe her. But Anis did.

His eyes meet mine. His stride breaks, and he takes me in, the way I'm standing alone and unguarded. Suspended in time, we all regard each other, and I hear him whispering, *I would have told them everything.*

Then Eli yells, "Get him."

Anis tears back around the corner. We race down the hall after him.

CHAPTER 16

THE GOLDEN RECORD

I feel the weeks of hunger, the weeks without running, in every stride. The boys, though, were never trained at all. Before we reach the hall's first turn, I've left them behind.

I push myself harder, rounding another corner just in time to see the door to the stairwell close behind Anis. Instead of following, I run past the door to the place where the hall opens up onto the balconies. Then I look back and wait for Matteo, Pieter, and Francisco to appear. "This way," I yell, beckoning, the instant they emerge. They sprint past the stairwell door and after me.

Remembering the cameras, I stop short of the entrance to the Residential Wing and point to another stairwell. "I saw him go in there," I pant.

"We need to split up," Francisco gasps. "Cover all the floors in the Residential Wing. Leigh, you take the third floor and exercise hall. I'll do four and five. Matteo, six and seven. Pieter, eight and nine, and be careful. His room's on the eighth floor."

Pieter pulls the pipe from his belt as we barge into the stairwell. I sprint down three at a time, praying Anis doesn't pass anyone in the treatment plant or catch anyone's attention by running, praying we can still somehow salvage the scraps of our plan. Could Sergei set off the diversion in the codehome while I control what happens in the bridge? At the very least, if Anis can get safely into hiding, maybe we can come up with something else in the three days before we reach the *Hermes.*

I do a cursory run through the third floor and the exercise hall. Then I emerge in the atrium. Dozens of the group are there, and they swarm me the second I emerge, clamoring to hear details about Eli's PA announcement.

"Who was it?"

"Did the hijacker—"

"Do you have—"

"Where—"

"It was a bluff," I call over them. "But her accomplice gave himself away. It's Anis Ibrahim. Have any of you seen him?"

Heads shake. Others aim their hungry eyes up toward the balconies, as if expecting him to appear.

"Wait here," I order. "I'm going back up to the bridge. Francisco will want to organize new hunting parties. Maybe we can catch him before he disappears."

"We should look now," someone protests, and another voice calls: "We can't wait!"

I ignore them. I run for the elevator bay, leaving the group in an uproar behind me. By the time I reach the bridge, Francisco,

Matteo, and Pieter are already there, huddled over something on the Council table, muttering with Eli.

"What is it?" I say. "Did you find him?"

They all look up. An instantly recognizable kind of silence falls, the abrupt hush that says they were talking about me.

Then I see the spread of yellow paper in front of them. I forgot to return my notebook to my cabin last week.

"Leigh," Eli says. The others' mouths are tight shut. Pieter is staring at me with eyes bright as fires. Gone is the eagerness to please me, any vestige of flattery or admiration. I see the suspicion burning in his face, but his eyes stray to Eli, and he doesn't speak. Maybe he doesn't think it's his place.

A survival instinct takes over, twisting my expression into bafflement. "Is that my notebook?"

"You admit this is yours, then?" Pieter snaps. "I found it in Anis's cabin."

"What?"

"He lives on her floor, Pieter," Francisco says. "He easily could have stolen it."

Pieter isn't listening. "And these entries! This is her hand-writing! This is exactly the reason the hijacker turned the ship around."

I let my expression morph smoothly into a mixture of bemuse-ment and pity. "Yes, I didn't need that explained, Pieter. That's why I haven't written in that book in months. Except . . ." I let a flicker of doubt show. "Hang on." I stride over to the end of the table. Matteo and Pieter recoil as if I'm diseased.

I grab up the book and riffle through the pages, then stop at the page I ripped out. I trace my finger down the torn edge. "I made notes on our plans for finishing the flight path," I invent, dropping the book back to the table. "I thought it might give me some fresh ideas if I wrote it out on paper. . . . He took them."

"What did you write down?" Francisco says at once, pulling out his tablet.

"Names of some of the guards Pieter wanted to station in the hall. The time we're sealing the door. Some of our theories on what they're planning."

Francisco exhales slowly. "Well, I'm sure they would have guessed we'd guard the bridge. That isn't too bad."

"Why did you keep this?" Eli says quietly.

I look to her. "What?"

"This book." As Eli reopens it, her control slips, and I see the disbelief that I'd keep this from her. "For months, we've been talking about— I thought you— Why are you even holding on to something like this?" The way she rushes and stammers makes me remember the first time we ever spoke, when I looked at her and saw someone unsure and in pain.

I take my seat at her right hand. "Eli, it was stashed in the back of some cabinet for weeks and weeks until I wrote those notes. With everything going on, I forgot about it."

Eli looks at me. Her eyes are shadowed. I see the girl who stood facing away from her mother's body, full of mistrust, hating herself for needing someone else, even in the most unimaginable circumstances.

She looks down at the book with a twitch of her head. "You actually care about this," she mutters. "I mean, I can tell. All these little . . . these details."

"I needed it for a while, Eli. I don't anymore."

I don't know what I'm hoping she'll do. Am I imagining the conflict in her face? Is it possible that the entries made her reconsider something—that she might soften in private, just us, the way we used to talk?

"If it doesn't matter," Eli says, "then you won't mind if we get rid of it."

My hope crumples. I feel a desperate impulse to snatch the book and sprint down the hall. Instead, I bob my shoulders. "Do what you want." I lean over the table, holding her eyes. "The important thing is that they didn't find out anything about our plans from this. I'm sorry, I shouldn't have left details lying around, but everything's going to be fine."

Eli looks at me a long time. Finally the line between her brows smooths away. She offers the book to Pieter. "Out," she says with a glance to the airlock.

I don't make a sound when Pieter grabs the book from Eli's hand. I watch him turn the metal wheel in the door until the hatch swings open. Beyond is an airlock with space suits folded in orange and white along a row of shelves. Pieter slides steel doors over the suits, sealing them away, and lets the notebook hit the floor. It falls open to pages I can't read from this distance. Details of a birthday party, maybe, or one of my first days of school with Lilly and Marcus.

Pieter closes and locks the hatch. With the press of a button, there's a quiet hissing sound that tapers almost immediately. I hear the outer hatch click open. Then there's an asphyxiated silence, the type I heard pounding in my ears as I stared down into the empty Seeders for the first time. I'm dizzied, but I have to pretend I'm still moving along the same trajectory. Eli is watching me to see if I will fracture. I scratch idly at my upper forearm. I look back at her unfazed, because I am not seeing her.

"Say goodbye," Pieter says, looking through the windshield. I glance over and see the notebook, its pages wafting open and shut, like a bird with many delicate wings. I watch the spiral binding shimmer like sterling silver, the book slowly spinning corner over corner. I have no idea how I'm so silent when a gravity well has opened up behind my sternum, pulling all of me toward a sunken center. You'd think it would make some sound, all my architecture falling in.

---

47 HOURS TO THE *HERMES*

It's 3:30 in the morning. Standing inside my cabin door, I dare myself to go out. I remember Pieter's spite, Eli's mistrust.

She seemed to believe my cover, but I can't be certain. What are the odds that my door is unwatched? Two days from now, we'll reach the moon, and when that happens, we need to have a new plan. The distance to the water treatment plant has never felt longer.

I press my thumb to the control panel. The door whirs open onto an empty hallway.

I creep down the eighth-floor hall. It's deserted, safety lights lining the intersection of floor and wall. I take the stairwell down to the fifth floor, then reroute to the balconies, my pulse beating hard rhythms on my eardrums, everything in me the attack of a blunt instrument. I fly through the darkened ship, my feet whispering over the mesh.

No one stops me. The *Lazarus* seems completely empty, but I don't relax until I'm unscrewing the panel in the tangle of the water treatment plant and crawling through.

"Caro?" I whisper, getting to my feet. "Anis?"

Caro darts out from beneath the silo, her eyes sleepless. "Leigh! God, you're all right," she whispers. "I thought we got you killed. Is Anis okay?"

"He's not here?"

She shakes her head. "He came here a minute after the announcement. He told me to stay here and said he was going to the bridge."

A lump swells in my throat. "He did go to the bridge. He got away, but his cover's shot."

"Where else could he be?"

"I'll find him. But we need to figure out a new plan."

"No, no, the old plan can still work," Caro insists, holding a tablet out to me. "Mostly. When we get close to the moon, Sergei needs to take this into the codehome and follow the directions in the notes. It'll dim all the ship's lights. You'll be in the bridge when that happens, and when the lights go down, you can pretend you've realized that Anis and I are both in the codehome."

I grimace. "They found my notebook in Anis's room. I talked my way out of it, but I don't know if my word is enough anymore."

"They don't need to trust your word. Take one of the other Council members with you to the codehome. When you get there, Sergei can play this for them. I recorded a load of dialogue to make it sound like I'm inside, and when you find Anis, get recordings from him, too. Then you and the others can go back to the bridge, tell Eli that the guards need to break into the codehome, and everything else is like we already planned."

She's all confidence, but I can still see the vicious triumph on the new Council's faces when Anis appeared at the end of that hallway, and I feel the impact of the knowledge that they will do it. If they catch Anis or Caro or Sergei or me, they will eject us from the ship and they will feel no guilt.

Our plan is growing thinner. We can still abandon it. The four of us can stage a surrender. I think I still have enough influence over Eli to ensure that she doesn't kill us if we turn ourselves in, and I know that if Irina were here, Sergei would forgo everything else for the chance to save his sister's life. What if I can do the same for him? For Anis? I look into Caro's face and I'm a coward, I'm afraid, I just want her to live.

I must be losing my mask, because she seizes my wrists and says, "You're not giving up on this now. I'm not letting you. We have to get inside that station—we have to see if there's someone there. Isn't that what we've been working for?" She presses the tablet into my hand, holds it there until my nerveless fingers close over the alloy. "You're not going back to what you were."

Don't trust me with that. The words catch on the tip of my tongue. The time has come again and again, and I've never been equal to it.

But Caro trusts me, the endless strategist, her mind as quick and hard as a diamond drill. Anis, stubborn and impossible to please—he trusts me. Marcus and Lilly and my parents trusted me. They saw something real in me, and even if I don't trust myself, I trust them.

---

46 HOURS TO THE *HERMES*

I toe the edge of a painted line. The lights in the exercise hall are down, but the place feels comforting, ghosts of my old self circling the space. Here I feel steadier, more confident.

"Anis?" I call as loudly as I dare.

Almost at once, a sound comes from a storage room, its door open atop a set of stairs. With a surge of hope, I run for it. Inside are bundles of equipment: braided ropes, weights anchored into racks, medicine balls the size of heads. At the back, exercise mats are stacked high, nearly to the ceiling. "Anis?" I repeat.

One of the stacks of mats shifts, and then he slips through, tousled hair, tired smile. He breaks for me, and I run forward to wrap my arms around him.

"I'm sorry," he says gruffly. "I ruined the plan. I should have known it was a lie. I'm an idiot. It was so—"

"Hey, stop, stop." I pull back. "You're not an idiot, and you didn't ruin the plan. Here." I hand Caro's tablet to him as we slip between the stacks of exercise mats into his hiding place, a strip of space hardly large enough for both of us to sit. As I explain her modifications to the diversion, his slumped shoulders lift.

"It's not so different from what we were planning before," he says, scrolling through Caro's bank of prerecorded sentences. "Do you think it'll work?"

I fight the instinct to give a bland nonanswer in return, although several spring to mind. *It could. There's a chance. We'll see.*

"I don't think it'll go perfectly," I say, "but it might be enough."

Anis half smiles, and I know he's savoring the reply, short but honest.

"You went to the bridge for me," I find myself saying, remembering him frozen mid-stride at the end of the hall. "You gave yourself away."

"I said I would," he says, steady as stone, his dark eyes unapologetic. "I keep my promises."

His gaze fortifies me. When I reach for his hand, he takes mine without question, then grips a bit too hard, and warmth spreads through me until my whole body tingles, because that's Anis in one motion. A ready sanctuary as well as a challenge. I don't think I knew before him that a person could be both. On Earth I saw friends and enemies, total agreement or total opposition. I never thought I'd find someone I trusted so completely—not just to reassure me, but to show me what kind of person I want to be.

I'm smiling, my whole face hot, and Anis smiles, too, his cheeks darkening. "What is it?" he asks, sounding a bit nervous.

"Nothing. I'm just . . . I'm scared, but I'm ready." I tighten my hold on his hand until my grip is as strong as his. "I guess it's weird to know that in a day, Eli will hate me."

"Yeah. And the Council. And most of the ship."

The words are blunt, and true, and I feel as if they should have a greater impact. Nearly everyone left in my world will think I'm a liar or a coward or a moral failure, but all these things that used to scare me so much, all the judgments in the universe, feel pale and abstract. Maybe it's because I can see myself more clearly now. I have lied. I have been a coward. I have failed in a way that other people paid for. So I will do what I believe is right, and let them hate me for it. They can have my reputation. It was never worth what I thought it was.

CHAPTER 17

FLYING LESSONS

16 HOURS TO THE *HERMES*

I wake up when my head hits the ceiling.

I'm drifting in midair, weightless. I thrash an arm out to grab a cabinet, but without knobs or handles, with only smooth surfaces, I can't find purchase. The sheets cling to the bed where they're tucked in at the sides. Otherwise, they waft gently, stirring like seaweed. Something's happened to the ship's acceleration.

I kick off the wall toward the door. My legs catapult me forward with unexpected force. I try to grab hold of the lintel, but my fingers slip from the metal, and my elbows strike the door hard.

As my body tilts backward in a reverse somersault, I close my eyes. It's a mistake. In the dark, I'm completely lost. I feel the air tumbling over my skin, but there's no center, no direction. My eyes snap open again, my hands folding behind my neck as I spin down through the room toward the opposite wall.

I seize the leg of my bed and finally get a moment of stillness. Who did this? Did something go wrong, a broken part on the ship? This could be just as much of a death sentence as our dwindling food supply. Maybe Caro miscalculated. Maybe some line in her new flight path made us lose gravity sooner than planned.

Navigating into the hall, I grab on to the mesh in the floor and pull myself along, skimming gently over the tangled surface. The ventilation at the intersection of the wall and the floor blows gently in my direction, fanning me as I move forward.

The first thing that comes into view past the balconies are a half-dozen of the youngest kids, hooting with laughter as they fly up toward the ceiling of the atrium. One of them hits the huge, warm sunspot and bounces back down. It's such a bizarre interruption from the grim silence of the last week that I wonder if I'm asleep.

I pull myself over the rail and kick off for the Pilot Wing. On the eighth-floor balcony, Francisco is pulling himself along the railing. "Hey," I say, "what is this? What happened to the gravity?"

"Don't ask me," he says. "The Pilot has everybody looking for a way to restart the acceleration." He spares an exasperated look upward at the zooming kids, who are shoving each other, pushed in opposite directions like repelled magnets. Then Francisco gives me a nod and continues his journey down the railing.

351

It takes a few minutes and a few bruises to reach the bridge. Eli sits strapped into the commander's seat. Pieter hovers redfaced by the entrance, and Matteo sits mute in the copilot seat to Eli's left, wearing the expression of someone recently berated into silence.

Eli cranes her long neck back in my direction. Her hair clouds around her face, still with inertia. She pushes it back in waves. "Leigh," she says. "Who do you think it was?"

"Who else?" I say, holding on to a bunk frame. "It has to be the hijacker, right?"

"Maybe." She turns back to the center screen, tapping in a long string of characters. "Or Ibrahim. Assuming he's not dead somewhere. Where are these people hiding? Where do they go?"

"Maybe he accidentally shot himself off into space," Matteo mutters. "Did the job for us."

I picture frost clinging to the tips of Anis's eyelashes. The image makes me feel ill.

I guide myself toward the third pilot seat and strap myself in until I'm held securely against the back of the chair. Eli's face is dour, her hands fixed hard over the arms of the commander's seat. "Whoever it is, what do you think they're trying to do with this?"

"Maybe they're not trying to do anything," Matteo says. "Maybe they're trying to make us ask questions. Get in our heads." He taps the side of his skull hard.

Eli and I look at him for a second, and then look back at each other without commenting. For a moment, this tacit decision makes me remember the way we used to be on the same side, the way I agreed so wholly with all her decisions, the way I thought of the Council as my only friends left in the world.

"It could be part of the flight path," I say.

"I don't think so. I can't access the specifics, but there are still hours on this countdown to orbit." She runs one hand over the dashboard screen. "I don't think we'll start syncing up with the *Hermes*'s orbit until the clock runs down. There's no reason for us to start losing gravity yet."

I feel a small pang of disappointment. This gravity malfunction has brought her attention to one of the few real advantages we had—the surprise of everyone suddenly entering zero-g.

"You could ask Min-ji," I say. "Not that I think she did anything, but I know she was in the advanced programming course. Maybe she learned something about gravity controls before the hijacker left."

Eli nods. "Matteo, find Min-ji."

Once he's gone, I unbuckle myself from my chair. I need to check in with Anis and Caro, make sure they had nothing to do with this, make sure this doesn't impact the plan. "I'm going to do a walk-through of the Residential Wing," I say. "See if anything came loose."

"Good idea," Eli says.

I consider her reddened eyes. "We just have to make it one more day. It's going to be okay."

Eli hesitates, then smiles. "I hope so."

———

As I head to the track, I glance into the exercise rooms lining the hall. We'd just done a gravity strapdown yesterday, so every item is strapped into its correct place, every room a single, cohesive object. The exception is a single five-pound weight that wasn't replaced in the track hall, which now hovers several inches off the ground. I slot it back into its rack and float up the steps toward the equipment room, which is difficult. The tip of my big toe nudged against any surface gives me more momentum than I'd expect.

Finally I slip into the equipment room. The top of Anis's head protrudes above his wall of exercise mats, a hemisphere of eyes, brows, forehead, tangled hair.

"Did you do this?" he says.

"No. So it wasn't you, either."

He shakes his head. "Why would I?"

"I don't know. To throw them off?" I sigh. "Do you think Caro—"

Then Anis's eyes affix to a spot over my shoulder, and a triumphant voice behind me says, "Look at this."

I try to turn and end up throwing myself into a tailspin. Pieter transforms into a smear of gold skin and black cloth. I seize one of the canvas handles on the exercise mats, and as I still myself, as everything comes to a halt, the world is transfixed into this instant.

There's no coming back from this. We're discovered, and there goes any chance to turn myself in, to earn that shred of goodwill that could have been a bargaining chip.

"I knew it," Pieter says with a grin so wide it splits his face in two. "Eli's going to be so disappointed. I told her, I *said* you were lying about that book. I told her you'd give the game away the second something went wrong. Look how good you are at following my lead."

"*You* did this?" I say. "You disabled the gravity?"

"Eli and I did it together. No one else knew. Don't feel too bad." His grin twists. "Now tell me where the hijacker is." He's braced in the doorframe, a stance like a crucifixion. He can't reach for the metal pipe hanging at his waist, or he'll lose his stability. I'm willing to bet on it. I have to bet, have to move, have to act.

"I don't know where she is," I say, adjusting my grip on the mats. I curl my legs up and back. "I swear, I don't—"

My feet slam into the mats and propel me forward with the force of pistons. Pieter moves but not quickly enough. "Go!" I yell back at Anis as I crash into Pieter and knock him from the doorway. We spin out into the huge emptiness above the track, limbs thrashing, making snow angels in the air above the painted concentric zeroes.

Pieter seizes a handful of my hair, twisting like a cat on its way to land. I lash a fist blindly upward at his throat and connect with something soft. He makes a strangled noise and yanks at my hair. I cry out as a patch rips away, but my eyes have fixed on the pipe at his waist. I lunge for it.

Too late. The pipe is gone from his waist and in his hand. It slams down on my back, once, twice. My vision whites out. There's a horrible tearing sound. It takes a second for me to realize it's coming from my mouth.

We roll toward the ceiling, everything sliding, the world a blur. The stripes of pain across my back throb. With my inner ear awhirl, bile rising in my throat, I retch. Something instinctive makes Pieter loosen his grip in my hair. At once I shove him back, and we rocket away from each other. Falling sideways through the room, I try to reposition myself, but I'm aimed face-first toward the wall. At the last instant, I pull my knees up in protection. My kneecaps slam into the white acrylic with a reverberant hit that goes all the way through my body.

I let out an agonized stutter and cling to the rail that runs along part of the wall. The pain forms hard bulbs over my knees, and multicolored streaks skewer my sight. I allow myself a moment of stillness, hunting for the door—Anis is nowhere to be seen—and straighten my legs. A guttural sound bursts from me as heat ladders up my thighs. *Ignore the pain,* I tell myself. *Ignore it all.* I kick out for the door.

My aim is good. I beat Pieter out of the exercise room, grab the railing that runs along the wall, and fly through the hall's curves, gaining momentum with every pull. When I emerge into the atrium, Anis is holding on to one of the tables, waiting for me. I propel myself from table to table until I reach him.

"The—" he starts, but then Pieter rockets into view at the mouth of the hall.

"Jump," I gasp, wrangling myself back into a vertical orientation.

"But—"

I grab his wrist. "Jump now!"

We kick off from the table. Pain erupts like firecrackers behind my kneecaps. We shoot up through the atrium, past balcony after balcony, air streaming down my cheeks. We narrowly miss one of the metal walkways. With our free arms, we reach out, hunting for purchase. Finally, at the ninth floor, Anis finds it. His hand seizes a railing, and my body snaps out like a cracked whip, fastened to him at his wrist. He tugs me over the railing and pulls himself afterward. "Go," he urges, "go, go!"

But Pieter isn't the only one chasing us anymore. Clusters of people are approaching us from every side, grappling their way down the balconies, soaring across the atrium. We're against the wall, the pair of us in tandem, scrabbling sideways down the hall, just out of sight, then toward the closest door: the Menagerie. My knees have heated to an unbearable temperature. The doors hiss open and we plunge into the arctic. Condensation wisps through the air, loose and erratic.

I hit the control panel to shut the door behind us, and at the last second, I hit the lights, too, hoping for a bit of camouflage. The white lights all around fade to deep blue, like a cave in a glacier reflecting the ocean. We fly through the vast grids of cubes, using the frames to direct ourselves.

I flinch, seeing a flutter of color. With the lights dimming, I wonder if my eyes are playing tricks, but no: Huge, colorful images are being projected onto the grids, videos of animals, showing which specimens are kept where. Jewel-toned beetles four feet in length flutter across one wall. Nearby, poisonously colored frogs the size of horses. I stare around and see lemurs, eagles, prowling wolves, an elephant at life size.

And there, in the corner, is a uniformed body. Francisco is floating beside one of the cryocases in the middle of some maintenance check, holding a diagnostic tablet in his hand.

His eyes move from me to Anis and back. "You . . ." he says in a small, choked voice. "You too."

I nod.

"And Sergei. Those visits you've been making."

"Yes."

Francisco lets go the tablet. It hovers beside the cryocase, turning end over end. He doesn't move toward us. He doesn't yell to raise the alarm. Instead he tugs himself across the cryocase, where a golden eagle is winging through the sky, and disappears without another word through the exit into the brightness beyond.

The shouts outside swell. Anis and I shy back and guide ourselves through a door set into the back wall, which leads to a darker chamber.

We've left the Terrestrial Wing. Here, in the blue murk, videos of white sharks pass peacefully by, their mouths gently open to reveal handfuls of teeth pointed askew. Minnows flutter in tremendous schools. Smooth pale ovals shine out from the sides of a pair of orca whales.

I hear a whir and look back. In the Terrestrial Wing, a long arc of white light has fallen across the tile. Anis and I maneuver ourselves farther behind the grid where the orcas are projected, but we only have so far to go. We're bottled up.

Pieter's voice resonates around the Menagerie. "They went in here. They're still here."

Then she's speaking. Eli. "Leigh," she says.

Somehow it kills me that she knows the truth. The raw betrayal in her tone hurts. *Think of what she's done,* I tell myself—but I am thinking of what she's done. Everything she's done, not just the knife she planted in Pieter's hand, but all the plans she made for our future, and the ways she thought she was keeping us safe.

"Why did you do this?" demands her voice, all around.

"You have to know why," I say, strong and clear. Everything is out in the open now. "Sergei already told us. Irina told us. They were right, Eli. Irina died because we were wrong."

"No, Irina died because of the girl you're helping! All this is her fault. We're starving because of her!"

Words pour out from me, words I didn't know had been circulating in me, coming together into something unbreakable: "Then I'd starve for the chance to save someone. I know you wouldn't, and maybe you're right, and there's nothing out here except us, and maybe we'd have a better chance if we pretended we were everything that mattered. But I don't want the worst parts of us to be what survives. I'm not going to cut out my heart to make it out here."

"Die, then!" Her shout ricochets. "That's your choice, that's your life! But you don't get to throw mine away!"

The only words that come to me are her own. "We all think we know what's best."

There's a brief silence. Then she says with cold anger, "Bring them out here."

Anis takes my hand. "Maybe we can get away," he whispers, his breath a pattern of white steam.

I try to imagine a way to dodge Eli and Pieter, despite my knees and back, despite the obstructed pathways. But then more voices sound, dozens of them, and my plans fall apart. The rest of the crew are out there with Eli. The others will be floating between the aisles of cubes, forming an unbreakable human rope, ill lit and faceless. This slow, anonymous murmur means we'll never get out.

"No," I whisper. "Lock us in."

Anis tilts forward. He grasps one of the brackets and pushes himself out into the air, unmooring himself from me. A moment later, I hear the door slide shut.

There's a faint laugh from the Terrestrial Hall, deadened by the door. "All right," Pieter says. "Your choice. When you start getting frostbite, we'll see you outside."

As Anis returns to the orcas, I hold myself against the wall, braced with one hand on a pipe and one on the freezing surface of cryocubes. The wipe of adrenaline, like whitewash, has started to drip away from my body, exposing a colorful map of pain. I feel the bruises purpling across my back. My knees are swelling with the trauma of collision. I thank God there's no weight on my legs, because even without gravity, they're shaking so violently that my muscles remember their old hobbies. Ten-mile runs in summer heat.

Anis sees my feet twitching. "You're hurt."

"My knees. And . . ." I turn away from him and lift up my uniform's shirt so he can see my back. He lets out a low sound.

"How bad is it?" I ask.

He doesn't answer the question, just tugs the cloth gently down. "Cold will be good for it. Here."

He helps navigate me toward the tile. I hook my feet into a grid nearby to keep myself against the floor. The surface is unforgiving, my vertebrae knuckled against the hard surface, but the cold is an instant relief, like pressing a slab of ice to the hot welts. Anis's hand slips into mine.

"We have to get to the bridge," I whisper. It's nearly lost in the hum of the freezers. "What are we going to do?"

"I don't know."

"Is there anything here we can use?" I scan the hall and blurt, "There!" Lying on my back, I can see something blurred in the blue shadows: a line of rungs leading up to a hatch in the ceiling. A service entrance? A ventilation shaft? I grab Anis's ankle and point.

"Wait here," he says, and kicks off for the Menagerie's highest reaches. He grapples his way across the ceiling, twists the wheel handle, and pulls the hatch free on its hinges.

Anis climbs into the chamber beyond. "It's an airlock!" he calls down. "This is one of the spots the solar sail is attached to."

"The airlock in the bridge," I say breathlessly. "We could still try to get in that way and catch them off guard. Maybe we could force them out into the hall, if there aren't too many."

I hear plastic slapping plastic, something whining, as he shuffles around.

"Anis?" I call. He's repeating something to himself over and over, but the size of the chamber distorts the words.

When he looks out of the airlock again, his excitement is gone. "There are no suits."

I shake my head. "There have to be. Isn't there something we could use as a makeshift suit? Anything?"

He's fastening the hatch back into place. "No. Neither of us is spacewalking without being absolutely sure we won't . . ."

He doesn't finish. I know we're both thinking the same thing. Space wreaks havoc on the unprotected human body. The suffocation is the least of it. Your spit boils on your tongue, and if you don't exhale, your lungs rupture, and any part of you facing the sun burns with radiant heat, and then, of course, you drift into space as if entering the darkest, deepest sea.

"I'll look around," he says, "and see if there's anything else."

Anis takes his time. He is as thorough and precise as ever. By the time he returns to our corner, I'm shivering. I don't need to ask if he found anything. We're alone with the beasts.

"Do you think they're still out there?" I ask. My teeth have begun to click in the cold.

"I don't know. They could have brought blankets and made camp behind the door. Maybe they're on the balcony."

"Do you think we could surprise them if we made a run for it?"

"I doubt it."

I'm glad for his pessimism. False optimism would be too sad to see on him.

"There's still Caro and Sergei," I say. "I gave her the new passcode for the confinement cells. She could get him out."

"They can't fight their way through fifty people."

"I'm not talking about helping us. I meant the *Hermes*. With the others here, maybe Caro and Sergei can make it to the bridge." I pause. "Also, once Caro's out in the open, Eli will make her a priority. We could make a break for it then."

"Even then, Caro won't leave the plant until tonight," Anis says. "And she doesn't have a diversion anymore." From his pocket, he pulls out the tablet she gave him.

At the sight of it, I manage a smile. My dry lips are close to cracking. "We can still give her one."

"How?"

I take the tablet and return to the door. "Eli," I call.

Pieter answers at once, dulled by the door, but I can still hear the smugness. "She's back in the bridge. Ready to come out?"

"No, thanks. The three of us are fine in here."

The self-satisfaction drains out of Pieter's tone. "Three of you?"

I scroll through Caro's list of prerecorded dialogue and press *Play* on one of the files. Her voice issues out from the tablet at full volume, tuneful and casual. *"It's so good to hear your voice. I've missed you all."*

"No," Pieter hisses. "How?"

I let out a laugh. "Why do you think we came this way? Caro's been here since we turned around."

"Then I hope you all freeze together!" he shouts.

"We'll be fine. It's warm behind the walls."

Something slams hard into the door. I jerk back. Anis grabs my hand, and we float to the back of the chamber again, behind a grid of cryocubes showing a blue whale, its massive body gliding up and over us.

Pieter strikes the door two more times. Then I hear the tones of an argument, and there's no more.

Anis and I exhale in unison. "Sorry," I say. "I should have realized he might try to break through."

"No, this is better. Now they'll focus everything on us. Caro might have a chance."

We brace ourselves between the grid and the wall so it's almost as if we're sitting beside each other. I let my head rest upon his shoulder, and we stay there for a long time, immobile.

When I look up at him again, his cheeks are no longer ruddy from navigating around the room. His forehead has a grayish sheen from the cold.

"What?" he asks.

"N-nothing." I look back down at myself, at my feet, which I can hardly feel, at my trembling hands. My skin doesn't look like itself anymore, but like a material, taut and textured, something I might have seen stretched over a tube in a fabric store for sale by the yard.

Anis takes my hands and rubs them between his. Feeling needles my fingertips. "Thanks," I say, smiling. I do the same for him, wrap his hands in my palms and force friction between us. Our skin is so dry that a susurrus comes from the contact, the sound of leaves brushed through in autumn.

Minute by minute, my thoughts grow sluggish and stupid. I was silly to think I would never see winter again. The world outside our windows is winter, colder and less forgiving than anything we had at home. This, in here, is winter, the world's natural state. What was miraculous was the tiny summer the engineers built for us, out in the body of the ship.

"Keep talking to me," Anis says. "How did P-Pieter know it was you?"

"I forgot t-to tell you. They found my n-notebook."

"No."

"Yeah. It's gone. Except . . ." I reach for the pocket of his uniform where I folded the single torn-out page. His bewilderment turns to surprise as I work the white corner of paper out from the fabric. He looks like a little kid taken in by a magic trick. I want to smile, but if my lips are stretching, I can't feel them.

He unfolds the paper, scans it. "Will you read it t-to me? I'm so slow at reading English."

Of course, I think. At first I'm sure that I've spoken the words, but that can't be right, because they haven't rung through the icy air like everything else we've said. I want to do it, want to read it to him, but the world is going gray.

"Leigh," he says, folding the page back into his pocket with stiff fingers. "*Leigh.*"

"Yeah?" I whisper.

The way he clutches my wrists makes my hands fill with blood, trapped in my fingertips, beating like wings. Then he gathers me gingerly into him. He's still braced firmly between grid and wall, anchoring our bodies, but my hair swirls around my face, shadowing us both. My knees are crooked over his hips, and we're chest to chest, forehead to forehead.

Our hands lose heat quickly, even entangled and soaked in our breath. Eventually we fit our hands into the warm hollows of each other's armpits, with nervous laughter at first, but it feels so good that we don't dare move. I can imagine us sun yellow in some thermal imaging photograph, the world around us as blue as snow at dusk. I remember sitting side by side in the water treatment plant, the warm hum, our hidden paradise. We should have fought our way there and hidden forever.

"I'm so tired," I say hoarsely.

He says something, and I realize my translator has died. I recognize part of the phrase from the nights he's spent repeating Arabic words for my benefit: "Don't." The rest is lost to me.

"I can't understand," I say.

He hunts for words a while before settling on, "Don't sleep. Not in the cold."

We slip our hands up the backs of each other's shirts, and I feel him arch against me with the iciness of my touch, and his hands feel like metal webs against my back. "Can you feel your fingers?" I whisper into the lower curls of his hair, which are crisp with sweat turned to ice.

"Not a lot," he says.

"Me neither." My words are slurring again. I rest my chin on his shoulder, tilt my head against his, and fight my eyelids. Time begins to skate on metal blades, gliding by with uncanny speed and smoothness. My vision blurs and darkens, but he shakes me awake.

"Anis . . ." I want to complain. Just a moment's rest.

He takes my cheeks in his palms and looks me in the eye. "No," he says, and adds something in Arabic. I imagine I understand. He will never let me rest. He will push me until the very end. He lets his forehead fall against mine. Our noses brush each other. His skin is so cold, but I put my hands up beneath the front of his shirt until my nails push against his sternum. Here, at the center, he's still warm. I imagine my fingers melting into water, my extremities dissolving.

"I'm sorry," I murmur. "Letting you down. Again."

"Leigh," he's saying. "Leigh." He's speaking so loudly. I want to cringe away into the quiet, where I can rest. He gives my head a little shake, gripping the back of my skull, making pain scurry over the patch of torn hair. My eyes are closing, my face feels like rubber. "Leigh," he says, "wake up, please, wake up."

He tilts his head, and after a moment I realize he's kissing me. The pulse of sudden heat burns, but I press back against him. Our teeth click, clumsy, against each other. My lips are graceless. I don't remember how to shift them, the movement of a kiss, anything, but I remember the light when I first kissed him, everything black and blue and silver. His hands bracket my waist, and his touch is featherlight, but even the slightest pressure hurts as if he's crushing the tissue irreparably. I try to lift my hands, to hold his face and stabilize the way he drifts before me, but we've lost too much strength to keep still. He curls around me as we hover away from the wall and the floor, whispering something against the nape of my neck that means nothing to me and everything: He's still here. As we revolve slowly, weightlessly, in the dark air, I realize we're going to die. But if we do, I will die knowing, at least, what I am. I could tell him if I could speak. My mouth is ajar, but the only thing issuing out is the white smoke of breath. Ahead, projected onto glass, are ghostly creatures I don't know: flat, rhomboid fish nine feet tall. Scales like chainmail. Looking up at the surface almost mirrored with frost, I imagine a cube our size; I imagine cracking its lid and slipping with Anis into its liquefied contents. The substance would be a cold sharper than a blade, a bath that would make our hypothermic bodies feel like firestorms. Maybe that's how we could save ourselves: by giving up the present to send our consciousness like a letter through time, waking up halfway through a trip that's elapsed without us. I'd like to think that if we woke up in five hundred years, this place would have found some of the peace I remember from before the announcements. Why do I feel that way about home, like we had peace? Earth was hectic and hyper-trafficked, an overloaded grid operating every second of every day, polluted and violent, brimming with hatred so strong it made people feel euphoric. Despite all that, though, I remember it as peaceful. Because—why? Because of Marcus's porch that creaked in summer? Because of a sunset I watched from the window of a plane, or the pleasure of running hard toward a thin chalked line? I know this tranquility is something I've picked and chosen, the way I've let the purr of the highway and the pollinated scent of spring air become the entire Virginia countryside. But those little utopias were everywhere. Now I let them expand to engulf the whole. Even here, adrift in the dark, I see lovely colors intermingled like abstract art, and I have the touch of somebody I've come to know. These graces might shrink, but I won't let them disappear. Anis was right. I will never let them go.

CHAPTER 18

OPEN SPACES

A film over my eyes makes everything hazy. Dreams have taken me, or maybe they're hallucinations. The Marine Hall has no windows, but I still see stars. We are the only life here, but I see something crawling down the wall, white as starch.

I can't move, can't speak. The crawling thing drifts away from the wall. It flies closer like a gliding seagull. Noise blares around me. I want to hide, but all I can do is let my eyelids fall shut. The dream is so vivid. Something squeaks against tile; the creature is upon me. I hear something click, then ragged breaths like the rip of card stock. I'm moved gingerly, eased upright against the wall, and I feel Anis's shoulder pushed against mine. I imagine us consumed by a hunter, throats torn away to reveal slick cavities.

Someone is speaking. "Leigh. Leigh?"

I crack my eyes open again. The dream figure is misty and unclear and surrounded by an angelic glow. It lifts an oblong bag from its shoulder, extracts blurry swaths of blankets that flap like wings in the absence of gravity, and wraps them around all three of us until we are cocooned. This last dream is a kind one. I close my eyes again and let myself imagine warmth.

Except that minute by minute, the warmth feels more real. Then it gives way to ferocious pain that attacks the suddenly sensitive nerves of my hands, wrists, cheeks, toes. All my digits quiver. Now, when I blink, my eyelids move smoothly, wiping away the film, and I realize why the figure is glowing. I recognize the shimmering fabric—an extravehicular activity suit, banded with mechanical pressure threads that hug to Caro's body. She wears bulky black gloves and boots, and bands of the same rubbery material coil around the EVA's elbows and knees.

"It's you," I rasp.

She replies in Swahili, throws herself sideways at me, and locks me in a stranglehold of a hug. Apparently my talking has convinced her that I won't shatter on contact. With my head tucked over her shoulder, I see Anis stirring on her other side. He's alive. Warmth spreads through my abdomen. The relief is so sluggish that for a moment I mistake it for nausea.

Caro pulls away and keeps talking, apparently unaware that I can't understand her. She's panting, clouded with breath, her eyes wet and shining. She looks unfamiliar like this, letting herself overflow with emotion.

She repeats something, and that much Swahili I remember from our lessons: "Do you understand?"

I shake my head, touching my translator. She tugs out her own at once, adjusting its settings to speaker, and talks into it. Caro's translation responds in English: "How about this?"

Anis's head bobs as he takes out his own dead translator and pockets it. "How did you come here?" he croaks in English. Caro's translator repeats in Swahili.

"I heard people shouting in the treatment plant," Caro says. "I knew something went wrong, so I snuck out. I have suits and helmets for you two in here." She shakes the duffel. "I took them from the Command Wing. The ship is almost deserted, since everybody is waiting for you two outside the Menagerie. This could be our chance."

It takes me a second to understand. "You think the bridge is unguarded?"

"Maybe not completely empty, but I wouldn't be surprised if only a few people are inside. If all three of us come in through the airlock, we might be able to overpower them."

"What about Sergei?"

She bites her lip. "I didn't want to risk being seen in the Residential Wing. Unless he can get to the bridge himself, I think we're on our own."

"And how much time do we have?" I ask.

"If my math is right, we'll reach the *Hermes* in around four hours. We actually should have arrived already, but when they killed the acceleration, we were moving slower than our average pace, so they stretched out the timeline by hours." She unzips the duffel and sorts through its floating contents until she finds three tablets. She hands one to Anis and one to me. "I duplicated the orbit sync program, one for each of us.

Remember, just like the old plan: We need to plug this in before we reach the moon, and then I need to get into the commander's seat."

I glance at Anis, who's staring at the translator as if he's trying to move it with his mind. "Have you been getting all this?" I ask.

"We will climb to the bridge?" Anis says. "Then plug in a tablet?"

"Perfect. You pass your English test." Caro takes our hands in her gloves, examining our reddening skin. "How are your hands? You need to be able to hold on tightly to make the spacewalk."

"Hold on?" Anis asks. "The suits don't have . . ." He repeats a phrase a few times in Arabic, then makes a hissing sound, pushing his hands out.

"Jet propulsion?" Caro says. "They do, but do you know how to use it? Are you willing to bet that you won't send yourself flying into space with it?"

Anis grimaces. "You're right."

"We'll use the rungs on the ship's exterior," Caro says. "Can you grip? The gloves are pressurized like the rest of the suit, so there'll be a lot of resistance."

I form a fist. Tears spring to my eyes. It feels like clutching a handful of broken glass. "I'll manage," I choke out. "Anis?"

He nods, slowly flexing his fingers.

"Good," Caro says. "Let's go." She returns the blankets to the duffel and tosses us our suits. My fingers are slow and blundering, but Caro helps me roll the elasticized material into place and fasten the seals at the elbow and knee joints. The suit is bulky over my back, where the air canisters are cushioned by protective layers. My body feels tight and secure, the pressure holding on to me like a hand, and the material straps all the warmth beneath my skin.

While Caro helps Anis, I climb up to the exit hatch, preferring the slow ladder rungs to kicking off. I still don't trust my knees. By the time I reach the ceiling, my arms are at least operating smoothly, even if stabbing sensations still accompany every movement.

Caro drifts past me to open the airlock, her hair up in mini twists that waft gently around her face. The duffel bag slung over her back brushes me as she crawls inside. Anis and I follow, pull the trapdoor up behind us, and turn the wheel until the airlock is sealed.

"Okay. We'll use these tethers for the first part of the walk." Caro removes three coiled tethering cables from the duffel and shows us the silver clips at each end. "Release like this, tighten like this, lock like this."

As Anis and I fasten the clips to our belts, Caro hands us each a helmet. "We'll climb to the bottom of this wing, then around the ship over the Systems Wing until we reach the Command Wing. Don't move too quickly, especially after we're untethered."

"Got it," I say, remembering my belabored attempts to navigate my bedroom in the morning.

She repeats the instructions more slowly for Anis. When he nods his understanding, Caro lets out a slow puff of breath, then manages a small, worried smile. "When we put on the helmets, the airflow is automatic. Are you ready?"

"Ready," Anis and I say together.

Caro reverts her translator to its original settings and plugs it back into her ear. We lower the silver domes over our heads. They fasten, and with a twist, mine emits a satisfying click.

We press buttons at our wrists with the microphone and head-phone symbols, and as the system turns on, the sounds of Caro's and Anis's breaths stir around my ears. Several small symbols light up in my helmet's interior: a tank, a droplet of water, a puff of air.

Caro holds up three fingers and lowers them. Three... two... one.

She pushes the depressurize button by the exit hatch. The vents reclaim the air around us back into the body of the ship, creating a vacuum in the airlock. Then the outer hatch springs open to reveal a perfect circle of stars. All this seems to happen in silence, my helmet's thick glass insulating me. We drift up and out onto the hull, a glimmering plain as smooth as fresh asphalt. I curl my aching fingers around the hatch's outer rail. To our left is the solar sail's top anchor, a metal ring five feet in diameter. The sail is like the fin of a sunfish, magnificent and thin, its fabric as iridescent as an oil spill.

I force my eyes away and survey the climb ahead, the trail of rungs that stretches down the exterior of the wing. Preparing to start downward, we clip our tethers to the outer rails and let go of the cables, which hang beneath our fingers, some of their coils unspinning. The sight of the braided material catching the starlight mesmerizes me.

Anis starts to seal the hatch. "Go," he says in English. "Quick."

Caro reaches from the hatch's rail to the first rung and starts down, looking like an acrobat walking on her hands. I don't allow myself to look out at the nothingness all around. I focus only on the ship's hull, a surface I know and understand, as I take the first rung and begin the journey after her.

From the airlock, this looked like a descent. Now everything reorients. I'm swimming across a flat surface, seizing the bars that have erupted out of the ground before me. The ship is an alien playground, or a model hung in the dark by invisible thread.

Halfway down the wing, my glove slips on a rung. My body sways. Sweat slicks my palms. I clutch tight to the rung, envisioning my body toppling into the distance as the ship sails back for the *Hermes*. My hands itch ferociously. I wish I could scratch them. I imagine the sore red flesh and squeeze the rung harder, trying to beat the blood back.

I touch the tether at my hip to reassure myself, then force myself onward.

Near the bottom of the Systems Wing, there's a gentle, insistent tug from the tether.

The others have stopped, too. I look through their gold-tinted visors for reassurance. As one, we untether ourselves and set off over the side of the Systems Wing, leaving our tethers drifting behind us like ribbons of quicksilver.

We follow the rungs, curving up toward the Preservation Wing. "Wait," Anis crackles through the helmet radio. I look in the direction he's pointing and see a long glass stripe: the window into the canteen.

"Wanaweza kutuona?" Caro asks, and although my translator is still zipped away, I understand. *Can they see us?*

"No," I say. "There shouldn't be anyone there. And our suits are good camouflage."

"But we should stay close to the ship," Anis says, voice halting as he searches for the words. "For less shadow."

Keeping our bodies close to the rungs slows our pace even further. Soon twenty minutes have passed since we left the

Menagerie. At thirty, the bridge's windshield finally comes into view, gazing out from the top of the Command Wing. I can see the hatch, a dark line cut into the glowing wall.

With the end in sight, I pull too eagerly on the next rung. My body sways like a rudder. I let out a high noise of alarm. Perpendicular to the ship, I tilt my head up at the rungs, my perspective readjusts, and suddenly I am hanging from a half mile of monkey bars.

I can't help myself. I look down, out, into space. The sight is as beautiful as it is horrifying. Is one of those pinprick lights a star whose system we'll reach someday? I imagine the galaxy watching us, and then my perception weightlessly realigns, and I imagine the galaxy utterly unconcerned. The flat fabric of the universe, rolling forever in every direction, never bothered with us. Nobody watched when Earth was destroyed. Nobody will watch if one of us lets go here, except each other. We are unspeakably small, bacteria clinging to an insect's body.

Then my legs swing back, and I'm looking up at Caro. She's four stories ahead by now, more agile, not hindered by the lingering effects of the Menagerie the way Anis and I are. She's reached the bridge. She twists her feet into the last rung to keep herself stable as she brings her hand down on something beside the airlock.

I wait for the hatch to click, to unlock, to make some sign. Nothing happens.

"No," I whisper.

"What is it?" says Anis over the radio. He's a story and a half behind me, still climbing, slow and deliberate.

"It's locked," I hiss. "Eli must have locked it; she must have realized we could try to get in this way."

"Xara," Anis swears—*shit*. He stops moving over the rungs, and we both scan the ship's exterior, looking for another way in, our breaths echoing in each other's helmets.

It's a moment before I realize how labored Caro's breathing is.

I maneuver myself around to look at her. She's trying to turn the wheel handle of the airlock, but she's moving with tedious slowness.

"Caro. What's wrong?" I say sharply.

"I feel . . . nina k-kizunguzungu."

"What does she mean?" Anis says.

"Dizzy, I think." The heat in my hands, in my whole body, increases to a burn. "She must be low on oxygen."

"Don't talk, Caro," Anis says. Though he's thirty rungs away, I can see his panic through the illuminated glass mask. "Door, Leigh!"

The closest entrance—

"There!" I point over the sheer face of the Command Wing. At the bottom is the hull door, the same entrance we hurried through that night in July.

"Let's go," Anis says, turning around. "Caro. Let's go."

He's in the lead as we climb back down the Command Wing, but we've hardly made it ten feet when I glance over my shoulder and see that Caro hasn't moved at all. She's still at the top of the row of rungs, a figurine at the airlock to the bridge, leaning over something that glints on the hull.

"Caro!" I say. "Come on!"

She mumbles something indistinct.

"What are you saying? Can you get it open?"

Caro doesn't answer. She reaches toward the glinting object on the hull. Halfway up the wing, she's the size of a doll.

"Caro, come on," I urge. "This way."

Her body turns fractionally toward me. She draws a scrape of a breath.

From far away, I see her grab for the next rung and miss. "Okay, don't move!" I say, my voice ricocheting around the interior of my helmet, high and scared, as I maneuver myself around to face her. "Just stay there, just wait for me!" Her left hand is still fastened to the ship, her only link. Flesh, blood, will.

Anis shouts something in Arabic. I make it three rungs toward Caro before she detaches from the ship, a glowing island.

"Caro," I yell. "Caro, grab back on! Now!"

Her arm moves feebly, but the motion does nothing. She hangs just above the surface of the ship like a helium balloon on its last day.

I contort my body until my feet find the rungs, crouching.

"Leigh!" Anis says. "Wait!"

But I'm already kicking off. I am flying upward toward her, parallel to the hull, rungs flickering by beneath me like a light show. Caro grows ahead. She's feet away from the ship now, but I'm nearly there. Close . . . closer . . .

I seize on to the rungs beneath Caro. My hands form a fulcrum, and the rest of my body swings around, slamming my back into the rungs, punching the air out of me. My jaw clacks shut, and my mouth tastes metallic, like pennies. Panting, I hook my feet into the rail at the airlock so I can reach for her. Caro drifts. "No," I gasp, groping for her, spreading my fingers so that the raw skin on my palms pulls like latex.

Still, her limp hands are hanging a foot above mine. Her face, beneath the glow of her helmet, is landscaped with hoops of light, her eyes half-open. And I see her lost like this forever.

She won't even have some burial on one of the Planter floors, repurposed into our closed system. She will float through asteroid belts, irretrievable and alone.

I look down at the controls on my forearm.

"Leigh, wait," Anis blares through my helmet's speaker. "Don't let go. Stop!"

I look back at him, still stories away. By the time he reaches us, even if we form a human chain, Caro will be out of our reach.

I tap the forward arrow on my wrist experimentally and hear a split second's hiss. There's a gentle force against my shoulders and back, like I'm a shy child gently ushered forward by a grown-up's huge hand. I tap the backward arrow, and puffs of nitrogen gas shoot out from my shoulders.

I unhook my feet from the rungs.

The second I let go, something miraculous spreads through my body. Certainty. I am swimming, weightless, suspended in space, held in by the designs of Earth's greatest minds. They are going to keep me safe. Delicate emissions come from my suit as I navigate myself toward Caro, tap by tap, puff by puff.

And then she's in reach. I lunge for her wrist with all my might. My hand closes around her arm. I let out a choked sound. "Got her. I've got her! Anis, go, get the door open!"

But she's horribly motionless behind the helmet, her eyes still half-open and unseeing. I grapple Caro backward into my arms, press the down arrow on my wrist, and with a hard exhalation from the propulsion system, we're thrust back toward the ship. We drift down over the hull, over the pathway of rungs, catching up to Anis. He's moving more quickly now, and by the time he reaches the door at the bottom of the Command Wing,

I'm at his heel, gripping Caro tightly, trying not to think about how still she is. When was the last time I heard her breathe? One minute ago? Two?

I grab a rung with one hand while Anis twists the hatch open. We bundle ourselves inside, the three of us, and as he fastens the outer hatch shut, I pull myself along the wall to the control panel and repressurize the airlock. A minute later, a light flashes from red to green, and I twist Caro's helmet off.

"Breathe," I gasp. I pull off my own helmet, and the warm air rushes over my skin, as tangible as butter. "Breathe," I say, seizing her by the shoulders.

Anis is grappling his way out of his EVA suit. Once he's freed one of his hands from its glove, he holds his palm in front of Caro's mouth.

"She's breathing," he says.

Every muscle in my body goes loose. I hold weakly to the wall and watch our helmets floating across the airlock, relief steamrolling over me. She's alive. She's going to be all right.

Another small victory: There's a charging dock at the door. As Anis secures Caro's limp, hovering form against a cabinet, I hook the dead translators into the dock. Red lights start to pulse on their sides.

We gingerly remove our suits, collect the helmets and gloves that have been revolving in the air around us, and stow them in Caro's bag. With every movement, I discover lingering effects of the hypothermia. My body feels like most of its parts have been substituted with near replacements. I've been given a mannequin's twistable joints, prone to sticking. And my hands are boiling hot, cast-iron gloves just pulled from a forge. Anis has stabilized himself near the floor to massage his ankle, face drawn, but when he sees me watching, he seems to forget what he was feeling. He plucks our translators from the charger, hands mine over, and says, "Is your back all right? Your knees?"

"They're awful, but it's okay. Are you all right?"

"All right."

Both our eyes move to Caro. "Is she asleep?" he says.

"Yeah." I wrap one of the floating blankets around her. "It's the middle of the night. Let's let her rest. I don't want her trying to dock the ship on no sleep."

Anis nods. "Is it safe to wait here until we're closer to the *Hermes*?"

"I think so. By Caro's last count, we're about three hours away. Also, everyone still thinks we're stuck in the Marine Hall."

"True. That's lucky."

Anis and I move toward each other unthinkingly. His hand presses to the soft part of my side, beneath the hem of my shirt. His skin is warm now, but I'm remembering how in the Menagerie we felt like twin sides of a single ice sculpture.

My eyelids are drooping. "Do you want to sleep?" he asks. "Have a couple of hours. I'll stay awake."

"Okay." I smile, hooking my translator back into the charging dock. "Wake me up if you want to switch."

I navigate downward, slipping one arm through the railing beside Anis to secure myself. Anis rests his hand on the side of my neck, and I rotate gently until my head has settled into his lap. I'm asleep, his hand stroking my hair, before my eyes are fully closed. There's no dream, only gray, only a feeling of immense comfort swaddling me.

Eli's voice wakes me. An announcement echoes through the PA: *The ship will resume acceleration in five minutes.*

Glancing around, I see Caro's awoken, too. "Caro?" I say. "Do you feel all right?"

She nods, gingerly unwinding the cable that Anis had used to hold her secure against the cabinet. "We still have time?"

"An hour or so," Anis says.

"And you can understand me?"

I smile. "Yeah. We let you sleep for a bit and recharged our translators."

"Right." The furrows in her brow ease but not completely.

"What were you saying out there?" I ask. "What happened? Did you see something at the airlock? In the bridge?"

"Yeah. It's the radio equipment."

"What about it?"

Caro licks her lips. "It's . . ." She looks from me to Anis, her dark eyes bright. "I don't think it's there."

Neither of us says anything to this. The words feel meaningless.

"The fleet's ships," she goes on, "are supposed to communicate with each other using lasercom. Optical communications. But to communicate to Earth, it's supposed to use regular radio, which means antennae and transponders near the bridge. And the amplifying equipment isn't there. Which means . . . I don't think the *Hermes* would have been able to receive any of our messages, or send any to us."

Realization makes my fingertips tingle and itch. "Then," I whisper, "the astronaut couldn't have sent out a distress signal."

"That would explain why we never heard from her," Anis says.

As we look at each other, I feel a powerful hit of hope. Like the feeling of lying in that bathtub with Marcus, three years and a lifetime ago, my head spinning, realizing I was drunk.

We're so close to the *Hermes* now, so close to fastening the *Lazarus* to the filling station. If we manage to get that door open—she could really be inside, alive, waiting.

"One more thing," Caro says. "Did Eli say the ship was going to accelerate again?"

"Yes," I say. "Why?"

Caro fumbles out her tablet, typing something into a calculator. "It'll compress the timeline. We won't be an hour from the *Hermes* anymore."

"How long, then?" Anis says.

Caro shakes her head. "I'm not sure. I don't know our exact speed, just that it's below average. We'll be accelerating toward the *Hermes*."

I think for a moment. "So we should try to take the bridge the second the gravity comes back on?"

"Yes. We can run for the elevators."

"Too noticeable," I say. "The elevator shaft is transparent; they'll see us going for the tenth floor."

"Then we'll go through the water treatment plant," Anis says. "We'll get out on the sixth floor and take the stairs the rest of the way up."

"Okay," Caro says, "but remember, the docking sequence has to be plugged into the dashboard before we pass the moon, and then I need to get into that commander's seat somehow."

We hover in the airlock, possibility pulsing between us like an invisible heart.

"Do you think anyone's there?" Caro says. "You don't think we did all this for nothing, do you?"

"Either way," I say quietly, "it wasn't for nothing. We're trying. That's—"

Eli's voice interrupts. *Ten. Nine. Eight.*

"That's the point," Caro finishes.

I smile. "Yeah."

Seven. Six. Five. Four.

Realizing we're all hovering four feet off the floor, I take hold of a railing in one hand, Anis's forearm in the other. "Get closer to the ground. Quick."

Three. Two. One.

A deep hum, and the ship begins to accelerate again. The few inches between us and the ground disappear. For a moment it feels as if someone is sitting on my back. Then my body remembers how it feels to resist. I push myself to my feet, alight with pain and purpose, with a sense of direction as pure and innate as gravity.

CHAPTER 19

ARTIFACT

C aro opens the inner hatch and we creep out into the atrium. I look upward at the flag of the Republic, at the nested circles of balconies, at the crisscrossing walkways. The ship is deserted, but the still-dark sunspot is a great eye overhead, watching us creep toward the treatment plant.

We're passing the hearth when there's a shout up in the balconies. Half a dozen faces have appeared, angled down toward us from fifty feet above. "They're here!" somebody yells, pointing. "They're in the atrium!"

As one, we break into a sprint across the atrium. I see one of the guards' metal bars lying on a table and snatch it up as I fly past. The last thing I see before the door to the treatment plant slides shut is a line of bodies running down from the elevator bay.

Every step on the walkway is an incriminating clang. From here, the sixth-floor exit is the size of a paper clip, waiting at the top of a steep incline. A maze of walkways lies between us and that exit.

As we tear up the ramps, beneath the strip lights, shouts chase after us. I glance back and see a knotted mass of limbs writhing through the dark. At first there are too many for them to gain much ground, but then the herd thins, and the third-floor exit opens. They'll take the elevator. They'll be waiting on the tenth floor when we reach it.

I've pulled ahead of Anis and Caro. To force myself to wait for them would be agony, even worse than pushing my injured knees. I move faster, holding the metal bar aloft. I'll use my lead to strike aside every obstacle for them.

I shove through the door onto the sixth-floor balcony, bar lifted and ready—but we've beat them. The elevator is pulling to a stop across the atrium. A full car pelts out onto the balconies and toward us, a faceless blur.

I shoulder through the door to the stairwell. Caro and Anis speed up after me, and the noise here, too, is excruciating, magnified off every surface. When I glance back, Anis is at my heel, nearly keeping pace, but Caro is gasping, folding over, clutching a cramp in her side. As we come up the final flight of stairs, she huddles over the rail and retches. It's a miracle she's gotten this far, after living beneath a boiler for five weeks.

Shouts come from stories below. Anis and I bolster Caro up the last few steps and emerge onto the balcony.

The hallway to the bridge is a hundred feet to our left. To our right is the elevator bay, where another search party is spilling through the elevator doors. I see Pieter raising his pipe like an Olympic torch, yelling as he leads the swarm toward us.

"Go," I cry out. The three of us run for the entrance to the Command Wing. Overhead, the light is slowly changing from night to day.

"Leigh!" Anis yells. I look back. Caro is twenty paces behind, staggering, hands flat against the wall. With a horror that makes the world approach slow motion, I see the search party closing in on her. Anis and I hurtle down the balcony.

But Pieter reaches Caro first. He catches her by the collar of her uniform, and she lets out a cry, twisting toward him, trying to shove him away. "Pieter," I yell, brandishing my pipe. I think about diving forward, finding an angle at which I can't possibly hit her if I swing for him.

Caro drives her foot into the side of his knee. Pieter's leg buckles horribly outward. He screams like stabbed livestock and grabs her shoulder, staggering, while she does the same, staying upright, and with their other hands thrust out at each other's necks and faces, they twist and feint and look bizarrely as if they're dancing, and the pipe in my hand is still raised and quivering, until a pair of strong hands grabs me.

Luke forces my arms down. "Stop," I yell, struggling, trying to slam my head into his, but he holds me fast, my back to his chest as I try to thrash free. At my side, two other guards have pinned Anis to the wall. Pieter and Caro are still locked in their fight.

Then Pieter stumbles, and Caro manages to knock him against the balcony railing. His head snaps backward on impact, and the railings tremble. I see hope on Caro's face right before he seizes her beneath the arm and lifts her. She cries out, flails, grabs hold of one of the railings, and kicks at him. They are entwined. They lurch. Then they're tipping over the railing into the atrium.

Caro's hands wrap onto the rail and hold tight. Pieter's grasping fingers find nothing.

I scream. He's hardly fallen before I'm screaming. He topples eight stories like a stone, spinning. His back and body slam into a walkway, but his neck is hanging over the side. I see it snap. Into my ear Luke releases a horrible, sick sound, even as the blade he holds nicks my side.

I go wild. My throat is raw from the noises I am making. I am torn in every direction, horror warring with relief, because Caro has clawed her way back over the railing and lies huddled on the floor, shivering—alive. I want to clutch her back from the edge. I want to dive after Pieter, somehow pull him up and correct him, undo all this, return him to who he used to be, evenhanded and levelheaded, a little too eager to please.

Yells come from behind me. I twist around. Anis has broken free, and he's running into the Command Wing, down that jagged hallway, and Caro is still curled up, hyperventilating, riveted by the red sight below, but Matteo—Matteo is running after Anis, howling.

No.

I slam the back of my head into Luke's face. His nose crunches softly beneath my skull. He bellows, and I throw myself forward, ripping free.

Pain tears through my side. Heat is pouring from me. It doesn't matter. My fingers button up the wound, holding me together. I'm running the way I ran the night we all knew this was the end. This is what I was made for. To fulfill the primal need to go, to chase, to burst free of everything that held me safe in place, and now I am running toward something, too. I see Matteo ahead and catch up with him. I slam my shoulder into his back. He ricochets off the wall like a pinball, trips, and falls. I dash past him.

When I sprint into the bridge, my hand clasped over my slippery side, the first thing I see is the moon, swelling in the windshield. Anis is wrestling with Eli at the far end of the dashboard. He has her in a headlock but looks up and sees me. "Leigh," he yells. "The tablet!"

I bolt down the stairs, but as I reach the dashboard and yank the tablet with the docking sequence from my pocket, Matteo storms over the threshold. He spots his mark and sprints for Eli and Anis, knife raised.

Time slows impossibly, and I could swear I see my future cleave apart, splitting into two passageways before me. Ten feet to my left, I see the port where the plug in my hand could fasten. But at the opposite end of the dashboard, Anis's back is a broad, vulnerable target. Matteo is tearing down the steps, blade positioned to scythe down. I'm standing in the atrium watching Pieter throw that first blow. I'm standing by the Council table and watching Francisco and Pieter disappear to retrieve Irina. I'm standing before the dashboard with my finger poised above the kill switch, thinking, *Stay or go?*

But I'm not frozen anymore. I hurtle toward Eli and Anis. I run, I fly, I've made my choice, and as Matteo swings the knife, I collide with Anis, ramming him out of the way.

A deep pain alights in the center of my back, between my shoulder blades. I sink to my knees, gazing at the cratered pearl through the windshield. The moon grows until it's no longer a sphere, until it's a flat surface sliding past us on our right. Everything is suddenly so quiet, so still. Anis and Eli are both before me, on the ground, staring at my face.

"Leigh?" Anis says. He sounds terrified. I didn't know his voice could sound that way. His eyes are shocked and wide and full of water.

Eli's mouth is open, her whole body rising and falling with every breath.

"Anis," I choke out. I see the *Hermes* ahead. It's just there, right there. Maybe we can still plug in the tablet. Maybe Caro is running toward us right now, preparing to dock us. "Anis," I repeat, and forming the syllables hurts me somewhere close to my center. But he isn't turning away from me, isn't moving, and we're too late to dock, and then the station is out of sight, and all that's left to see is Earth.

I gaze into the planet's face, uncomprehending.

There should be smoke from wildfires, snarls of clouds from the eruptions. There should be evidence of wreck and ruin, flooding and disaster.

Anis has moved to my shoulder. I keel back into him. He touches the thing protruding from my back, and I cry out. He doesn't touch it again.

"Do you see it?" I whisper, eyes fixed on Earth. "Is it real?"

"Yeah," he whispers back.

Eli shakily rises. She collapses into the commander's seat. She's crying now, so hard that she's shuddering. I look over my shoulder. The motion shoots pain down through my back, every muscle reminding me it's connected to the rest.

The threshold of the bridge overflows with people. They're all withered away to bones, all stock-still, and all gazing down at me. Francisco is standing at Sergei's shoulder, both their eyes reddened. Caro stands at the forefront of the pack, tears running down her cheeks.

"Look," I say.

As one, they look into the windshield, as bright as a video screen, an impossible sight. There are startled cries, breath catching. Francisco's face fills with the rapture I've only seen him show once before.

There's no layer of ash over North America, no sea of atmospheric vapor shrouding the planet. No sign of the eruption's aftermath. I see the tapering root of Central America connecting to the top of South America. I see Sardinia hovering beside Italy. I see the golden stripe of the Sahara wrapped over Africa, and blue seas, and the scattered shrapnel of white cloud. I swear I can feel sand crunching beneath my heel, smell the damp salt of the ocean.

I remember the fiery lights and trembling impacts of the night we left Earth. I close my eyes and see them again, and I realize the truth.

Those weren't eruptions we saw. They were bombs, striking the *Lazarus*'s launch complex. Inside the blast radius, in the sea of smoke, we looked at what we were doing to one another and saw the end of the world.

I find that I'm not even curious who struck the blow. We were dozens of political targets crowded together on a single complex. It might have been anyone, and as for why, I've learned the list of reasons by now. A perceived threat. A sense of righteousness. Someone's fear or rage or incomprehension.

But now the smoke has cleared, and we're gliding high above, looking down at the blue marble, and I see more than the blast site. Satellites in orbit slide like silver beads across the stratosphere, and I wonder how many of them are filling stations like the *Hermes*. Clusters of lights glow on the dark swath of the planet, spray-painted across continents that are gazing up at the moon, still hoping, praying for more time. I see the way beauty lies flush against the wreck.

The *Lazarus* will reenter. Everyone around me will step out onto the earth, wrung out with disbelief, and return—for a last small moment—to their lives. In the caps of ice and the rosy plains, I see days, months, the spell of time they still have before the end. I can see Francisco's fingertips sliding across cello strings. Caro's distant parents welcoming her back with a frantic relief she'd never have expected. Sergei's yellow-painted house, too quiet without Irina. The dog burrowing under Anis's bed in a thunderstorm. And if I could go back—

The pain turns to choking. Something is collapsing inside me. The windshield has fallen away, and I see white ceiling, and a single face looking down at my own. I'm curled on my side, and Anis is holding my head in his lap, smoothing my hair back from my forehead with shaking hands.

"Anis," I whisper.

He can't seem to speak.

"My parents," I say. "Lilly and Marcus."

"No," he whispers. "Please."

I twitch my head one way. Try to smile. My vision is beginning to drift. "You have to tell them," I say, reaching up to touch the pocket of his uniform, where a sliver of paper protrudes.

His hand clasps mine, and his head dips in a nod. Then his shoulders are shaking.

"It's okay," I breathe. "Hey. We're home."

He's holding my hand too tightly, and I know he won't let go. As I look up at him, I remember standing outside in winter back home as snow toppled from the black sky. I looked up, and the snowflakes, illuminated by the streetlamps, were huge white tatters like carnation petals, drifting and spinning and lifting themselves up again. The farther back I tilted my head, the more it looked like the world was moving toward me, like everything was falling my way. I felt like everything hovered just beneath my fingertips at those moments, the universe's every possibility available to me, like the cold air was regenerating me and I could start my life again from nothing, and this time I'd get everything right. Now, looking into two eyes that recognize me as we emerge from the expanding night, I feel the same welling sense of consequence. I am not afraid. I have never felt less alone. My eyes are closing, and the world is ending. Ending. Beginning again.

ACKNOWLEDGMENTS

First, the science. For anyone who's already suffering from climate anxiety, please know that I have taken a lot of dramatic license. There's no evidence that Earth is at risk of methane-release-turned-runaway-greenhouse via death volcano. Chalk that up to plot, with my apologies to climatologists.

That said, obviously the symptoms of extreme weather, heat waves, polar ice melt, and global flooding will not sound new to anyone. Something doesn't have to be a planet-killer to endanger the lives of millions upon millions worldwide. So, every day is a good day to urge your elected officials to support renewable energy initiatives.

For the writing and revision of this book, which happened in four feverish lumps divided between the past eight years, I owe lots of thanks. To Li An, Noelle Wells, Anne, Rose, and the rest of the O'Brien clan, thanks for nearly two decades of making life brighter. Thanks to Piper Thomson for reminding me of the benefits of a countdown clock, and to Foss Baldwin for talking stakes in bars. Thanks to Hunter Lehr for listening to every separate aspect of this book out of context. Thanks to my sister and parents for talking me back up the spirals.

Publishing is a weird place. You'll hang out every one to two years with authors you admire so much it feels almost para-social, since you only see each other once in a blue moon. And those hangouts might last for an hour or for an adventurous weekend, but either way, the conversations will be honest and energizing in a way that it's difficult to find in other contexts. All this to say that I feel lucky to know Janet McNally, Emily Henry, Bri Cavallaro, Jeff Zentner, Jay Coles, Rebecca Hazelton, Traci Chee, and Samira Ahmed.

Additional thanks to Dyer Pierce, Kshipra Hemal, Nate Winer, Dylan Tatum, Emma Brown, Liam Horsman, Clara Mooney, Annie Bonello, Eamon Levesque, Ben Jacoby, Aaron McIlhenny, Chelsea Finn, Sarah Lackore, Nina Corcoran, Kevin Anderson, Lauren Michael, Kendall Theroux, and Lilith Bachelder, plus cherished e-pals Maddie and Ramona, for everything from movie nights to catch-up calls to book opinions to just bein' you.

I'm also very grateful to the team at Hyperion, especially my editor, Heather Crowley, whose patience and guidance were invaluable throughout this process. Last, thank you to my agent, Caryn Wiseman, for believing in this one.